THE
LIBRARIANS

TITLES BY SHERRY THOMAS

The Librarians

THE LADY SHERLOCK SERIES

A Study in Scarlet Women
A Conspiracy in Belgravia
The Hollow of Fear
The Art of Theft
Murder on Cold Street
Miss Moriarty, I Presume?
A Tempest at Sea
A Ruse of Shadows

OTHER WORKS

My Beautiful Enemy
The Luckiest Lady in London
Tempting the Bride
Ravishing the Heiress
Beguiling the Beauty
His at Night
Not Quite a Husband
Delicious
Private Arrangements

THE
LIBRARIANS

Sherry Thomas

BERKLEY
New York

BERKLEY
An imprint of Penguin Random House LLC
1745 Broadway, New York, NY 10019
penguinrandomhouse.com

Copyright © 2025 by Sherry Thomas
Penguin Random House values and supports copyright. Copyright fuels creativity, encourages diverse voices, promotes free speech, and creates a vibrant culture. Thank you for buying an authorized edition of this book and for complying with copyright laws by not reproducing, scanning, or distributing any part of it in any form without permission. You are supporting writers and allowing Penguin Random House to continue to publish books for every reader. Please note that no part of this book may be used or reproduced in any manner for the purpose of training artificial intelligence technologies or systems.

BERKLEY and the BERKLEY & B colophon are registered trademarks of
Penguin Random House LLC.

Interior illustration by vectortatu/Shutterstock

Library of Congress Cataloging-in-Publication Data
Names: Thomas, Sherry (Sherry M.), author.
Title: The librarians / Sherry Thomas.
Description: First edition. | New York: Berkley, 2025.
Identifiers: LCCN 2025001039 (print) | LCCN 2025001040 (ebook) |
ISBN 9780593640456 (hardcover) | ISBN 9780593640463 (ebook)
Subjects: LCGFT: Detective and mystery fiction. | Novels.
Classification: LCC PS3620.H6426 L53 2025 (print) | LCC PS3620.H6426 (ebook) |
DDC 813/.6—dc23/eng/20250113
LC record available at https://lccn.loc.gov/2025001039
LC ebook record available at https://lccn.loc.gov/2025001040

Printed in the United States of America
1st Printing

The authorized representative in the EU for product safety and compliance is
Penguin Random House Ireland, Morrison Chambers, 32 Nassau Street,
Dublin D02 YH68, Ireland, https://eu-contact.penguin.ie.

To all the libraries, big and small,
and to all the librarians, then and now

THE
LIBRARIANS

The man captured by the library's surveillance camera does not appear to be in desperate straits.

CCTV footage in real life is not always black-and-white or grainy—this one has medium resolution and somewhat desaturated colors. Viewing the footage, it's easy enough to make out that the man sports a light blue Oxford shirt, open at the collar, sleeves rolled up.

With his slightly long hair held back from the forehead by a pair of bronze-tinted sunglasses, he looks like a young Hugh Grant, someone who has enough charm, talent, and privilege to survive a hooker scandal with his career intact.

He strolls along the stacks, occasionally crouching down to examine a row of books on the bottom. Several times he pulls out a volume, flips through it, then opens it until the front and back covers almost touch—as if to test the binding.

The next day's footage is even longer, fifteen uninterrupted minutes of Kit Asquith wandering about the library.

What was he doing? And did he know then that in less than three weeks he would be dead?

In the final recording, Kit Asquith enters the library with a cardboard box. It looks heavy. He disappears from frame for a few minutes. When he reappears, he is still holding the same box. Again he strolls the stacks, sometimes taking down a book to drop into the box, sometimes putting one from the box up onto the shelves.

After ten minutes of this, he leaves—never to be seen on these premises again.

Maybe it's for the best that no one can figure out what Kit Asquith did in the suburbs of Austin, Texas—or where he hid the twenty-five million dollars he stole. Late-stage capitalism is the golden age of fraud, and financial crimes are thick on the ground. In a year Kit Asquith will become a footnote. In five years he won't even merit an ancillary remark.

Provided, that is, his widow stays far, far away from this insignificant little library.

CHAPTER ONE

Austin, Texas
Monday, two days before Halloween

In the fortunate places of the world, libraries are everywhere to be found. Some are architectural marvels. Some are touchstones of civilization. Some awe by the depth and granularity of their seemingly infinite collections.

But the greater wonder is perhaps not the phenomenal libraries proudly associated with illustrious universities or storied seats of power. The greater wonder lies in the ordinary ones, the ones that in the fortunate places are everywhere to be found.

They exist and serve quietly, standing apart not at all from their unexceptional surroundings. Sometimes they are squeezed into tight corners; sometimes they share walls with grocery stores and sellers of electronic cigarettes. There is rarely anything unique or unforgettable about their collections, humble aggregates of popular novels, standard reference volumes, how-to books, and DVDs for those who don't yet stream all their audiovisual entertainment.

Yet their ubiquity is their most fundamental virtue. Their unremarkable holdings would have dazzled scholars from the Age of Enlightenment. And as much as anything, they represent a community's investment in its members, a commitment to care for and nourish hearts and minds.

Or libraries can be merely another place to work, another place of mundane chores, minor dramas, and mediocre compensation.

I have become a pessimist, thinks Hazel Lee.

Or perhaps she has long been a fatalist in an optimist's athleisure, her acceptance of the inexorable sweep of fate and entropy masked by her willingness to put some effort into the here and now.

Her grandmother wanted her to take a position with the library system and Hazel acquiesced. But she didn't think she would be assigned to this particular branch. Nainai, on the other hand, is delighted. "So close by. And you loved going there when you were a little girl."

One should be wary of revisiting childhood icons. Epics she adored turn out to have undertones—and overtones—of sexism and colonialism. People she loved embody a large spectrum of human frailties. Places that occupied hallowed ground in her heart are demolished or become something else entirely, such as the old noodle shop that is now an establishment called The Furless Kitty, specializing in Brazilian waxing.

The branch library too has changed. The current incarnation is a red-brick building, its aluminum roof covered with solar panels. Two hundred yards away, a highway meets a local thoroughfare, but a shopping center separates and shields the library from the intersection. On the library's large lot, much of which has been left unpaved, mature live oaks flourish and further foster a sense of comfortable seclusion.

Pleasant. Not impressive, but pleasant. And Hazel is satisfied with pleasant. She parks her e-bike on the rack at the front of the library and hooks her helmet to her backpack. Nearer to the entrance stands a stack of a free regional weekly. She remembers the publication from decades ago and is happier than she thought she would be that it still exists.

A hesitant question comes as she browses the latest issue's guidance on the upcoming off-year election. "Hi. Are you Hazel?"

Hazel turns around; a young white woman in her late twenties waves. Other than the red streaks in her sandy hair, she looks a lot like a hobbit: round-faced, with pink cheeks and brown eyes. Hazel can see her dancing, in the exact dusty-rose sweater vest and long corduroy skirt she's wearing, at Bilbo Baggins's eleventy-first birthday party.

In other words, absurdly cute.

She smiles. "Yes, hi, I'm Hazel."

They shake hands. The young woman, who speaks with a Scandinavian accent, introduces herself as Astrid, a librarian at the branch.

"It's great to have you here," says Astrid, looking a little shy. "Let me open the place up and show you around."

The library's two sets of automatic doors slide apart to reveal ten computer terminals set up for the public. To the left of the computer terminals are the stacks. To the right, the circulation area. An L-shaped children's department wraps around the circulation area on the farther side, making the latter feel like a snug island, the warm heart of the library.

Behind the stacks, a long rectangular work gallery unspools with desks, chairs, and plenty of outlets set beneath a bank of wide windows. Outside the windows, thick vines on metal trellises form natural sunscreens.

Beyond the work gallery, invisible from the front entrance, nestles a reading area. There are fewer magazines on the periodicals shelf now—the times have not been kind to print publications—and the spin racks of audio CDs are gone. But DVDs still take up half a wall and the collection of graphic novels has proliferated.

Given that Halloween is right around the corner, there are a fair number of skeletons scattered around the library, mostly on posters that will be taken down on November first. But there is a fully articulated skeleton in the children's area, peering intently into a shelf of image-heavy compendiums on dinosaurs. Not far away, three chubby and friendly-looking ghosts cluster around a Brambly Hedge collection.

Astrid has Hazel deposit her personal items in the librarians' office, sandwiched between the circulation area and the drive-through pickup at the very back. She helps Hazel turn on the public terminals and the checkout stations' computers, then introduces Hazel to Sophie, a striking Black woman in a perfectly fitted hunter green suit and sky-high heels, and a tall, bearded white man named Jonathan—Sophie is the branch administrator, Jonathan their program director.

She also presents two other librarians, but Inez and Raj protest that they are only clerks, not real librarians. Hazel takes that to mean that they, like her, do not have an advanced degree in library and information science. Not everyone at an attorneys' office is a lawyer and not everyone on a flight crew is a pilot—Hazel, no information specialist, will shoulder relatively humble duties.

"To the public we are all librarians," insists Astrid. "And you're one of us now, Hazel. You're going to love it here."

Before Hazel left Nainai's house this morning, the venerable old lady said, "Go on. Start a new life for yourself."

Except Hazel does not want a new life. She would simply like to have her old life back, that untroublesome existence she hadn't appreciated enough when she still drifted along its placid currents.

She smiles at everyone. "Thank you. I'm delighted to be here."

Astrid has done a lot of fantasy casting over the years, putting faces—mostly those of well-known actors—onto characters from her favorite books. Hazel, she is sure, would have been perfectly cast as a woman with whom a chance encounter alters the course of a protagonist's life.

Or at least costs them sleep and focus for a good long while.

She is beautiful—perfect forehead, wide-set eyes, complexion as smooth as fondant on a wedding cake. Yet it isn't her loveliness that instantly fascinates Astrid.

Near the university campus where Astrid spent her undergraduate years, there was a lake that teemed with expensive properties along its shores. One was finished right as Astrid began her freshman year.

The house stood empty for a few weeks, then one day, curtains appeared. A few days after that, some downstairs curtains were pulled back to reveal a spotless living room, a baby grand piano set against a far window, a blue settee to the side.

Those downstairs curtains never closed again. No matter what season of the year or day of the week Astrid walked, biked, or rollerbladed by, the curtains were always open, the settee plush and inviting, the piano placed just so to silhouette against the lake beyond the house.

Never in her four years there had Astrid seen a single person inside, a car in the driveway, or a stray toy on the lawn. The house seemed to exist in its own separate reality, so much so that it was always a shock—and a profound thrill—when a fully lit Christmas tree appeared next to the piano each December.

Hazel, like that house, also seems to exist on her own plane.

Her attire is simple, a black blouse over a pair of black trousers, but they drape beautifully over her tall, elegant frame. When she speaks, though her accent is North American enough, Astrid hears echoes of distant lands, a life lived globally. (And her instinct is proven correct within the hour, when Hazel tells Inez that she's spent most of her life in Singapore and moved back to the US only recently.)

For someone who should exude glamour, though, Hazel manages to be marvelously low-key. Shortly after she meets the morning crew of librarians, it's as if she's always been there. She moves about at an unhurried pace, yet when Astrid looks in on her around lunchtime, she finds that Hazel has culled all reserved titles that have not been picked up on time, pulled all the new requested transfers, and restocked two entire rolling carts of sorted returned items.

And then sauntered out of the library.

Astrid retreats into the Den of Calories, the affectionate term for the staff breakroom. Jonathan is there, munching on a bag of Indonesian cassava chips. When people think of librarians, they don't immediately conjure a six-foot-four, blond, blue-eyed former college football player. Jonathan is all that and more and he is a great librarian.

"Why, hello, Divinely Beautiful," he says, holding out his bag of chips. "Want some?"

The name Astrid means "divinely beautiful."

"Yes to chips, always." She reaches into the bag and grabs one. "Unfortunately, I've only ever looked like a younger version of Mrs. Weasley—like when she's had two kids, rather than seven."

Her Swedish genes have not endowed her with either height or svelteness, and the pale hair she was born with turned brown sometime in her teens, a common enough occurrence for those of Scandinavian heritage.

Jonathan recoils in mock horror. "How dare you! I'll have you know Molly Prewett Weasley is and has always been an absolute babe."

Astrid laughs and thanks him. They chat another minute while Astrid's lunch heats up in the microwave oven. Then Jonathan cleans up after himself and goes back to work, leaving Astrid to slurp down her chicken chow mein by herself.

When she first arrived at the library, she ached for Jonathan to become her long-awaited gay best friend. But while Jonathan has always been kind and helpful, a special bond has not blossomed between them.

The gay men of the world are too busy with their own lives to revolve around her, and the hetero ones have no use for her if she isn't willing to immediately proceed to the "chill" part of Netflix and chill.

And the one exception, a man she met at this very library, crushed her as if he were a junkyard compactor and she a 1982 Datsun.

One does not become a librarian dreaming of luxury and acclaim. Astrid wants to be useful and she wants to achieve quiet contentment. But quiet contentment is beginning to feel like the hardest boss level in the game of life.

At least the noodles from Trader Joe's, a store famously geared toward the "overeducated and underpaid," of which librarians form exhibit A, are chewy and flavorful.

Astrid wonders what Hazel is having for lunch. Something low-key molecular, she hopes.

Hazel returns from lunch in perfect time to sit down for her first desk session, an hour at the checkout station facing the public.

Not every librarian enjoys dealing with patrons. Astrid does. Other than an occasional best-forgotten battle with the toilet—what exactly *is* the correct way of retrieving a loaded diaper that has been knocked inside?—she likes the "public" aspect of working at a public library.

Patrons don't need to tell her why they need to use the library's terminals, but their tales of visiting grandchildren accidentally destroying the CPU with a water-soaker rivet her. She has good conversations every November with those who need to prepare a Thanksgiving feast that accommodates every dietary restriction under the sun. And she loves helping people find correct tax forms and fill out employment applications.

Obviously, iffier members of the public show up too. But early afternoon on a Monday, with kids still in school, isn't a heavily trafficked time slot.

Hazel, who, like all new hires, has received training at the central library downtown, checks out books like a pro and processes two new library card applications without a hitch. She even fields an I-don't-know-the-author's-name-or-the-title-but-can-you-help-me-find-this-book inquiry with panache. Astrid, the list Hazel generated in hand, takes the patron to the stacks and the older gentleman exclaims with excitement at the second book she pulls out—precisely the one he's been looking for.

Her delight in Hazel's excellence is polluted by a bit of melancholy: At the rate Hazel is going, she won't need any help from Astrid. But when Astrid returns to the circulation desk, she finally has a chance to be useful.

A youngish South Asian couple want to know about Game Night, taking place the next evening, and Hazel, new to the branch library herself, puzzles over the flyer the couple hand her.

"Oh, I can answer your question," Astrid says eagerly. "The library will provide all the board games; you only need to bring yourselves. Because it's so close to Halloween, the inaugural Game Night will be murder-mystery themed. We'll have Halloween decorations and snacks, and you can even come in Halloween costume, if you'd like."

The wife, whose lavender headscarf matches the embroidery on her cream tunic, does look tempted. But she frowns a little. "Do we need to sign up and commit?"

"Oh, no, not at all," Astrid reassures her. "You *can* sign up via the library's website, if you'd like, but you don't need to. Just show up tomorrow evening. And you don't have to dress up either—only if you feel like it."

The couple promise they will think seriously about attending and disappear beyond the stacks in the direction of the work gallery.

"Can I come too?" asks Hazel. "I like board games."

She smiles a little, as if to herself. And Astrid feels as electrified as when a Christmas tree appeared in the house by the lake, tinseled and festooned, lights gently twinkling.

To Astrid, tabletop gaming is like gardening: something she might look into later in life. But if Hazel will host board game nights, then Astrid doesn't mind taking it up right away.

"Of course you can come. You'll be most welcome!"

"Does the library have that many murder-mystery games?" asks Hazel.

The central library downtown has a decent collection of tabletop games, but their little branch does not have that nice touch yet. Astrid is about to explain that the difficulty they're having with Game Night is not the number of games required but a lack of interest on the part of the patrons when a man north of seventy makes a beeline for Hazel.

"Why, hello, are you new here?"

Oh, no, not this guy. If this were a cartoon, his eyeballs would be bouncing all over Hazel, maybe even stuck to the front of her shirt.

Hazel smiles—for someone who feels so enigmatic, she has a very friendly smile. "Yes, today is my first day."

"Welcome to the library!" The old dude, his pale skin slack and crepey, returns an unctuous grin. "I love this branch. All the librarians here are so nice and helpful."

Yes, and all the nice and helpful librarians would love it if he never came back.

"That's wonderful," says Hazel in her low, soft voice. "How can I help you?"

The man sets a pair of reading glasses on his nose and pulls a slip of paper out of his pocket. "Let's see."

If he doesn't say *Fifty Shades*, then the enshittification of the internet ends today.

"*Fifty Shades*," says the man, glancing up as he smooths his stringy comb-over. "That's the book my lady friend recommends."

Social platforms erode, water is still wet, and Astrid will bet her collection of BTS photocards that said lady friend is of the inflatable variety.

Calmly Hazel taps on her keyboard. "We have a great many titles that begin with the words 'Fifty Shades.' What is your book's subject matter, sir?"

"Really? I thought there was just the one."

"There are a lot of them. There is *Fifty Shades of Grace*, which looks to be a spiritual memoir. *Fifty Shades of Bipolar*, for essays on the subject.

And in the realm of cookbooks, we have *Fifty Shades of Kale* and *Fifty Shades of Chicken*, if you are interested in trussing poultry."

Astrid suppresses an urge to laugh.

"Oh," says the old guy. "I see. I see."

Is the troll wondering whether he is being trolled? *Yes, you are, troll!*

"I think mine is fiction," he adds gamely.

"All right. Let me adjust my search parameters, then," answers Hazel, clicking and scrolling. "Still a ton of titles. *Fifty Shades of Crystal. Fifty Shades of Haiku. Fifty Shades of Hell.* There appears to be a fifty shades of everything."

The old guy clears his throat. "Maybe there's a color in the title?"

"*Fifty Shades of Black? Fifty Shades of Greyhound?*"

Astrid coughs so she won't giggle.

"Gray, yes. That's the color."

"*Fifty Shades of Dorian Gray, Fifty Shades of Earl Grey,* or plain old *Fifty Shades of Grey?*"

"Plain old *Fifty Shades of Grey*," mutters the old guy in relief.

"And would you like to read it from the point of view of the female protagonist or the male one?"

"There are two versions?"

"Yes. Or perhaps you'd prefer the cinematic version instead? We have it on DVD."

"I . . ." The old man perks up a bit. "Do you have any recommendations as to which version I should go for?"

"Ah," says Hazel, "I'm afraid I can't help you there. I've never read the book or watched the movie."

"But I thought librarians read everything."

"Maybe some librarians do but I haven't yet. And when I do read erotic fiction, I prefer the male-male variety. I can recommend many good titles in that subgenre. Would you like a few, sir?"

Ah, what joy to behold the unwelcome patron's hasty retreat. The *1812 Overture*—or whichever tune plays on Fourth of July right before the fireworks start—should be blaring out of the PA system right now, all pomp and triumph. *Serves you right, dirty old man, wasting public servants' time for your stupid titillation.*

The automatic doors open. The old man wobbles out. Astrid at last allows herself to grin openly. She sits down at the idle terminal next to Hazel and looks into the library's catalogue. Hazel has not exaggerated: The system does own all those titles and more for the delectation of the public.

It would be rude to discuss patrons out in the open, so she leans toward Hazel and whispers, "Do you really read male-male erotica?"

Hazel smiles a little. "Librarians read everything, right?"

What a mysterious and unsatisfying answer. Can Astrid press a little—maybe even confess that she has read more than a few fanfics on what BBC Sherlock and Dr. Watson get up to after hours at 221B Baker Street?

Or maybe that would be too much, given that they met only this morning.

Reluctantly, Astrid straightens, tells Hazel that she's doing a great job, and flounces out of the circulation area. There's a middle school less than a mile from the library. After school a fair number of kids come to the library, and Astrid usually spends part of her afternoon in the children's area, supervising and helping with homework.

Her path takes her near the front entrance, the automatic doors of which part at that exact moment to admit the man who made her feel cherished and understood—and then ghosted her without a backward glance.

CHAPTER TWO

George A. Romero is likely spinning in his grave, but someone who ghosts you and then reappears back on the scene as if nothing happened is called a zombie.

Yet as Astrid's personal zombie apocalypse looms, she is elated. She always hoped that there was a legitimate reason behind Perry's abrupt disappearance, that someday he would return to explain everything.

And here he is, looking strong and healthy. Eager. She wishes, all at once, that she hadn't worn such a hobbitcore outfit today. She actually has an oxblood suit that's quite sleek. And he—

He walks right past her, as if she were one of the public computer terminals, and heads for Hazel.

Astrid, her hand half-raised in greeting, turns into stone.

"Hi!" says Perry to Hazel.

He sounds breathless.

Astrid understands. She really does. In front of Hazel, she too has a hard time keeping her cool.

"I have an oddish question I hope you can help me with," Perry continues.

If he enunciated better, he'd sound like a Shakespearean actor, someone who bellows *Once more unto the breach, dear friends* eight times a week to thunderous applause. But he lacks that perfect elocution because of a speech impediment—and she once found it so very charming.

"I can try," says Hazel. "A friend of mine is a movie producer. Occasionally, when he evaluates a script, he wants a little on-the-ground research."

This is beginning to sound eerily, grotesquely familiar. Is his next sentence going to be about a thriller that takes place in a library?

"The script he's looking at is a thriller that takes place in a library very much like this one. And he wants to know, realistically, how long a book can sit undisturbed on the library's shelves. And what library policies or procedures might shorten or elongate that time frame."

Is this what it feels like to have her eardrums blown out?

"Interesting questions—must be a fun script," says Hazel. "I'm probably not the best person to answer since I'm new here. But I'm sure my colleagues can help."

She looks behind herself. "Jonathan, could you come here for a second?"

Astrid thought she'd turned into a pillar of salt. But at that moment she moves fast enough to give Usain Bolt whiplash.

On the day Perry first came into the library—with those same questions—Astrid too asked Jonathan for help. She wasn't exactly sure how RFID technology worked and wanted Jonathan's input.

Another librarian might not have remembered Perry, but Jonathan would have taken note of a handsome Brit who respectfully acknowledged his expertise.

And she couldn't bear it if Jonathan were to see her now.

Not at the moment he realizes, as she did, that Perry is just a younger, posher version of the *Fifty Shades* dude.

Six and a half months ago

Astrid stares across the parking lot of the library.

With the vine-laden trellises behind her, she can only see cars, asphalt, and the apartment complex beyond. But she knows that less than a mile ahead, the land folds into small canyons thick with yaupon and ash juniper—the first undulations of Texas Hill Country.

As long as it isn't stuck under a heat dome, Austin, ribboned with greenbelts and rich in reservoir lakes, is a great place for the active lifestyle. Despite having always loved books and libraries, Astrid also adores open air and an unpaved path.

When the very outdoorsy Becky became her roommate, Astrid was delighted. She envisioned them hiking, cycling, and paddleboarding around town. She even imagined road trips to Marfa and Big Bend.

Then Becky showed a normal amount of interest in Astrid and Astrid became Greta Garbo, noted recluse.

Now Becky is moving out. She and her boyfriend might even buy a place together, if they can find one they'll qualify for. Astrid is happy for Becky. But Becky progressing to the next stage of her life only highlights that Astrid is stuck.

No, worse than stuck. Her life has shrunk year by year.

"Hi, is this seat taken?"

Astrid looks up. It's the British guy who asked about a movie script's verisimilitude earlier. And he's gesturing at the bench on the other side of the picnic table.

"Ah, no," she said. And then, after a moment, "Feel free."

He sits down across from her and smiles. "Spring in Texas is less sweltering than I feared—I thought I'd have to stay inside all the time."

He has a nice smile and bright, even teeth—have Hollywood standards of glamour swept aside the supposed British disdain for orthodontia and cosmetic dentistry? The smile also brings out attractive wrinkles on the outer corners of his eyes. Earlier she gauged him to be in his midtwenties, but he must be her age—twenty-nine—or thereabouts.

"April is unpredictable. Last week the temperature went up to"—she calculates in her head—"around thirty-three degrees Celsius."

"You mean more than ninety Fahrenheit?" He grins again. "In the UK when it's cold, we use Celsius and say it's below zero. But when it's hot, we switch to Fahrenheit, because it's much more dramatic to shout, 'Blimey, it went over a hundred!'"

She chortles, even as the gears in her head smoke from trying to figure out if he's flirting with her.

It's not as if patrons never do, but usually she shuts it down right away.

In this instance, though, she might not mind. He's good-looking in a slightly dorky way, which is exactly up her alley. And his gaze feels kind.

"Would you like some cookies?" she asks, pointing to a couple of sealed packets on the perforated picnic table.

He takes one packet. "I'm Perry, by the way."

"Astrid."

"That's an Old Norse name, isn't it?"

Astrid tenses. People being knowledgeable about Old Norse anything makes her nervous. "Yes."

She hopes he can hear the disinclination in her voice—she's not interested in being an accessory to his Viking fascination.

"I spent two semesters in Sweden, first when I was in school, and then again in uni. Do you speak Swedish by any chance?"

A very reasonable question, given that they'd had a fairly lengthy conversation earlier in the day with her speaking in a Swedish accent.

The day is mild; it can't be more than sixty-eight degrees. Astrid, however, feels as if she's chosen to sit on this thermoplastic-coated metal bench when it's one hundred and eight in the shade.

It had happened once before, at a party in grad school. Someone came up to her and started speaking in Swedish. She was surrounded by her fellow library science students, her skin on fire with desperation. Thanks to the two shots of tequila already in her, she ground out, "I prefer to speak English when I'm Stateside."

The Swedish student shrugged and walked off. And Astrid has zero recollection of the rest of the night.

But today there's no one else within hearing range. And the man opposite her . . .

"Do you live in Austin," she asks, "or are you passing through?"

"I don't live here. I'm just here on business—for a short while."

"I don't speak Swedish."

He's taken aback. "Oh, I apo—"

She holds up her hand—she realizes belatedly that she was still speaking in a Swedish accent. These days, it's not as easy to switch back. "And I don't speak Norwegian, Danish, or any other Nordic languages. I don't speak any language other than English."

He blinks. Does he hear her new accent? Her real accent, the one she grew up with, as American as Jell-O salad and interstate highways?

"I'm sorry if you wished to practice your Swedish. I'm just an American from flyover country. I've some Swedish ancestors, but that's about it."

"Oh," he says.

The hush that follows feels like a thousand paper cuts. She doesn't know why she told the truth. It doesn't even feel like she made any major decisions at all. She was just too tired to act out the same old charade for yet another person, a transient who will soon be gone from her life.

Maybe she should have made the effort. The perplexity and reproof she hears in the awkward silence—that's why she could never own up to her little hoax, isn't it?

"Actually"—he laughs a little—"I wanted to speak to you not to practice my Swedish but because you have lovely eyes. And you were very patient with all my silly questions earlier."

It becomes her turn to say "Oh," unable to follow it up with another word.

"I am, in fact, profoundly relieved that I don't have to speak Swedish— I'm absolutely rubbish at it." He again laughs a little—does he laugh when he's embarrassed?—and clears his throat. "I hope it's not unseemly, but now I want to know why you were maybe pretending to be Swedish. Can I—ah— um—buy you a drink when you get off work?"

This feels like a dream sequence from *Inception*. Are the placid neighborhoods around the library going to rise up and fold in on themselves? "You want to go out with someone like me—someone fucked-up?"

He shrugs. "It's the twenty-first century. Everybody is fucked-up. Maybe there's a chance that we're fucked-up in ways that are mutually comprehensible."

He fidgets a little as he waits for her response, and the hopefulness in his gaze causes an abrupt swell of tears in her eyes.

"Thank you," she says thickly.

So this is what gratitude feels like, a fountain bubbling in her heart, iridescent and inexhaustible.

And then, after a long moment, she remembers his question and adds, feeling as shy as an adolescent, "Yes, I can do drinks after work."

Present day

When Astrid was in high school, she read Ted Chiang's *Story of Your Life* and thought it achingly beautiful. During the pandemic, when she streamed *Arrival*, the movie based on the novella, she was forcefully reminded of the point of the story: that by studying the aliens' language, the female protagonist begins to see time as they do and chooses to marry her colleague and have a child with him even though she has foreseen that the marriage will fail and that their daughter will die from a rock-climbing accident when she is twenty-five years old.

Astrid often ponders the protagonist's choice, as she both understands and does not understand it. If she could see the future, she would have made so many decisions differently.

Those right swipes that led to only self-doubt and emptiness? She wouldn't have installed the app in the first place. The youthful stupidity that had her believe that pretending to be Swedish would be fun and broaden her horizons? Her kingdom for a time machine.

And that extraordinary week with Perry?

"Hi, Astrid."

She stills—then continues with her book pulling. In a few days, the display of Halloween and Día de los Muertos picture books will be coming down and she will exhibit a new batch of books on Diwali, Bon Om Touk—both of which take place in November this year—and Thanksgiving.

"Hello, Perry," she says, not looking at him.

"When I spoke to your colleague just now—it wasn't what you think it is."

He sounds as sincere as he always did, but the fountain in her heart has tumbled down and become trash-choked, rusty, broken pipes gaping at nothing and no one.

She kneels and finds the two Diwali books on her list. "I'm sure you're right."

Silence. And then, into that silence, the arrival of the middle schoolers. They talk at half volume, but they are still chatting and chortling. Several boys settle down at the children's area's computer terminals, their backpacks landing on the floor with solid thumps.

Perry lowers his voice. "Can we speak somewhere more private?"

She takes him to the empty meeting room—the last thing she wants is a scene.

"Please, Astrid, believe me, none of this is what you must think," he repeats as soon as the doors close behind them.

She knows that his voice is not echoing from the blank walls of the meeting room. She also knows that the folded tables and stacked chairs are not revolving dizzily around them. It's only the sudden eradication of hope, leaving her weakened, unsteady.

"What is it, then, you showing up here and playing the same charade with my beautiful new colleague?"

Perry grimaces. "I'm sorry that I can't explain anything yet but I want you to know that I hate that I've made you unhappy. That was never my intention."

Astrid bristles. Yes, he's made her unhappy, but how dare he bring it up as if of course he has that kind of power over her. "Perry, let's not be dramatic. We had a situation. It was always going to be short-term. I didn't dwell on it after you left and you don't need to dwell on it now."

He has the audacity to look hurt, which only makes her angrier.

"Excuse me. I'm still at work," she says—and marches out.

CHAPTER THREE

Tuesday, one day before Halloween

The second day of Hazel's tenure at her childhood library begins with three boxes of book donations dropped off overnight—and the young Brit who wanted to know about how long books remained on shelves pacing beside them. She asks him jokingly whether he brought in the donations. He answers, his manner preoccupied, that he hasn't read enough for that.

The boxes are practically the size of shipping containers. The library's hand trolleys cannot be inserted under them, let alone lift them up. Even Jonathan, with his great height and mighty biceps, can budge them only a few inches along the ground.

But the boxes must be dealt with, because they block the path to the front entrance—and because rain is in the forecast. What self-respecting librarian will allow hundreds of books to become waterlogged through sheer inaction?

In the end the work falls largely to Hazel to scoop books out of the boxes into plastic bins and then wheel the bins on a hand trolley into the storage room behind the Den of Calories. Patrons arrive and greet her, including the couple who inquired about Game Night yesterday afternoon. They assure her that they will be in attendance tonight.

The Brit, who keeps wandering in and out of the library, offers to carry some donations for Hazel. She turns him down—the library wouldn't wish to assume that sort of liability. But also, she rather likes performing the task by herself, repeating her motions as if taking part in a walking meditation.

The day before, she didn't want to let sentiment cloud her judgment of the newer, larger version of the library. But after a decent night's sleep, she still likes it a lot. The ceiling is the right height for the entire space to feel open and roomy, but not echoing or cavernous. The light is restful *and* mood-lifting. Even the storage room, accessed through the breakroom and crammed full of donated books, would have been a booklover's wonderland, if anyone other than the librarians ever saw the inside of it.

After a while, Jonathan comes to help her.

Though he's careful never to stare at her, she feels his attention—she felt it the day before too. There is a Chinese saying, *When someone is nice to you for no apparent reason, they want either sex or money.* Whoever first quipped so had probably never met missionaries, but in general the rule holds.

Hazel, however, is a little puzzled by the nature of Jonathan's interest: The pensive quality of his glances does not suggest either greed or attraction.

They empty out the boxes enough to push them under the library's extended front porch as the first drops of rain splatter down. Jonathan ushers her to the breakroom. "Have something. You deserve it."

The breakroom must have acquired its moniker of the Den of Calories because of its large open-back shelf, referred to as the Wall of International Snacks. The typical selection of Oreos and Ritz crackers is on display, as well as bags of Doritos and cans of Pringles. But also, Swedish candy fish, Mexican caramels, and Indian chakri mixes, among many other items that might be considered curious and unusual from an American perspective.

Astrid, when she was Hazel's tour guide the day before, explained that Sophie is open to having fun snacks, but only allows those that are individually packaged to avoid roaches and other pests. Sophie's policy must be working. The Den of Calories, all old fridge, older microwave oven, and mismatched furniture, is nevertheless as spotless as a Japanese lunch counter.

Thinking of Astrid makes Hazel recall how cheerful the young woman was yesterday morning. By the end of Hazel's shift, however, Astrid appeared distracted—actively unhappy, one might even say.

Today Astrid's shift doesn't start until the afternoon—Hazel hopes she will be in a better mood by then. In the meanwhile, Hazel makes herself a cup of tea. Jonathan tears open a pack of roasted seaweed.

She estimates him to be a little older than her, maybe around thirty-seven or thirty-eight. She would not call him handsome, exactly, but he is blond and blue-eyed, has an appealing smile, and fills out his *I'm with the banned* T-shirt very nicely. The patrons certainly love him. They chat him up when they come into the library and find him to say goodbye when they leave.

He holds out the roasted seaweed toward her. "How's working at the library for you?"

"So far I like it," she says, taking a sheet of seaweed from the packet, "but it's only my second day. How long have you been working as a librarian?"

"Almost eight years."

"How do you like it?"

"I love it. But then again, my aunt was a public librarian for thirty years, so I didn't come in with rose-colored glasses. Having realistic expectations helped."

The roasted seaweed crunches rather loudly inside Hazel's mouth. "So you also plan to be a public librarian for thirty years?"

"Longer if they'll let me. But I'm lucky—my mom moved to a retirement community and I get to live in her old house. If I started out as a librarian today, I'm not sure I could afford a place in Austin."

Hazel, very naturally, asks about the local real estate market.

It should have worked perfectly: He gives her a brief rundown, and she thanks him for the roasted seaweed, sails out of the Den of Calories, and avoids any potentially awkward subjects.

But she forgot to factor in her tea—or rather, the cup of water that's been slowly spinning inside the breakroom's medieval microwave. How quickly one becomes sloppy in one's practice of minor Machiavellianism.

The former space-age marvel dings. She has no choice but to put in a tea bag to steep. Jonathan gathers seaweed bits from the table and drops them into the empty wrapper. "I know this might sound weird, Hazel," he says. "We met only yesterday, but if I may, and if you are single and hetero, I'd love to introduce you to someone."

In the silence, the tiny plastic tray inside the wrapper emits sharp, fricative sounds as his palm closes over it.

Hazel warms her hands with her mug. "Oh? What kind of someone?"

Jonathan seems relieved that she is willing to hear more. "He's my high school buddy's roommate. He's hot. My friend thinks highly of him. And I think he'd be super into you."

Now Hazel is amused as well. "Why is that?"

The packaging in Jonathan's hand makes more crinkly sounds. His tone turns tentative, almost uncomfortable, as if he hasn't prepared for the conversation to get this far. "Well, you're a tall, beautiful woman, well-dressed, well-spoken, sophisticated—pretty much exactly what he's searching for."

News of my sophistication has been greatly exaggerated, Hazel wants to tell him. The primary culprit is her wardrobe, which consists largely of her mother's cast-off designer pieces. Now, there's a woman of cosmopolitan tastes.

"That's a very flattering assessment," she answers. "And thank you for bringing this interesting prospect to my attention. I am single and hetero, last I checked, but I lost my husband only a short time ago. I won't be jumping into the dating—or even the fooling around—pool for a while."

"Oh! My—I'm—" stammers Jonathan. "I'm terribly sorry for your loss. And please allow me to apologize for throwing random dudes at you without first getting to know you better."

Hazel shakes her head and discards the tea bag from her mug. The tea is fragrant and scalding, the way she likes it. "There is nothing to apologize for. I'm charmed by your offer. I'm sorry I can't embrace it."

Trying to hook up a woman he met only twenty-four hours ago with a man about whom he knows just as little was not a great idea. Jonathan was deeply aware of that even as he made his laughable attempt.

Except the guy is Ryan Kaneshiro's roommate and Jonathan is desperate for an excuse, any excuse, to contact Ryan Kaneshiro again.

Thank God he edited down the roommate's description of his ideal woman, because Jonathan distinctly remembers the words "Asian" and "mysterious" too. Altogether wouldn't that have made for a fantastically fetishizing stereotype.

Despite Hazel's gracious reply, he is sure his face is the shade of Santa Claus's suit. What should he do? Carry on as if he hasn't stepped in it or flee clumsily, as he longs to?

"How is the local dating scene, by the way?" comes the unexpected question from Hazel. "I've been in town only a short time and don't know the first thing about it."

"Rough," answers Jonathan, as grateful for her interest in this legitimately adjacent topic as Oprah must be for the discovery of semaglutide. "Sometimes it feels as if there's no etiquette or even ethics anymore, when it comes to people getting together for whatever purpose and whatever duration."

"That does sound dangerous, almost a little unsavory."

"I know. My mom likes to antique. She used to say that you have to get through a lot of fakes and a lot of mediocrities to find something worthy of love and investment. The dating pool is like that."

Except he often wonders whether *he* is the fake, the sheer mediocrity made acceptable by the West Texas good ole boy–ness he still carries, despite having left Lubbock when he was all of six.

"Oh? How does your mom figure out if something is authentic?"

Hazel's face is alight with curiosity. Jonathan has seldom felt more flattered by someone's interest. Maybe it's because she's beautiful. Certainly not because she shows no interest in anyone else. In fact, she seems to want to know both the patrons and the librarians. Yet when that friendly inquisitiveness turns to him, it still induces a frisson of pleasure.

He finds himself telling her about his mother's reams of reference works at home, her online friendship with appraisers all over the United States, and even her appearance on *Antiques Roadshow* when the juggernaut last came to Austin.

Not until Sophie comes inside wanting a word with him does Jonathan realize that Hazel smoothed over the situation so impeccably that he, accustomed to berating himself over stupid mistakes, completely forgot his faux pas.

No, more than that. Though she said nothing else on the subject, she has somehow persuaded him that he has not put her on the spot or embarrassed himself.

"I think we got lucky with her," says Sophie, as the door closes behind Hazel.

That is high praise indeed, coming from Sophie.

They go into the storage room, in which they barely find enough space to stand. And there is still an assload of books under the porch. Sophie shakes her head, her palm over her temple.

"Entropy reigns supreme even in a temple to systems and organization," she mumbles.

"You know we public librarians always exist on the edge of chaos," says Jonathan, giving her a pat on the shoulder—a brief one.

He likes Sophie a lot. She is capable, fair, and kind. Under her stewardship the branch library has thrived as a community center and the staff enjoy a harmonious workplace. But Sophie is also extremely professional. After all these years of working together, Jonathan knows her opinions on a lot of books and he can guess which way she votes. But of her personal life, other than her devotion to her daughter, he hasn't gleaned much, if anything.

"We're going to have to do something," laments Sophie.

The solution to their problem is fairly obvious, but even with Hazel joining the roster, the branch is still shorthanded.

"Don't worry," Jonathan says. "I'll—"

They both turn at the bellows coming from the public area.

Jonathan sprints out, Sophie in his wake. Part of the reason the administrator likes having him around, even though she's never said so openly, is that he's an ex-military big guy. The library is open to the public and sometimes the public bring their worst tendencies to the library.

A leathery-tan man in a tattered T-shirt and pair of stained camo shorts and the man to whom Jonathan explained the library's culling system twice are braced together, each trying to shove the other out of the way. They are next to the computer terminals. Patrons at other terminals have jumped up and stepped back, but patrons elsewhere in the library, drawn by the brouhaha, have filtered in past the stacks to see what's going on.

At least the combatants don't seem to be armed. Nor does Jonathan see, as he scans the crowd, any "Good Samaritan" about to whip out a Glock—thank God for small mercies.

He steps forward to forcibly separate the two men. But before he can do so, Astrid, who must have just arrived, screams, "Stop! Stop or you'll both be banned from the library!"

The guy with whom she dealt for a minute back in spring stills. His opponent decks him across the cheek. He goes down, knocking over a chair to rendezvous with the floor. Onlookers cry out in alarm. The other man glances about, mutters a few unintelligible words, and bolts from the library.

Sophie is at Jonathan's side with the first aid kit. "Do we need this?"

"Thanks." He accepts the case and rounds the computer terminals.

The man on the floor, his face bloodied, the top buttons of his shirt ripped open in the tussle, appears unconscious. Jonathan can't help a glance toward where Astrid stands, stark-eyed, at the back of the small crowd. For a week or so the guy came to the library every day and Astrid walked around with a huge smile on her face. Though she never did anything unprofessional on the library's premises, once Jonathan saw them in the reading area, the guy sitting, Astrid on her haunches next to his chair. They were turned toward each other, their foreheads almost touching, and Astrid gazed at him as if she were a *Star Wars* fan circa 1998 and he the first image ever released from *Episode I—The Phantom Menace*.

Then he disappeared. For months, so did Astrid's smile.

In the moment of Jonathan's distraction, a man with a beanie pulled low enough to obscure his eyebrows sinks to one knee next to the guy and checks his pulse.

Sophie steps closer. "Sir, are you a medical professional?"

Jonathan would have asked the same. He too is unwilling to allow interference by some random dude.

Beanie, a light-complexioned man whose ethnicity isn't immediately evident, rises and greets Sophie courteously. "Yes, ma'am. I'm a combat medic, serving with the 10th Mountain Division. I can show you—"

He reaches into his pocket, presumably for a military ID. The Brit on the floor rears up, startling everyone.

"Sir, are you okay?" Sophie asks immediately.

He clutches at his head. "I—I suppose so."

Serves you right, thinks Jonathan. It was low, the way he barged in here to try the same schtick on Hazel. When Hazel innocently passed on the questions Jonathan had already answered six months before, Jonathan had to try hard not to freeze the guy out.

Or look toward Astrid—it would have mortified her.

Sophie crouches down. "Would you like some water?"

"No, thanks." The guy gets up, unsteady on his feet. "I don't need anything."

"Sir, you have a cut on your face," Jonathan makes himself say. "You might need to clean it."

The guy, now upright, gingerly touches his cheek. He studies, as if in a daze, the small smear of blood on his fingertip, then glances in Astrid's direction. "Do you—do you have anything I can borrow?"

Jonathan opens the first aid kit. The man accepts several large bandages and a packet of antibiotic cream with a mumbled "thank you" and heads toward the restroom.

"Would you like to file a police report?" Sophie calls after his retreating back.

He stumbles slightly. "No, no need."

Sophie sighs and looks around. Jonathan is the first to spot the army medic, now seated in the work gallery, behind an open laptop. They approach him.

"Sir, you were going to show me something?" asks Sophie.

"Oh, right." The medic offers up a military ID to Sophie. "I hope the gentleman will get himself some medical attention. The cut looks dramatic, but the greater worry is a concussion. I'd be surprised if he doesn't exhibit the symptoms of one in a few hours, but hopefully it will be a mild case."

Sophie passes the common access card to Jonathan. *Tarik Ozbilgin*, it says. Jonathan's unit once trained with various NATO counterparts and this looks like a Turkish name. The CAC is unexpired; Tarik Ozbilgin is in active service with the army. His pay grade is E7. According to the birthday on the back of the card, he is thirty-six years of age. And if he's been in the army sixteen to eighteen years, then E7 tracks.

Jonathan hands back the CAC. "Thank you for your service."

Tarik Ozbilgin chuckles. "Thank you for the tax dollars that support my service."

Now that Jonathan has seen his name, he hears a slight accent also. They leave Tarik Ozbilgin, possible first-generation American, to his work. The other patrons who gathered to watch the brouhaha have also dispersed back to various corners of the library.

Jonathan finds Astrid in the children's department, which is mostly empty this time of the day, when kids need to be fed. "Are you okay? You don't look too good."

Astrid picks up several picture books that have been left behind on a pair of tubby hassocks. "I'm okay. I just hate it when things like this happen at the library."

Jonathan wants to put his arm around her and tell her that she deserves so much better. But she's never confessed any heartache to him and it doesn't look like she's about to start now.

He sighs. "I'll go take a look at the guy."

The guy is already out of the restroom. Sophie again offers him the option of not only filing a police report but calling EMS. He thanks Sophie repeatedly but rejects any further action and leaves.

Except he then proceeds to stand outside. Waiting for an Uber?

Can the man not even do a dramatic exit properly?

Hazel comes up to Jonathan. "Does the library have CCTV cameras?" she asks softly.

"We do. But they're not currently working and they're not exactly a priority on the city's maintenance list," Jonathan answers, distracted. A second passes before he gets the gist of her question. "You want to see footage of what just happened?"

"I thought it was strange—completely one-sided. The patron who got beat up—I don't think he had any idea why the other patron went after him in the first place."

Jonathan shrugs. "Our cameras wouldn't have recorded anything. But last time there was a fight in the library, a couple of years ago, somebody caught it on their phone and uploaded it. It could happen again this time."

He studies Hazel's expression, afraid he might see a distress similar to Astrid's. But Hazel does not appear disturbed, only puzzled.

She shakes her head. "Much more of a thrill ride than I anticipated, working at the library."

Sophie needs to write up the brawl. But the day doesn't want her to file an incident report in peace.

By the time the aftermath of the fight has been dealt with—chairs righted, carpet sprayed, terminals disinfected—a potty emergency arises. And by the time Sophie, who keeps a pair of heavy-duty tongs for just such occasions, extracts a sippy cup stuck in the drain hole of the family restroom toilet bowl, the on-again-off-again drizzle outside has turned into a downpour.

"The rain is supposed to stop in about forty-five minutes," Jonathan says.

He means that weather shouldn't be a factor for Game Night's attendance.

Sophie's sixteen-year-old daughter, Elise, adores tabletop gaming and has been trying to find a local club with people her age where she won't be the only girl or the only Black person in the room. Game Night is Sophie's attempt to see whether Elise can find that community of younger and more diverse players via the library.

It hasn't been billed as a teen event or an event aimed at traditionally underserved segments of the population. But in terms of marketing, Sophie targeted area high schools—specifically, teacher and parent sponsors for clubs for girls in coding, STEM, and leadership.

Unfortunately, registration numbers have been sluggish, to put it kindly.

Astrid has been hyping the event to kids who attend the library's teen book club and LGBTQ+ social club. She's even started to pimp the event to the young parents who come to her baby and toddler storytimes, telling them to think of it as a pre-Halloween treat for themselves.

Jonathan has reassured Sophie, using historical data, that usually more people show up than those who register ahead of time, but Sophie is secretly convinced that everyone is going to find something more fun to do and Game Night will end up a complete dud.

"I'm sorry, what?" She realizes that Jonathan has said something else and she hasn't heard.

"Nothing, really. Just that I disinfected the toilet tongs and put them back," answers Jonathan.

"Thank you, Jonathan." She rests her hand on his arm for a moment. "You're a godsend."

He really is a great person, always respectful and always helpful. And gets better-looking every year in the way that sometimes happens for men in their thirties and forties. If he were a woman she'd have no choice but to date him.

Behind him, in the middle of the circulation area, stands Astrid, staring at nothing in particular.

"Astrid, isn't it almost time for your next program?" Sophie asks, momentarily jolted out of her own problems.

"Oh, right," says Astrid and hurries off.

Sophie sighs. She recognized the beat-up man: She saw him once, in the grocery store, the loading zone of which abuts the edge of the library's lot. He and Astrid had their arms around each other, whispering, oblivious to their surroundings.

But something went wrong within days—pain had been written all over Astrid's face. It was only in the past month or two that she had regained some of her liveliness and interest in life.

Sophie sighs again and heads for her office. She now has two incident reports, in addition to all the reports she must generate at the end of every month. And a slew of emails to get through before six p.m.

She opens her door and almost steps directly on an origami love knot—

the things one learns to identify from library summer programs over the years. Puzzled—and a bit excited—she picks it up. Can this possibly be an old-fashioned love note? With Elise nearly grown, maybe it's time for Sophie to think about herself again.

The unfolding of the knot is a barrel of ice water upended on the tiny fuse of her anticipation.

I know you're keeping a secret. We should talk.

CHAPTER FOUR

On Saturday, three days ago, Astrid led a Halloween-themed scavenger hunt. Sophie, coming back from a volunteer park cleanup outing with Elise, stopped by to see how that was going. As she was about to leave, two other staffers had a question about swapping hour blocks. Sophie stepped into her office for the master schedule. Just inside the door, one of the props from the scavenger hunt stared up at her, a small gray card that declared, in a swooshy scarlet font, *A great secret lies here.*

Sophie chuckled, tossed the card that must have been accidentally kicked under her door into the recycle bin, and sorted out the schedule. Then she and Elise went home, made spaghetti, and watched *The Great British Bake Off* together in the evening.

When the library hosts events, especially events involving kids, things tend to end up in unexpected places. But this new note . . .

I know you're keeping a secret.

Sophie's fingertips shake. The note drifts free of her hand. She doesn't want to believe it. She can't even bear to think the thought. But—is this about Elise?

She whips around and yanks open her door. Her office is next to the Den of Calories, separated from the circulation area by five feet of carpet.

Inez, at the nearest checkout station, turns her head and smiles at Sophie. Sophie smiles back woodenly.

Inez resumes helping the patron in front of her. Sophie tries to imagine herself as Annalise Keating from *How to Get Away with Murder.* But her mind spins like a tire in mud. All she can recall is Annalise's resolute face and those fantastic sheath dresses, and not a shred of the law professor's devious, ruthless tactics.

Okay, first she needs to have an idea of the note writer's identity.

She is sure the note—written on a slip of paper from the box next to the catalogue terminals—wasn't there before she left at lunch to get her car inspected in the shopping center next door. When she came back, she'd investigated the secondary storage room, which is also completely full and not going to be of much use for holding donated books.

After that she'd gone to the Den of Calories to talk to Jonathan. Then the brawl happened, followed by the sippy cup incident.

During all that time she'd rushed in and out of her office a few times and might not have immediately noticed a tiny origami love knot on the floor. But it's a virtual certainty the note writer was in the library between twelve thirty and two o'clock.

It could have been any of fifty people, but if that person also slid the *A great secret lies here* card under her door on Saturday, the number of suspects would reduce sharply, since weekday patrons tend not to come in on the weekend, and vice versa.

In fact, the most likely individuals to have been around on both occasions are the librarians on duty.

Can it be one of Sophie's subordinates?

She walks around. Inez and Raj are at the front of the circulation area, handling the public. Jonathan, stationed at the book return/drive-through pickup, answers phone inquiries via a headset as he empties out a bin of returned books onto different rolling carts.

On the other side of Sophie's office is a passage that leads to the meeting room and the by-appointment passport office. The double doors of the meeting room are open: Astrid's program is finished and she is talking to a pair of younger teens who have stayed behind.

Hazel appears at Sophie's elbow, holding a box of movie posters that are to be the decorations for the evening's program. "Do you have any preferences, Sophie, as to how they should be arranged?"

Sophie is prone to micromanaging if she isn't careful. But today she only waves her hand. "Your judgment will be fine."

Hazel didn't even start working at this branch until yesterday and can probably be eliminated from suspicion. But the other librarians too look perfectly normal and innocent.

Okay, Astrid *is* acting strange, but that is inwardly directed. And if anyone is planning to remove Sophie from her position, only Jonathan is senior enough to occupy the vacancy.

But Jonathan, really? *Jonathan?*

It's difficult to predict what people might do; it's easier, sometimes, to take a stab at what they won't do. Sophie doesn't believe Jonathan capable of blackmail. And he doesn't seem in a great big hurry to helm his own library, either, though he is more than capable of it.

Then who can it be? A patron? A patron who wants to shake down a *librarian* for money?

What would Annalise Keating do, if she had a child to protect? Is it time for Sophie to give *How to Get Away with Murder* a rewatch?

An in-depth study?

CHAPTER FIVE

At six thirty, Jonathan announces the imminent Game Night event over the PA system. Elise texts Sophie to say she's arrived.

Sophie rushes out to the parking lot. Before the girl can complete her "Hi, Mom," Sophie wraps her in a bear hug.

Elise laughs but good-naturedly endures the embrace. "I'm touched, Mom. You last saw me this morning."

So tolerant of her crazy mother, this child. "That's too long to go without seeing you," Sophie mumbles.

But she pulls herself together and helps Elise carry two huge boxes of board games into the library. "We still only have three people registered and they might not all show up."

The weather, as Jonathan predicted, has cleared. But it's the day before Halloween; there are plenty of other ways for people to amuse themselves.

Elise spares a hand and rubs Sophie on the back. "That's okay, Mom. I brought my homework in case nobody comes."

The girl is so reasonable and all-around fantastic that Sophie's feelings shot past wonder and smugness years ago to land squarely in panic. She cannot think about it too much, or she invariably becomes terrified that Elise is too lovely for this world, and that the world will somehow find a way to punish her kindness and crush her spirit.

Has that day come?

"Let me." Jonathan comes out of the circulation area and relieves Sophie of her burden. "Hi, Elise."

"Hi, Jonathan." Elise beams at him. "You get more daddy every time I see you."

"Elise!" cries Sophie.

She knows Elise would not say anything of the sort to Jonathan if he weren't queer. But that's still inappropriate.

Elise chortles. She does enjoy getting a rise out of her mother from time to time. And being reminded that Elise is still a teenager and not truly perfect is unexpectedly reassuring.

"Sorry, Jonathan," Elise laughs. "It's just that guys from school suck and you can't say anything nice to them without them thinking it's the equivalent of a right swipe."

Jonathan smiles and opens one of the meeting room's doors to let Sophie and Elise through. "You can say all the nice things to me, Elise, as long as my boss here approves."

Good. Sophie approves entirely of this kind yet firmly limit-setting statement.

"Wow, creepy," says Elise.

The meeting room has long been the most boring part of the library. It's a blank box with no books and only stacks of folding tables and folding chairs lined up along the walls.

But tonight its fluorescent fixtures bathe the room in a reddish light, thanks to filters inside their covers. The movie posters, which Sophie thought would be placed around the room in a perfectly equidistant and symmetrical fashion, are instead thrown up crooked. Some are torn; others have been slashed through; a few even drip blood.

In the dim, scarlet illumination, the effect is straight-up spooky. Sophie rushes over to one poster and sighs in relief: It is indeed visual trickery, the slashes and the blood splatters both large adhesive stickers printed on clear plastic backing.

"Wow," Elise exclaims again. She spins around, wallowing in the atmosphere. "Hey, Astrid! Is everything here yours?"

Sophie didn't even notice that Astrid had come into the meeting room.

"Yeah," answers Astrid quietly. "I had all these props and decorations hoarded. I decided I might as well use them here, for Game Night."

Might as well use them here, for Game Night? What is the elsewhere and other occasion that didn't work out?

"I love your costume, by the way," murmurs Astrid. "Nakia, right?"

"The one and only." Elise preens. "But I think my mom looks even cooler. I mean, how can anyone be cooler than Nick Fury?"

"That's what all the old, half-blind brothers out there tell themselves," says Sophie. But she can't help smiling a little.

They set the games up on bookstands so that they can be better admired. Elise hops over to the refreshments table to give herself a sugar high—Sophie is still surprised that food and drinks are now allowed in the library. Only in the meeting room, true, but all the same. Welcome to the library of the future.

Just then Hazel walks in. She sports a long beige coat, a T-shirt with a rainbow stripe over her chest, and culottes—really, culottes?—worn with suspenders over a pair of brown boots. How the woman manages to look breezy and stylish in this odd getup Sophie has no idea. She also has no idea who in the world Hazel is supposed to be.

"You're the Thirteenth Doctor!" cries Elise.

Sophie mentally slaps herself on the forehead. Of course. *Of course.* The first female Doctor Who.

"Hey, the Thirteenth Doctor!" Ana Maria, Elise's BFF, comes in, a heavy-looking backpack over one shoulder.

Elise squeals as if she doesn't see Ana Maria every weekday and most weekends. "Hey, you made it."

"Of course I was going to make it. You're auditioning new friends. As your OG friend, I have to be the Simon Cowell of this reality show. I have to reject everyone except a select few."

"There may not be anyone to reject."

"That's why I brought my APUSH homework."

"Me too—minus the AP part."

The girls break into peals of laughter. They're still bemoaning the fact that they can't watch *Hamilton* without having to write an essay about it when a pair of actual attendees arrive—Sophie recognizes the two as the kids who spoke to Astrid a few hours earlier, in this very meeting room.

And then more patrons come. By the time seven o'clock rolls around, there are twelve attendees who are not library employees or Elise or Ana Maria.

Sophie can't believe it. The program is a success. The attendees skew younger, they skew female, and they do not skew entirely white. Maybe there is indeed an overlooked need the library can continue to serve in the future.

"We'd better bring out more snacks," she says to no one in particular.

And decides to seize the hour. Who knows what will happen after tonight? She'd better enjoy every moment with Elise while she still can.

Elise takes on the role of the host for the evening. The attendees divide into two equal groups, one tackling a more involved game, the other trying out several faster games.

Elise helps the group that chooses the deep dive of Sherlock Holmes Consulting Detective with a summary of the rules. Sophie would have loved to stand by and listen to her—the girl speaks with such conciseness and authority. And joy too. But instead Sophie explains the rules of a shorter game to the second table to get them started.

A woman asks Sophie if Elise is her daughter and then compliments her on that terrific young woman. Sophie basks.

A similar sense of pleasure and relaxation unfurls in the meeting room. When the very atmospheric lighting proves a little too dim to study maps and other clues by, the players turn on the flashlights on their phones. And when someone mentions that it feels as if they are up at night at summer camp after the counselors have gone to sleep, half of the attendees chime in, expressing agreement.

To Sophie's surprise, even more people arrive around seven thirty: first a South Asian–looking couple, both in tunic and trousers. On their heels, a white woman at the sight of whom Sophie takes an actual step backward.

The woman, costumed in a brown vest over a floral peasant dress, is clearly meant to be a fortune teller. A glittering orange scarf covers her hair and frames her slightly oversized forehead, from which gazes a large third eye. The eye is nearly photorealistic, each lash distinct, and stares at Sophie with something between pity and malice.

Sophie is thrown back to a documentary she saw long ago about the aftermath of Chernobyl. Without warning, the camera panned to a fetus floating in a jar of formaldehyde, cyclops-like, its one eye directly above its nose.

The woman's third eye, a mere artistic flourish, can never achieve the impact of a tragic deformity. But nevertheless, in the hazy red light, it jars.

"Wow, what an entrance," pronounces Elise.

Everyone laughs and the tension breaks.

The new arrivals considerately do not demand to join the games already in progress. Instead they decide to try Clue: Two out of the three have seen the movie.

"I'm pretty sure I saw it on a bootleg DVD when I lived in Karachi," says the woman of the South Asian couple. "It was weird, but good."

Three players suffice to start the game, but Elise feels that four would be more fun. Sophie thinks of Astrid first—Astrid is likely to find the third eye cool. And being at a table with other people might take her mind off the young man who should have known better than to come around again.

But Astrid is still on the clock and needed at the checkout station. Whereas Hazel, who is attending on her own time, has been busy as a beaver, getting extra snacks and napkins from the supply closet and fresh pitchers of ice from the Den of Calories. Not to mention, she seems familiar with the games on hand, helping out the players when Elise is engaged with another table.

The third-eye woman issues an invitation to Sophie. "You are most welcome to join us."

"Let me find you someone better," says Sophie—and beckons Hazel over.

Soon the foursome at the table is busy unmasking the killer of Mr. Boddy. Outside Jonathan and Astrid are holding down the fort; inside the meeting room Elise handles it all with aplomb.

If only there weren't that stupid note under her door . . . Sophie would have felt the spheres of the universe sliding into alignment, the Venn diagram of professional success and personal happiness merging into a perfect circle.

However briefly.

———

Twenty minutes after the late arrivals sit down, the fast table finish their first game. Over at the Sherlock Holmes table, still digging into the details of the case, someone remarks, with satisfaction, "Aha, we have ourselves a Mata Hari." And the younger players need that reference explained to them.

Sophie, her Nick Fury eyepatch now in her pocket, tries not to think about the fact that the note writer could be among the attendees. That potential blackmailer probably isn't someone Elise's age or younger. But eliminating the underage crowd still leaves six full-grown adults, without counting Hazel.

After her earlier frenzy of doubt concerning her longtime colleagues, and after those colleagues persist in not coming forward to extort her, Sophie now wonders whether the person threatening the foundation of her existence is instead a relative stranger. She can't be sure why any stranger would know or care about the distant past of an anonymous librarian, but all the same, she finds herself drifting repeatedly toward the Clue table, occupied by four such strangers.

It so happens that at the Clue table, players are furnishing one another with their life facts. The couple and the fortune teller are all new to town: The former are relocated techies from California; the latter used to live in North Carolina. Hazel, who does not seem to be interested in talking about herself, merely says, when she is asked by the South Asian couple, that she hasn't lived in too many places besides Austin, which is a bit brazen as deflections go, considering that Singapore is halfway around the world.

"I really wanted to move to Austin—I loved it when I came here on work trips," says the fortune teller. "But now that I'm finally here, home prices have gone through the roof. You guys are lucky, coming from California."

The wife of the South Asian couple waves both hands in vigorous denial. "No, no, we are definitely not those Californians buying up everything when they come to town. We were in Silicon Valley only for a short time and were renters, so we didn't have any home equity."

The not-so-illuminating conversation continues, with no one saying anything that immediately makes them out to be a prime suspect.

By eight thirty-five, players at the fast table finish another game. Players at the Sherlock Holmes table correctly deduce their killer. They congratulate one another, pack up their games, and place tables and chairs back along the walls.

Folks at the Clue table, seeing the commotion, abandon their game, given that they will not be able to finish before the library closes at nine. Hazel confesses that she is in fact the killer and gets a laugh from her tablemates.

The patrons leave happily. After an orderly cleanup, Sophie locks up the building for the night; Elise side-hugs her as they make their way to Sophie's car.

"Thanks, Mom. This was *elite*."

Sophie kisses her on the cheek. "Anything for you, nugget. *Anything*."

They pass a black Audi in the parking lot. Elise's head whips around. "Look at those bumper stickers. Perfect for Halloween."

Maybe too perfect. The two stickers declare *It's okay to decay* and *The dead know how to speak, if you know how to listen*.

Sophie shivers, looks away, and says, "You know, we can have another Game Night in January. And—"

From behind her, someone calls out. "Ms. Claremont, can I have a word with you?"

CHAPTER SIX

Hazel parks her grandmother's Miata in the garage and immediately picks up her phone.

During the pandemic, when anti-Asian sentiments ran high, Nainai proactively put up a dozen cameras in and around her house. They are connected via Wi-Fi to her home security company's app. Hazel checks the feed from cameras that overlook the street and does not see any cars drive by.

She isn't sure she's being followed, but she also can't be sure she isn't. She had the same feeling for a few weeks in Singapore, over the summer, then the microsensations went away and she thought that was the end of it.

Perhaps not.

She gathers her things, heads into the house, and stops for a minute in the formal dining room: On the usually gleamingly empty dining table there is a piece of paper, a flyer for a school trip fundraiser.

Well, Nainai is very charitable by nature.

She crosses the living room and peers into a book-lined space where a thin woman with a sweep of silver hair and a pair of large headphones is ensconced in a Lamborghini of a zero-gravity chair. The back of the seat rears up like the spine of an alien creature, then expands into a canopy from which suspends an enormous monitor. Nainai's hands, cradled in armrests of equally impressive curvature, fly over a pair of ergonomic keyboards.

Hazel wouldn't dream of distracting Nainai from the blood sport on her monitor. She merely waves and then goes to the front door: While she was at Game Night, Nainai texted to let her know that a big package had arrived for her.

Hazel hefts up the box and carries it to her bedroom upstairs. She slices open the heavy-duty carton and pulls out a smaller box stuffed with drafts of rules, palm-sized cards cut from double-thick stock, polymer clay miniature books, and three different versions of a game board—one printed, two hand-drawn, and none remotely resembling what she really wants.

Perhaps she didn't abandon development on this book-themed game only because of unforeseen circumstances in her life. Maybe the game just plain sucks.

Underneath the box that contains the half-finished game is another box. Judging by its weight, inside are the books she borrowed from her mother, a semiserious collector, for inspiration. But inspiration, sorely lacking for months, is no more forthcoming tonight.

She sighs, picks up the whole carton again, staggers a little under its weight, and carries it to the hall closet for storage. She's about to shut the closet door when she glances up and recognizes a still-sealed package on the very top shelf.

She knows what's inside: a two-thousand-piece jigsaw puzzle of a sailing ship cutting across a cobalt blue sea. An old wistfulness takes hold of her. Reaching up a hand, she touches the edge of the box. A fine powder clings to her fingertips—her hopes, turned to dust.

"Hazel!"

Hazel closes the door on her past and heads downstairs. "Did your team win, Nainai?"

"Yes, but it was an ugly victory," grumbles Nainai, standing by the newel post.

Hazel doesn't have to ask what kids these days are doing; she only needs to check what Nainai is into, and then look online to find out that it's either the hottest trend going or, even better, the next big thing.

"I forgot to put cilantro on the shopping list I gave to you earlier," says Nainai. "Can you stop at H-E-B again tomorrow?"

Hazel strikes her own forehead. "I can't believe it. I didn't go to H-E-B at all. I'll go now—and I'll put cilantro on the list."

She glances at her watch—nine forty, not too late.

"How was Game Night, by the way?" asks Nainai.

"Uneventful," replies Hazel, pulling on her boots. "Which is all anyone can ever ask for."

Closeted

I did not say yes because
If I opened my mouth
I would say far more than yes

I would say, don't stop
I would say, kiss me
I would say, what is your middle name, if you have one

So I did not say anything
I let you touch me, your tongue on my skin

And then, I said, how dare you,
I did not say yes

Jonathan submitted the poem anonymously to his university's literary magazine when he was nineteen, before the injury that ended his college football career. Two months ago, after his high school class's belated and rather disorganized twenty-year reunion, he came back home, dug up a copy of the magazine, and took a picture of that meager confession.

Ever since then, he's been on the verge of forwarding the image to Ryan.

Jonathan shifts on his living room couch, which is beginning to sag. Chimney, his cat, climbs onto his stomach, studies the glowing screen in his hand, and looks up at him, as if asking, *Are you going to do it tonight? Finally?*

He doesn't. Instead he texts Ryan, Tell your roommate I've found his perfect woman.

Hazel, of course, has not agreed to meet with Conrad, Ryan's roommate. To his astonishment, a few minutes later his phone vibrates softly.

> He's out of town.

Jonathan's heart rate surges. Does this mean Ryan will pass on the message to Conrad at some point? And does this mean Ryan will then get back to Jonathan?

He sits up straight, startling Chimney. In the next ten minutes he taps and deletes a dozen different responses.

Dare he read any significance into it? Or is Ryan's casual reply merely their generation's equivalent of his mother's willingness, at times, to talk to telemarketers and pollsters because there's nothing good on TV?

In the end he tosses aside his phone and holds his cat close, because only one of the two has affection to share.

When Astrid returned to her condo, it seemed the most natural thing to contact Perry.

> Are you okay?

> I'm home.

> Come and let me take a look at you.

But now, after she's taken a shower and ordered a pizza, he still hasn't responded, as if his desperate pleas the day before were just so much pollen, there to cause headaches and itchy eyes.

The bag of Halloween decorations she brought back from the library sits limply on her dining table, all illusion and fakery.

In the beginning, everything went so well with Perry she actually looked forward to telling the truth about her accent to people and at last unburdening herself. Looked forward to having friends again. She would organize potluck parties, binge-watching parties, and maybe even a book club for her condo community.

In that moment of blind optimism, she bought the Halloween decorations in anticipation of a whole new life.

But he ghosted her the next day and her hopes, castles in the air, fell prey to gravity.

Astrid's phone dings. Her doorbell rings at the same time.

She whips around in surprise. He *hasn't* stood her up?

Yet she does not feel buoyant. To the contrary, she feels as if someone has poured concrete over her feet. A deep dread curls around her heart.

It's the moment of truth and moments of truth are always, always the worst.

A little before eleven, Sophie totters into her house.

Almost immediately Elise appears at the top of the stairs. "Hey, where have you been?"

Oh, shit. Sophie does not want Elise's observant eyes on her now. She manages a smile. "You're still up, nugget?"

"I just got done with my *Hamilton* essay. How long does it take to buy some cookies? I texted you."

For the first time in her life Sophie wishes she had a sullen, self-involved teenager who shuts herself in her room, blasts music 24/7, and would never notice her mom briefly leaving the house at night.

Sophie has no choice but to brazen it out. She sets the cookies on the kitchen counter and sorts other items into the fridge. "I decided to get more stuff since I was already at the store. I got cupcakes too. Frozen burritos. Frozen tamales. But don't touch the cupcakes—they're for the library."

"Oooh," says Elise. "What's come over you, Mom?"

Sophie considers frozen prepared meals processed food and tries not to indulge in them too often.

"I guess the success of Game Night went to my head." She laughs a little.

Even though she feels like crying.

No, a nervous breakdown, that's what she feels like having.

She shoos Elise out of the kitchen. "Okay, go to bed, now that you're done with your essay. I need to sleep too."

But how can she ever sleep again, knowing what is to come?

CHAPTER SEVEN

Thursday

Halloween passes without incident at the library. On Thursday, November 1, Jonathan announces that he will organize a book sale to clear out the donated books. The task of coming up with publicity posters for the sale falls to Astrid, who tackles most of the branch's graphic design needs.

That afternoon, she and Jonathan sit in the staff office, she fiddling with a Christmas tree made of books in Photoshop, he looking on the *Austin American-Statesman*'s website to see how much coverage the paper has given to branch library events in the past year.

"I love the board you did for the poetry workshop, by the way," said Jonathan.

"Thanks," she murmurs.

Jonathan hosts the monthly poetry workshop and gets a nice roster of regulars. But given how many people have moved to Austin recently, Astrid thought it would be a good idea to publicize the workshop a little more with a standing blackboard display at the front of the library.

"I'm thinking of also updating the board for the open mic night," she adds.

"That's a great idea. You're so talented, Astrid."

He is being deliberately kind. She should be too proud for it, but she is desperate for such care and generosity.

"Wait—what?" Jonathan exclaims softly.

Astrid looks up. "What's going on?"

"Come and see."

A frowning Jonathan gets up from his chair and steps out of the way for Astrid to read the article on his monitor.

NEW AUSTIN RESIDENT FOUND DEAD

The Austin Police Department has confirmed that the body found in a vehicle parked on Fanfare Drive in Northwest Austin is that of Jeannette Obermann of Twin Courtyards Apartments.

Obermann, until recently a resident of North Carolina, moved to Austin in August to take a job with Apple as a technical writer. Those who knew her describe her as helpful and responsible, "someone who's interested in everyone and everything."

The police have not yet released Obermann's cause of death. They have also declined to state whether the incident is being investigated as an instance of homicide.

"Twin Courtyards Apartments?" says Astrid, feeling faintly alarmed. "That's right across the street from where I live. And why does this woman look familiar?"

An image of Jeannette Obermann accompanies the article, a professional portrait that makes Astrid think of real estate agents, the kind whose faces are prominently displayed on open house placards.

Then shock hits her like a hammer, jolting her out of the lethargy of the past few days. "My God, was she the fortune teller with the third eye on her forehead? She's dead?"

A knock comes at the glass door of the office—Sophie, in a tangerine skirt suit that only she and Lupita Nyong'o can carry off. Astrid is used to seeing Sophie in vibrant outfits. It's Sophie's expression—at once hollow-eyed and . . . guilty-looking?—that takes her aback.

Sophie pulls open the door and admits a handsome woman of about Jonathan's age and possibly Middle Eastern heritage and a freckled young white man. Sophie closes the door again, then says quietly, "Astrid, we have two detectives from Austin Police Department who would like a word with you."

"Are you Ms. Brittany Sorenson?" says the woman detective. She sports a blue vest over a crisp white shirt, her dark, abundant hair pulled back into a high ponytail.

"Maryam?" Jonathan cries. "Is that you?"

The woman nods, her manner impeccably professional. "Hey, Jonathan. It's been ages."

Jonathan glances toward Astrid, confusion and inquietude written all over his face.

With some reluctance, Astrid answers, "I'm Brittany Sorenson, but I usually go by Astrid."

At least that is her real middle name, from her real Swedish great-grandmother.

"I'm Detective Maryam Shariati and this is Detective Branson Jones," says the woman. "A moment of your time, please, Ms. Sorenson."

"Y-yes, of course."

"I'll take the detectives to our meeting room," says Sophie. "Why don't you log out of your session, Astrid? Detectives, this way, please."

"Do you need a lawyer?" asks Jonathan urgently, as soon as the cops are gone. "If you aren't comfortable, you don't have to answer questions without legal representation."

Astrid dry-cackles from sheer astonishment: He thinks she might be in trouble. Is that why Sophie guided the cops ahead to the meeting room? To give her a minute or two to gather herself and form a strategy?

"I'm fine," she declares. "Let me go see what they want."

All the same, her mind becomes a swarm of whirling thoughts. Maybe the police want to know about Jeannette Obermann, but Astrid doesn't know anything about her. She doesn't have any late bills or outstanding traffic tickets. She's never even abandoned a shopping cart in a grocery store parking lot.

Sophie stands in the passage leading to the meeting room. She raises a brow in question. Astrid smiles in reassurance, but her cheeks feel rigid.

Inside the meeting room, a table and three chairs have been set up, but not in a confrontational configuration of two chairs on one side of the table and one chair on the other side. Instead, the chairs are placed all around the table, looking haphazard, as if three buddies who are working on a project together have deserted their station at lunchtime.

The detectives ask if she is all right with being recorded. Astrid, after a moment, nods. Detective Shariati motions her to a seat. Detective Jones turns on the equipment. And Astrid states, when prompted, her name, age, address, and occupation.

"Do you recognize this person?" begins Detective Shariati and shows Astrid a picture on a piece of printer paper.

Perry! In the not terribly sharp image he sports the kind of formal attire people wear to English society weddings, and there is a church looming up behind him.

Astrid's confusion congeals into dread. "Is—is he okay?"

"Can you identify him for us?"

Why won't they answer her question? "He told me his name is Perry. I don't know his last name."

"Can you tell us what you do know about him?"

What *does* she know about him? That is her entire problem, isn't it? "Can you tell me if he's okay?"

"Please answer the question," says Detective Jones in a kind but implacable tone.

Detective Shariati merely waits.

Will they tell her what they know if she tells them what she knows? "I met him in April when he was in town on business. We had a fling that lasted all of one week. I never heard from him again until he showed up at the library two days before Halloween."

"What business?"

"I asked him one time and he said it was tedious business, so I didn't ask anymore."

"You didn't dig around a little?"

Astrid shrugs, a stab of futility in her heart. "We were a hookup, plain and simple. I didn't know his surname—I can't even be sure Perry is his real name. I would have *liked* to know what he was doing in town—and a lot of other things besides. But I didn't have the means to find out—or the standing, really."

"When he came back, you didn't take the opportunity to ask questions?"

She realizes belatedly that they last spoke in this very space, she and Perry. They were standing near the doors, the stacks of brown folding chairs behind him. "Frankly, I was trying not to have anything to do with him."

"But then you changed your mind?"

Her heart drops straight into a vat of nuclear waste.

How? How do they know she changed her mind? And why does it matter, in the greater scheme of things, that she ended up sending a few more texts to a man who clearly didn't care enough about her?

Yet for the police to ask, it must matter to some degree. Also, they would need access to his phone or phone records to know that she'd messaged him.

If everything were okay, they wouldn't have either and they wouldn't be here.

Her fingers clutch at the edge of her cardigan. "On the day he returned, he tried to put some sort of gloss on his disappearance. I refused to listen. But the next day, he was in the library again and was struck during an altercation. He left quickly enough that we didn't speak, but I worried. So that evening, after work, I sent him a few texts telling him he could come over if he wanted, but he never responded."

"You didn't try to get in touch with him after that?"

Astrid shakes her head. "What was the point?"

Detective Shariati is silent for some time. They must know that what Astrid said is true, that there was no more exchange between her and Perry after her unanswered texts.

"Does the library have CCTV cameras?" Maryam Shariati asks instead.

"It does, but they haven't worked for a while." Astrid gathers her courage. "Perry—is he okay?"

Maryam Shariati again does not answer her question. "Can you give us an account of your movements in the twenty-four hours after the altercation here?"

Maybe he is lying in a hospital unconscious. Maybe he kidnapped someone. Maybe he stood up people far more important than Astrid—a judge or a parole officer—and is now being considered a fugitive.

Anything but the bleak possibility that is now a maelstrom in her head, swallowing up all hope and coherent thought.

"I was at the library until it closed at nine p.m. that night. I texted him after I got home," she answers. "At one point someone came to the door. I thought it was him, but it was only the pizza I ordered. I went to sleep and came back to work the next morning and didn't leave again until the end of my shift."

She clasps her hands together and prays this will be the end of the interview. Instead, Detective Shariati starts again from their first meeting and wants to know everything Perry said and did—or at least, everything that wasn't NC-17.

Astrid does most of the talking, yet she feels as if she is the one forced to listen to something endless and miserable. She wants to cover her ears and beg for it to stop.

At last Maryam Shariati asks, "And you've answered everything to the best of your recollection?"

Astrid's voice quakes. "Yes."

At a signal from Detective Shariati, Detective Jones turns off the recording equipment.

Astrid leaps to her feet. "Can you please tell me now what happened to Perry?"

"He is dead," says Maryam Shariati, her eyes softening slightly. "I'm sorry. Thank you again for your cooperation."

CHAPTER EIGHT

The police call Jonathan into the meeting room next. He has no idea what he can possibly tell them, until they show him an image of Astrid's "situation."

Jonathan gives an honest if pared-down version of the Q&A between the British guy and himself. He describes the bit of the brawl that he saw the following day between the guy and an apparently homeless patron. He hesitates when Maryam asks him whether he remembers the man's visit from earlier in the year, but in the end answers yes, though he does not volunteer anything about Astrid looking adoringly at the man.

As soon as the police leave, he sets out to find Astrid. She is in the children's area, setting up a display of November holiday books.

"Hey, are you okay?"

Two days ago, he asked her the same thing. Then she kept him at arm's length; today she turns around and grips the front of his shirt with both hands. "I don't know, Jonathan."

Several parents with young children milling about look curiously in their direction. Jonathan tucks Astrid under his arm and ushers her into the Den of Calories. Sophie brought in a bunch of Halloween-themed cupcakes a couple of days ago and there are still a few left in the fridge. He takes one out, sets it in front of Astrid, and asks, "You want something to drink?"

Startling them both, Hazel pokes her head out of the storage room. "I brought a hot water dispenser from home. If you want tea, now you can have it right away."

And then, after a moment, "I'm sorry. The gentleman the police wanted to know about, is he okay?"

Like Jonathan, Astrid, and Sophie, Hazel too was interviewed by Maryam and her partner.

Astrid shakes her head. "He's dead."

Hazel's already grave expression turns even more somber. She glances at Jonathan. And when he nods, she comes into the Den of Calories and puts a mug under the hot water dispenser. "Is there anything we can do?"

Astrid tents her hands over her forehead, as if by doing so she can shield herself. She takes several deep breaths and looks up. "Jonathan, you know Detective Shariati, right?"

"We went to high school together." Jonathan chooses his words carefully. "But before today I hadn't seen her in ages."

Maryam was not at the reunion.

"Still, you must be friends, right?"

Maryam was in fact Jonathan's girlfriend for two years—two Christmases, two Valentine's Days, two proms. His mom still has their senior prom picture up on her mantel.

He hesitates. "I guess."

"Can you find out from her what happened? All they'd tell me was that he died, but not when or how or—why." Astrid clutches at Jonathan's arm. Her grip is tight, but her fingers shake. Her eyes brim with desperation. "Jonathan, do you think the police came here as part of a murder investigation? Am I being investigated for a murder?"

Jonathan sits at the bar of a midtown restaurant, nursing a martini.

The restaurant is a local favorite. To be a favorite in a town trying to hang on to its bohemian roots while swimming in a tsunami of tech money, it doesn't hurt to be a bit kitschy. The kitsch here is of the romantic variety: There are twinkling fairy lights everywhere, cascading in garlands and curtains. And overhead, crisscrossing the beams, hang pendant lights that are orange and red glass bubbles, because Halloween is over and everything has become Thanksgiving-themed.

Two months ago, close to a hundred of Jonathan's former classmates thronged the banquet room of this very establishment. Eleven o'clock that night, outside the restaurant, he finally managed to talk to Ryan Kaneshiro for a few minutes. It was the tail end of a brutally hot day. Heat still radiated from the asphalt lot, and Ryan's shirt was open a few buttons at the collar.

Shadow pooled in the hollow of his throat. He placed a hand on his roommate's shoulder and the motion pulled on his shirt, enough to show the indentation of a collarbone.

And Jonathan hasn't stopped thinking of him since.

Which is part of the reason that instead of contacting Maryam, he fixed up a time with Ryan. But it's also possible that Ryan, who works for the Travis County Medical Examiner's Office, might be able to tell him just as much.

"Is this seat taken?"

Ryan.

Without waiting for an answer, Ryan settles himself next to Jonathan. He is wearing glasses—and looks so hot it's a moment before Jonathan can say, "Hey."

The bartender comes over. Ryan orders a local beer. And Jonathan wants to roll his eyes at himself. The dry martini in front of him resulted from half an hour of last-minute online education, in the hope of appearing grown-up and sophisticated. If he knew Ryan had a beer in mind, he'd have ordered a beer too. At least he knows what he likes in a beer.

The bartender slides a pilsner glass of pale lager to Ryan, who takes a sip and turns toward Jonathan. He's waiting for Jonathan to begin, a faint gleam of amusement in his eyes.

Jonathan swallows. "Thanks for meeting with me."

"Sure. I'm sorry for what happened to your colleague," answers Ryan. "It's never fun getting mixed up in police business."

And Jonathan suffers his next bout of regret. He shouldn't have gone for such a no-nonsense opening, because now he must go straight to the problem, when he'd have preferred to ask Ryan what he's been up to lately—and in the past twenty years.

Does he still play basketball? When did he start wearing glasses? Has life been kind to him? Has he been kind to himself? Does he ever kick himself for giving the time of day to the dumbass high school quarterback?

"She has a list of questions, my colleague," Jonathan says, so that he can look down at his phone and stop staring stupidly at Ryan. "She would like to know the victim's full name and when and how he died, at least. I know I'm asking a big favor, so please don't hesitate to say no if anything goes against rules and regulations."

"That's okay. I can tell you a thing or two without getting into trouble." Ryan, like Jonathan, consults his phone. "Full name of the deceased: Heneage Pericles Bathurst."

"What?"

Ryan shows him a slightly fuzzy screencap. Jonathan squints to take in the full-throttled nonsense—at least Pericles was an important Athenian; what's Heneage? No wonder the guy went by Perry.

"Midmorning on Halloween, the police received a call from the management of an apartment complex in Northwest Austin. Mr. Bathurst was judged to have been dead at least ten hours by the time he was found in his rental car.

"As for how he died, I don't want to say too much, but I can tell you that it was not from natural causes. And I can also tell you that, for the moment at least, it isn't considered homicide."

"*Not* a homicide—and two detectives interview everyone at the library?"

"From what I understand, his parents don't believe their kid died of his own fault."

Not from natural causes. Isn't considered homicide. The parents refuse to accept their son's culpability in his death, but the police differ in their assessment.

An overdose, then?

No parents ever want to believe that their precious child is only one bad hit away from being a statistic. But a rich kid filling his existential void with illicit substances is all too common a story.

"The parents apparently have lots of connections. Nobody at APD wants them to hold a press conference saying that the police aren't doing their job, so the force is looking hard. Or at least they want to appear so."

Is this good news for Astrid, if the investigators themselves don't believe that they're looking at anything more than an accidental overdose? Or does it mean the opposite—that the detectives, under pressure from above, will in turn tighten the screws on Astrid?

"Anything else you can tell me?"

"Okay, you didn't hear this from me, but at the moment, your colleague is Detective Shariati's only lead."

Jonathan swears under his breath.

"I can also tell you that the fried pickles here are pretty good. Try some, if you still deal with gluten."

Jonathan's heart thumps. "Will you share some with me? My treat. I don't think I can handle a whole order."

"Sure," says Ryan.

He smiles slightly into his beer and Jonathan's heart becomes a racquetball ricocheting at a hundred miles an hour.

A large, festive party comes into the restaurant. Ryan gives the newcomers a cursory glance, then leans toward Jonathan. "Do you have a picture of the woman?"

For a moment Jonathan has no idea what he's talking about. Which woman? Astrid? Oh, Ryan means the perfect woman for his roommate. Jonathan finds the group selfie he took on Game Night and texts it to Ryan. In the picture Hazel stands at the very edge of the frame, almost hidden behind an exuberant Jeannette Obermann, her arms thrown up.

With Perry Bathurst and Jeannette Obermann both dead, it hasn't been a very good few days for the branch library's patrons.

"You can hardly see her in the back," Jonathan says apologetically. "She is beautiful, though, and . . ."

Ryan looks closely at his phone. "And what? Charismatic?"

"'Charismatic' might not be the right word. 'Enigmatic,' I would say."

"I'll have to take your word for it, because the picture doesn't convey much."

Ryan puts away his phone and takes a swallow of his beer. Jonathan's eyes are glued to the motion of his Adam's apple, the smooth skin of his throat sliding over the protuberance.

"But even if she's all that, I'm not sure anything will happen," Ryan continues.

A second passes before Jonathan hears his words. Hastily he raises his gaze to meet Ryan's. "And—why's that?"

Again the gleam of amusement in Ryan's eyes. Jonathan wishes he evoked a more substantial response in the first man who ever went down on him.

"Remember Conrad telling people about his perfect woman at the reunion?"

How can Jonathan forget? When Ryan and Conrad walked in that night, a hush fell upon the gathering. Ryan is hot, but Conrad is stunning, and their combined height and beauty were such that despair instantly swamped Jonathan.

And then, late in the reunion, some women managed to corner Conrad.

Ryan came over, a little hammered, and said to Conrad, "Hey, Davoud Asadi isn't coming. So you can be straight now."

Conrad, who might have been completely wasted, tilted his head back against the top of his high-backed chair. Perhaps because of his thick hair, slightly long and just beginning to curl, and his simple white shirt with a couple buttons open, he managed to look like an eighteenth-century aristocrat. "Brilliant. Whatever you say."

He spoke clearly, if slowly, and with a British accent, no less.

The women hooted.

"Wait, you're straight now? I'm straight too. Let's get together!" cried one, three sheets to the wind.

Conrad squinted up at the chandelier over the table, as if he weren't addressing his admirers but some invisible entity. "If you're at least five-nine, beautiful, stylish, and articulate, you may apply to be my girlfriend. Bonus points if you're Asian—and mysterious too. And if you satisfy all of the above requirements, I don't mind if you're a few years older."

Thanks to a decades-long influx of techies, Jonathan and Ryan's high school had a large plurality of Asian students. One of the women at the booth—Jonathan actually remembered her name, Maggie Liang—shouted, "Omigod, if I was six inches taller, I'd be your perfect woman!"

Her friends shrieked with laughter. "Shut up, Maggie. You're the least mysterious person ever. We know how many tampons you used last month."

Jonathan, who had been spying from a nearby table, finally went over and asked, "Is it true, you two aren't actually together?"

"It's true," Ryan answered. "He's just my roommate and you still have a chance with me."

He winked at Jonathan, then kicked Conrad in the tread of the latter's shoe. "Come on, let's go home."

Jonathan's hopes, like Jon Snow stabbed and left to die in the cold, miraculously resurrected.

So yes, he remembers every detail of that exchange. "And?"

"And the next day I asked him about it and he swore he couldn't have said anything of the sort because he doesn't date Asians."

Their fried pickles arrive, piled high on a plate. Jonathan eats a few pieces and screws up his courage. "Ryan, can I ask you a personal question?"

Ryan grins, the corners of his eyes crinkling. "Let me guess. Is it about how I became a forensic pathologist?"

No, not really. But if that's what Ryan considers a personal question then Jonathan had better go along. "Yes, that one."

"I had a boyfriend in med school. His dad specialized in litigating medical malpractice. One Thanksgiving with the dad was enough to convince me I didn't want to work on anyone who might sue me."

"What about the boyfriend? He wasn't scared?"

"Nope. He's been doing heart surgeries on babies left and right—which goes to show that I was probably just looking for an excuse not to save lives." Ryan dunks a slice of fried pickle in the tangy dip. "It worked out okay. I would have been matchmade to death if I were a doctor. But you tell people you do two hundred fifty autopsies a year and they can't wait to leave you alone."

Jonathan laughs in spite of himself. "I can't imagine why."

"Me neither." Ryan flashes another smile. "But it is what it is."

Could it have been like this for them, drinks together after work, making each other laugh, had things been different?

Had *Jonathan* been different.

So many times he'd wondered, especially since the reunion, what would have happened if they'd met each other not in high school but later. After he left the navy. After he finally learned not to run away from himself.

Well, you're sitting on adjacent barstools, aren't you?

There was no need for a face-to-face meeting—Jonathan could have asked his questions over a phone call. But Ryan agreed to come in person.

Does that mean he isn't, after all, averse to seeing Jonathan again?

Ryan looks at his watch. "Oh, sorry, gotta run. I have a date tonight. Wish me luck."

Jonathan's heart shrinks into an asteroid, a lonely rock lost in the vastness of space.

"Good luck," he replies mechanically.

Ryan hops off his barstool. "And good luck to your colleague," he says cheerfully. "Let me know if she needs anything else."

The intelligence Jonathan gleaned from his old friend at the county examiner's office does not comfort Astrid. Why did she think that it would? Sometimes there is no good news and the more one knows, the worse the situation becomes.

Jonathan hugs Astrid. "Don't worry. The whole thing will sort itself out."

But he doesn't sound convinced. He sounds hollow—and he looks worn out, as if the news weighs fifty pounds and he has carried it on foot all the way from midtown.

After he leaves, Astrid does the fifteen-minutes-before-closing announcement. She, too, sounds hollow.

Hazel appears at her elbow. "Astrid, do you want to grab a drink after work?"

Astrid freezes. She does not get drinks with her colleagues. She doesn't do anything with anyone, really. She simply cannot make up any more stories about her fictional Swedish parents' fictional farm in southern Sweden, a little more than a stone's throw from Copenhagen in Denmark.

And the last time she agreed to drinks after work was with Perry. Look how that turned out.

"I—I would love to, but most restaurants will be closed by the time we get there and I don't know any good bars."

"We don't need to go anywhere."

Hazel tilts her chin at the Den of Calories and the Wall of International Snacks therein. She hasn't dressed in anything half so luxe as what she wore her first day to work—today it's only a white long-sleeve tee over a pair of loose-fitting jeans—but she still looks as if she stepped out of an inspiration board.

Astrid wants badly to be her friend, as she wants badly to be Jonathan's and Sophie's friend.

"Having a drink right here?" her voice squeaks. "Will Sophie be okay with it?"

Sophie gets off at six most days and is long gone.

Hazel is unfazed. "Text her and ask her if it's okay for you and me to stay a little extra time to work on the donated books."

Some portion of Astrid's brain blares with alarm, but she obediently does as Hazel suggests. Sophie replies almost right away.

Astrid looks up from her phone. "Sophie says go ahead. She says thanks besides."

Hazel smiles. "It's settled, then."

"Okay," mumbles Astrid. Someone else must be speaking through her numb lips.

Shortly after nine p.m., Hazel slips out to H-E-B, which is five minutes away on foot, and returns with a combo tray of sushi and a bottle of screw-top white wine. She sets all the sushi on a paper plate and pours white wine into mugs.

Only after Astrid takes her first bite does she realize that she's starving. She devours five sushi in a row before pausing to take a sip of wine. The bottle doesn't look expensive, but the wine is brisk and delicious. She eats another sushi, savors the acidity of the rice, the crispiness of the tempura shrimp, the spicy smoothness of the drizzle of sriracha mayo on top.

"I don't remember supermarket sushi being this nice."

Hazel laughs a little. "I don't remember supermarkets selling sushi before I moved to Singapore—at least not this one. It used to have fried chicken and mac and cheese."

"Oh? When was that?"

"Gosh, almost a quarter century ago. I was ten when we left."

She really shouldn't, because if she asks Hazel personal questions, then in turn, she will be expected to reciprocate with information about herself. But the question slips past her tongue anyway. "If you don't mind me asking, why did you move to Singapore?"

Hazel opens her purse and pulls out, from a slender case, a pair of metal chopsticks. Astrid is completely charmed. Hazel pops a sushi into her mouth. "My mom is from Singapore. She and my dad divorced, so she went back to Singapore and took me with her."

"Was it hard, moving to another country?"

"It was. But even more than the displacement, I had a tough time dealing with my parents' divorce."

Astrid is amazed that she's learning so much, so easily, about Hazel. *And* that she hasn't put a stop to it.

"Are your parents still together?" Hazel asks.

This question Astrid can answer truthfully, so she does. "They are, but they're hardly hashtag goals. They might as well be roommates, rather than a couple. The only thing they do together is watch the evening news, and then my dad goes off to his man cave and my mom watches her shows and plays games on her iPad."

"Are they here in the States?"

The question is a jagged rock scoring the inside of Astrid's skull. It takes her a while to understand that Hazel hasn't called her bluff. She's only wondering whether Astrid's parents have emigrated from Sweden.

"They—" Astrid stuffs another sushi in her mouth to buy a little time.

Unbelievably, the sushi still tastes good—clean and sharp, unlike the mess she's made of her life.

She grabs her mug of wine and takes several sips. But there's only so much she can do to put off answering a simple question. The old answers, long practiced, long perfected, surface. "Have you ever heard of Malmö?"

"It's a city in Sweden, right?"

"Sweden is almost a thousand miles long north to south and Malmö is maybe fifteen, twenty miles from the southernmost tip of the Scandinavian Peninsula."

She stops—she is speaking in her own accent and Hazel, judging by that flicker of bafflement in her eyes, has noticed. But she waits patiently for Astrid to continue.

Astrid lifts her mug, but it's empty. Hazel unscrews the cap from the bottle and refills it. But the mug now feels glued to the table. Astrid can't make it budge.

"Most people here think of Sweden as reindeer and snow but in the southern reaches it has a decent growing season."

She is still speaking in her own accent and Hazel still regards her with infinite patience.

Astrid drags the words past her parched throat. "Potatoes, wheat, and sugar beet all do pretty okay there."

Oh, God, why did no one ever tell her that she sounds like an AI reading from Wikipedia?

"What about dairy?" asks Hazel. "I seem to recall that the Scandinavian diet is fairly high in dairy."

Astrid gulps. Not because she can't answer the question, but because she can. This is where she used to say that her fictional Swedish mother drinks a glass of milk every day at lunch. And if anyone was still interested after that, she could give a mini TED talk on Swedish cheeses, especially the ones people are likely to encounter in IKEA.

"Yes, lots of dairy. Have you ever had Hushållsost? It's a cow's-milk cheese and I like using it for quesadillas."

She laughs shakily.

Hazel takes a sip from her own mug. "I'm always interested in what people eat. Do you make quesadillas as a snack or a meal?"

Holy shit. Have they moved past the question of where her parents live?

Thank God. She can talk about quesadillas for days—not that she knows much about them, but she will blather on about anything now.

She opens her mouth and out comes, "Ever since I left home for college, I've been telling people that my parents live in southern Sweden, not far from Malmö. But that's not true. They live—and have always lived—in a tiny little town in Iowa."

Hazel's eyes widen. She thinks for a moment. "May I ask why?"

Astrid wishes she had a good answer. "I lost my mind briefly—I mean, figuratively, of course."

The southernmost counties of Iowa were hit hard by the Farm Crisis, which made her grandparents, formerly prosperous farmers, into paupers overnight and severely limited her parents' options in life. Her hometown has lost 40 percent of its population in her lifetime. And in spite of being surrounded by agricultural land—or perhaps partly due to the relentless production of corn and soybean—her entire county was—and is—a food desert where most non-meat cooking has to be done with shelf-stable ingredients.

"I don't want you to think that I was Don Draper, escaping some kind of horrible Midwestern past. I could have been any other small-town girl, leaving home for better opportunities elsewhere."

Hazel chews slowly. She doesn't look at all as if she's been turned off by Astrid's revelation, but nor is she burning with the sort of curiosity that would make Astrid feel like a monkey in a zoo. She is just waiting for Astrid to reveal more at her own pace.

So Astrid does. "I had a boyfriend in high school. We were serious—at least serious enough to plan to go to the same college. But he was a year ahead of me and two months after he left for college, he texted to break up with me—like he was Taylor Swift's boyfriend or something."

And she was so devastated and livid at the time, not realizing that in another decade, people wouldn't even text to break up anymore. They would simply disappear.

"Not very grown-up of him," says Hazel.

"No. And I had to find out from his sister that he fell head over heels for a Portuguese exchange student. Years later he would apologize, but at the time it didn't feel like one teenage boy broke up with me, it felt like the whole world rejected me. I became obsessed with female exchange students from Europe—they seemed to be everything I wasn't.

"Next thing I knew, I was spending the summer before college immersed in Swedish writers and Scandinavian travel shows."

"That doesn't sound so bad."

"It wasn't. Showing up at college telling people I'm from a little farm outside of Malmö wasn't bad either, to be completely honest."

Hazel pushes up her sleeves—it's a bit warm inside the Den of Calories. "Sounds a bit like Matthew McConaughey. Supposedly he went around for a whole year at college with an Australian accent."

"No way!" Astrid can't believe she doesn't know this. "What happened after that year?"

"I think he just sat his friends down and said 'haha, gotcha' or something of the sort."

Her kingdom for Matthew McConaughey's chutzpah! Instead, she was the girl who had absolutely no idea how to unwind the lie.

"I wish I'd done that. I was so happy when I started library school in a different state, only to meet someone who used to live down the hall from me on my first day. And when I came to Austin, guess what, someone from a year ahead of me in library school got transferred here too."

If she'd had the courage to admit her lies when she first realized their negative impact, two months into her freshman year, she might have lost some friends but she would have gained her life back. Instead she dithered and vacillated and let a silly charade become the ever-crumbling foundation of her life. And she's not even in touch with anyone she met in freshman year anymore!

"Sometimes it's easier to come clean to strangers." Hazel pours soy sauce over the dot of wasabi paste she'd put on her side of the paper plate and mixes the two with the tips of her gleaming travel-size chopsticks. "You don't need to answer if I'm being too intrusive—but I'm guessing that you also told the truth to Perry?"

Instead of embarrassment, Astrid feels an overwhelming sense of relief: Hazel knows and she understands. "Perry happened to strike up a conversation with me on a day when I didn't feel like lying. Sometimes I don't know whether I fell in love with him or with that euphoric feeling of finally being myself for once. For sure when he ghosted me, I didn't just lose a guy, I lost all hope that a new, different life was still possible."

She exhales shakily. "Then he came back. Now he's dead. And maybe I'm in big trouble. Is it terrible that I can't even feel anything about his death? I just want the police to understand I had nothing to do with it."

Ever since her interview with the police she's felt precarious, like a Jenga stack in a room full of overactive kids.

"You're in shock," says Hazel firmly. "Grief will come. And when it does, you might wish you were still in shock instead. But in the meanwhile, don't worry too much. The police will move on when they realize you were just a bystander."

"Thank you." Astrid suddenly feels shy. She lowers her head. "Thank you for everything."

"It was a low-risk offer on my part, to be a pair of willing ears. For you the stakes were much higher. So I should thank you for putting your trust in me. It's an honor."

No one has ever said such a thing to her, that it's a privilege to listen to her story. A warm, liquid sensation spreads inside Astrid. She stares at the paper plate of supermarket sushi and the two mugs of room-temperature wine—what a rare, beautiful sight.

In the end they manage to eat all the sushi—and share a pack of Pocky sticks from the Wall of International Snacks besides. Hazel asks if she can take the rest of the wine home.

"We're running low on cooking wine and this will last us until I can go to 99 Ranch."

Astrid must be a bit tipsy, because that strikes her as impossibly funny. She's still giggling as they lock up the library. Out in the parking lot, she hugs Hazel.

Hazel giggles, too. "Are you sure you can drive home?"

"Yes. I live barely a mile away and I'll be careful."

Hazel makes Astrid show her the location of her condo on a map app to make sure it really is close by before she hugs Astrid again and walks away. Astrid gets in her car and reels—not from alcohol, but the realization that maybe she finally has a friend.

When she's back home, she finds Hazel's number from the librarians' message group and texts, Please tell me that a new, different life is still possible for me.

Her phone buzzes almost immediately. I believe it has already begun. Good luck.

CHAPTER NINE

Friday

Sophie runs. She's not exactly comfortable being on foot alone in an unfamiliar neighborhood, but it's five thirty a.m. right before the end of daylight saving time and the sky is pitch-dark. She comes across only one other jogger, who raises a hand respectfully as they pass each other.

She does a mile and a half before she grits her teeth and ventures onto Fanfare Drive, that cursed street. The moment she does, she sees neon yellow police tape in the distance, flapping in the wind.

The air is cold and clear, yet her nostrils fill with the stench of acetone and rubbing alcohol.

But at least the RAV4 is gone—and the body too.

She reaches her car at five minutes past six and decides to take a risk. She drives to a side street not far from Twin Courtyards Apartments, parks, and runs toward the apartment complex. Yesterday, she, the not-so-proud owner of a brand-new burner phone, used it to call the apartment office while sitting in the parking lot of Home Depot.

Hi. I'm going to take a job at the new Apple campus and I'm looking for a place to live. Do your buildings have exterior cameras? That would make me feel much safer.

I'm sorry, ma'am. We don't. But the lease doesn't prohibit tenants from having them, as long as the installation doesn't damage the buildings.

She has her beanie down to her eyes, her mask up to her lower lash line. Dressed like this, even if individual tenants have cameras, they wouldn't be able to identify her, especially when it's still so dark.

Now she's on the street that leads to Twin Courtyards Apartments, but on the opposite side. As she slowly jogs alongside a wall, she realizes that the wall forms part of the boundary of Astrid's gated condo community.

Before she can think more about Astrid, a group of four people, dressed in athletic attire, come out from Twin Courtyards. Or rather, they stand right near the entrance, stretching.

The street T-junctions onto a more heavily trafficked road. Sophie crosses to the Twin Courtyards side and starts back. The folks meeting to work out are still there, probably waiting for more people to show up. They step aside courteously as Sophie approaches, but in doing so, they block the entrance.

For a split second she almost asks them to move but doesn't—she can't afford to draw attention to herself. So she nods and runs back to her car, parked out of sight, and leaves the neighborhood from a different direction.

Three hours later, she arrives in the Den of Calories. Jonathan, who just made a pot of coffee, hands her a cup. "I meant to tell you about an article in the paper yesterday, but the police showed up and it slipped my mind. You remember the woman who came to Game Night, the one with the third eye on her forehead?"

Sophie's eye twitches, but she has her response ready. "I saw that article last night when I tried to find some news about Astrid's ex."

"Do you think we should contact the police?" asks Jonathan.

Sophie's other eye now twitches too. "If she was missing, then maybe we could provide a time and place where she was seen alive and well. But she's dead and try as I do, I can't think of anything I observed that night that would help any investigators."

The door to the Den of Calories opens and Astrid comes inside. "You two are here early!"

She seems chirpier than Sophie would have expected. "How are you?" Sophie asks. "Are you holding up okay?"

"I—I think so." Astrid nods rather hesitantly, but she nods. "I just hope everything will blow over soon."

"Good attitude," says Jonathan. "Everything *will* blow over soon."

For Astrid, maybe. For herself, Sophie senses only impending doom.

When Hazel arrives for her shift early in the afternoon, Astrid waves at her from the picnic table under a sprawling live oak. A dappled ray of sunlight falls on Astrid and picks out the red streaks in her hair.

Hazel smiles as she approaches. "Taking your break?"

"Taking advantage of climate change before it roasts us alive next summer."

Fall and winter were always the best seasons in Austin, as spring is liable to bring sudden hailstorms and summer, which sometimes lasts for what feels like half the year, turns the whole region into an oven. But in recent years winter too has become thorny—Nainai lost both water and power for days during the Snowpocalypse. And persistently balmy days in November, however enjoyable, are a worrisome anomaly.

Hazels sits down opposite Astrid. "How are you?"

"I'm—" Astrid stops. "Oh, I spoke in my fake accent again, didn't I?" She plunges her fingers into her hair. "This morning when I got here, I wondered if I could start speaking normally. But then Sophie and Jonathan were there and without thinking I just did what I always do."

With her smooth, round face and large, wide-open eyes, she looks so young, like a high school student. And she wants so much to do the right thing. Hazel, not terribly maternal by nature, feels a surge of protectiveness toward her new friend.

"Power of habit," she says. "You can't eat an elephant in one day."

Astrid giggles. "That's—"

She leaps to her feet, all mirth gone from her face. "That's a cop car."

Hazel scans the parking lot but doesn't see any vehicle with a telltale light bar. Then her gaze lands on a blue sedan with a reinforced front bumper. A man and a woman emerge from the vehicle, but they are not the same pair of detectives who came to the library the day before.

"I hope they didn't send meaner cops this time," mumbles Astrid.

The plainclothes officers disappear into the library. But by the time Hazel and Astrid enter, they are nowhere to be seen.

Jonathan waves them over and whispers, "I think they're here about Jeannette Obermann."

"Oh, God!" Astrid sounds choked. "I hope they don't think I have anything to do with her."

Sophie's door opens. She beckons stiffly. "Jonathan, Hazel, will you two come in here for a second?"

"Sure," says Jonathan.

"What—what about me?" Astrid pipes up.

"You can keep getting ready for the teen book club meeting tonight, Astrid. Thank you."

Astrid doesn't look so much relieved as befuddled.

Hazel gives her a squeeze on the arm before she follows Jonathan into Sophie's office. It is a nice size for one person, but with five people crammed in, Hazel can barely find a place to stand without crowding into a silk ficus tree or a file cabinet.

Sophie introduces the visitors as Detective Hagerty and Detective Gonzalez, Hagerty being the man and Gonzalez the woman. And they are indeed on the premises to investigate Jeannette Obermann's death.

Detective Hagerty, a white man with a craggy face and military bearing, gives his email to Jonathan and asks for the list of patrons who registered for Game Night as well as photographs taken during the event by library staff.

"Can we have everything ASAP, Mr. Webster?" asks Detective Hagerty.

"Call me Jonathan, Detective," says Jonathan. "And I will take care of this right away."

He glances at Hazel before he leaves. Hazel, on the other hand, keeps an eye on Sophie. The administrator, her hands braced on the back of her swivel chair, looks a normal amount of rattled for someone who likes order and orderliness dealing with a sudden influx of chaos. But behind a wastepaper basket, which blocks the detectives' view but not Hazel's, Sophie is grinding the toe box of her gleaming black heel into the carpet, as if the pressure from her left foot is the only thing that keeps the seams of Hell from ripping open.

Detective Hagerty turns his attention to Hazel. "Now, Ms. Lee, you sat next to Ms. Obermann during Game Night, at the same table."

Hazel does not request the use of her given name. She is perfectly comfortable being addressed as Ms. Lee. "That is correct, Detective."

"Would you mind answering a few questions for us?"

"Of course not," says Hazel.

"Normally you'd be able to use the meeting room, but our English conversation group is in there right now," says Sophie. "Hazel, why don't you show the detectives to the staff office? I'm sure everyone will understand."

Hazel nearly raises a brow. Is she reading too much into it or is Sophie implying that the police are inconveniencing the librarians?

She smiles at the detectives. "This way, please."

At the door, Hazel glances back at Sophie, who is slowly sinking into her chair, her face a rigid mask.

The staff office boasts a decent tally of square footage. But with four full-size desks, two on each side of the traffic lane leading to the drive-through pickup on the far wall, as well as a number of rolling bins, rolling carts, and crates, luxuriously spacious it is not.

The other librarians have decamped elsewhere for now. Hazel thought she and the detectives would move some chairs around and maybe even push a desk out of the way so they can all fit around the same desk. But after Detective Gonzalez sets up the recording equipment, Detective Hagerty sits down directly behind that desk, and Detective Gonzalez takes Jonathan's usual spot across the traffic lane, which leaves Hazel no choice but to lean on the fore edge of the desk opposite Hagerty's: She'd be too far away if she sits down behind this desk, the space between the desks is too narrow to fit a chair, and she does not feel like dragging a chair to the side of the desk currently occupied by Hagerty,

Astrid, temporarily free from the gaze of the law, brings in a few cans of chilled sparkling water and a plate of individually packed gluten-free cookies. Hazel smiles as she thanks Astrid, but Astrid departs looking no less stressed: Hazel is wedged between two desks, which cannot be a reassuring sight for Astrid.

"Ms. Lee, please state for us your name, age, occupation, and place of domicile," begins Detective Hagerty.

His opening is nearly identical to Detective Shariati's from the day before. But Hazel already knows that his interview will be conducted in a very different tone. She also knows that she will not cooperate to anywhere near the same extent.

She answers his inquiry. The edge of the desk cuts just under her bottom, not exactly comfortable, so she boosts herself up to sit on the desk.

This apparently jaunty position does not please Detective Hagerty. He taps the pen in his hand twice against the top of his desk. "You started working here only one day before this Game Night event."

"That is correct," she replies.

It occurs to her that if the police are in the dark, desperately seeking clues, this coincidence might not appear one hundred percent benign.

Sure enough, a small silence descends, as if the detectives too must ponder the likelihood of her stumbling into a job that throws her into the environs of not one but two suspicious deaths as soon as she starts working.

"Where was your previous place of employment, Ms. Lee, and how long did you work there?"

"This is my first job in the United States. I was born in Austin but lived in Singapore most of my life. And while I was there, I was a freelancer."

Detective Hagerty leans forward. "Oh? What made you return to the US?"

Does the fact that she literally traveled ten thousand miles to take the job make her more suspicious? "My grandmother is in her late eighties. She doesn't have other relatives in town so I thought I'd come and keep an eye on her. But while she enjoys my company, she doesn't want me in her house 24/7. In fact, she was the one who trawled through job listings on the city's website, found this opening, and insisted that I apply."

She pauses a moment. "Would you like her contact information?"

Detective Hagerty contemplates her offer—he has a dour face and grim eyes, as if everyone he's ever come across has disappointed him somehow. "We'll appreciate her info, should it become necessary to speak to her directly later on. Will you give us your recollection of Game Night?"

Hazel has given Game Night a great deal of thought, but she takes a minute to sort through her recollection. "I attended Game Night not as a library clerk, but someone who enjoys board games. Still, at first I restricted myself to helping out. It was only when Jeannette Obermann and another couple showed up that I was asked to join them for a game of Clue. We played but didn't finish the game, but I don't think anyone minded as it was a social event more than anything else. Then the staff on duty took some pictures. By roughly eight forty-five all the patrons cleared out of the meeting room. I helped with the cleanup and was home by ten after nine, since I live less than two miles away."

Detective Hagerty gestures at Detective Gonzalez, who brings over a tablet that shows the group photos taken that night—Jonathan indeed sent the requested material ASAP. But Hazel can only identify the librarians, Elise, Elise's friend Ana Maria, Jeannette Obermann, and Ayesha and Ahmed, the Pakistani couple.

"Do the others not frequent the library on a regular basis?"

"Perhaps they do. But I'd worked at the library a grand total of two days by the time Game Night took place."

Detective Hagerty takes back the tablet and turns off the display. "I assume you didn't participate in the planning of the event?"

"Correct."

"Ironic that Jeannette Obermann played a game about murder in her last public outing."

A loaded statement. Hazel smiles. "To me it was less ironic than unsettling, as I was the one who played the killer in that game."

The detectives exchange a glance. Are they surprised by her honesty? Or will they consider it a form of taunting?

She wants to tell them to relax. She isn't some blasé killer out to lead the police on a merry chase, she's just been . . . sleepwalking through life these past few months and can't be bothered to react to their minor intimidation and negligible traps.

She *is* troubled about Jeannette Obermann—and Perry Bathurst. They struck her as people with things to do and places to be who would have been enormously upset if they'd known that they were about to die. But Perry

Bathurst likely fell victim to an accidental overdose. And Jeannette Obermann—it's not Hazel's place to speculate on what might have led to her death.

Detective Hagerty tools his expression into one of stony impassivity. "What did you think of Ms. Obermann's demeanor that night?"

"She seemed excited to be there."

"What makes you say so?"

Hazel thinks for a minute, her knuckles against her chin. "She kept looking around. She talked as much as the other two patrons combined. She definitely had the best costume—or maybe I should say the best makeup for Halloween."

Detective Hagerty, who hasn't written down a single word, spins his pen with his squarish fingers. "Do you remember what she said?"

"Everybody at my table was new to Austin. The three of them talked about when and why they moved, the price of housing, and how they felt living in Austin, as opposed to visiting as tourists."

Detective Hagerty begins to sound impatient. "What did Jeannette Obermann say on those topics?"

Behind him hangs a framed poster that states simply, in rainbow letters on an iridescent background, **WE DO NOT POLICE WHAT YOU READ**. The word "POLICE" hovers right above his head, which strikes Hazel as droll.

"She really liked Apple's cafeteria," she says solemnly. "She liked that there's a Trader Joe's within five miles of her apartment. But she worried that on a single income she'd only be able to buy a tiny condo, unless she was willing to drive an hour each way for work."

Detective Hagerty frowns. What Hazel tells him is too generic, almost worthless for someone on the prowl for a killer. "What else did she say?"

"We didn't play for that long. There were times when we discussed the rules of the game, and the other couple also talked about their lives."

Detective Haggerty stares at Hazel. It is not pleasant to be the subject of his unblinking study, not because of any creepy or suggestive undertones but simply due to its sheer, unrelenting, possibly sociopathic intensity.

Without breaking eye contact, she pulls off the slim black band on her wrist and gathers her hair into a low ponytail. And if he persists, she plans to make a whole-ass decorative braid from the silk scarf around her shoulders while she stares back at him.

"Anything else you can tell us about her?" Hagerty finally asks his next question as Hazel reaches for the scarf.

She flicks a bit of nonexistent dust from the scarf. "When I left, Ms. Obermann was still sitting in her car. She was parked not far from me and there was enough light to see her costume."

"Were you also able to see what she was doing in her car?"

"Looking at her phone, maybe—it didn't seem that she was doing anything unusual."

"It was late and the library was closed. You did not think it was unusual that she stayed in her car?"

Hazel shrugs. "I've sat in a parked car scrolling on my phone. I assumed Ms. Obermann was doing the same."

Detective Hagerty's jaw moves. "Were there any details—any at all—during her time at the library event that stood out for you? Did she pay special attention to someone or something? Say anything a little off? Appear nervous or afraid? Or did anyone else at the gathering strike you as being, doing, or saying anything out of the ordinary?"

Hazel shakes her head as she continues to withhold information. "At the moment, I really can't think of anything else, unless you want to know about her favorite dishes at the Apple cafeteria."

"You are sure about that, Ms. Lee?"

His voice edges lower, more menacing, which might have intimidated a woman of less privilege. She meets his gaze straight on and answers, with a perfectly clear conscience, "I'm sure, Detective."

"Well, should you recall anything later, please do let us know."

It sounds like a threat. She smiles as she accepts his card—and is done with her first adversarial police interview.

Her first in the United States of America, in any case.

CHAPTER TEN

Singapore
Seven months ago

Of the ten police officers who barged into Hazel's penthouse apartment shortly before midnight, only three remain seven hours later, two men and a woman.

They sit around the coffee table, a large, mirror-smooth oval of polished steel shot through with veins of equally reflective brass. The two junior cops stare at the floor-to-ceiling windows, an eight-meter-high wall of glass that overlooks Marina Bay, now bathed in the reddish-gold brilliance of sunrise. A third, their superior, studies Hazel as he drinks his coffee, a scowl on his face.

Hazel, trying not to slump in her accent chair, isn't so much unafraid as she is dead tired. She had yet to go to sleep when the raid began. And now, after an entire night watching her home being systematically torn apart, she just wants to be alone.

Does she owe Kit an apology? she wonders numbly. A bit pedestrian for her to suspect that he was having an affair, isn't it, when instead his failed speculations on cryptocurrencies led him to—allegedly—embezzle twenty-five million dollars?

"Where is your husband, Ms. Lee?" asks Detective Chu, still drinking coffee and still scowling.

Briefly she considers the possibility that the coffee might be too bitter. Carmela and Marisol, her Filipina housekeepers, both make excellent coffee. But they too spent a sleepless night and are probably in no mood to show hospitality to the invaders.

"Detective," she says, "I have not received any news from the outside world since you seized my devices. All I can tell you is what I've already told you. My husband, as far as I know, reached London ten days ago to attend a weeklong art fair.

"Now that the art fair is over, according to his original schedule, he should be in the Sussex countryside, at his father's place."

"'According to his original schedule'? You don't know for certain that he's in the Sussex countryside, at his father's place?"

Hazel suppresses her desire to repeat *But I've already told you.* "That is correct, Detective."

"Because of this 'trial separation' of yours."

"Correct."

"Which is known to no one except the two of you."

Do you *blast the news of your trial separation to your family and friends?*

"Correct."

"A bit convenient, don't you think, just when the police come knocking?"

Hazel crosses her feet at the ankles. "In that case, it would have been far more convenient for me to have gone with him and be out of the country too."

Detective Chu takes another sip of his coffee—and finally bends forward to add sugar and cream to the remaining brew in his cup. He stirs it with an antique silver spoon, part of a set of twelve, a family heirloom from the Georgian era that Hazel's mother-in-law received from her own mother-in-law upon her wedding to Kit's father.

I don't know about the luck attached to those spoons, Hazel's mother had commented in private, as Kit's parents are not only divorced but acrimoniously divorced.

Hazel shrugged. *It's their tradition. You have to let people keep their traditions.*

Now she wonders whether her mother was right and the gift was tainted with the senior Asquiths' marital failure.

Or maybe she is trying to deflect blame elsewhere, and even a set of spoons will do for a scapegoat.

"Ms. Lee, I hope you understand that these are extremely serious charges," Detective Chu begins again, fortified by less bitter coffee.

She makes no reply, waiting for him to go on.

"Explain to me again what he does."

"He is an art dealer. He has two art galleries, one on Lock Road, the other in Soho, in London." Words dribble from her lips, a listless trickle of syllables—she sounds like a street vendor at the end of the day, too tired to hawk her wares anymore. "He sells art that he acquires, or sometimes on commission, depending on the preference of the artist. He works with museums and corporations, connecting them to emerging artists or older works that have been overlooked. He also works for an art investment fund."

The one he stole from, apparently.

"He is properly credentialed for this line of work?"

"He has a postgraduate degree in art history and experience working at both the Tate Modern in London and the Museum of Modern Art in New York—if those are what you would consider proper credentials."

Detective Chu's lips slant—maybe he heard a rebuke in her sluggish reply. Who knows, maybe she intended one, too.

"Have you ever been to his galleries?"

"Yes, both."

"Did you not notice the scarce foot traffic?"

"Art galleries are not grocery stores or movie theaters. Foot traffic is not how one judges their success or lack thereof. A large portion of sales can take place in the back rooms, or by catering to the tastes of art collectors who may never set foot inside a showroom."

Now she sounds like the audio track for a self-guided tour, giving out a string of archaeological details.

"My husband has always appeared busy. He always has calls to take and travels to arrange. And he has always paid into our pool for household expenses promptly—and bought me gifts and holidays."

"You are not acquainted with the actual financials of his enterprises?"

She shakes her head, too weary to be going over everything yet again. "I believe I've mentioned that our prenuptial agreement specifically precludes that."

"And you and your family allowed it?"

She deliberately sat with her back to the sunrise, but even the light sweeping across the policeman's face sears her vision. She blinks, which somehow only makes her eyes feel grittier.

"He and his family allowed much more, if that is your line of reasoning. My grandfather's lawyers drafted the document, which bars my husband from not only touching my inheritance but also any involvement in any Kuang family holding or venture. It did not seem terribly unreasonable, then, for him to ask that I and my family also stay out of his business. I know my grandfather gladly agreed to it and even commended my then-fiancé's attitude, which he gauged as cooperative without being obsequious."

"What did your husband think of the document?"

She desperately wants to rub her eyes but forces her hands to remain still on the armrests. "He thought it was par for the course—no man marries Bartholomew Kuang's granddaughter without such a document, especially if he's a foreigner."

"He is considered some sort of a relation, though, is he not? And your union an example of intermarriage upon intermarriage?"

This is at least a new question. Perhaps as his subordinates searched fruitlessly, the detective read up on Hazel and her husband to greater depths.

"My grandfather's mother was an Atwood. And some branch of the Asquith family and some branch of the Atwood family are related by marriage. The precise details escape me but my grandfather was able to pinpoint my husband's lineage. He conceded that Kit comes from good stock, but the prenuptial agreement remained inescapable."

A prenuptial agreement, however, even an ironclad one, will not protect her reputation, once it becomes known that the police want him. And of course it could have never protected her heart from the chill that slowly crept in over the past year.

"So there you have it, Detective. I did not—and do not—have access to the financial records of his ventures. His conduct within our marriage gave me no reason to suspect that he might have been in money trouble."

"You had no idea at all that anything might be wrong?"

"That is not what I said. I said that I never thought he might be having money trouble. What I suspected was that he no longer loved me—and was perhaps in love with someone else."

"Because?"

She props up her elbow on the armrest and drops her cheek into her palm—it's either that or let her head fall back against the padded top of the chair. "Because he was distant and easily distracted. He stayed later and later at work. And sometimes when I went to his gallery in the evenings, he wasn't there, even though that was where he'd said he would be. You know, all the classic signs, at least according to movies and TV shows, that someone might be having an affair."

"Did you not ask him?"

"No."

If I asked him, and he said yes, then that would have been the end of us, we who have no children and no financial entanglement to hold us together.

Every hour or so, it occurs to her that she might never see Kit again: Her grandfather will insist that the dissolution of their marriage be conducted via lawyers, and only via lawyers.

But she wants to hear everything from Kit's lips. She wants him to tell her why.

It's respectable enough, I guess, art dealing, he'd said wryly. *My parents don't have to apologize for it, or explain what I do, especially if they label me as a gallery owner. People understand then that I'm a shopkeeper. Actually it might have been better if I became a bookseller, but I've always been slightly dyslexic and would not have done a very good job.*

She'd laughed.

They'd met on her Singapore–Frankfurt flight and had hit it off right away. From Frankfurt she was headed to Brussels, to meet her board game publisher, he to Basel, to attend Art Basel, of course.

As they readied for disembarkation, he proposed that they meet in Bruges afterward, for a second date.

Oh, we already had a first date?

I don't know about you, but I'm deeply relieved to have that behind us.

So there they were, in Bruges, ambling along canals lined with cake-colored town houses.

Why would it have been better if you'd been a bookseller?

Booksellers don't have to travel as much. Or it's possible that everything I know about bookselling is wrong because everything I know about bookselling comes from Notting Hill *and that rom-com in which Tom Hanks was basically Barnes & Noble in its heyday, right before Amazon came along and ate its lunch.*

After that, their conversation had promptly veered off to his mother's love of romantic comedies—and her mother's equally strong adoration of celluloid tragedies, romantic or otherwise.

That had established a pattern: his charming deprecation of his profession, a few anecdotes here and there of his days working in museums, and perhaps an analogy or two on what it was like trying to get artists and billionaires to see eye to eye. But no more than that—never more than that.

It was a refreshing change from the men of her family, who talked about work to the exclusion of almost everything else. She never suspected that this modesty, this disinclination to take up all the air in the room, was in service of deception.

"You are sure you've had no communication from him for the past five days?"

She nods slowly. "Before he left we agreed that we'd check in with each other once a week—to exchange photos, so that if anyone asked we'd still appear up-to-date on each other's lives."

"And you did not try to keep tabs on him through social media, his or his friends'."

A good guess—or does Detective Chu already know her entire browsing history?

"No," she replies simply.

"No, indeed. But you spent a great deal of time looking up the island of Madeira. More specifically, clicking through fifty Airbnbs and thirty different real estate listings—in the last three days alone. Thinking of relocating?"

Has she looked at that many? She remembers only an indistinct continuity of hope, regret, more hope, and more regret.

"I visited Madeira once, when I was much younger. I've always wanted to go back. At a time like this—or rather, at a time like the past few days, more than two weeks into my trial separation with little hope that it would be followed by anything but a real separation, I wanted to lose myself in something that made me happy, however momentarily."

But, of course, truth is that unfiltered, unedited photo everyone skips over. Detective Chu shows his disdain immediately. "Come now, Ms. Lee. What is your real interest in Madeira?"

A deep green canyon. Tall, speckle-limbed plane trees casting leafy shadows on the terrace. Two young people, leaning on the parapet separating them from a precipitous fall. They were having a conversation about happiness, of all things, the way it is sometimes possible to have substantive discussions with a complete stranger.

So, asked the young man, *what do you do?*

He had pierced ears, not just lobes but cartilage, yet wore no earrings. She didn't normally care one way or another about men wearing jewelry, but she was curious what he would look like with a barbell that spanned the width of one helix and a big spiky cuff on the other ear.

But in the meanwhile, she had to confess, rather embarrassed, *I don't have a job yet.*

What? But you are like a million years older than me. I thought you must already be a senior director, plotting to dethrone the chief executive.

She laughed. *Hey, I got my master's only this past summer. And I've been traveling since.*

He smiled. Ah, those dimples again. *Okay, rich lady who obviously doesn't need to work, what did you study at uni?*

Architecture. My mom wanted me to be an architect, because she herself would have liked to have been one. But it's not for me.

What is for you, then?

She wanted to give him a good answer. A great answer, unique and fascinating. But all she had was an honest and honestly boring *I don't know.*

He considered her. His gaze was warm and curious—her heart sped up from his nearness, his attention.

What makes you happy? he asked.

They'd circled back to happiness again.

When she was small, her dad sometimes asked if she was happy. When they rode the teacup at Disneyland. When he took Mom and her to see fireworks on the Fourth of July. When he got her a new bicycle. She'd always nodded hugely and hugged him hard.

But after she moved to Singapore, she didn't remember anyone asking about her happiness anymore. Maybe it was an age thing—kids understood and handled happiness much better than their adult counterparts. Or maybe it was because everyone was overwhelmingly concerned that she not squander her great good fortune. She was a real live instance of *The Princess Diaries*, an ordinary girl who became a great heiress overnight. With that kind of exceptional luck, it would be downright vulgar to aspire to happiness too.

I don't know what makes me happy, she said after a while.

Hmm, said her companion of the past ninety minutes—or had they even known each other for that long? *Fair enough—I'm not sure I do either. Do you have anything you look forward to, either on this trip or when you get back home?*

She did. She'd stumbled into an all-women tabletop gaming group back in Singapore and it quickly became one of her favorite monthly experiences. And on this cruise, she met up with a bunch of fellow passengers who played in the evenings; some even brought their own favorite games from home.

Umm, board games?

Okay, you really are much older than me. I see that now.

She laughed again. It was funny because earlier she'd indeed tried to convince him that there existed a real and substantial age gap between them.

Design tabletop games, then, he suggested.

What do you mean?

Every game you play was designed by somebody. They didn't spring fully formed onto retail shelves. Someone conceived them, developed them, and published them.

But I don't know anything about designing games.

You don't need to be a game designer to design games. Monopoly—or the game it was based on—was designed by a writer who wanted to illustrate certain economic principles. A woman, by the way.

How do you know that?

Because I was the idiot who, when my cousin told me that Monopoly was developed by a woman, shouted "Not a chance! It says 'Parker Brothers' right here on the box."

She laughed some more.

Would she have tried to create a board game if she'd never heard his gentle exhortation? She doesn't know—certainly no one else ever lobbed that idea at her. But he did suggest it, and she did give it a shot—and the rest, as they say, is history.

Her first two games did well; the third one took off in a way no one anticipated, least of all her. The trip to Brussels was a celebratory one. But as she sat by herself on that Singapore-to-Frankfurt flight, she wished only that she could have told the lovely young man that his long-ago idea had given her life structure and purpose.

But since she couldn't, since that ship had sailed, capsized, and sunk ages ago, she chose to smile when Kit sidled up to her.

And never told him that he was the one she'd settled for.

"My real interest in Madeira?" She uncrosses and recrosses her ankles. "I received this apartment as a wedding gift, Detective Chu. I believe I can get my grandfather to splurge on a little divorce present, too. Frankly I didn't find any appealing properties on Madeira. Maybe a place in Lake Como would be more my speed. Or even Scotland."

Detective Chu's lips thin—he believes it.

Hazel exhales, exhaustion rolling over her like a fog.

Her doorbell chimes, the otherwise ordinary sound harsh and ominous under the circumstances. She blinks, her eyes as dry and brittle as glass.

"Your colleagues, Detective?" she asks Chu.

The police look at one another. "No."

She specifically instructed Carmela and Marisol not to tell her mother—or anyone, for that matter—about the police raid. She has no next-door neighbors—her grandfather's generous present occupies the top three stories of the building. Who can it be, then, so early in the morning?

The doorbell shrills again.

Hazel rises. *Kit.* Normally the sound would not make her think of her husband, but two days ago she changed the code and deleted his fingerprints from the authorized list.

For the first time she's glad of Detective Chu's presence: She won't have to explain the lock change to Kit. And then alarm finally spikes through her depleted brain.

Kit has returned home at the worst possible time.

Detective Chu is ahead of her, charging for the door. She picks up her pace. Shit. She owes it to Kit, doesn't she, to at least shout a warning—*Fly, you fool!*

But as the intercom comes into view, it is her mother on the screen, raising her hand to ring the doorbell yet again.

She taps on the intercom, intending to tell Lillian Kuang that it's not a good time.

But before she can even offer a greeting, her mother's voice blares. "Hazel, are you okay? Why didn't you answer your phone? I've been calling and calling. Your mother-in-law has been trying to reach you for three hours."

A strange chill pools at the base of Hazel's spine. "Why is she calling me? Is everything okay?"

Did she find out that her son is now a wanted man?

"No, everything is not okay. And why don't you open your door? Hurry up!"

Hazel opens the door—at this point her mother might as well learn the whole truth.

Lillian Kuang barges in and enfolds Hazel in a hard embrace. "You have to be strong now, Hazel. Don't panic."

Their contact jolts Hazel more than anything else. Fifteen years in the

United States of America had failed to turn her mother into a hugger. Whatever news she is bringing will be a calamity far worse than mere financial crime.

"What's the matter?" Hazel croaks.

Her mother pulls back, but now her hands are braced on Hazel's shoulders, forcing Hazel to look at her.

"Kit's plane went down over the North Sea," says she, her eyes full of pity. "I'm sorry, sweetheart. I'm so sorry."

CHAPTER ELEVEN

Sophie does not have an outright fear-and-loathing relationship with the police. Still, they unnerve her—her mother's car was stopped at least three times a year, leaving the tony private school in Chicago where she taught and Sophie attended.

And that was under the best of circumstances, when she had absolutely nothing to hide.

It is not the case here.

Detective Hagerty makes the hair on the back of her neck stand. As he contemplates her, his silence heavy and broody, he seems to already know everything.

Her toes tremble in her heels.

But her interlaced fingers at the edge of her desk still look steady enough. Her Halloween manicure of slime-green half-moons on deep matte black is five days old yet just might pass muster if no one looks too closely.

People only see what you show them. Right now she needs to show the police Ms. Claremont, library administrator. Ms. Claremont may be unsettled by the situation, even a little vexed—why are there two unnatural deaths associated with her library all of a sudden?—but she is not guilty of anything.

Why, she was barely involved.

The code-switching that has served her well all these years kicks into gear. She receives every question with grave attentiveness. She gives considered answers. She cooperates.

The expression on Detective Hagerty's face, as he rises to leave, is one of disappointment, but only a mild variety—he did not anticipate game-changing information from Sophie after all!

They exchange parting pleasantries. The detective asks about a good time to speak to Elise. Elise has a prom committee meeting after school. Sophie informs Hagerty of it, having no idea whether he will let Elise attend the meeting in peace—and let Sophie have the rest of the evening to prepare the girl for her first police interview.

She closes the door behind him and collapses against it, her mind a blazing blank.

Knocks come, heavy strikes that thud against her spine.

It's Detective Hagerty again. He appears excited. Her heart is the stock market in 1929, dropping straight down.

"Sorry to take up more of your time, Ms. Claremont. But while we were speaking earlier, Detective Gonzalez had a look around the library and came across Ayesha and Ahmed Khan, who sat at the same table with Jeannette Obermann. Would it be all right if we borrowed your meeting room to interview them? Jonathan said that the English conversation group is done and there is nothing else scheduled in the meeting room the rest of the day."

Sophie has no reason to refuse him, so she takes the initiative and walks the cops and the Khans, who look reverent, nervous, and more than a little curious, into the meeting room.

She offers a silent prayer for the couple—*May they not be innocent bystanders caught up in this country's justice system.* Then she stops by Hazel, on duty at the checkout station, and asks if she's all right.

Hazel nods with all gravity. "Thank you, I'm fine."

And then she asks, "And you, Sophie? How are you?"

There is real concern in her eyes and Sophie comes precariously close to blurting out, *Oh, God, I'm so scared my face is numb.*

She pastes on her most librarian-ish expression. "I'm all right. Except now I'm behind on my emails."

The cops interview not only the Khans but Jonathan and Astrid, neither of whom spent much time in the meeting room during Game Night. Jonathan at least came in to take some photographs; Astrid didn't even have that much contact with the attendees.

When the detectives are done at last, Sophie walks them out of the library. Then she catches up with Astrid in the children's area. Thankfully this police interview does not appear to bother Astrid as much as the previous one. At least when Sophie asks about it, Astrid replies with no small relief that she can feel these cops are just being thorough, that they are not really interested in her.

Sophie wishes she could say the same: Even though she can *reason* that they haven't zeroed in on her, she feels her peril.

On her way back to her office, she sees Ayesha Khan at the checkout station, speaking to Hazel.

"I hope this won't prevent you from coming to other library events in the future," says Hazel.

"I don't think so, but it's spooky, isn't it?" Ayesha Khan's features scrunch together in distress. "What a horrible thing to happen. Everything was so nice and normal at Game Night. Now to think that we might have been among the last people to see her alive . . ."

Hazel nods in sympathy. "It is a very great shock."

"Will this affect the library? It won't be closed or anything like that, will it?"

"I don't think so," Hazel says slowly. Then she sees Sophie and beckons her over. "Sophie, will the police investigation affect the normal operations of this branch?"

Once again Sophie pastes on her head-librarian-in-charge face. "At the moment, we are not expecting disruptions."

"Thank goodness," says Ayesha Khan. "This is such a great place to work."

"I agree," says Hazel smoothly. "And we do apologize for any inconvenience."

Ayesha Khan, after reassuring Hazel and Sophie that she has not been unduly troubled, departs for the work gallery, where her husband is already back before his laptop, typing away.

"This won't become a publicity problem for the library, will it?" asks Hazel in a low voice.

Sophie shakes her head. Not that she believes the negative publicity that might arise wouldn't impact the library at all, but people still go to movies and concerts despite the danger of a mass shooting. It will take a lot for patrons to abandon their favorite library. "The library will be okay."

Whether Sophie will still be here to oversee the library, however, is a very different question.

"Will *you* be okay?" asks Hazel.

A frisson of chill climbs up Sophie's inner wrist. This is the second time Hazel has asked whether Sophie is okay. Why? Does she know something?

"Yes," says Sophie with as authoritative a smile as she can manage. "Now I'd better reply to all those emails in my inbox."

"Hey, Jonathan!" chirps Maryam. Her toned arms are on display in a sports tank top and her face is flushed and slightly damp—she might have just finished a workout before getting on their Zoom call. "I was wondering when I'd finally hear from you. But of course you met up with Ryan first."

Jonathan's heart does a somersault. "Did Ryan tell you?"

"He asked me ahead of time—wanted to know if I'd be cool with it."

That is *not* the same as Ryan calling her afterward with all the deets. Jonathan hopes his disappointment isn't obvious. "I didn't know you guys kept up all these years."

"We didn't. He looked me up after the reunion—'Hey, why weren't you there' and all that—and we picked up from there." She leans forward, her dark eyes gleaming with curiosity. "So, are you still into him?"

Jonathan, his face burning, can only defend himself with rhetoric. "What do you mean, *still* into him—when was I ever into him? But enough about me. How are you?"

Maryam, as it turns out, taught middle school for a few years before she decided that seventh graders were the bane of her existence and she'd rather deal with criminals instead. "At least now I can drive past a school without breaking out in hives."

They chortle over that. Then she says, "So, about your question..."

Sophie, concerned for Elise, who has to speak to Hagerty and Gonzalez, asked Jonathan if he could find out a bit more about the case. Jonathan figured Maryam was the best person to ask.

He pulls his chair closer to the screen. "Yes?"

"Sorry, I don't have a ton to tell you," says Maryam. "Theoretically they and we could be working on the same big case—"

"Wait, what?"

"Currently, the link between the two deaths is highly circumstantial but not nonexistent."

"You mean, they both passed through the library in the final hours of their lives?"

"A bit more than that, but not much. She was found one mile from her apartment, he one-and-half miles from his hotel, and they were found about two miles apart—like I said, not much to go on." Maryam brings what looks to be a turkey sandwich from offscreen and takes a bite. "Detective Hagerty has stated, in his professional opinion, that Bathurst was an idiot who trusted the wrong dealer in an unfamiliar city. He doesn't want to waste his time on Bathurst when the real interesting case is Obermann. And he has some pull with management so Jones and I got Bathurst instead."

Jonathan shoves a forkful of scrambled eggs into his mouth, which leads to a digression on what they usually eat for dinner and what they can throw together quickly when they don't feel like either cooking or breaking the bank ordering in.

All at once it doesn't feel like decades have passed since they last talked.

It's ten minutes later that Jonathan remembers he's not there just to chat with an old friend. "Do you also think that Bathurst is a waste of time?"

Maryam dabs her lips with a napkin and drinks from a water glass. "I was definitely not happy to be saddled with the case, but let's say I'm not as unhappy as I used to be."

"Oh?"

"Sorry, can't divulge." She grins, looking a bit like the Cheshire Cat. "But to get back to your original question, Detective Hagerty and I agreed to exchange relevant information with each other, but I haven't heard a thing from him since. So I can only assume that whatever he's found out doesn't impact my investigation. Do you want me to ask him some questions?"

Jonathan sucks air through his teeth. If Maryam becomes too curious about Hagerty's case, Hagerty might wonder why. And Sophie, Jonathan feels, would prefer to fly under Detective Hagerty's radar. "Have the rest of your dinner. I'll get back to you on that."

As he is about to log off, however, Maryam asks abruptly, but with a sly look on her face, "Do you remember my cousin Davoud?"

Where did Jonathan hear that name recently? "Barely—we had one class together in high school. The only reason I remember him at all is because he's your cousin. Why?"

Maryam grins again. "No reason. Let me know if you want me to speak to Hagerty."

CHAPTER TWELVE

Sophie finally gets rid of her Halloween manicure that should have been wiped off on the night of October 31 itself, after the last of the trick-or-treaters left. She has always made sure to use a base coat. Still, the keratin of her nails has become slightly yellowed and vulnerable-looking.

She picks up her phone. There's a message from Jonathan, informing her that Detective Shariati doesn't know much about Jeannette Obermann's case, but does Sophie want her to ask?

Sophie deletes the text and rubs her faintly throbbing temple. Does she?

The front door bursts open, startling her, but it's only Elise. "Mom, Ana Maria is here to help me with chemistry!"

Sophie shakes her head. "We do chemistry on Friday nights now?"

"What? It's Friday night?" Elise laughs. "Did you hear that, Ana Maria? I refuse to study on Friday nights."

"Hmm," says Ana Maria, "guess I'll have to stay until tomorrow to make sure you do your trig homework. Hi, Miss Sophie. Thanks for letting me sleep over."

The sleepover has been in the works for several weeks. But Ana Maria, who is locked in an epic struggle for valedictorianship with three other kids at their ultracompetitive school, does not have the luxury of taking an entire Friday evening off—she has to get in an hour of APUSH reading so she doesn't fall behind.

Sophie takes advantage of this window of time to talk to Elise. Elise, who pops a bag of kernels in the microwave to take upstairs to Ana Maria, ends up shoving popcorn into her own mouth as she listens, wide-eyed, to Sophie's account of these wild days at the library.

What? Is Astrid okay? She's such a nice person!

No, you can't be serious. Jeannette? The woman with the third eye, the one who asked me about graphic novels the Saturday before—she's dead too?

We're not the last people to see her alive, are we, Mom? Didn't she want to talk to you about volunteering at the library? My God, she even waved at me when we drove away from the library that night.

Sophie nearly breaks out in hives at Elise's comments. "The police want to talk to everyone who was at Game Night—we are all considered to be among those who saw her last. They already interviewed the library staff. They will want to ask you questions too."

Elise's expression turns somber.

"I don't think you'll be in any danger for speaking to the police about Game Night. All the same, I want you to take it extremely seriously," says Sophie. "No jokes. No glibness. Don't draw their attention. Just give them all the facts they ask for and get out. Got it?"

"Yes, ma'am."

Sophie pats the girl on the arm and sighs. "Okay, pop a new bag of popcorn and take it to Ana Maria—and tell her that the police will want to talk to her too."

Elise jumps up from the couch. "They won't give her a hard time. She's an A-plus-plus student."

You could be an A-plus-plus student too, Sophie wants to say. But Elise's chillness extends to her schoolwork and she cannot be bothered with AP classes or extra credit assignments.

Elise delivers a hot bag of popcorn to Ana Maria, then comes downstairs again, without being urged by Sophie, to prep for her upcoming police interview. She asks questions as if she were the cops, answers those questions as herself, and covers the entire timeline from the conception of Game Night to when they drove away from the library.

In the end it is Sophie, both proud and shaken, who shoos Elise upstairs.

"Tell Ana Maria forty-five minutes of school reading is enough for any sixteen-year-old on a Friday night."

Elise, who seems to have already brushed off the oppressiveness of a mock police interview, shouts up the steps. "Ana Maria Estevez, you are hereby commanded to live a little."

"I'll party when I'm in college."

Elise glances back at Sophie. "You know she won't. She'll pick such an expensive place, work every spare minute, and then eat nothing but ramen for ten years after she graduates just to service her student loans."

Ana Maria sticks her head out over the banister. "I heard that!"

Elise grins and bounces upstairs. "Miss Estevez, hi. I'm Elise Claremont, your burnout prevention counselor. How are we doing tonight?"

Sophie wants the girls to have fun and de-stress. But now that they are doing so, yakking it up in Elise's room, she grows deathly afraid that everything Elise loves will be taken away from her.

She wants desperately to do something. To reconnoiter Twin Courtyards Apartments, at least. But the burner phone, the feverish browsing at random coffee shops from a reformatted old Chromebook, Jeannette Obermann's address that she bought from an online background-check service with a prepaid debit card—will everything Sophie's doing simply make cops laugh harder when she is caught breaking into Jeannette Obermann's apartment?

She shivers.

Elise storms down the stairs—she is strong and compact, like Simone Biles if Simone Biles were seven inches taller—and sticks her head in the fridge.

"What are you looking for?" Sophie demands.

"Buttermilk. Nope, we don't have any. No worries, Mom, Ana Maria and I will get some in the morning and then we can make Grandma's buttermilk pancakes."

Is this the excuse Sophie has been waiting for to leave the house? Moments later, she stands outside her garage, car key in hand, and vacillates.

Overhead, light spills out of Elise's room—light and muffled laughter. Somewhere in this tight cluster of town houses, someone is baking an apple pie, the aroma of butter and cinnamon warm and delicious in the air. Were this any other Friday, Sophie would have wrapped up her hair and been snugly ensconced in bed, a biography open on her lap.

The beauty of her ordinary life burns a hole in her heart. Will she ever have that again, that safety, that normalcy, that belief in the possibility of building a small haven for herself and Elise in the midst of a big, scary world?

A small, bright red car parks not far from her house. A tall, slim woman emerges, the surface of her wafer-thin puffer jacket gleaming under the glow of a streetlight. Hazel. What is she doing here? Surely she should know that it is inappropriate for her to show up uninvited at Sophie's house.

Or is it a coincidence? Is Hazel meeting a Tinder date nearby?

Hazel sees Sophie and comes forward. She smiles easily, as if there is nothing odd about her presence. "Hi, Sophie. Sorry to bother you on a Friday night, but I have a question and the library may not be the best place for it."

"Oh?" Sophie is wary, but Hazel's demeanor is completely unthreatening. Disarming, even. "How can I help you?"

Perhaps Sophie's reassurance to Ayesha Khan wasn't enough for Hazel. Perhaps she's worried about the library and therefore her job?

Hazel tucks her hands into her pockets. The two of them must appear like neighbors who happened upon each other, chatting a bit about kids and weekend plans.

"I've been thinking about Detective Hagerty's visit to the library," says Hazel, her tone soothing, her voice dulcet. "I can't help but think we haven't seen the last of him. And I was hoping you could tell me, if he comes back, whether there's anything I should keep in mind. Anything I should not remember, if I'm questioned again."

She gazes at Sophie expectantly, as if Sophie should know what she's talking about.

Sophie's stomach lurches. "Do you mean to tell me that you saw something that you kept from the detective?"

"Yes," says Hazel. Almost six feet tall in her thick-soled sneakers, she steps closer until she looms over Sophie. Then she lowers her head and murmurs, "I went home after Game Night, realized I forgot to get groceries, and went out again. I drove past the library around nine forty-five, stopped at the red light just outside, and saw you there, talking to Jeannette Obermann."

CHAPTER THIRTEEN

Sixteen years ago

Sophie's phone rings. It's Jo-Ann. *Again.*
What is wrong with that woman?
Sophie sets the phone on silent. But the device buzzes like a frustrated bee.
She gets in her car and starts the engine—don't want to let the good people of Newark Public Library see her lose her temper right there in their parking lot, not when she's just answered every interview question with the calm, helpful demeanor befitting a future public librarian.
But dear God, Jo-Ann makes her want to take a drill to the phone.
A year ago, things were going so well between them, when Jo-Ann suddenly got it in her head that they should have a baby. She brought it up on a Saturday evening, after first serving Sophie a Jamaican chicken curry on the balcony of their Hoboken apartment. There were candles and a vase of flaming amaryllises on the table, with Manhattan in the distance, draped in sunset.
Sophie was feeling a rare bout of effervescence—it was summer, her first year in grad school had gone well, and she was with someone who managed to make an uptight girl like herself laugh every single day.
Jo-Ann's proposition punctured her bubble instantly.
"No," she said. "I'm not ready."

She was only twenty-five and had a year left in her master of library and information science program. She didn't want to have a baby while she was still in school, nor did she want to become a mother immediately after getting a job.

Jo-Ann, across from her, smiled indulgently. Her skin, the color of myrrh, glowed in the candlelight. "I didn't say *you* have to give birth. I have a perfectly good uterus, too."

Sophie threw up her hands. "Right. And you'll then quit your high-power-attorney job to look after this kid."

"Neither of us has to give up our work. Together we'll make enough to hire a nanny."

Sophie would be lucky if she made a quarter as much as Jo-Ann. She'd feel terrifically impoverished if she had to contribute a half share toward the cost of a nanny. But she might feel even worse if she contributed only 20 percent, as if she had only a 20 percent stake in this child.

"And what if the nanny doesn't work out for some reason? What if the nanny gets sick or has to leave for a while to look after her own family? Then who looks after this baby?"

"Then we get another babysitter. They have services now that'll have vetted, experienced childcare providers in people's homes in the blink of an eye," said Jo-Ann breezily.

Her confidence was one of Jo-Ann's most attractive qualities. That same damn-the-torpedoes-full-speed-ahead attitude was also, at times, her most exasperating trait. Sophie was not a damn-the-torpedoes kind of person. She needed to carefully map out the locations of all the pitfalls, then engineer a path to avoid every single one.

Jo-Ann's blitheness struck her now as not only inappropriate but wildly irresponsible. Fine, never mind the money—in a relationship like theirs, with a personality like Sophie's, it might always be a bit of a sore point that she couldn't be an equal financial contributor. But this was about a lot more than their domestic arrangement. They were talking about a baby in a world hostile to same-sex parents.

"You're a lawyer. Have you taken a proper look at current law—and the legislations that are brewing everywhere in this country? What if something happens to you? I will have no rights to make any decisions for this child."

"Not after you adopt the child."

"But that is not an instantaneous process. What if something happens in the meanwhile? It'll be your mom who becomes the kid's legal guardian."

At last some of Jo-Ann's cheerfulness drained away. Night was falling. The wind picked up. The candles flickered and cast shadows across her face.

Time magazine had published an article only a few months ago, asking if Jamaica was the most homophobic place on earth. Jo-Ann had pooh-poohed the clickbait-y hypothesis, but she had not disputed her homeland's entrenched homophobia. And Jo-Ann's mom was the most homophobic person Jo-Ann had ever met.

"Nothing will happen to me," Jo-Ann declared, but she sounded a little shaken.

"You don't know the future," Sophie pointed out, pushing away her still half-full plate.

"Don't you see?" Jo-Ann reached across the glass table and took Sophie's hand in hers. "That's why it would be better for you to have the child. Then my mother will never be able to take it away from us."

Sophie had always loved the warmth and care of Jo-Ann's touch. But she was annoyed enough to pull her hand away. "Aha! Now we come back to that. And I already told you I am not ready to have a baby."

"And are you ever going to be ready to have a baby?"

The sadness on Jo-Ann's face made it impossible for Sophie to be sincerely angry. It was true: Sophie might never be ready to have a baby.

Maybe someday her biological clock would tick like a B-movie nuclear bomb with a flashing countdown. But even so, would it ever out-glare her internal chaos meter, which always judged the world as too threatening, too unstable, and too inherently untrustworthy?

"I'm thirty-four, Sophie, and every day I get older," pleaded Jo-Ann. "I mean, I don't feel older, but I also don't want to be having my first biological kid at forty, for both my own sake and the kid's."

Jo-Ann's drive to have everything right here right now accounted for much of her success, but it was also the reason Sophie held her own plans close to the chest: They'd just moved in together and she was already talking about a baby next year.

Of course Jo-Ann had wanted to move in together by the end of their second date, but Sophie held out. And she believed that a good five years should elapse before a relationship passed the durability test to undertake the addition of a baby.

At which time she, though not naturally inclined to having kids, would be much more open to persuasion.

But not now. Not when she hadn't finished school, found a good job, or reassured herself that she and Jo-Ann would be able to stick it out through thick and thin.

"Can we please not discuss this any further today?" Her head was beginning to throb.

Jo-Ann rubbed her own arms, as if she felt cold. "Is this going to be one of those things that no matter when I bring it up, it will always be the wrong time?"

Can you not just wait five years? Sophie wanted to shout.

She was crazy about Jo-Ann, she who had almost decided that a spinster life would, in fact, suit her just fine. She loved Jo-Ann's expansive love of life, she loved how kind and deeply decent Jo-Ann was, and she had never known how wonderful it felt for everything she wanted to do to sit absolutely right with someone.

But Jo-Ann was a force of nature and it was all Sophie could do to hang on to her own plans and her own self. If Jo-Ann learned that she might be persuadable in five years, she was going to be hell-bent on cajoling Sophie to do it in four, three, two years. Hell, right now!

And Sophie could not allow that.

"You're right. It's always going to be the wrong time, at least until I'm out of school."

She considered it a perfectly reasonable answer. And what did she get for her honesty and transparency? An out-of-left-field request for them to take a break three months later!

"What is this, *Friends*? Real people don't take breaks. We're either together or we're over!"

Sophie rarely raised her voice, but doing so on this occasion did not make any difference. Jo-Ann was possessed. If Sophie would not agree to a baby then they had to take a break from each other.

The break has not been kind to Sophie. She does not like changes and does not make changes lightly. Going back to being single after she finally became accustomed to thinking of her future not in "I" but in "we" was like being locked out of the house cold, wet, and shivering.

Their mutual friends, unable to believe that they won't get back together any moment now, keep bringing her Jo-Ann's news. *Did you know she bought a house? Did you know she nailed a huge deal for her firm? Did you know she managed to negotiate four months of leave for pro bono work? That's Jo-Ann for you, always giving back to the community.*

Now Sophie is finally—reluctantly and still somewhat resentfully—getting used to being on her own again. It sucks, having no one to text during the day, no one to meet after school, and no one to hug her when her mom issues another strong disapproval of her "lifestyle."

But hey, no one to break her heart and crush her dreams either. That's gotta be worth something, right?

And she doesn't believe that she'll hear from Jo-Ann at the end of the "break" either, unless it's to tell her that Jo-Ann has already found the perfect baby mama and would be welcoming that prized child very soon.

So why is Jo-Ann calling today, all of a sudden?

Her phone buzzes throughout the drive home. As Sophie walks into her tiny apartment, she jabs the red phone button yet again—and belatedly notices that there are fourteen voice mails.

They can't be from Jo-Ann, can they? Jo-Ann likes to talk on the phone but never cares to leave voice messages. Instead she prefers to send a text if she can't reach Sophie by calling, the reason Sophie had to switch to a plan with unlimited texts.

The voice mails *are* from Jo-Ann. The first few sound almost identical. "Hi, Sophie, sweetheart. It's me, Jo-Ann. I know I've been an asshole but please call me. This is important. Super important. I love you, okay? I never stopped loving you for a second."

Sophie sneers. *Right.*

But as message after message plays, the iteration begins to get to her, especially as Jo-Ann's voice becomes more earnest, more urgent.

The ninth voice mail is longer. "Hey, Sophie, you know I don't leave messages if I can help it. And I really wish you were here, by my side, so I don't have to keep annoying you with these voice mails. But it's important and I don't want to blurt out what I need to say to you in a stupid text. So please, please, please call me. Please."

On the next one Jo-Ann starts to sound desperate. "I'm sorry, Sophie. I'm sorry for everything I've put you through. Will you at least let me apologize properly, which I can't do talking into an electronic device?"

Her voice breaks on the thirteenth message. "Oh, God, I don't know why it never occurred to me before. You haven't moved on from me—from us—have you? I think about us all the time. I've been so inspired. I bought a house for us, Sophie. You never talked about it, but I know you weren't sure yet whether you should invest in a lifetime with me. This is me telling you that I'm so sure of us still being together decades from now that I will literally bet my house on it. Just say yes and I'll transfer the house to your name. But please at least listen to my messages. If you delete them unheard then what am I going to do?"

All at once Sophie knows why Jo-Ann's calling. And she knows what Jo-Ann has been up to since she last saw the impulsive, preposterous bitch. Dear God, if Sophie is right, then Jo-Ann used the "break" to get herself artificially inseminated. The whole thing was just so that they didn't have to actually break up because she went to a sperm bank over Sophie's objections!

The house isn't a gamble. It's a baby-I-done-did-you-wrong present!

What was Jo-Ann smoking that she thought she could spring a baby on Sophie and it would be okay?

Sophie deletes the messages, one by one, with vicious satisfaction. You think you're too good for compromises like the rest of us mortals? Then enjoy this baby all by your lonesome self, because I will not be coming by with flowers and casseroles.

The final message is over a minute long. Sophie hesitates. What would be better if they ever run into each other—to tell Jo-Ann that she expunged this last voice mail without hitting play, or that she listened to it, laughed at its futile pleas, and hit delete anyway?

She envisions herself as her most terrifying auntie, the church organist who never made a single mistake in thirty-odd years, declaring, with a genteel sneer, "Oh, I heard. But no reason for me to answer, was there?"

Sophie goes for it.

Jo-Ann is now frantic. "Sophie, help me!"

Sophie stops eating her imaginary revenge bonbons.

Jo-Ann sounds scared.

Jo-Ann is never scared. She is one of those individuals who glide through life certain of their specialness, convinced that nothing will ever stand in their way, not really. And people don't maintain such attitudes in adulthood unless it's been demonstrated again and again that life will always stand down where they are concerned and that they can always behave like kids going wild at a buffet.

"I was so sure I could handle this on my own, but now I don't know anymore. Ahhhh! Oh, fuck. Ahhhh!" Jo-Ann wails.

"Breathe now. I know it hurts, but you need to relax and breathe," says a woman. "You have to remain calm for the baby."

Jo-Ann doesn't exactly have a high tolerance for pain.

Sophie stands up.

"Oh, God, that was a motherfucker of a contraction and they won't give me anything because I'm not five centimeters dilated yet. But Sophie, Sophie, listen, the baby is in trouble. I don't know what's going on. This whole pregnancy was so easy—I never even had morning sickness. But now they say her heart rate has dropped and they have to do an emergency C-section."

Sophie falls back into her couch, her hand over her open mouth.

Black women in the United States are three times as likely to die from pregnancy and childbirth. But surely statistics don't apply to Jo-Ann Barnes. That shit is for others, not Jo-Ann Barnes. Never Jo-Ann Barnes.

"Can you please come? I'm at St. Paul's Hospital in Albany, room 435. Please help me. I know you don't agree with this but please come. You're already listed as my emergency contact—cuz you're my sister, don't you know, and—"

"Ms. Barnes, we need you to put the phone away. We have to sedate you right now."

"Okay. Okay. Sophie, I love you. I love you. Please, if anything happens to me, please look after the baby. Her name is Elise—I wanted something beautiful and sophisticated like yours. You know you are family to me. You *are* my family. Please, Sophie—"

"Ma'am, you have to hang up now."

"I'm sorry—I will. Just come, Sophie. Please. Soph—"

The message ends abruptly. Did someone yank the phone from Jo-Ann? Sophie springs up. The time stamp on the message is fifteen minutes ago. How long does a caesarean take?

She turns on her desktop computer and looks it up online. Forty-five minutes to an hour.

So Elise is about to be born. Or maybe she's already out of the womb and the medical team is just stitching Jo-Ann back up.

Sophie taps her fingertips against her phone. Her mom hates to see her fidget; Sophie deplores it no less. The *dak-dak-dak* of keratin on hard plastic drives part of her up a wall, yet she cannot make herself stop.

After a few minutes, she finally sets her phone aside to google post-C-section care.

She is not going to get back with Jo-Ann. A woman who pulls a trick like this—having a baby and expecting that Sophie will eventually go along with it? Lord knows what else she might do in the future. Pop culture can preach spontaneity all it likes, but spontaneity is for people who can afford it, people who have comfortably situated parents and personal social standing to cushion them for when that spur-of-the-moment decision turns sour.

Jo-Ann's spontaneity has cost Sophie a lot and she will not put herself through that again.

But she also doesn't want Jo-Ann to be all alone after a major operation. And Baby Elise—Jo-Ann wanted her so badly, someone ought to take that child some balloons and a teddy bear, mementoes that she can point to, when she's much older, that show she was welcomed into this world, heartily and with great joy.

Sophie makes up her mind and calls Jo-Ann. It immediately goes to voice mail. The operation might be over, but Jo-Ann is probably still under anesthesia.

She listens to the message again to write down the name of the hospital.

Why did Jo-Ann choose to have her baby in Albany? Wouldn't she have preferred to give birth at a hospital either in Manhattan or on this side of the Hudson River in New Jersey?

Sophie groans. Of course she isn't the only person from whom Jo-Ann is keeping the pregnancy a secret. That four-month leave from work might have been devoted to pro bono work, but its ultimate purpose must have been to keep her law firm in the dark about her impending motherhood. After all, a woman with a child, especially an infant, is more likely to be passed over for major assignments and further promotion.

Jo-Ann, already a partner, is dead set on making managing partner. And as long as she still hopes that Sophie will come around, why not keep the maternity of the baby a secret so that later on she can say it's Sophie's, in the expectation that this way, having a baby won't affect her career any more than it would any of her male colleagues?

To do that, she must give birth where those in her normal life are unlikely to run into her.

Sophie groans again and packs a small bag for herself.

The three-hour drive turns into five with traffic and Sophie becomes increasingly antsy.

Jo-Ann should have regained consciousness long ago. A conscious Jo-Ann would have asked for her phone in short order. She would have asked for it to be plugged in if the battery had died. And she would have asked with such amiability and wide-eyed gratitude that the nurses would have been delighted to help.

So why hasn't she called yet?

Midway through the drive Sophie veers into a rest stop and calls Jo-Ann. It goes to voice mail yet again. A chill creeps into Sophie's heart. Potential disaster is the language she speaks most fluently, having been raised to consider risks arising from all quarters every step of the way. Yet now, as she merges back onto the highway, for the first time in her life, she finds herself reasoning the way Jo-Ann must.

What can possibly happen to Jo-Ann? Nothing, that's what. After the agony of labor, the strain of an abrupt operation, the joy and relief of learning that the daughter she's yearned for has arrived safely into this all-too-imperfect world, Jo-Ann must be sleeping, completely knocked out by the events of the day and the painkillers sloshing through her system.

That's it. No catastrophic scenarios. Occam's razor all the way.

Occam's razor all the way has Sophie sweating despite the AC in the car blasting on the highest setting. When she finally reaches the hospital, she nearly clips another vehicle in the parking lot. Jo-Ann still doesn't pick up her phone. Sophie grabs a couple of random items from the gift shop and charges up to the maternity ward.

"Hi, I'm here to see Jo-Ann Barnes. She was in room 435 earlier, but she had to undergo an emergency C-section and I haven't heard from her since. Do you know if she's back in the same room?"

The young Black woman at the nurse's station does not even look up. "Let me check for you. What's the name again?"

"Jo-Ann Barnes."

"Oh, honey!" exclaims a voice from behind Sophie.

Sophie turns around to see a South Asian nurse in her forties, the name *Amiru J.* on her badge. "She was calling you and calling you. We barely managed to take the phone from her right before the operation started."

Guilt, sharp as teeth, sinks into Sophie at the woman's gentle yet weary statement. "I'm sorry," she says, her voice breaking a little. "I had a job interview today. And then I had to drive five hours to get here. Can you tell me if she's still in 435?"

Nurse Amiru shakes her head. She turns to the young woman behind the nurse's station. "I'll take this one."

Then she beckons Sophie. "Come with me."

Sophie scampers in her wake. "Is everything okay? Is her baby okay? Last I heard, the baby was in distress and they were going to do an emergency C-section."

"The baby is fine—I'm taking you to see her now. Her bilirubin is a bit high but that's not uncommon for newborns. Everything else looks good and she should be strong and healthy. She's really cute too."

They turn the corner and come upon a nursery. Behind the large window, there are half a dozen babies in bassinets.

"There she is, second row on the left," says Nurse Amiru.

All the babies are tiny. The nugget that is Elise seems even smaller than the rest, a barely there bundle with a scrunched-up little face. Sophie is only halfway through her breath of relief when a new worry pummels her. "She isn't premature, is she?"

"She might be a couple of weeks short of her due date but that's considered full-term, so no worries there. She doesn't need to be in the NICU or anything like that."

Sophie sets one hand on the wall next to the window. "That's wonderful. So Jo-Ann can take her home when she's discharged?"

Her shoulders are as tight as clenched fists from driving all tense for so many hours. Her right calf too threatens to cramp. But at least Elise is doing well. Now Sophie just needs to drop off the gifts she's bought for the sweet little nugget and—

"I'm afraid that's what I need to talk to you about," says Nurse Amiru. "Ms. Barnes—your sister—she won't be able to go home from the hospital."

"Oh?" Sophie tears her eyes from Elise. She's never been a baby person but she wants to cradle Elise with infinite care and gaze at her for hours—she'll have trouble saying no to Jo-Ann if Jo-Ann wants to come over with Elise. "Were there complications from the C-section?"

"Yes, great complications."

A prickling sensation spreads from between Sophie's shoulder blades. She is suddenly four years old, listening to her mom tell her that her firefighter dad won't ever come back home from work again.

"Is—is she okay?"

The nurse shakes her head. "I'm sorry."

Jets of heat and cold zip up Sophie's neck into her skull, spiking a pain that expands and implodes at the same time.

Were this a movie, she'd have interpreted the information Nurse Amiru is trying to impart very differently. But this is real life. This is Jo-Ann of the infinite vitality. Jo-Ann, unlike her exuberant personality would suggest, has never been careless with money, because she always says, somewhat jokingly but mostly meaning it, that she's going to live to a hundred and ten and needs a large enough nest egg to be comfortable in her long golden years.

And Sophie has always believed her. When she used to plan a whole life together for them, she even experienced pangs of jealousy, imagining herself dead at sixty-five—not unusual for women of her family—and Jo-Ann living it up in her seventies with a younger, hotter new girlfriend.

Surely this isn't what Nurse Amiru is trying to tell her. Surely it isn't too much to expect that Jo-Ann will live at least to her eighties, ditching her pantsuits to exist free and easy in the bright plaid caftans of her island youth, a glass of tongue-scrapingly spicy ginger beer always at hand?

"You mean she isn't okay now but she will be soon? She's here in this great hospital"—Sophie googled the hospital earlier and it has a sterling reputation, especially its maternity ward—"and—and you'll make her all good, right?"

Nurse Amiru, her eyes solemn, places a hand on Sophie's arm. "I'm sorry. She passed away about an hour ago."

Childbirth is dangerous business and Sophie is willing to consider postpartum hemorrhaging. She is willing to picture Jo-Ann weak and ashen, surrounded by beeping machines and a tangle of tubes.

Her brain refuses to understand "passed away," yet something crashes to the floor—the bag of gifts for Elise.

"That can't be true. You must have her confused with someone else."

"I wish that were the case. But it's hard to mistake her for anyone else. When I checked on her, she took one look at my name tag and asked if I was from Kerala. She said that she had an intern at her law firm whose mom is also a nurse from Kerala. It was delightful to talk to her—she knew so much about my home state."

Sophie's stomach twists. She knows a thing or two about the beautiful South Indian state too. The intern is now a full-fledged attorney. During their time together, Sophie and Jo-Ann had drinks with him a couple of times. They even attended a grand Christmas feast at his parents' place.

Still she persists. "Are you sure?"

Nurse Amiru glances down—belatedly Sophie realizes that she is clutching the woman's hands.

"She developed a pulmonary embolism after her C-section and had to be rushed into surgery on a different floor. I kept thinking about her. So on my break I went up and asked how she was doing and that was how I learned."

When Sophie was in college and going to football games, her friends, who cared a lot more than she did about the fortunes of the home team, got tense and weepy in the final minutes of hotly contested matches. Some even sank to their knees and prayed right before a Hail Mary pass. Sophie used to shake her head at them. Chances are, a team going for a Hail Mary pass has already lost. Why get so worked up?

Now she too is putting all her hope into one last attempt to hold off the reality crashing toward her like a fishtailing semi.

"But she is—she was—" Dear God, does she really have to talk about Jo-Ann in the past tense? "She was so healthy. She could play racquetball for hours and then go out and dance like she was in a music video. And she was saving her money because she was going to live forever."

Nurse Amiru envelops Sophie in a fierce hug. Sophie hears herself panting. *Please don't let go. Don't let go of me.*

But the kindly nurse eventually does. "I'm so sorry. But I have to make my rounds now. We have a chaplain on the second floor if you need to talk to someone. The baby is okay for now—she'll be staying with us at least tonight and probably tomorrow night too.

"You go get some rest. Tomorrow you'll have to come back as the next of kin to deal with paperwork."

She hugs Sophie again, this time more briefly. "Take care of yourself. I'll pray for you and the baby."

Sophie stares at her departing back. Then she turns toward the window to Baby Elise on the other side, sleeping like a cherub, with no idea that she is now an orphan.

Sophie glances again down the corridor, but Nurse Amiru is gone; the empty passage glares back at her under a pitiless fluorescence.

Something wet falls on her. She looks down. Her hands are clamped together. A large droplet is rolling off the side of her right hand, just as another large droplet splatters onto her left hand.

Tears, from her own eyes.

Sophie doesn't cry. By nature she is more stoic than expressive, and what little tendency to weep and fuss in the hope of receiving more care and attention was stomped out by her mother's hard nurture.

And she isn't even that devastated—yet. She's in shock. Hell, she's still in denial. So why have her eyes become leaky spigots?

Because, she realizes slowly, as teardrops continue to rain down, she's scared, terror coursing through her like a tsunami crossing the deep ocean at five hundred miles an hour.

Her worst fear has come true—the very first objection she raised when Jo-Ann blithely declared that she could be the one to have the baby. Jo-Ann is dead. Sophie has no blood relationship to Elise. She and Jo-Ann weren't in a civil partnership. She has no eligibility to apply for any legal status that will allow her to make decisions for the baby.

Even sunny, ebullient Jo-Ann was damaged by her upbringing. Even she sometimes stood before a window and stared out into the middle distance, lost in old arguments and old hurts that never quite lost their power to wound anew.

Aubrey Claremont disapproves of Sophie's queerness. Yet it isn't, for all her devotion to her church and her Savior, a line-in-the-sand condemnation. Aubrey disapproves because Aubrey considers queerness a luxury for rich white people, just as marijuana is a luxury for rich white people, something for which *they* will not be punished. But a Black woman from a family hanging on to middle-class respectability tooth and nail indulging in an alternative lifestyle? It will not end any better than a brother caught smoking a fat one on a street corner, bothering no one in his mellowness.

Cora Barnes, however, is a real believer. Cora Barnes regards homosexuality as a great and willful perversion, a deadly offense against God and Nature. Cora, hardworking, enterprising, hospitable Cora, a lioness of a mother and the maker of the best goat curry in all of Kingston, Jamaica, banished Jo-Ann because Jo-Ann refused to live a lie.

I'm glad your dad is already dead, she once said to Jo-Ann, *because this would have killed him, to see his baby grow into an abomination.*

While they were together, Jo-Ann sent home a card one Christmas, a photocard with Sophie and Jo-Ann in front of the pyramids, from a surprise trip organized by Jo-Ann to celebrate the one-year anniversary of their first date, a rare true splurge on Jo-Ann's part. It was returned unopened. Jo-Ann spent a whole weekend barely speaking, as dejected as Sophie ever saw her.

Sophie replays Jo-Ann's last message. *Please, if anything happens to me, please look after the baby. Her name is Elise—I wanted something beautiful and sophisticated like yours. You know you are family to me. You* are *my family.*

Stupid, stupid Jo-Ann. How dare she die on this beautiful baby, knowing that the girl would be raised by an old woman who considers her own wonderful child deviant and detestable?

Suddenly she wonders what death was like for Jo-Ann—and hopes with all her strength that she died on the operating table, blissfully unaware of her impending mortality. The thought that she might have been lucid, unable to draw her next breath, unable to see Elise, unable to make any provisions for the baby's care . . .

Sophie rubs her chest, but the rib-crushing pressure persists.

And then a different vision comes to her. Jo-Ann, at death's edge but holding on to life with her last shred of strength, trying desperately to crane her neck to look up and out, waiting for Sophie's silhouette to appear at the window, the door, anywhere. Because she knew that Sophie would come.

That Sophie would not abandon her—or Elise—at a time like this. She would not leave them to the vagaries of fate.

Sophie's tears flow like streams. She had no idea the lacrimal gland could hold this much fluid. She is also shaking despite the jacket she always puts on to go into air-conditioned buildings.

What is she supposed to do? Oh, God, what is she supposed to do?

She already knows, doesn't she? She's frightened not because she doesn't know but because she not only knows but has already decided to damn the torpedoes, full speed ahead.

"You were right about me, Jo-Ann," she murmurs to the echoing corridor. "You were right about me."

Beware women who always follow the rules. Because when they stop, they will blow up everything in their path.

CHAPTER FOURTEEN

Saturday

Elise and Ana Maria are in the middle of making their buttermilk pancakes when Detective Hagerty and Detective Gonzalez knock on the door. Sophie, out for a jog to clear her head, sprints back after she receives Elise's text.

When she arrives, her fingers cold and numb despite her hard run, Elise is seated in one of the two lawn chairs on Sophie's tiny front porch, talking to the cops. Hagerty has taken the other chair, Gonzalez standing behind him.

Sophie has no legal objections to raise—in Texas, cops do not need a parent's permission or presence to question minors. After a stilted greeting, Sophie moves closer to Elise and lets the police continue with their official business.

Elise must have told the cops that she conversed briefly with Jeannette Obermann in the library the Saturday before Game Night. They ask her whether she paid any special attention to Jeannette Obermann on Game Night itself.

Elise shakes her head. "Not after I put her at a table with the couple that also came late. Clue is a fairly straightforward game and I think Miss Hazel, the librarian who sat with them, knew the game well enough to help out. I didn't have to guide them or give any extra explanations."

Hagerty asks a number of other questions. Elise displays a steadiness that almost dispels Sophie's terror at this near home invasion. Almost, but not quite. She starts out standing immediately next to Elise but quickly moves six feet away, so that the cops—and Elise—cannot see that she's shaking.

They are back so soon. On a Saturday morning. At Sophie's house. Are they just eager to do their job or have they already found a trail of clues that led them directly to her door?

But at least Elise is not giving them any reason to pay extra attention to her, and that's—

From inside the house Ana Maria yowls. Elise springs to her feet. Sophie places a hand on her shoulder. "I'll go see what's going on."

In the kitchen Ana Maria is sucking on her finger—she nicked herself while trying to slice some fruits to go with the pancakes she's just finished making. Sophie hauls out her first aid kit, disinfects Ana Maria's small cut, dabs it with a bit of ointment, and wraps a bandage around it.

"Thank you, Miss Sophie," says Ana Maria. "Are they treating Elise okay out there?"

As if she summoned the cops, the door opens. Detective Hagerty lets Elise back into the house but asks, "Ms. Claremont, can I also have a few minutes of your time?"

Elise looks apologetic.

Sophie's gut twists. What did the child say? But she puts on the deflective shield that she forged during an adolescence spent at a private school full of rich WASP kids. Hopefully the shield still works; hopefully it will still convince people she belongs *and* make her fly under the radar.

"Of course, Detective. Elise, don't let Ana Maria do any washing up. Her bandage should stay dry."

She goes outside to the porch and sits in the same chair Elise occupied earlier. Across from her Hagerty takes up her entire field of vision. There is a window to his right, a tall, dark-stained wooden fence just behind his head, and beyond his left shoulder, trees and an open field—yet all she can see is the keen gleam in his eyes and the pores on his nose.

He asks the same questions he asked earlier—or at least, very similar questions. Sophie gives similar but slightly different answers—she doesn't want her testimony to sound copied and pasted from one occasion to the next. Human recollection is unreliable. People forget details; they recall new details; they fabricate details that they then convince themselves have always been the details.

She is so caught up in the give-and-take of the interview, going over completely inconsequential events, that her pulse slows, her nerves settle.

They've reviewed the evening. They are now in the parking lot of the library. And Sophie repeats her story of how she stepped aside to speak to Jeannette Obermann, who, God rest her soul, was interested in volunteering at the library.

Because Elise had been there with her in the parking lot, Sophie made sure to confess that encounter the first time Hagerty interviewed her. She also informed him that it was the last she saw of Jeannette Obermann.

But this is a lie and Hazel knows it.

Last night, Sophie fled from Hazel in a panic. It wasn't until she was behind her own front door, perspiring despite the coolness of the night, that she was able to reassure herself that if Hazel didn't rat her out when she was face-to-face with Hagerty, then she wasn't going to rat on her now.

But there's still the matter of what Hagerty might have found in Jeannette Obermann's apartment. If that woman conducted any internet searches on a device that wasn't her phone...

"Ms. Claremont?"

"Sorry, I was trying to recall some more details. But I'm afraid I've already told you everything. Ms. Obermann looked and acted completely normal when we talked about her interest in volunteering at the library. Then my daughter and I went home."

"But when I spoke to your daughter just now," Hagerty says innocently, "she told me that after you came home, you left again and didn't return until pretty late in the evening."

Sophie stands at the edge of a caldera and the erupting magma threatens to melt her whole.

"That's right," she hears herself say. "I believe I mentioned it last time we spoke. I belong to a running group and we had a Halloween cookie swap the next morning, but I was so busy getting Game Night off the ground that

I forgot about it until we got home from the library. So I had to go and get some cookies from the store."

This is the weakness in their defense. Sophie would never make Elise fudge the timeline for Sophie. And because she didn't want Elise asking about what she was doing that night, their preparation had ended at the point Elise returned home.

"You told me that you were back from the grocery store at ten-ish. But your daughter said you got in right before eleven."

The muscles in Sophie's back spasm. "Was it that late? I experienced a huge adrenaline rush from the success of Game Night. I knew I wouldn't be able to go to sleep right away. Since I was already out, I drove around for a bit."

Sophie already checked. On that night, during the most critical window of time, she didn't pass by any of the city's listed traffic cams. Which supposedly do not make recordings unless the city is doing a traffic study. But what if the city is doing one? And what if there are hidden, unlisted cameras?

Hagerty leans forward, blocking the sky, blocking everything. "You're sure you never saw Jeannette Obermann again, Ms. Claremont?"

Sophie's blood vessels constrict—her head pounds from a lack of oxygen. "I am sure," she insists. "I never saw the poor woman again."

When Astrid walks into the library, Jonathan looks up from the patron he's helping. "Hey, Astrid. How did it go at the dentist's?"

But before she can reply in an American accent—*her* American accent—he adds, "I'll get the answer from you later," and returns his attention to the patron.

So much for her jangling nerves.

All the tables in the work gallery are taken. Astrid sits down in the reading area by the periodicals and brings out her laptop.

Right after she learned about Perry's death, terror muddied her reaction—she was convinced the police would somehow pin the responsibility on her. She wanted to bar her condo and insulate herself from the case—as if that would somehow minimize her problem.

Denial, writ large.

But as she lay trapped on the dentist's chair this morning, cursing him for being open on Saturdays, unable to even grit her teeth at the sound of the diabolical drill because of the device that held her mouth open, she was suddenly desperate to find out what happened.

She wants to know why Perry died. And maybe who he was. In that order.

But the internet, which loves to speculate, has no theories on Perry's death—it doesn't even seem to have learned of his overdose. On the other hand, it knows all too well his romantic history.

Most images online showed him escorting one of two slim, beautiful women to various fancy occasions. One woman was apparently his college sweetheart, someone whose appellation starts with the word "Lady." The other one looks weirdly familiar until the caption informs Astrid that she was on an extremely popular show—not one Astrid watched but very much in the zeitgeist for nearly a decade.

For Perry wasn't just Perry but the Honorable Heneage Pericles Bathurst. Although, contrary to what she'd first supposed when faced with a name like that, the family title—his father is Baron Bathurst—isn't that old. It was granted only after WWII, among the last hereditary peerages ever created in the United Kingdom.

She wonders whether he was saddled with a try-hard name to make the other aristocrats forget how recently the family arrived at the party.

But it wasn't as if they held it against him, since he went everywhere and dated women with marquesses for fathers and former prime ministers for grandfathers—the actress appears to be from a family both older and posher than his.

Mortification sears Astrid. Would she have bared her soul to him had she known about the kind of life he'd led and the confident, sophisticated women in his past? What could he possibly have thought when she prattled on about how happy she was not faking being Swedish?

She forces herself to browse on and reads an article about his parents' separation. She remembers his bewilderment. *Four children and almost thirty-five years together—down the drain.*

She told him then of her parents' divorce, which happened when she was fifteen. Really, at that age, what could they do that *wouldn't* be disappointing and disillusioning? Her newly freed parents each went on a semi-epic search for love and companionship. But given the demographic trends of their hometown, there was no one available among the five hundred or so residents who hadn't already been rejected for one reason or another.

Commiserating about their scant luck out there brought them back together, but not to a rom-com happy ending. Her parents live in separate parts of the house and haven't bothered with a new marriage license—it's just that they are no longer motivated enough to seek replacements.

Perry sighed. *Listening to you makes me realize, for the first time, that I should try to be happy for my parents. It's not such a bad thing that they don't have to settle for each other if they don't want to. And it's not such a bad thing that at their age they can still look ahead to a different and perhaps better life.*

Some of the shame gnawing at Astrid fades away. Maybe she is a naive bumpkin who has made a lot of stupid choices in life, but that doesn't mean there wasn't, however briefly, a genuine connection between them.

She caresses a rare solo photo of his that somehow found its way to the interwebs.

But Perry's parentage and dating history offer no clues as to why he came to Austin.

Astrid sets more search parameters by suppressing coverage from *Tatler* or anything having to do with romantic relationships or the social scene. Now up pops a database maintained by the UK government that provides information on limited companies.

Perry was apparently a director of no fewer than half a dozen business entities.

Astrid clicks through to each company and discovers that most are under the umbrella of the Bathurst family holdings—Perry was being groomed to take over at some point.

A point that will never come now.

There is one company, however, that doesn't seem related to the family businesses. It has a different address and features a codirector who is at least a fresh name.

Valerian de Villiers.

Someone sits down next to her. Hazel.

"Hi!" Astrid, happily surprised, side-hugs Hazel. "How are you? I thought you didn't work today."

"I don't. My grandmother went to a potluck without me so I'm picking up some food next door." Hazel looks Astrid over. "You look . . . energized."

"Do I? I guess I feel energized."

She turns her laptop toward Hazel. "Look what I found. Perry was involved in a bunch of companies related to his family's holdings. But then there is this outlier."

"Valerian de Villiers," Hazel murmurs.

"What do you think—a man or a woman?"

"A man, I would say. Have you ever read *Valerian and Laureline*?"

Astrid shakes her head.

"French space-opera comic—I read the English translation when I was twelve or thirteen. In that, Valerian is definitely a dude."

"Okay." Astrid feels silly to be relieved that for Perry's sole venture outside the family aegis, his partner was not a woman—but she is relieved nevertheless.

Hazel turns the laptop toward Astrid again. "Good work."

Astrid glances at her watch—her shift is about to start. All at once her heart pounds. "Today will be the first day I don't speak with a Swedish accent at work."

Hazel smiles. "Sounds like a great way to start the rest of your life."

How many times did Astrid see the *Today is the first day of the rest of your life* poster in her high school library? Enough for the exhortation to have lost all its power. But now she feels it, the joy and urgency of a new beginning.

And this time she will rise to the occasion.

The shopping center next to the library is pretty white-bread—an H-E-B, a nail salon, a car wash, and an old-fashioned diner. The shopping center across the street, however, has always boasted a wide selection of ethnic restaurants and businesses.

Hazel stops before the door of the South Asian mart, pretends to look at her phone, and glances about from underneath her lashes. The parking lot isn't the carnival of a 99 Ranch on a weekend, but cars flow, and shoppers and diners mill about in pairs and clusters.

She's had some training in spotting would-be kidnappers, but Jason Bourne she isn't, and she can't pinpoint exactly what gives her that slight yet unmistakable sense of unease. Inside the store, she wanders about and casts a look here and there out of the glass front of the establishment. Still nothing.

Giving up, she walks to the vegetable section to inspect a crate of bitter gourds.

"Hi!" says a man's voice. "Hi, I thought it was you!"

She looks up. Elderly white male, comb-over, overkeen expression: the *Fifty Shades* patron.

"Do you come here regularly?" he asks eagerly.

"Occasionally," she says. "You?"

"At least once a week. The samosas here are fantastic. Have you ever tried them?"

She has and likes them very much. "No," she says. "I have to stay away from gluten, unfortunately."

That does not discourage him. "Try the dhokla, then. It's made from rice and lentils, perfectly gluten-free."

"Okay. Thanks for the recommendation." Might as well agree with him since she has no good objections.

The old guy grins, as if she's given him all the approval in the world. "Do you still enjoy working at the library?"

"Yes, I do. Thank you."

"Oh, oh, oh," he cries excitedly, oblivious to her attempts at killing the conversation. "Were you there when a fight broke out at the library?"

"You know about the fight?" She doesn't remember him being there that day. In fact, she's pretty sure she hasn't seen him since her first day of work.

"Didn't see it in person but somebody in my neighborhood was there and put a video on Nextdoor. You've got to see it—I cribbed it and uploaded it to Facebook."

"I'm not sure I want to relive it again," she protests.

He's too busy fiddling with his phone. "Let me open my Facebook app—"

A woman comes up behind him. Ayesha, who was at Game Night with her husband. And on her face is the universal expression of female sympathetic horror: *Oh no, are you cornered by this guy too?*

"Hazel!" She waves. "What are you doing here?"

Hazel drops a pair of bitter gourds into her basket. "Getting some vegetables. You?"

"Dal. They have a whole aisle of organic dal and spices now. You want to check it out?"

"Absolutely. Excuse me," she says to *Fifty Shades* and ducks around him.

"Look me up on Facebook if you want to see the video—Gus Anderson is the name!" he cries after her. "And hi, Ayesha! See you ladies around!"

Ayesha leads Hazel nearly to the other end of the store before she rolls her eyes. "Can you believe him? I was working at the library the other day. That fellow sat down at my table, started talking, and refused to take any hints. I had to flat-out ask him to please be quiet. He shut up but still wouldn't go away until Ahmed came back from taking a call outside. What a nuisance. The library is such a great place to work but because of him I almost didn't go back the next day. Thank goodness he hasn't been around since then."

"Well, thank you for coming to my rescue today," says Hazel sincerely. "That's a lovely salwar, by the way."

Ayesha preens a little. The gauzy green scarf over her hair flutters, the golden embroidery along its edge matching perfectly with the neckline of her fitted green tunic—very pretty, if a little formal for grocery shopping.

She asks Hazel the best way to cook bitter gourds. Hazel shares her grandmother's practice of blanching in salted water to get rid of the bitterness but warns that Ayesha still might not like it.

Out of the corner of her eye Hazel spies *Fifty Shades* leaving, the large paper bag in his hand presumably full of crispy, delicious samosas. Earlier she was more concerned with getting away from him. But now she wonders why he wanted to show her the video. Was it just an excuse to scoot closer to her? Does he know that Perry is dead? Why was he interested in the video in the first place?

Jonathan, waiting for his weekly bowl at Peng's Noodles, assesses his life.

He seems to be doing that a lot lately.

He isn't in a bad place at all. He has his mom's old house, his dad's old truck, and a job he enjoys. The poetry workshops, the open mic nights, and the young writers' programs that he leads every summer are deeply gratifying—in encouraging others, he nurtures himself. He is plugged into Austin's large network of creatives. Not to mention, a small university press published a slender volume of his poetry a few years ago, mostly poems that had already appeared in literary magazines and other anthologies. Royalties have been negligible, but the satisfaction? Immense.

His lackluster romantic life has felt almost par for the course—half of his colleagues are single, as well as a good portion of his friends. Even at the reunion, where presumably only those classmates who feel at least somewhat good about their lives showed up, there was a lot of commiseration about being on the dating app merry-go-round after ending marriages and major relationships.

But seeing Ryan again at the reunion upended Jonathan's relative passivity.

To want someone with such intensity—to long for that spark, that connection—is disconcerting. Almost like being a teenager again. Jonathan is not exactly scared, but—

The door of the tiny noodle shop opens and in walks a man who makes Jonathan think that AI must have installed filters in his eyes—surely this level of good looks can only be achieved with pixel manipulation.

His hair, which Jonathan remembers as bouncy and a bit rumpled, has been sheared off. The dark buzz cut serves only to emphasize the celluloid-ready angularity of his features. He wears a white T-shirt under a structured charcoal blazer, but instead of jeans or trousers he sports a pair of charcoal joggers that taper at the ankles.

That is not a look most men should attempt. But Conrad, Ryan's roommate, has the long, lean physique and the slightly otherworldly air not only to pull it off but to convey the impression that he happened to be wearing the T-shirt and joggers at home and simply grabbed the nearest item of outerwear as he headed out the door.

Conrad stills and studies Jonathan for a moment before approaching his table. "Hi. Jonathan, right?"

Jonathan finds his voice. "That's right. I thought you were out of town?"

That was what Ryan had said when Jonathan texted him after Game Night to tell him that he'd found someone who could be Conrad's perfect match.

"I came back a few days ago. Ryan says he met you because your colleague was in some trouble with the police. Has she been cleared yet?"

The idea of Ryan mentioning him, even if in passing, makes Jonathan's heart skip a beat. "We can't be sure. At least she doesn't seem to be in bigger trouble than before. So . . . small mercies."

But what is Conrad doing in this part of town? Is Ryan with him, by any chance? Did they—or Conrad by himself—go to the library, which is right across the street, to check out Hazel?

As if Jonathan has conjured her, the door of the noodle shop opens again, and in strides Hazel.

She is dressed in the exact same color palette as Conrad, a figure-hugging sweater with white-and-gray Breton stripes tucked into a knee-length gray suede skirt. With her bare face and pulled-back hair, she looks like Hollywood's idea of an ivy league grad student, one whose arrival tolls the death knell for more than one department chair's long-term domestic arrangement.

Conrad certainly stares as if he were a fellow student who has already jeopardized his doctoral candidacy for her.

She goes straight to the counter. "To-go order for Hazel, please."

Her transaction takes all of thirty seconds. She turns around, spots

Jonathan, and covers the distance between them. "Hi! I was in the library and didn't see you."

"I must have been in the back," he answers. "I thought you didn't have any hours scheduled."

"I don't. But I wanted to talk to Sophie and she wasn't there."

"She called this morning. She's taking a personal day off."

"I see," says Hazel, some significance to her words that Jonathan can't quite grasp.

Her gaze at last slides over to Conrad, who is still staring at her. But she gives this Adonis only a cursory glance before her attention returns to Jonathan. "You'll be at work tomorrow, right?"

"That's right."

She waves. "Okay. See you then."

And because Conrad still hasn't stopped gawking, she acknowledges him with a slight nod as she makes her way toward the door.

Then she stops and slowly, very slowly, turns around.

This time, she studies Conrad as if she were a conservation biologist and he a species long thought to be extinct.

"Conrad?" she murmurs, her tone uncertain. She takes a step toward him. "It's you, isn't it? Madeira, twelve years ago?"

A look of wonder comes over her—wonder, astonishment, and no small measure of melancholy.

"I think so," answers Conrad, his voice low and hesitant.

You think *so?* marvels Jonathan. *You don't* know?

At least five-nine, beautiful, stylish, and articulate. Asian. Mysterious.

That's why he thought the words fitted Hazel to a T! A plastered Conrad had been describing none other.

And now they've found each other. After more than a decade.

Perhaps Hazel has just realized the same thing. She smiles, a smile that grows and grows until it reaches Julia Roberts–level wattage and the dingy interior of the noodle shop is suddenly a few thousand lumens brighter.

Jonathan had no idea that Hazel came with a more exuberant setting. No idea that she could radiate such hope and joy. Something catches in his throat at this flash of pure happiness.

"Are you busy? Can I buy you lunch—assuming, that is—" Her expression sobers. "Assuming that it won't lead to any misunderstandings for you at home."

"I live with a gay man," says Conrad. "There will be no misunderstandings."

The way they continue to stare at each other, as if the other person might evaporate at any moment—Jonathan's chest constricts with a futile longing.

"Ah," says Hazel, smiling again. "Let's go, then?"

"Sure." Conrad turns to Jonathan. "See you later."

They leave. Jonathan's name is called and he goes to the counter to get his bowl of tomato-and-egg noodle soup.

To eat by himself.

CHAPTER FIFTEEN

Madeira, off the northwest coast of Africa
Twelve years ago

It was raining hydrangea petals. Flights of white doves crisscrossed the sky. Hazel's silk scarf streamed in the breeze, a long gossamer ribbon sparkling under the sun.

It was nothing of the sort, but it might as well have been.

What does Hazel actually remember of that day, a third of her lifetime ago? What was real and true, and what has been photoshopped in by her mind in the long years since?

The steep gradient of the streets was real—confirmed by Google Earth. The seemingly endless upward slant was real enough—she's never encountered other residential lanes that climb with such steady ferocity. San Francisco's got nothing on Funchal, Madeira.

The early October weather was lovely. Hazel was comfortable in her T-shirt and cargo shorts, her face shaded by the giant visor that is part of the stereotypical Asian Auntie travel uniform. Her mother would have shaken her head at this getup—Lillian Kuang has never once in her life looked like a tourist, not after she returned to Singapore, in any case. But Nainai always had on her visor and Nainai was a lot cooler.

Hazel is also sure that during the long ascent to the Jardim Botânico, she was thinking of her father. Crazily tilting neighborhoods were a sentimental favorite. She lived the first ten years of her life in such a neighborhood at the edge of Texas Hill Country. Some streets there were so steep they were scored diagonally across to provide traction in bad weather. Dad walked up those streets for exercise; he liked to have her with him, and he was always happy to hoist her onto his back when her little legs protested.

When she left, he was a bawling mess. She was the one to reassure him, through her own tears, that she would be back every summer and every Christmas. But the only time she ever returned to her old house was four months later, to attend his funeral and pack up all the remaining memories of her American childhood.

Yes, she thought of him on that climb. But she wasn't too sad. Her mother had put her in therapy for two years. She knew it was okay to wish that he was still around, that he could have shared this trip with her; it was also okay that he wasn't and couldn't.

Such was life. Life had never been unfair to her parents or herself. Life was simply like video games: It was normal to try hard and fail spectacularly; it was normal to invest untold hours only to realize that the game itself sucked; it was normal to love a game to bits and still, with the passage of time, never go back to it again.

Here is another certainty. At forty minutes past nine that morning, she turned around and took several panoramic photos: ocher roofs and white walls amidst subtropical greenery. The pictures failed to capture the vertical nature of the vista or its sweeping expansiveness. Looking at them in the years since has always felt like listening to someone talk about a movie whose original footage has been lost.

And then what happened? Flower petals, doves, and scarves streaming as if on a soundstage, with wind machines whirling just outside camera range.

She doesn't even remember what he wore.

Okay, not entirely true. She definitely remembers the canvas deck shoes, which she thought to be a fashion affectation, until he told her that he'd come to Madeira as a cabin boy on a sailing ship.

Because she remembers the deck shoes, she also recalls bare ankles and long, shapely calves. But not his knees. Was he wearing something three-quarters length?

And his T-shirt, what color was it? Blue, gray, faded indigo? The only thing that really comes to mind is the small hole in the left shoulder seam. He tried to do the gentlemanly thing and walk on her outside to protect her from traffic, but she didn't like to be hemmed in and insisted on walking on the outside. So every time she glanced at him, the little aperture was always in her line of sight, tempting her with a hint of very light freckles underneath.

Hi. Excuse me, I'm completely lost. Are you by some chance also headed for the botanical garden?

She was texting her mother. She looked up to see a cute boy standing a few feet away, a hopeful expression on his face.

He might be hitting on her, but she didn't mind the possibility. They walked around the Jardim Botânico together, admired its famous green-and-oxblood parterres, which overhung a panoramic view of the island, and shared beverages at the Jardim's café.

It was while she was drinking her can of sparkling water that she learned he was only nineteen. Or rather, not even nineteen.

I'll be nineteen in three days, he said, chugging down black coffee as if he worked three jobs. *And how old are you, if you don't mind me asking the same question?*

Me? Twenty-three next month.

He appeared delighted. *We're the same age, then.*

A twenty-two-year-old woman and an eighteen-year-old boy are not the same age.

Ouch, he said—and laughed.

He had dimples and spectacularly clear skin. His dark hair was thick and wavy. He spoke with a British accent and was most likely some sort of Eurasian mix, the kind who looked like he could hail from 60 percent of the world's land area.

You're not going to try to persuade me otherwise? she asked, not sure why she was hanging on to the subject.

He shook his head, a mischievous look in his eyes. *No. What if you like boys who aren't the same age as you?*

She'd snorted—and laughed too.

After refreshments at the café, they took the cable car across a deep canyon to a place called Monte, and there rode a toboggan launched down narrow, steep streets by two local experts—even though he admitted to not enjoying that sort of rushing, descending motion. Then, on their way back to Funchal, they stopped by a roadside eatery and had lunch.

One hears a lot about photographic memories. What Hazel would have liked is a phonographic memory. They spent close to five hours in each other's company and talked for most of that time. But though she retained a fair amount of information—he just learned to make Bolognese sauce from the ship's cook; the espresso machine on board, prone to blockage, was the bane of his existence; it took his vessel five days to sail from Gibraltar to Madeira, relying solely on wind—she could recall only a few snatches of conversation in their entirety.

If those five hours were an archaeological dig, they would be akin to a site with a handful of well-preserved artifacts, the rest only shards and weathered foundations. She could still generate a floor plan and maybe even a forensic blueprint for how the villa must have looked in its heyday, the gardens here, the baths there, a lovely pergola for the occasional alfresco dinner. But mostly, just a lot of rubble.

Sometimes a night watch at sea feels as if it will never end. But there are also times when all the stars are overhead and it's overwhelmingly beautiful. Times like that I'm almost sad that this won't be my life forever, that I will go back to land, to people, traffic, a desk job.

They were waiting for the cable car to Monte, standing atop a terrace with magnificent views.

You don't like normalcy? she teased.

Oh, I do. If I ever get to live in a full-size room again, with internet on demand and a shower that's wider than a telephone pole, I will cry. I miss those amenities so much that I have to remind myself nobody forced me to sign up for the mariner's life. The opposite: I fought hard for an opportunity to sail the seven seas.

He turned and smiled at her. Those dimples again. She felt covetous.

It's a good lesson. It tells me I can never have everything—not at the same time, in any case. Adventure has its costs; stability has its own costs. And I should stop thinking about what I don't have.

Zen and the art of cable car tourism, she murmured.

He laughed and escorted her up to the cable car's boarding point.

I came here for work. How did you end up in Madeira?

They'd alighted from the cable car some time ago and now stood looking over the deep green canyon they'd just traversed.

Hazel's mother, unable to stop her from finally leaving home to travel on her own, had booked her a long cruise from Singapore to London. Hazel had not minded: Nainai had stepped off just such a cruise to visit her in Singapore six years ago.

It took her a few days aboard to perceive Lillian Kuang's Machiavellian brilliance: For the entire journey Hazel was lumped in with several hundred septuagenarians.

The ship departed most destinations by eight o'clock in the evening—five o'clock in the afternoon, sometimes—well before local nightlife kicked into gear. And even when it stayed in port for more than a day, the itinerary worked against her—Cape Town on a Monday night was not exactly lit.

And Hazel had barely minded. *I'm here in Madeira because I finally ran away from home.*

It felt good to say that aloud.

At your advanced age? he teased her.

She giggled a little. She deserved that. *Better late than never, I guess. My mom's always been overprotective.*

He studied her. There was a steadiness to his eyes, an intelligent focus. *But you seem to have yourself very much in hand. What is she trying to protect you from?*

Her heart thudded, whether from his gaze or his question she couldn't be sure. *From life itself, perhaps.*

How can anybody do that?

People will try. They don't want to accept that pain is simply a part of life; they still think, after thirty, sixty, or even ninety years on this earth, that something can be done, if not for themselves, then for those they love.

A leaf fell from the tall plane trees overhead and landed on the parapet that separated them from the canyon. He picked up the leaf. *Have you accepted that pain is simply a part of life?*

She could not label the question invasive as she herself had brought up the concept, but it was ... discomfiting. And then she saw, all at once, that it was discomfiting because no, she had not accepted the inevitability of pain. She had simply come to believe that she had sufficiently equipped herself to keep pain at bay—and would not need her mother's feebler measures.

She tapped her fingers against the parapet. *The honest answer is no. I probably believe that by living very carefully and making no mistakes, I will not hurt.*

Will you be happy that way?

I don't know. How strange that she was speaking of such a deeply personal matter with a stranger. But then again, who better than a stranger to listen to a conversation between a woman and all the forces of the universe? *I don't often think about happiness. Do you?*

He expelled a breath. *I do, but I'm not sure that I approach it the right way. I don't seem to care whether I'm happy today, but I worry over whether I'll be happy when I'm forty-five or fifty.*

Well, are *you happy today?* she asked impulsively.

He glanced at her, then smiled down at the leaf in his hand. *Yes, today I am.*

It would be maybe a quarter hour after this, with his suggestion that she try her hand at designing tabletop games, that he sealed his place as one of the most influential individuals in her life. At the time, though, the idea made no impact—it was so out of left field, barely plausible, let alone practicable. At the time she was busy laughing over his purposefully entertaining description of his absolute terror of rapid downward motion because as a child he'd once fallen off a high slide and broken an arm.

And yet he'd come with her on the tremendous downhill rush that was the toboggan ride.

For lunch, once he recovered, they shared an enormous traditional Madeira beef skewer, enjoying it with warm fluffy buns and a glass of local wine each. Afterward, they bought popsicles from a tiny grocery store.

The early afternoon sun was liquid and warm. As they walked past little squares filled with locals lingering over their luncheon—it was a Saturday—

she asked him where he was headed next. He told her that after three days in Madeira, his boat would sail to Ponta Delgada, in the Azores, then cross much of the Atlantic to Bermuda, before arriving in Miami. In Miami their current guests, an old couple, would depart and they would welcome a trio of retired siblings and herd them around Cape Horn.

I'm scared. Rounding Cape Horn is the sailing equivalent of climbing Mount Everest—the waves there can toss a yacht end over end. It's no joke.

But his eyes were undimmed as he looked at her.

They did dim a few minutes later. By then they were back on the waterfront. Her plan called for her to take the hop-on-hop-off bus to Cabo Girão, a nearby scenic point, but he could no longer accompany her, as he had to be back at work by three in the afternoon—it was his turn to cook for the crew.

She had never believed in the parting-is-such-sweet-sorrow nonsense. Yet there was indeed something pure and fresh about the sadness that permeated her heart.

Seven years would be insufficient to make some people acquainted with each other, wrote Jane Austen in *Sense and Sensibility, and seven days are more than enough for others.*

They'd had less than seven hours. Seven days would be such a luxury.

Good luck crossing the Atlantic, she told him. *And safe passage around South America. You'll be fine.*

Thank you. And happy travels to you too.

She smiled. The corners of his lips lifted slightly, but he didn't quite smile back. He only took her in with his eyes. She raised her hand, intending to offer it for a shake, but instead settled it on his shoulder.

Surprising herself even more, she leaned in and kissed him on the cheek.

A quick peck for a lovely and all-too-brief day. Maybe this was exactly the experience she had sought on the trip, this serendipitous connection, this freedom that she never felt at home.

But as she stepped back, he banded an arm around her. He did not crush their bodies together. In fact, he kept two inches between them—and did nothing except study her intensely.

His eyes were light brown, almost golden, the lashes long and thick. A breeze stirred his dark hair. Under her hand—her hand was still on him?—the thin cotton of his T-shirt was warm, the shoulder beneath hard and sinewy.

He leaned in, but still did not do anything, as if he was only interested in breathing the same air as she. Her heart scarcely beat, her fingertips trembled, waves roared and crashed in her ears.

The space between them disappeared—*she* had closed it. Her hand that had been on his shoulder was now behind his nape, pulling him to her.

He tasted of lime sherbet and latent heat.

Excuse me! Excuse me, madam! I'm sorry to interrupt but you need to board the bus now. It's leaving.

They pulled apart. Vaguely she was aware that she must smile, wave, and turn away, but her body wasn't yet capable of doing anything to follow a predetermined schedule.

He unslung his backpack and pulled out a pen and a small notebook. *Conrad*, he wrote. *Funchal, Madeira*. Then the date and a number.

He tore out the page and handed it to her. *Will you take this?*

I will take it, she said lightly. *But I make no promises*.

She leaned in to kiss him again on the cheek, but he embraced her instead, holding her tight against him.

I wish I didn't have to let you go, he whispered in her ear. *I will always remember you.*

———

In the coming months and years Hazel would marvel that she actually got on that bus, climbed up to the open-top upper deck, and waved a final goodbye to him. But she did all that, and then, as the bus peeled away from the curb, jacked her earphones into the box on the seat before hers and listened to the audio guide that introduced the sights along the route.

At Cabo Girão she took lots of pictures—it was a spectacular headland above a heart-stoppingly sheer cliff. She made it back to her cruise ship just before the crew pulled up the gangplanks and barely had time to take a shower before the vessel pushed off from the long quay.

Rushing up to the top deck, she scanned the marinas along the shore.

But she didn't see any watercrafts that matched the description of his ship, a big sailing catamaran over forty meters in length.

Her heart ached dully. Not because she didn't see his catamaran but because she wished now that he hadn't held her close and that she hadn't kissed him.

Had they remained platonic friends, she would have felt free to contact him, to ask at some point how he was getting on. But that sudden turn into romance—that complicated things.

The short acquaintance, the age difference, the fact that she had no idea where he called home when he was not a cabin boy sailing the seven seas—all those things paled in comparison to the baggage she would bring to this—or any—relationship.

She could be fun and attentive for a day—or maybe even a month. But over time, she would revert to the reserve instilled in her by her mother, who believed emotional stasis to be the best defense against life's slings and arrows. Why would anyone want to love a puddle when there were lakes, rivers, and oceans out there?

Madeira receded. The panorama, at first that of Funchal's endlessly upward slopes, was now the entire silhouette of the island, a beautiful rock four hundred miles off the coast of Morocco.

A place that held her spellbound and wonderstruck.

But it was the nature of enchantments to wear off. And it was the nature of reality to rush back in.

She recalled his candor, his curiosity, and the rather threadbare texture of his T-shirt under her palm. *I will always remember you,* he'd said.

Yes, let him remember her as she had been this day, spellbound and wonderstruck. And let her remember him as he had been this day, gentle, wise, winsome.

She took out the piece of paper from the inside pocket of her small backpack. *Conrad. Funchal, Madeira.* The date. His number. And underneath that, *If I never see you again, have a wonderful life.*

She hesitated. A wonderful life, what an outrageous aspiration.

But she proceeded to carefully tear out the part of the piece of paper that bore his number. She would keep his name, the time and the place of their meeting, and his heartfelt inscription. She would simply remove the temptation to ever find him again.

She pressed the number to her lips, then ripped it to pieces and let the wind carry away the confetti.

Now it would never not be perfect.

CHAPTER SIXTEEN

Hazel might not have recognized Conrad had he not stared at her with those distinctive eyes: amber, downturned, a rim of white showing just above his lower lash lines.

Now she is the one staring, trying to merge the flesh-and-blood man with the impressionistic clutter of her memories. Trying to make sense of the monumental significance of those memories against the awkward silence of two strangers sitting down to coffee.

Coffee, not lunch, because he has a flight to catch and only a quarter hour to spare.

The pure elation that surged through her a minute ago has dissipated, like effervescence fading from a glass of champagne. She realizes she has no idea what to say.

But she took his number, so she must account for her lack of a response all these years. "I'm sorry that I never called or texted."

"That's quite all right—I didn't expect you to."

His voice is so distractingly lyrical—how did she not remember this?—that it takes a moment for her to understand that his courteous and understanding answer is also cruel. He implies that it didn't matter and he didn't care. He implies that she was but a fling on a sailor's shore leave—less than that, in fact, because they never got around to having sex.

She presses on because of the way he looked at her in the noodle shop.

The sheer disbelief on his face, as if he'd buried her himself and here she was, alive, prattling, without the least recollection of said interment.

She couldn't have been entirely trivial, could she, if her reappearance provoked this outsized reaction?

"Will you give me a chance to explain?" she asks but does not wait for an answer. "Until I was ten, I grew up in a happy home. My dad was a family doctor and my mom ran his clinic. He adored her. Whenever I butted heads with her—and we did that a lot—he always pulled me aside and told me that she'd sacrificed so much for us.

"I had no idea what he meant until one day, in fifth grade, I came home to find her crying happy tears. That was when I learned that she'd been born into a wealthy family in Singapore."

His brow raises slightly. *"Crazy Rich Asians?"*

"Close enough. They fell in love when they were in college. Her family objected to her choice and threatened to disown her. She said 'bite me' and married him, giving up an enormous inheritance in the process.

"But that day, her parents finally relented and called her. And they told her that not only did they miss her desperately, they also admired her. That she, raised in the lap of luxury, had managed perfectly well without their money. Now would she please come back into the fold, so that they could have her company—and mine—in their old age."

He slowly peels the wrapper from the cupcake before him, no longer looking at her.

She wishes he would—when they met on Madeira he rarely took his eyes off her.

She presses on. "To me my mom's story sounded like a fairy tale, the banished princess finally allowed back into the castle. For my dad, however, it was a cruel twist of fate. My mom would come into so much money that his income would become utterly irrelevant, and he had always prided himself on being the provider for our family. He simply could not deal with that existential crisis.

"It marked the beginning of the end of their marriage. Five months later, my mom took me and moved back to Singapore. Two months after that, they formally separated. Another two months after that, he died of a stroke. His father too had died of a stroke, but in his fifties. My dad was only thirty-eight.

"In the wake of the news, I overheard my mom saying to her own mother that if he was fated to die anyway, why couldn't he have died a year sooner, so that she would always remember him as a wonderful husband and father, and not as a man who could only be happy with a wife financially dependent on him. A man who lacked the maturity and confidence to face his much wealthier in-laws, as if all his achievements in life evaporated the moment my mother regained her birthright."

His cupcake's wrapper now lies in a perfect circle. Hazel looks down at her cup of mocha. The barista had drawn a heart with latte foam.

"That was my first lesson in romantic love. That time is its great enemy. That, everything considered, an early end might very well be the kindest possible outcome." She dips in her spoon. The foam heart elongates but still holds its shape. "It was the reason I tore up your number, so that I would never be tempted to get in touch with you."

"Wow," he says softly, his tone undecipherable.

She deserves it, this cool unresponsiveness. He still isn't looking at her but at a point somewhere beyond her—the polka-dotted walls of this cute but unremarkable suburban cupcakery.

"If it's any consolation, I regretted my decision almost immediately. I was in Miami for a month, checking the marinas every day to see whether a new hundred-foot sailing catamaran had come in. I checked all the marinas in Fort Lauderdale too."

He takes a sip of his black coffee. "We docked in Charleston, South Carolina, instead. The new guests we were taking on were from Charleston and the guests already onboard decided that they preferred to visit Charleston over Miami."

Something she would have known had she not torn up his number.

He puts down the coffee cup. It makes a soft *thud* that nevertheless makes the hair on her forearms stand up. "I guess some things are not meant to be," he says calmly.

She'd come to that same conclusion years ago, hadn't she? Then why does she feel so bleak?

It was that stupid surge of warm, buoyant hope. That moment when all the shards of all the dreams, disturbed from their somber vaults, rose and swirled into a perfect, spectacular vision—before falling victim to gravity again to lie quiescent and powerless.

"I bought a jigsaw puzzle for us," she murmurs, a futile appeal. "I still have it."

He stands up. "I'm sorry. I really must go now. It was nice to see you."

She rises to her feet and scrapes together enough pleasantries to see him off. And then she sinks back down. Next to his barely sipped coffee, the cupcake he bought sits naked, untouched. She picks it up and eats the whole damn thing.

"If I never see you again, have a wonderful life," she says to the man who should have remained a perfect memory.

"Spill the tea!" exhorts Ryan, his voice full of anticipation.

It's been almost an hour since Jonathan texted him about Conrad running into Hazel at Peng's Noodles. The wait was dispiriting, but now Jonathan is buzzing because Ryan has bypassed texts and called him directly.

He takes out a carton of eggs from his city-mandated reusable grocery bag and gives what he hopes is a punchy version of events.

"You know what makes this interesting?" Ryan demands gleefully.

"What?" Jonathan obliges.

And belatedly realizes that he's been walking around the kitchen holding that carton of eggs instead of putting it in the fridge.

"Not that Conrad's been carrying a great big torch for your colleague all these years, but that he lied about it with the not-dating-Asians crap. Now I'm dying of curiosity."

It would be nice if Ryan would spare a bit of that curiosity for Jonathan but Jonathan can't complain. Even he is invested in Hazel and Conrad now.

"But is that all you know?" continues Ryan. "Did she not give you a report on their little one-on-one?"

"No. Them walking off into the sunset was the last I saw of her."

Not that he expects details from Hazel even otherwise, but Ryan doesn't need to know that.

"Well, let's talk to her. Bring her over for dinner."

"Wh—" Dinner? Jonathan forgets how to breathe. "You mean tonight?"

"Why not? I've got some good Bolognese sauce in the freezer. I'll make some salad and we'll be set. And if your colleague doesn't eat meat or gluten, let me know; I'll order something for her."

"But wait. Wait." Somehow Jonathan is still able to think despite his wildly drumming heart. "How do you know the two of them aren't together right now, being really busy—if you know what I mean?"

"Oh, I know what you mean, and I'm sure they would love to be really busy with each other, but they can't because he has a flight to catch—and right before I saw your message I texted him and asked if he got to the airport on time and he said yes."

Now Jonathan's heart rate is through the roof. If Hazel says yes, then he gets to hang out with Ryan tonight. "Let me get in touch with her and see what she says."

"Okay. Let me know."

Ryan hangs up. Jonathan takes several deep breaths. Good Lord, he's *still* holding on to the carton of eggs.

> Hi Hazel, this is Jonathan. Hope it's okay to text you privately. My friend Ryan, Conrad's roommate, would like to invite us to dinner at their house tonight. I hope you'll be able to come?

It's only after he sends the text that he finally puts away the eggs and the rest of his groceries, so he won't just stare at his phone on pins and needles.

But what if things didn't work out after Hazel and Conrad were reunited? What if seeing each other in person isn't a dream come true but finally waking up from that dream instead?

He realizes that he's standing in the middle of the kitchen, biting his thumb, an old pregame nervous tick that he thought he'd banished ages ago.

His phone dings.

Thanks, says Hazel. I'd love to.

Jonathan leaps up, his head nearly hitting the recessed ceiling, relief raging through his body as pure happiness.

In a few more exchanges he gets Hazel's okay on the menu and arranges to pick her up at seven thirty p.m.

He showers and agonizes over outfits before changing into a chambray shirt and a pair of chinos. Then he goes out and buys a six-pack of highly rated local IPA and a bottle of red wine that his mom likes to drink when she has Italian food.

After that he still has almost two hours to kill. He heads back to the library—Hazel lives nearby. Also, there's a book about human cadavers that he keeps seeing in the stacks. Maybe he can flip through it and sound more knowledgeable in front of a man who does two hundred and fifty postmortems a year.

His stomach grumbles as he parks and it's a no-brainer to march directly into the Den of Calories.

Astrid is there, eating an apple. "Hi, Jonathan."

"Hey, Astrid. What's good here?"

"Hazel brought some interesting Chinese crackers. They're super flaky, like eating pie crust, except savory. They're right next to the choco pies."

He finds the individually wrapped crackers and sits down opposite Astrid.

"How come you're back again?" she asks.

"I—wait, why do you sound different, Astrid?"

Astrid clears her throat. "I'll tell you if you promise to still be my friend afterward."

Are they friends? He likes Astrid a lot and would like to be her friend, but despite her seemingly sociable nature, she's always felt rather closed off—he's known her for years without really getting to know her any better.

Is that about to change? "Of course," he says.

Astrid sets her apple core on a napkin on the small table. "I sound different because I dropped my Swedish accent. And I dropped my Swedish accent because I've never been Swedish."

It takes a moment for his mind, full of visions of a perfect first date, to compile her words into meaning. "Come again?"

"Do you want the long version or the short version?"

He glances at his phone. "I have time."

He'll just have to walk into Ryan's place completely ignorant about cadavers and ask Ryan to fill him in.

Astrid laughs, a nervous sound. "But I have to be back at work in a few minutes. So basically, I'm from the Midwest, but I was young and stupid and wanted a different background. At college I made up this story about my parents and grandparents being prosperous Swedish farmers, rather than Iowans of Scandinavian extraction who pretty much lost their shirt during the Farm Crisis.

"In the reductionist vein of things, somehow my fake Swedishness became my entire personality. And everywhere I went, there was already someone who knew that I was 'Swedish.' So I've had to keep it up all these years.

"Of course, now I understand that I never *had* to keep it up. I just couldn't face the consequences of telling people that I'd been lying to them. I'm sorry, Jonathan. I'm sorry that I lied to you when we met and that I kept up the pretense all these years."

Jonathan tries to digest everything that has just been fire-hosed at him. Across from him, Astrid fidgets as if her chair is sprouting nails.

"I won't say I'm not shocked—I mean, I feel like I've just been told that pizza is actually French in origin," he says slowly. "I'm disoriented. But I don't think how I interact with pizza will change, whether pizza is French or Italian. Am I making any sense?"

"I . . . think so? Are you saying that my nationality doesn't matter or that the fact I've lied about it doesn't matter?"

There is such fear in her eyes—and such hope too. Jonathan can't remember the last time anyone looked at him with such hope. He feels a stab of protectiveness. "I guess what I'm really trying to say is, have you been okay all these years? It must have been a real drag."

Astrid bites her lower lip. "You know, Jonathan, ever since we first met, I have wished that you were my friend, because you are such a generous soul. I should have realized a lot sooner that what stood in the way of our friendship was me—and my lies."

Jonathan always feels a prickle of his conscience whenever he is labeled as kind or generous. Is he? The look on Ryan's young face at that pool party... it haunts him to this day.

Maybe the barriers Astrid's pretense formed between herself and the world isn't the only thing that has prevented the growth of their friendship. Maybe there is also Jonathan, feeling unworthy of the trust of this sweet, gentle young woman.

"I should probably get back to work," says Astrid.

She looks awkward as she stands up and collects the apple core. Jonathan realizes that she must have misinterpreted his silence. He rises, takes the apple core from her hand, puts it in the compostable bag Sophie brought from home for organic trash, and hugs Astrid.

"I would like to be your friend, Astrid," he tells her. "And when you have time, I would love to hear all about you."

Nainai makes Hazel walk the runway, the runway being the corridor outside Nainai's bedroom, where she installed one of the security cameras. During the pandemic, she used to dress up in her best outfits, sashay, and send the footage to Hazel.

Hazel tosses back her hair, squares her shoulders, and slinks in her best imitation of Naomi Campbell—one does not half-ass a strut down Nainai's runway, even if one's heart has been left behind in pieces at the neighborhood cupcakery.

"Good walk," Nainai says. "Dress is basic though."

Hazel grins. Her little black dress is indeed extremely inoffensive, long-sleeved, the hem grazing her knees.

"When you said dinner with two handsome men," continues Nainai, "I suspected that neither is into you. Now I know for sure."

Hazel laughs out loud, grabs Nainai, and kisses her papery cheek. "I can have handsome men anytime I want. This is just dinner."

Her first reaction upon receiving the out-of-the-blue invitation was that Conrad would not like for her to be there. Her second reaction was that she herself did not want to be in his home without his express permission. But then she recalled Jonathan's effort to introduce her to his high school classmate's roommate. At the time she hadn't picked up on it, but was Jonathan interested in Ryan, the old classmate? Conrad wouldn't have told Ryan about meeting her today. It had to have been Jonathan, putting out a feeler under the guise of conveying gossip.

She erased the answer she'd already tapped out and replied in the affirmative. Yes, she would go. If there was to be no future for herself and Conrad, their fizzled reunion could at least serve as a stepping stone for Jonathan.

"Make sure you wear your blue light glasses if you play games after eight o'clock," she tells Nainai as she takes out the container of Italian trifle she made in the afternoon.

Her grandmother might be all kinds of wise, but she's still liable to neglect her sleep hygiene when battle arena bloodlust overtakes her.

Jonathan arrives several minutes early; by seven thirty they are on their way. Hazel asks about Dr. Ryan Kaneshiro, their host for the evening, who is apparently good-looking, charming, and athletic, not to mention handy with a scalpel. No doubt about it. Jonathan has it bad. Hazel can only hope that he hasn't had it this bad since high school.

Ryan—and Conrad—live at the foot of Mount Bonnell, noted Austin scenic spot, where Hazel and her parents used to go to watch sunsets. And Hazel used to marvel at the pretty houses on the lake below, which seemed to her the epitome of luxury, not realizing that her mother had grown up in far more opulent surroundings.

The house sits in a bend on a dark, twisty lane. A set of wrought iron gates set in a low wall swings open as the car approaches. The architecture is a mishmash of vernaculars. The steeply pitched slate roofs feel Parisian here and there thanks to half-hipped dormer windows, but then slant almost to the ground in other places in the manner of an A-frame house. Some walls have a half-timbered mock-Elizabethan look, only to meet other walls that look like stacked dry stone.

It should be ridiculous, but in the lamplight, with its abundance of natural material and brilliant mullioned windows, the house is strangely attractive.

Ryan comes out of the front door as they pull up. The two men shake hands and slap each other on the arm.

"Hazel, this is Ryan," Jonathan says. "We went to high school together. Ryan, Hazel, my colleague."

Ryan shakes Hazel's hand. "A pleasure. You're tonight's guest of honor."

Hazel smiles, befitting tonight's third wheel of honor.

"Come on in. You'll love the house."

They walk across a high-ceilinged hall into a dream space. It is a living room, with two double-length leather sofas facing each other across a long coffee table made of a single eight-foot-long, five-inch-thick slab of wood—a dramatic grouping of furniture.

But what makes Hazel and Jonathan suck in a breath and crane their necks back in unison are the two walls of books behind the sofas. Cabinets with table-like surfaces become shelves that climb up and up, two stories in height. A rolling ladder is hooked over horseshoe-shaped rails that run along three sides of the room. And the higher shelves are recessed just enough for a careful booklover to stand on a narrow gallery to look her fill at all those thousands of volumes.

The room has no other decorations save two small trees in large wicker baskets, a smattering of lamps with plain round shades, and a chandelier overhead. And yet it is immediately one of the most beautiful indoor spaces Hazel has ever beheld.

The books are all large coffee-table volumes. The first one Hazel sees is a compendium on the treasures of the Forbidden Palace, the next about the fauna and flora of Patagonia, the next a collection of historic photographs of a hundred and fifty years of Black cowboys. The randomness of the shelving excites her—she can give herself a whole education by grabbing any one book and starting from there.

A few covers are set facing out—the pink palaces of Jaipur, a spiral galaxy in breathtaking detail, a gilded and ornately illustrated A the height and width of a nightstand.

Tucked in among the books, Hazel finds a handful of personal touches. A tiny origami dragon in dark red paper, a glass jar of used tickets in faded green and ocher, a large, intricate ship in a bottle, so detailed it even has a sailor on deck about to throw a message in a bottle overboard.

She trails her fingertips over the smooth exterior of the ticket jar. After she'd torn up Conrad's phone number—and after she'd come to her senses—she'd found the tickets for the botanical garden and the cable car ride. And those were all the souvenirs she had of their time together.

She turns around to find both Ryan and Jonathan watching her.

"You're right," she says to Ryan, "I do love this house."

"Sometimes I get on the ladder, swing around, and pretend I'm Belle from *Beauty and the Beast*," says Ryan. "Except, you know, around here Conrad is Beauty."

Everyone laughs.

"Let's go to the kitchen. You'll love it too."

And he is right again because the kitchen too is book-lined, with one shelf of cookbooks, one shelf of food anthropology, and one shelf of food memoirs.

"Whose books are these?" Jonathan asks the question on Hazel's mind.

"Conrad's. He inherited most of them—he says people leave him their book collections for some reason." Ryan slides the food and drink the guests brought into the fridge. "A lot of them are pretty old."

Hazel has already noticed that. Many of the cookbooks have lost their jackets; some even have food stains. A random one she picks up is in Spanish, published in Chile in 1955, and has handwritten notes in the margins by at least two different people.

Ryan moves to the stove and puts a pot of water to boil. "Tell me how you guys became librarians."

"I'm just a clerk," Hazel says quickly. She can recognize when a query isn't meant for her. "Jonathan is the only properly credentialed librarian here."

Ryan stirs an adjacent pot of pasta sauce that is already simmering. "Color me amazed when I found out, Jonathan. I don't remember you being particularly bookish back in high school."

Jonathan seems surprised that Ryan knows this much about him. "Good memory. I didn't really become a reader until I was in the military—it took very little bandwidth to download an electronic book, as opposed to an episode of television. I borrowed most of the books from the library—"

"From Austin Public Library?"

Jonathan nods. "I used my mom's account. So when I started to plan my discharge, I thought, why not become a librarian? Can't be a bad thing to go to work surrounded by books."

Ryan, still standing at the stove, listens attentively. But he does not look at Jonathan the way Jonathan looks at him. If anything, he reminds Hazel of a less determined version of Conrad in that cupcake shop.

Jonathan, on the other hand, does not see that which is blindingly obvious to Hazel. He basks in Ryan's presence, in their proximity. Hazel feels less like a third wheel now and more like guardrails at the edge of a precipice, there so that Jonathan won't plunge to his annihilation.

Or maybe Jonathan exists on a higher plane. Maybe he's like the man in the Zen story, hanging from a vine, a tiger on the cliff above, a tiger in the ravine below, a rat gnawing away at the vine, who still manages to savor a wild strawberry he finds growing in the fissures of the rock face.

"I always enjoy it when people like their work," says Ryan. "Good for you, Jonathan."

He takes them on a tour of the house. When they come back, Ryan puts pasta in to cook and serves salad in the adjacent dining room.

Hazel anticipated that the space would have books on entertaining and such. Instead its shelves are jam-packed with history and social sciences, including a boatload of titles on politics and religion.

Both Hazel and Jonathan chuckle.

"Okay, a bit difficult to avoid politics and religion at *this* table," says Jonathan.

"It's usually just Conrad and me, if there's anyone at all, and we don't avoid politics or religion."

"How did you and Conrad meet?" Hazel finally gets to ask her question.

"My ex from medical school"—Ryan, distributing the salad, glances at Jonathan—"the one I told you about the other day—we've kept in touch over the years. His colleague and Conrad are friends. One day he was out and ran into them so they got to talking. Conrad was about to move to Austin and my ex said, hey, I know someone who's an Austin native and I'm sure he'll be happy to show you around."

"Conrad came. I showed him around. We got along pretty well. And when I was at the end of my lease he asked if I wanted to stay here—he travels a lot and didn't want the house to be empty half the time. So that's how I became the world's happiest house sitter."

He leans forward. "Hazel, after you move in, can I please stay on? I can decamp to the guesthouse and I promise you'll barely know I'm here."

If only. The ache in her heart threatens to erupt into outright pain. "Conrad and I are not rushing into anything, so no worries."

"Not rushing into anything? But life is short, I can tell you that—I see all the short-lived ones."

"Excellent point. We're still not rushing into anything."

But I would if it were up to me. I would rush in like it's the opening minutes of Black Friday.

"Huh." Ryan leans back in his chair. "Can I ask you how *you* and Conrad met?"

"Sure. We met when we were traveling, spent a very nice few hours together—" At the look of great interest on Ryan's face, she adds, "Fully clothed and in public. And that's the entire extent of our acquaintance. He gave me his phone number. But I didn't act on it right away, and when I decided I did want to keep in touch, I'd lost it."

The words cut a little upon her lips, the first she has ever spoken about her non-history with Conrad.

"Why didn't you want to keep in touch? Oh my God, did he get his looks from plastic surgery? Was he an ugly kid when you met?"

Hazel laughs. "No. I mean, he didn't look exactly like he does now, but all the building blocks were there."

How strange that he would turn out more spectacular than she remembered, when she had already elevated him beyond perfection.

"Then why?"

"He was three days short of nineteen. I was almost twenty-three."

"That's it? But you seem like a much cooler person than that."

Hazel shrugs. "That's always been my problem. I'm not cool; I just have resting enigmatic face."

She is only an heiress raised not to rock the boat. Yet ever since she was a teenager, people have wanted to ascribe to her a life—and a soul—far more compelling than her own.

Jonathan coughs into his napkin.

Ryan laughs—and jumps up because his timer has beeped on the spaghetti. Jonathan goes with him to the kitchen to help.

The pasta they bring back is delicious. The sauce clings thickly and is so savory and satisfying that it takes Hazel two servings to realize what it is. Spaghetti Bolognese, so different from the insipid, gloopy mess that resulted from her own attempts to learn something Conrad knows how to do during the month she waited for his boat to sail into Miami.

Did Conrad make this?

She does not ask.

After dinner they move back to the living room. Inspired by a coffee-table book about Austin set on the actual coffee table, the two native-born Austinites and Jonathan, who has lived here some thirty-odd years, reminisce about all the changes that have swept over their city.

Remember when the Children's Museum used to be right downtown?

Remember when the airport *used to be just about downtown?*

Remember when breakfast tacos weren't everywhere?

Actually, no need to remember that.

Hazel does not go near the ticket jar again, but she feels Conrad's absence all the same. He is not the elephant in the room. He is the room. He is the house. He is the price she has paid for the generational belief that it was better never to begin than to end badly.

"Come during the day next time," says Ryan toward the end of the evening. "This room is even more beautiful in daylight, when you can see the lake."

She probably will return to this house, even though she shouldn't. It's only in *Pride and Prejudice* that stalking one's not-quite-ex pays off. For mortals it's but an exercise in futility and mortification, the death of impulse control.

Ryan walks them out. Jonathan, possibly in an attempt to prolong the goodbyes, points to a car in the parking pad behind theirs and asks Ryan, "Is that yours?"

"Yup. Want to have a look?"

Hazel didn't pay attention to the car earlier—upon their arrival her eyes had been riveted to the house. But now the car begins to look familiar.

There are two large stickers on the rear bumper of the black Audi. *It's okay to decay. The dead know how to speak, if you know how to listen.*

Hazel stares. Has she been caught in a time vortex and transported back to Game Night? She walked by this car on the way to her own and even stopped for a minute to reread the rather creepy declarations.

At the time she considered them Halloween-themed, but they are in fact—

"A bit of occupational humor," says Ryan.

A gong goes off inside Hazel's head, a loud clang followed by maddening reverberations. She glances at Jonathan, who seems to find nothing amiss. The two men launch into a conversation about the car's specs.

"Excuse me, gentlemen, I don't mean to interrupt," she hears herself say. "Ryan, I just realized that I left my dessert container in your fridge. You're welcome to have all the rest of the trifle, but my grandmother is a bit paranoid about losing her favorite containers."

Ryan, ever the gracious host, says immediately, "Oh, I know what you mean—except more in a work context. Well, come on."

"I'll be right back," she says to Jonathan, to prevent him from returning inside with them.

"I feel like I've seen your car before," she says. Did their footsteps echo so loudly across the entry hall earlier? "Those stickers are distinctive."

Ryan laughs. "Have you been visiting the medical examiner's office?"

Mirthful, this man. Does that make it easier for him to laugh off uncomfortable inquiries?

"I have no idea where that's even located," she answers.

Ryan makes a turn toward the dining room and holds open one of its double doors for her to pass. "You must like gay bars, then."

"I've been to a couple in Singapore, but never in the United States."

They are now in the kitchen. He opens the fridge, takes out her container, and spoons the few remaining mouthfuls of Italian trifle inside into a Pyrex dish of his own. "Come to think of it, it's been a busy couple of weeks at work. The only time I drove somewhere else was after Halloween, when I met with Jonathan."

Hazel grits her teeth and gets more specific. "I feel like I saw this car before Halloween."

Ryan frowns, then snaps his fingers. "Now I remember. The day before Halloween I borrowed Conrad's car to have dinner with my family—my dad wants to try a non-Tesla electric car and Conrad has a Taycan. I didn't think anything of it because he was supposed to be away the entire week. But he came back that evening and took my car somewhere. I almost had a heart attack when I got home and my car wasn't there—and only then did I see his message on my phone."

A few days after she gave up Conrad's number, Hazel misjudged the last step on a flight of stairs and took a hard spill. The impact was such that she couldn't move for half a minute, convinced she'd broken everything inside.

She feels like that now, so jolted she can't even react.

"Let me give your container a quick wash," says Ryan, turning to the sink.

The sound of water splashing pulls her back into the fabric of space-time.

So . . . when she last saw the car, it had been driven by *Conrad*? What in the world was *he* doing at the library, which is what, twelve, fifteen miles from his house? At that time of the night, in that part of the town, only grocery stores, fast-food restaurants, and bars are still open, and frankly he can find better selections of any of those much closer to home.

Come to think of it, what was he doing hanging out near the library today?

She feels a breath of ice at her nape.

Taking the now-spotless container from Ryan, she says, "Thank you again for dinner. When Conrad comes back, tell him I said hi."

And then she flees.

CHAPTER SEVENTEEN

Jonathan walks into his living room, puts his phone to charge, and falls on the couch. Chimney, his tabby, tiptoes onto his stomach and makes himself comfortable.

"Hey, big fella," he says absently, caressing Chimney's head.

Chimney, his eyes wide, stares at Jonathan.

"Must you gaze into the depths of my soul?" Jonathan murmurs. "Why can't you just be my superior overlord?"

Most cats regard humans with varying degrees of condescension. Chimney, for some reason, has world-weary eyes that seem to say, *I've been there too, buddy, and I know how you feel.*

Jonathan sighs. "I feel sad. There, I can admit it, my feline counselor—I feel sad."

Maybe this sadness is easier to acknowledge because it's about Hazel. He remembers her euphoria this afternoon. A moment of such deep, intense, *transparent* emotion that he has to believe it was a glimpse into her real self, beneath all that ingrained low-keyness.

But this evening she was again a kindly observer, rather than a participant, of life.

And the pain that coiled around his heart was completely out of proportion to his recent and very slight connection to her.

"We all need fairy tales," he tells Chimney.

Okay, maybe not everyone. Some people are perfectly fine believing that the world is going to hell in a Wi-Fi-enabled handbasket. But everyone else, or at least Jonathan, still wants some reassurance that there is a point to all this striving, all this confusion, all this existential melancholy.

And if not for himself, then for someone more deserving—after all, happy endings are never given out willy-nilly, but only to the select few, the unimpeachably worthy.

It hurts to be reminded so bluntly that life is hard and love near nigh impossible. It shakes him to the core that all the hopes Hazel has carried over the years could extinguish in the blink of the eye. There was a moment, in that almost mythically beautiful library of a living room, when Hazel caressed a glass jar of ticket stubs and a lump formed in his throat at the longing in her simple gesture.

He knows, even if he doesn't want to admit it, that much of the sadness is for himself too. For his impossible dream with Ryan.

Chimney climbs up and nestles his head in the crook of Jonathan's shoulder. Jonathan rubs his cheek against Chimney's warm, smooth fur. "At least I have you," he says, his voice thick. "At least I have you."

A sheriff's car is parked outside Twin Courtyards Apartments.

Sophie curses under her breath.

Jeannette Obermann's case is being handled by city police, not the county sheriff. So the sheriff's car, which doesn't have its light bar on, could be anything from an off-duty officer visiting a friend to an off-duty car parked there specifically to deter crime.

But still, Sophie drives away without going inside.

If she were white, would she have simply walked into the management office and said that she was Jeannette Obermann's friend/colleague/sister, and could she please have access to Jeannette's apartment to sort out her things?

She doesn't know.

All she knows is that she has no idea whether she ought to try something desperate that could get her arrested today, or to keep her head down until Hagerty comes for her with the deceased's phone records.

She drives back home.

Elise is at a birthday party sleepover. Sophie gives herself a matte burgundy manicure, with a thin strip of gold above each lunula. Normally she enjoys having her house to herself once in a while, and she dearly loves a well-executed manicure. But tonight, as she stares at her newly perfect nails, she can't help but feel that she's just visited the spa on the *Titanic*.

She still has several months before the police get their hands on Jeannette Obermann's phone records, right?

She fishes the reformatted Chromebook out from the bottom of her closet, turns it on, and ignores nagging questions in her head about the wisdom of using it on her own Wi-Fi. She's deleted her browsing history at the end of every session on this notebook, but it doesn't take long before she finds the article she's looking for.

She taps the article open, scans the lines, and freezes.

The key sentence doesn't say it takes "months" for the phone companies to cough up records. It says "several days to several months, depending on the circumstances."

How many days has it been since Jeannette Obermann's body was discovered? The police may already have her phone records. Or, if not yet, they will obtain them any day now.

What is Sophie going to do the next time Detective Hagerty demands to see her?

Even on that day sixteen years ago, standing in the hospital, feeling as if someone had strapped a hundred-pound backpack to her shoulders, she didn't feel quite so alone as she does now.

She still had her mother, then. And she had Eileen Su, Jo-Ann's best friend from law school—Eileen had cousins who knew people and those connections netted a birth certificate for Elise with Sophie as her birth mother.

But Aubrey Claremont passed away four years ago. And Sophie did not contact Eileen again after she and Elise moved to Austin—she was still terrified of being found out in those early years and the last thing she wanted to do was to bring down Eileen too, while she was at it.

Since then she's kept Elise and herself safe by not getting too close to anyone—or at least that was what she thought she was doing. Only to end up not safe, and without allies.

—⁓—

Waking up at two thirty in the morning sucks.

Astrid reaches toward her nightstand and groans: She forgot to bring a glass of water. She closes her eyes. Maybe she'll fall asleep again. Then she won't care that she's thirsty.

But now she notices she's also cold. Wait a minute, did she fall asleep on top of the covers? Yes, she did. After the library closed, she came home, ate a sandwich, and then settled down on her bed to do French-language searches.

She worried about swimming in a sea of Google-translated gobbledygook, but machine translation—at least for straightforward, journalistic language—has become more or less readable. Her problem remained the same: the scarcity of usable results. All she has to show for her detective work—which literally put her to sleep—are some biographical details of an old, dead French diplomat named Valerian de Villiers. He led an interesting, globe-trotting life but breathed his last twenty years ago, so he couldn't have been Perry's business partner.

Astrid yawns and rolls off her bed. She might as well tidy away her laptop and get some water, and then take off her clothes and crawl under the covers.

After she plugs in the laptop on her dining table, she turns around. The front of her condo features a large window to either side of the door. By falling asleep unceremoniously, she neglected to draw the curtains shut.

A silhouette appears against the sheers. Astrid starts. The silhouette moves and disappears behind the door. After a brief silence, she hears faint but distinctly metallic scratches.

The situation is so irregular that she simply stares. Only then does alarm slam into her. Someone is trying to break into her house!

She covers her mouth. Her phone. Where is her phone?

She can't think, but her body takes over. Her feet march to the utility room deeper inside the condo; her hands reach up and yank down the attic ladder. She climbs up, draws the ladder back up and pulls the entire hatch door shut as tight as possible.

When she was a little girl, she was traumatized by the first zombie movie she saw. The idea of her parents becoming the undead and coming to devour her made her demand that they always speak in full sentences as soon as they saw her. And then she spent days figuring out where she would be safest in the event the house was overrun.

In the end, she decided on the attic, because zombies didn't seem to look up very much. What she would do after she'd shut herself off in the attic, she didn't quite think through. But wherever she stayed from then on she always knew the way to the attic or the roof.

The wooden beams she lies on, spaced six inches apart, dig into all the wrong places on her body. The house is eerily quiet. The silence makes her think of that movie in which aliens pounce on anyone who makes the least sound.

Her heart thumps. She doesn't dare move, except to cover her face with her sleeve so she won't breathe in dust and sneeze at the worst possible moment.

Wait, but why did she come up here in the first place? Now she's stuck. Her condo doesn't have a garage, but it does have a back door, accessible right through the utility room. She should have just gone out. And if she had any presence of mind, she could have even put on the old sneakers she keeps next to the dryer.

In the darkness, it becomes impossible to draw enough air through the fabric over her nose and mouth. She's chilled to the bone—*and* perspiring freely. She can't breathe and yet she breathes all too loudly, sibilant whooshes ricocheting against the unimproved interior of the attic.

Just when she thinks she can't take it anymore, the door to the utility room opens. Fear seizes her. Whimpers gurgle in her throat; she swallows them, sick to her stomach.

Now fear is a shriek rising from her lungs. She grits her teeth together. Her hands grip rough wood. Her knees shake. She lifts them up so they won't knock against the beams, and her calves scream with strain.

The door closes. Heavy tears spill down her cheeks, but not tears of relief. The intruder could still be in the utility room, simply with the door closed. And that would mean he has homed in on her location. What would he do? Would he come up or simply wait for her adrenal response to overthrow her self-control?

How much time has passed? Where *is* her phone? At least wherever it is, it cannot ring on her person and betray her whereabouts.

She begins to count. Is there any use to her hiding? If the intruder finds her phone and her car keys, they will know that she has to be here somewhere.

But seconds pass—she counts past one hundred, two hundred, three hundred. When the count hits three thousand she decides that she's been in the attic long enough.

No one attacks her as she descends the ladder. Nor is anyone waiting for her outside the utility room. The condo is silent. Standing with her back against the utility room door, she realizes that, as she didn't change out of her pants, her car keys are in her pocket. And her phone—she remembers now—she forgot the device inside the center console of her car. She meant to go and retrieve it after dinner, but it was chilly and she'd parked some distance away because the neighbors were having a party. So she didn't bother in the end—the phone isn't visible to passersby and she could do without it for the night.

Did the intruder, finding no phone, no key, a still-made bed, and her car not anywhere nearby, conclude that she wasn't home after all?

Her head spins at the thought of her lucky escape.

But why was there an intruder in the first place?

She begins to shake again.

———

Hazel wakes up at four in the morning—or what would be five if daylight saving time hadn't ended two hours ago.

She doesn't feel well rested but jittery and overbuzzed, as if someone hooked her up to a coffee IV overnight.

Conrad. Walls of books. Spaghetti Bolognese. The jar of ticket stubs.

Bumper stickers. Ryan's car. Ryan's car that he said had been driven by Conrad on Game Night.

Does she believe Ryan? She is not at peak confidence on her ability to judge men. But Ryan's response to her questions was one of reciprocal curiosity: He wanted to find out—and not in a sinister way—where and how she might have seen his car. She'd even say he was a little surprised when she abruptly abandoned her quest.

As for the invitation to dinner, now that the event is in the rearview mirror, her sense is that while he did want to meet her, it was probably just as much an excuse to see Jonathan in a plausibly deniable way. True, he didn't look at Jonathan the way Jonathan looked at him. But she, the third wheel, very much felt the undercurrents beneath the general amiability of their conduct.

If she absolutely must give a yes-or-no answer, then yes, she believes Ryan about Conrad's possession of the black Audi on Game Night.

Does it matter where Conrad was that night? People are free to park at an ordinary branch library at nine p.m. on a Tuesday night, twelve, fifteen miles from home, aren't they?

Obviously it matters to her.

Hazel flings aside the covers. Vaguely, she understands that she is applying a very different standard to Conrad. Forty-five minutes after the library closed on Game Night, Sophie was there in the parking lot, talking to Jeannette Obermann—and Hazel is more than happy to consider a dozen other possibilities that do not involve Sophie being culpable in the death of another.

Yet with Conrad, she cannot shy away from the worst possibilities. If he had anything to do with . . . anything at all—already she feels like the *Hindenburg*, about to crash to the ground engulfed in flames.

She grabs her laptop and heads downstairs to the breakfast table—her room is beginning to feel claustrophobic.

Almost twelve years ago, at this very table, she slumped over her breakfast while Nainai tapped on her giant tablet. She was trying to convince herself that she wasn't hurting, merely sulking, a rich little girl denied her latest favorite toy, who failed to sail into Miami as he said he would.

But why couldn't she breathe?

THE LIBRARIANS

She made herself sit straight and take a bite of the H-E-B hash brown patties that had been a childhood favorite. *What are you looking at, Nainai?*

Nainai gave her a long look, then said cheerfully, *I'm finding out how much my neighbors pay in property tax—you're too young to understand how much fun this is.*

She smiled in spite of herself. *You can do that?*

I think you always could, answered Nainai, *if you were willing to schlep down to county offices. But now it's all online. And I never knew Deb's last name—you know, the nice woman across the street—but now I do.*

So there is a way to find out, from public records, the identity of the homeowner. And Hazel needs Conrad's full name before she can begin to learn anything useful about him.

It does not take her long to discover that the county's appraisal office has that information. The name that comes up when she types in last night's address, however, is An-Nian Lo.

Is that Conrad's legal name? It's not uncommon for Asians abroad—or in Singapore, for that matter—to use a Western name in daily life instead of their official name.

She taps on the function that lets her search the same address year by year. An-Nian Lo has owned the property only for the last few years. Before that, as far back as the online tax records go—which isn't very far, only six years—the house belonged to someone named Romy Lonstein.

Typing *An-Nian Lo* in the search bar returns no meaningful matches, especially when restricted to Texas. But when Hazel looks up Romy Lonstein, she finds out that Romy Lonstein died of an apparent overdose in that lovely house at age thirty-seven.

She bore a slight resemblance to Conrad—could they have been related? Hazel digs further into her life. Her poetic obituary gives scant biographical data, but thankfully someone commenting on the memorial post on her long-abandoned Facebook account directs mourners to her Tumblr.

The worst thing about being a fuckup, Romy Lonstein wrote there eight years ago, is that I feel overwhelmingly guilty about being a fuckup. I'm Jewish and Asian. I'm supposed to be a striver, a clear-eyed success, practical and levelheaded. Yet with all the resources available to me, all the help I've had over the years, it's arduous for me just to breathe.

Okay, part Asian, confirmed.

A photograph of a single candle on a cupcake. This is for you, Aunt Anaïs, one of the few who haven't abandoned me. Happy birthday. I wish I had a fraction of your grace, fortitude, and aplomb.

As Hazel spelunks further and further back in time in Romy Lonstein's posts, she becomes convinced that the woman scrubbed her account at various points: There are multiple references to romantic disappointments, but never any photo evidence.

So Hazel is surprised when, with very few posts left, she comes across an image of a shirtless man. He's shot from the back, against a setting sun, his spine a deep channel in a lean, strong torso.

> My little cousin Conrad is all grown up now and can take his big cousin Romy sailing. Where did the time go? I remember when I used to hold him in my arms and call him "my baby"!

Conrad! On Madeira he mentioned a cousin. Can Hazel take this as sufficient evidence that Conrad is indeed An-Nian Lo?

But she already looked up An-Nian Lo and found nothing useful.

On a hunch Hazel searches for *Anaïs Lo*, and up pops an article from *Tatler Hong Kong* dated a year ago.

LEGENDARY TAIWANESE ENTREPRENEUR AND STYLE ICON ANAÏS LO MARRIES HAYDEN CHENG, SON OF HONG KONG HOTEL TYCOON SOO-YAT CHENG

Anaïs Lo, who needs no introduction in these pages, tied the knot with filmmaker Hayden Cheng on the 9th of September. His feature-length works have premiered at such venues as the Cannes and Toronto International Film Festivals. The two have known each other for more than thirty years, having met as students studying abroad in the UK.

Hayden Cheng, in his speech at the wedding, poked fun at himself. "When I met Nian Jie (Elder Sister Nian, the appellation by which Anaïs Lo is often affectionately referred, both in the media and by her friends and associates), I was a shy, awkward young man. I was gobsmacked by her presence, her beauty, and her competence— and I was completely intimidated. I only dared hang around the edge of her circle, hoping she would notice me. She did. She was very kind to me but dated more confident men.

"When our paths crossed again five years ago, I was gobsmacked anew. I was no longer a young man, but I remained shy and awkward. This time, however, I screwed up the courage and asked her out. Best decision I've ever made. Nian Jie, thank you for coming to dinner that night. Thank you for coming to other dates. Thank you for allowing me into your life and thank you for agreeing to be part of my life forever and always. I hope you'll never get tired of me telling you that I am the luckiest man alive, because I plan to tell you that a lot in the coming years."

Cheng's daughters from his previous marriage and Lo's son from her previous marriage all spoke at the wedding. Cheng was married for seven years to cinematographer Francine Tam. Lo was briefly hitched to French diplomat and businessman Hubert de Villiers.

Hazel lurches out of her chair. De Villiers.

Romy Lonstein could have had other aunts and uncles. Her cousin Conrad isn't necessarily her aunt Anaïs's child.

But what if he is? What if his surname *is* de Villiers?

For a moment her mind is as blank as a wiped whiteboard, all information gone. And then she remembers: Wikidata. Astrid's searches.

She somehow pulls up the company registration page Astrid was looking at yesterday. This time, she sees that there are various tabs at the top. One such tab leads her to a pdf of incorporation papers.

And on those, where full names are required, under *Heneage Pericles Bathurst* is *Valerian Conrad de Clausonne de Villiers*.

CHAPTER EIGHTEEN

Sunday

Nobody is ever prepared for the worst. Especially not those preparing the most assiduously: They are the ones most desperate to avoid that particular outcome.

Hazel feels as if she's just opened the door to a battalion of cops again.

Could the young man she met on Madeira have turned into a killer? Could she have conceived, when she tossed the confetti of his phone number to the wind, determined to make him the sweetest memory of her life, that someday she might ask this question?

Her phone buzzes. A text.

> Hi, Hazel, it's Conrad. I apologize for yesterday.
> I'm sorry. I don't know what I was thinking. I'll be
> out of town until the end of the week. Would it be
> possible for us to meet again when I'm back in
> Austin? Please say yes.

She yelps.

"You okay?" comes Nainai's creaky morning voice.

Hazel glances at the atomic clock on the wall. It's almost eight—she has no idea when the night ended and the sun rose.

"I'm fine," she calls out. "I just won the lottery!"

Nainai cackles. "There's no one more deserving. You want some baozi for breakfast?"

Hazel closes her laptop and stands up. "I'll do it."

She puts a trio of small frozen bao to steam in one Instant Pot and sets a batch of rice porridge to pressure-cook in another. While breakfast takes care of itself, she goes back to her room and parses Conrad's text again.

If she hadn't gone to his house last night, she wouldn't be just saying yes: She'd ask if she could fly out to meet him wherever he happens to be. But now she's spooked.

Is he sending a conciliatory note because he sincerely regrets not giving them another chance—or because he learned from Ryan that she saw Ryan's car when she shouldn't have?

She stares at the message for ten minutes before she types, It's a lot to decide. Why don't you text me when you're back in town? That'll give me some time to think.

She doesn't want to give the impression that she's had a sudden change of heart. But after his brusque rejection, it would seem reasonable for her to hesitate before committing herself.

Her phone buzzes right away. She flinches.

> Hi, Hazel. So sorry to impose, but I really need to speak to you. Could you meet me at the library? I'm available any time you are.

Two seconds pass before Hazel sees that the text is not from Conrad, but Sophie.

It's eight twenty-five.

Hazel frowns, then taps, I can be there at 9am. Will that work?

Sophie can only pray that she's made the right call in reaching out to Hazel. Hazel, who knows that Sophie met with Jeannette Obermann well after the end of Game Night, has kept that from the police and not asked for anything in return. And Sophie has no choice but to gamble that it will prove enough of a foundation for a crisis alliance.

When she reaches the library at five minutes to nine, Hazel is already there, standing by her Miata.

Before Sophie can thank her, she says, "I could be wrong, but is that Astrid's car?"

Sophie has certainly never seen another Prius with a bumper sticker that says *My book boyfriend is a billionaire archaeologist astronaut vampire.*

What is Astrid doing at the library three hours before it opens?

Another vehicle enters the parking lot. Sophie recognizes Jonathan's ten-year-old pickup truck.

He sees them as well and rolls down his window. "What are you guys doing here?"

"You're early, too," answers Hazel.

Jonathan shrugs. "It's the time change. I got up and didn't have anything I wanted to do at home, so I thought I'd put in some work on those donated books."

That could have been Sophie's excuse if she'd been quicker on the jump. She points at her tracksuit. "I'm going downtown to run. Just stopped here cuz I couldn't find my lunch tote at home."

"I went out for breakfast tacos and thought I saw Astrid's car," says Hazel smoothly.

Jonathan frowns. "Astrid?"

He and Sophie exchange a look. Astrid is always on time and enthusiastic about her work, but she isn't even on the schedule today.

"Let's go inside, shall we?" says Jonathan. "Maybe she can give me a hand."

―――

The couch in the storage room looks like a Garfield plushy left outside too long, but the cushions under the pilling upholstery still have some support to offer. Astrid, her feet pulled up, her arms around herself, wonders if it was a dream, what took place in the middle of the night. Can she go home and pretend that none of it happened?

She scrambles off the couch at sounds coming from the Den of Calories. "Who's that?"

The door to the storage room opens and Jonathan pokes in his head. "Astrid? Are you okay?"

"Jonathan!" She rushes over, nearly knocking over two stacks of books, and throws her arms around him. He is huge and solid, like a mountain. "I'm so scared. There was somebody in my condo last night."

"What?!" exclaims Jonathan.

As well as two other voices behind him.

Before she knows it, Astrid is ushered to the old Mod-Podged table in the Den of Calories. Sophie fills a mug at the hot water dispenser, Jonathan ventures back into the storage room to fetch Astrid's sneakers, and Hazel empties foil-wrapped breakfast tacos onto a melamine plate.

"I have eggs and potato, eggs and bacon, brisket, and beans. Two of each kind."

"You brought enough to feed a party," Sophie says quietly.

Hazel turns to her and smiles. "The Chinese diaspora believe in shoving food at trouble. That way at least we're facing problems with a full stomach."

This sounds like a general statement to Astrid, yet somehow it also feels like reassurance aimed specifically at Sophie.

"I guess I could use some food too, since you're sharing," Sophie murmurs.

Hazel smiles again and sets out small containers of salsa. "Help yourself."

But Sophie doesn't sit down to eat yet. Instead she brings Astrid a Tazo English breakfast tea bag and a Republic of Tea Asian jasmine one. These are Astrid's two favorite teas to have at work. She had no idea Sophie ever took notice of her tea selections.

Jonathan comes back with Astrid's sneakers. Now her feet are no longer cold.

Astrid's eyes swim with tears. They are all so wonderful to her, despite her stupid fake life.

She takes a deep breath and begins her account.

Sophie was already wound up tight. She nearly vibrates listening to Astrid's ordeal. Even though the young woman is sitting right in front of her, safe and sound, she still can't breathe until the Astrid in the narrative puts on her sneakers, slips out through the back door, and drives to the library for refuge.

She grips Astrid's hand. "I'm *so* glad you're okay."

Keeping her distance from everyone means Sophie doesn't always let herself think about how much she cares about her colleagues. She would be devastated if anything happened to Astrid.

"But are you sure they didn't take anything?" Jonathan looks puzzled.

"They didn't take my laptop, the single most valuable item in my house. I can't imagine what else was there that anyone would have wanted."

Sophie does not say it aloud but swallows at the possibility that the intruder didn't come for any objects but for Astrid herself.

The likelihood must have also occurred to Astrid. "So I'm thinking—based on very incomplete data, of course—that either they came for me or—" She takes several rapid breaths; her fingers clench around the napkin she's been using to rub out a tiny dot of salsa from her cornflower blue Austin Public Library hoodie. "Or they came because of Perry."

Perry, Astrid's situationship. It feels bizarre to be reminded that there is more than one active police investigation involving the library and its staff.

Astrid looks around the room, her eyes wide and beseeching. "I know it sounds outlandish, but is it any more outlandish than that I'm suddenly attracting housebreakers who go through my house and take nothing?"

Vaguely Sophie notes that Astrid seems to have lost her accent. Don't people's accents usually become stronger under stress?

Hazel, who has been leaning on the door—there are only three chairs in the Den of Calories—says, "It doesn't sound outlandish to me."

She speaks with such solemnity that little centipede feet march up the insides of Sophie's forearms. Astrid, the one who gave voice to the idea in the first place, stares at Hazel, as if she can't believe someone agrees with her.

"In my early twenties, I had a—let's call it a missed connection," continues Hazel, a hint of wistfulness in her voice. "For a long time I held out hope that our paths might cross again. Yesterday it happened: We ran into each other at Peng's Noodles."

Sophie blinks. In her early twenties, Hazel would have been on the other side of the world. For her missed connection to materialize a decade later, on a different continent, in the most unremarkable, if delicious, of strip mall noodle shops . . . But wait, what does this have to do with the intruder at Astrid's place?

"His name is Conrad. Unfortunately, Conrad was not interested in rekindling anything." Hazel's tone remains even, but she does stop for a second, as if the rejection is too monumental to be brought up without creating a momentary void. "But he happens to be Dr. Ryan Kaneshiro's roommate—I think we've all heard of Ryan?"

Jonathan spoke to Ryan to find out more about how Perry died—Sophie remembers that. Astrid nods likewise.

"And Ryan was curious enough that with Conrad out of town last night he invited Jonathan and me to their place for dinner."

Despite Sophie's panic for herself, anxiety about Astrid, and sorrow over Hazel's razed-to-the-ground dreams, she can't help but feel a sliver of envy that Jonathan and Hazel socialized outside of work.

Jonathan, on the other hand, regards Hazel with rising uneasiness.

"When we were leaving, we saw Ryan's car and I realized that I'd seen it before, parked right here on Game Night, a black Audi with two unmistakable bumper stickers. One says, *It's okay to decay*, and the other, *The dead know how to speak, if you know how to listen*."

Sophie starts.

"Really?" Astrid finally sets down the napkin in her hand. She pulls her chair slightly closer to the table. "I don't remember seeing a car like that."

"Me neither," says Jonathan slowly.

"I do." Sophie's voice sounds raspy in her own ears, as if she hasn't spoken in days. "It was parked one over from mine. Elise pointed out the bumper stickers to me. They were creepy."

"They were, as it turned out, forensic pathologist humor," says Hazel, her tone still devoid of inflection. "I left my dessert container in the house. Ryan and I went back to get it. I used the opportunity to question him and learned that on Game Night, Ryan took Conrad's car and Conrad, who returned unexpectedly from out of town, used Ryan's car instead."

"You didn't say anything about it on the drive back." Jonathan's voice is quiet.

The words he does not say echo in Sophie's head. *Are you okay, Hazel?*

"I needed some time to process the information," answers Hazel softly, in a tone that also says, *I don't know if I am but thank you for asking.*

Astrid scoops up the big fat mug in front of her, looking both alarmed and befuddled. "But why was Conrad hanging out at the library on Game Night?"

Sophie is only confused.

Hazel pushes off the door, takes a few of the empty foil wrappers on the table to the sink, and rinses them. "The question bothered me last night. I woke up this morning and it still bothered me. So I did some digging on the internet and now I can say, with ninety-five percent certainty, that Conrad is Valerian de Villiers."

The name means nothing to Sophie. Jonathan looks as lost as Sophie. But Astrid shoots out of her chair, nearly upsetting the table. "What? Are you sure?"

"At this point, if he turns out *not* to be Valerian de Villiers, I would be very surprised." Hazel shakes the water from her hands, turns around, and explains to Jonathan and Sophie, "Astrid looked up Perry Bathurst and found that he was in partnership with someone named Valerian de Villiers."

So Hazel's long-lost ex used to know Astrid's recently dead ex well enough for them to have a business together.

Sophie's next thought isn't about Perry Bathurst or Valerian de Villiers, but that there is enough trust and camaraderie between Astrid and Hazel for Hazel to know what Astrid knows. This is . . . encouraging. For Sophie, that is. Hazel now bears Astrid's stamp of approval, a peer-reviewed confidante.

"I always wondered what Perry was doing in Austin," says Astrid, sinking back down, looking dazed. "I guess he really did have business here."

"My God," murmurs Jonathan.

They all turn toward him.

"No, it's just that when Hazel and Conrad met yesterday, I was there at Peng's Noodles, too. Conrad walked in first. We said hi. He said he heard that Ryan and I had drinks. We talked about Astrid's troubles for a bit and—and he never once mentioned that he knew Perry."

All attention swivels to Hazel. Apparently, this is news even to her. She looks down and adjusts the strap of her watch. "I don't have anything to add to that. Conrad and I didn't talk about anything having to do with the cases."

Jonathan now looks desperate to remove his foot from his mouth. "You know what, I overreacted—it's not so strange that Conrad didn't mention Perry to me. He and I met exactly once. He'd be crazy to discuss the ins and outs of his business partner's death with me."

That is a reasonable thing to say, but it is also a gallant attempt to make something questionable sound less so.

"Thanks," says Hazel. "But this makes me wonder even more whether Conrad might have had something to do with the break-in at Astrid's place."

They all stare at her.

"Let's suppose he is in some way responsible for Perry's death—"

The Den of Calories isn't large. The sink is right next to Astrid's chair. Astrid puts a hand on Hazel's arm. "We don't have to suppose that."

Hazel smiles slightly, a meaningless yet proficient expression, as if she's trained for it the way a CrossFitter deadlifts. "I'm not saying I believe he is Perry's killer—I fervently hope he isn't. But can we confidently declare that Conrad being here on Game Night had nothing to do with Perry being in the area on that same night?"

No one can say that.

But Astrid bites down hard on her slightly chapped lower lip, giving away her continued reluctance to regard Conrad as a culpable party—and she's never met the guy.

"Maybe he was looking for Perry," suggests Jonathan. Another romantic.

"If he was," answers Hazel, her tone soft yet implacable, "then shouldn't he have been talking to his roommate? After all, if your business partner goes missing, and your roommate works for the county medical examiner's office, wouldn't you ask him to keep an eye on John Does arriving in the meanwhile? And if Ryan knew that Conrad was looking for Perry, and he already learned from Jonathan that Perry was in touch with Astrid right before he died—"

"Then *I* should have heard from Conrad," says Astrid slowly, her nail scraping at the stubborn salsa stain on her hoodie. "He would want to know what Perry was doing with me and what I might be able to tell him."

"An extremely reasonable supposition," deems Hazel. "And it didn't happen."

"But Conrad was out of town last night, wasn't he?" asks Jonathan, still unwilling to go down this path all the way. "That was why Ryan invited us over, to take advantage of his absence. If he was out of town then he couldn't have been the intruder in Astrid's condo."

"Ryan is Conrad's roommate, not his mom. If Conrad says he's going out of town, Ryan isn't going to get a flight manifest for verification."

Jonathan rubs his knuckles along the grain of his beard. "So you think that Conrad, who was supposed to be out of town, stayed in Austin and broke into Astrid's condo?"

This isn't even Sophie's problem, yet her nails are digging into the palms of her hands—she can barely conceive Hazel's distress. By Hazel's own admission, she hoped for years that she and Conrad would find each other again. And listening between the lines, she said only that *he* wasn't interested in rekindling anything, which meant that she was. Less than twenty-four hours ago, she wanted them to be together.

"It's a possibility," says Hazel.

"I don't believe it!" Astrid cries. Then, as if embarrassed by her small outburst, she reduces the volume of her voice. "Okay, we have no evidence one way or the other as to the identity of the intruder. But I don't think it's that weird that Conrad was hanging out near the library yesterday. Or on

Game Night. He could have been in the area in the hope of meeting you, Hazel."

Under different circumstances Sophie would have been the first to pooh-pooh the idea. But now she almost wishes that Hazel would at least consider it.

Hazel does not refute it outright. She even smiles briefly—or perhaps it's only an upward flick of the corners of her lips, meant to imitate a smile. "Sure, that's also a possibility, which is why I have no idea what to do next. But *I* don't need to do anything right now. *You*, on the other hand, Astrid, you must decide whether you're going to call the police about the break-in."

Astrid grimaces. "I already looked at the online submission form for residential incidents and I don't know that it'll be any use at all."

"I think Hazel means," says Sophie, "if you plan to tell Detective Shariati about the break-in."

"Oh, God, I haven't even thought about that." The expression on Astrid's face is outright horror at the notion of dealing with homicide investigators again. "Do I have to? I really don't want to."

She looks at everyone in turn, seeking permission from one of them—or perhaps all of them—for her to turn her back on the police.

Sophie, at best an awkward hugger, badly wants to hold Astrid and tell her that she understands exactly how she feels.

"If you hold off getting in touch with Detective Shariati, I'll be grateful. Because if you do, you'll probably have to tell them what you now know about Conrad. And—" Hazel exhales. "And I'd like a little time to find out more about his involvement in all this before we sic the police on him. After all, there is a chance he is not involved."

And now it's Hazel whom Sophie wants to hug, Hazel who feels that she must game out all the worst possibilities so that she will not be ambushed by them. Sophie understands that too—all too well.

Astrid sets her hand on Hazel's sleeve again. "Even if I do go to the police, I don't need to say anything about Conrad."

Hazel presses two fingers between her brows. "But if you don't say anything and I don't say anything, even if the police eventually figure out that

Valerian de Villiers lives in Austin, there will be nothing to tie him to not just one but possibly two suspicious deaths."

Sophie notes how Hazel is careful not to say the word "murder." The next second she feels as if someone has run her through with a lightsaber. *Two* suspicious deaths—Hazel is putting Jeannette Obermann's death on her never-quite-lover too? "But I thought Jonathan already asked Detective Shariati and the police are treating the cases as separate."

"Separate until they learn otherwise," Jonathan adds hesitantly. "That was the impression I got."

"I didn't consider the cases connected—frankly I didn't ponder the cases at all except for their impact on everyone here—until I found out that Conrad is Valerian de Villiers and that he was here that night."

Hazel does not say this, but Sophie knows what she means: At that time, Jeannette Obermann was also in the library's parking lot.

Hazel turns to Astrid. "Remember the night when we stayed behind at the library? I asked you to show me where you live on Google Maps."

"Yes?"

"I drove past Twin Courtyards this morning, after I picked up breakfast tacos, and your gated community was right across the street. If Perry was waiting for you to come home on Game Night, he could have parked either right outside Twin Courtyards Apartments or somewhere on the grounds, since it's not gated."

"Ryan did mention that Perry was found in an apartment complex in Northwest Austin," says Jonathan. "He didn't say which one though."

Was that the possible connection between the two cases, that both Perry Bathurst and Jeannette Obermann might have been at Twin Courtyards that night?

Hazel glances at Sophie but doesn't say anything.

Sophie's heart thumps. Her head is a cacophony of half-formed ideas. She is desperate for Detective Hagerty to latch onto someone else. But what if this Conrad guy was no different from her, just another hapless individual who happened to be in the wrong place at the wrong time?

It occurs to her that Hazel didn't need to say anything at all about Conrad, especially not in front of everyone. There is no evidence against the man, only theories. But she did it so that they would have all the relevant information—and perhaps to pave the way for Sophie to come clean?

Certainly Sophie does not think that Hazel misjudged in taking the three librarians present into her confidence. Nor does it surprise her in the least that they are all doing their best to be supportive and worthy of her trust.

Astrid rubs her face, looking as tired and underslept as she must feel. "So if we do pass on what we know about Conrad, we'd have to tell not only Detective Shariati but Detective Hagerty too?"

Sophie grips the front of her tracksuit.

"Detective Hagerty is a bulldog," says Hazel. "I never knew Jeannette Obermann existed until Game Night, and still he thought it suspicious that I started working at the library right before she died. I would not want him to have any goods on me. It would—"

"Help!" The word that Sophie has been screaming into the universe finally leaves her lips, a low, hoarse syllable.

Astrid turns toward her in bafflement. Jonathan, who's known Sophie longer, looks both alarmed and concerned. Hazel, her hands braced against the counter behind her, waits patiently.

Sophie isn't one hundred percent sure that she would have told Hazel the truth had their scheduled meeting not been preempted by unexpectedly running into Jonathan and Astrid. Perhaps she would have taken the plunge; or perhaps she would have chickened out in the end and made up some bullshit story about why she was talking to Jeannette Obermann in the parking lot, on the last night of the latter's life, forty-five minutes after the library closed.

But now she walks herself to the edge of that cliff—and leaps over.

"Detective Hagerty will have the goods on me very soon," she says, her nails once again digging into the palms of her hands. "That is, if he doesn't already."

CHAPTER NINETEEN

Game Night

"M s. Claremont, can I have a word with you?"

Sophie turns around. It's the woman with the third eye. The sodium vapor streetlight at the edge of the library's parking lot casts a yellow glow on her face and gives the photorealistic eye that takes up her entire forehead a sinister tinge. "Yes?"

"Great, thanks," says the woman—and walks away to an SUV that's even more loudly orange than the scarf on her head.

Sophie doesn't see what the woman could have to say to her that Elise can't hear. But she's in a good mood and willing to indulge a patron who helped to make Game Night a success.

"I'll be just a sec," she says to Elise, who probably wants to spend some quality time with her phone, in any case.

Elise slides into the passenger seat of Sophie's Mini Cooper with a cheerful "Okay!"

Sophie approaches the woman. "Can I help you?"

"Hi, I'm Jeannette." She grins and points to the name tag on her chest, to which she affixed an Austin Public Library sticker, given out during Game Night. "It's nice to meet you."

She is pretty enough but Sophie is wary of the keenness in her eyes—this is someone who wants to know stuff and Sophie prefers a little less curiosity.

"Hi, Jeannette," she says, her tone noncommittal.

"We've never met but I know a lot about you." Jeannette, her left hand braced on her RAV4, leans forward. "I met Jo-Ann Barnes in an LGBTQ-friendly tabletop gaming club in Albany, New York."

A grenade goes off inside Sophie's head. "*You're* the one who sent me those notes?"

Jeannette holds up both hands. "I didn't mean anything by them, I swear."

Grenades are still going off but one thing is clear to Sophie. "I have to drop my daughter home—she has school tomorrow. But I will be back here in twenty-five minutes."

Perhaps Sophie's tone is too grim. Jeannette chortles awkwardly. "Actually, we can talk another time. It might be a bit dangerous for me to wait here by myself for that long."

"You can wait somewhere else but I'll be back here in twenty-five minutes."

For the worst conversation of her life, Sophie realizes, as her shock turns into a frantic dread.

"At least give me your phone number, in case some axe-wielding murderer charges through here and I have to hide somewhere," wheedles Jeannette.

Sophie would have liked to refuse, but the woman already knows where she works. And she can't in good conscience tell a lone woman to meet her past nine thirty without giving the latter a means to contact her, not even if said woman is a potential blood leech.

Jeannette offers her phone in a slightly obsequious manner. Sophie jabs in her number, then turns and leaves.

"What does Jeannette want?" asks Elise when Sophie gets in the car and pulls on her seat belt.

"She wants to volunteer at the library and I told her to apply online," says Sophie, trying not to sound too worked up. "There's a whole process for it."

Elise unscrews the cap of her large metal water bottle and takes a sip. "I didn't get a chance to tell you but she came over and talked to me in the library on Saturday."

"She did?" Sophie's voice, at least in her own ears, sounds sharp enough to key cars.

"I was looking at graphic novels and she asked if I had any recommendations—you know I always have recommendations. Then she asked me for cool things to do around town. Then things like how's school, where do I want to go to college, et cetera. I think she might have had more questions if we hadn't left the library at that point."

Sophie, already tense all over, draws as taut as a bowstring. "I hope she wasn't being weird?"

"Not in the way it might sound. At no point did I ask myself, 'Is this person trying to groom me?'" Elise chortles—entirely unaware of her peril. "Just, you know, for a grown woman, she seemed more curious than she had reason to be about some rando teenager in the library."

"That's it?"

"That's it. She didn't try to talk to me tonight and I also didn't make it a point to approach her."

That's because the damn woman already decided to target Sophie. "Let's hope she's just one of those people who ask too many questions because they don't know how to end a conversation, and not because of anything else."

After that, Elise might have talked a bit about Hazel, who is apparently cool because she's played board games that Elise has never heard of. Sophie listens with half an ear. When they reach home and put away the games, Sophie tells Elise that she needs to go out and get some cookies for the next morning's running-group meeting.

Elise doesn't doubt her. After all, Sophie has been careful all these years never to do anything to draw excess attention to herself, not even from Elise.

But after Sophie settles back behind the wheel again, she can't simply start driving. She's freaking out. Two years. In less than two years Elise will be an adult and no one will be able to part them from each other. Why couldn't this Jeannette woman have arrived in their life a little later, when her knowledge would no longer matter?

But Elise is still only sixteen. If it gets out that Sophie is not her biological mother, will child protective services take her away and place her with strangers? And dear God, is Jo-Ann's queer-hating mom still alive?

What is she going to do if things go badly with Jeannette, as they most likely will?

Shit. How long has she been sitting in her car, losing her mind? Now there is no way she will make it back to the library on time, and she hates it when she fails her own standards of punctuality.

Sophie swears and burns rubber. Half a mile from the library, her phone dings.

> It's looking a bit desolate here.

Will Sophie arrive to find an empty parking lot, leading her to drive herself crazy—crazier—with all the worst possibilities of what Jeannette could be up to?

But Jeannette is there when Sophie's Cooper swerves to a stop in front of the library.

Sophie gets out of the car. "Sorry. It took a bit longer than I thought it would."

Jeannette refashioned her scarf so that now it covers her forehead and conceals the third eye—small mercies. "No problem. I was in H-E-B getting some shampoo. Anyway, I'm sorry to alarm you, I really didn't mean to."

At the look on Sophie's face, she says, "Please understand, I had the biggest crush on Jo-Ann. She was so warm and embracing—being near her was the best kind of self-care."

That was Jo-Ann, all right. After all these years, for Sophie there is still nothing like putting her head on Jo-Ann's shoulder. That must have been how a well-swaddled baby felt, all snug and safe.

"She loved to talk about you," murmurs Jeannette. "She had this sixteen-month pocket calendar that she used to pull out of her purse anytime someone new joined our group, to show off your pictures. Like, she bragged about how many books you read and I used to feel all salty about it. You were a librarian. What were you going to do? Not read?"

Sophie crosses her arms over her chest.

Jeannette again holds out her hands placatingly. "Don't worry. My feelings were completely unrequited—Jo-Ann was all set to go back to New Jersey for your life together with the baby. I just couldn't help falling a little more in love with her every time she found a reason to bring you up. I wish..."

She smiled rather sadly. "I wish someone would talk about me with such a glow on their face."

The long-buried ache of everything that could have been—Sophie, Elise, *and* Jo-Ann... How delighted and proud Jo-Ann would have been about Elise, how tightly and protectively she would have held them to her.

Sophie's throat tightens.

"She used to show us her sonogram pictures too—I already had presents all wrapped up for Baby Elise. When I heard that Jo-Ann died in childbirth, I couldn't believe it. I went to the hospital, thinking I'd find a way to pass on my gifts, but all I found out was that Jo-Ann's sister took Baby Elise and that Baby Elise would most likely live with her grandmother in Jamaica.

"So imagine my shock on Saturday when you guys walked into the library. You haven't aged a day from when Jo-Ann used to shove your pictures in my face, and Elise is a carbon copy of Jo-Ann."

That she is. And she inherited Jo-Ann's easy way with people.

"I talked a little to her," continues Jeannette. "I didn't dare ask too many questions but it was pretty obvious she had no idea she was supposed to have spent her life in another country. I became suspicious. I'm sorry if what I'm about to say sounds offensive, but I wondered if Jo-Ann had a trust settled on the kid and you erased Jo-Ann from her life in order to have total control over the money."

"What?!"

Jeannette scratches at the side of her cell phone case, as if embarrassed. "I'm sorry—I worked in a retirement home for a while and saw some wild schemes to get old folks' money, even when there wasn't a lot of money to be had. That's why I passed you the notes. But tonight, when I was home changing, I got results back from the Hudson County probate record search I paid for and found out that—"

"That Jo-Ann didn't leave a will?" Sophie can't help a hint—or a large, dripping heap—of sarcasm.

Jeannette smiles sheepishly. "Right. Her estate had to go into probate and was then divvied up among surviving family members according to New Jersey's succession law. Your name was nowhere to be found in the records.

"But according to the filings, there was also no mention anywhere of a child. Could it be possible? The sister they'd mentioned at the hospital, the one who took the baby, could that have been you? I mean, theoretically that shouldn't have happened, because Jo-Ann was Jamaican. Why would they let an American woman take her baby? Was it because Elise was a Black baby that no one paid attention?"

It had helped that Jo-Ann had put Sophie down as her sister and emergency contact, and that Sophie's grief was real and palpable. But still, it had taken lying, cheating, and document forging on a breathtaking level—thank you, Eileen Su and your cousins who knew everybody under the sun—for Sophie to become Elise's mother. At every step along the way Sophie had quivered like a Jell-O cube in a commercial, convinced she would be caught and sent to jail.

Instead of a too-merciful Almighty, as her mother had thought, had Sophie's salvation been, ironically, the system's indifference to the fate of little Black girls?

"I mean, obviously it was possible—you already did it. But why? That's what I had to know. Elise is obviously flourishing—what an impressive young woman. And you guys clearly love each other very much. But why did you steal her?"

Jeannette sounds sincere rather than threatening. But the threat is ever present.

What business is it of yours? Sophie wants to shout. *You were just Jo-Ann's acquaintance. That you fell for her doesn't give you any say in the matter.*

But Sophie broke the law—she broke *all* the laws. And lawbreakers don't get to claim privacy for their lawbreaking. All she can do is to somehow get Jeannette on her side.

A gust blows. Sophie took off her Nick Fury pleather coat even before the library closed and without it she shivers in the wind. "I took Elise at Jo-Ann's request—she realized much too late that she'd made no arrangements for contingencies. Without my intercession, Elise would have gone to Jo-Ann's mom in Jamaica, who'd disowned her for being queer."

Silence. The traffic light on the street beyond changes; a small red car goes through the intersection, then turns into the H-E-B lot.

"I never want to make another queer woman's life more difficult," says Jeannette. "But how do I know what you're saying is true? How do I know that you didn't steal Elise because you couldn't handle the pain of losing Jo-Ann?"

Just Sophie's luck that instead of a blackmailer, she gets a self-appointed arbiter of truth and justice.

Sophie's voice turns hard. "I already lost Jo-Ann. All the times Jo-Ann waxed poetic to you about us? We were done. We broke up because I wasn't ready to have a kid, so she went ahead and had one without telling me—until she needed the biggest favor anyone's ever had the gall to ask.

"But if you want proof, I can let you listen to the last voice message she left on my phone, on the day Elise was born. The recording, however, is in a safe-deposit box at my bank. I can retrieve it tomorrow morning and you can come by my office at one p.m."

"Fair enough."

And then I want you out of our lives. There is another perfectly good branch library less than five miles away—use that one in the future. Whatever good intentions you may have about other queer women's lives, you've already made mine both more difficult and less secure. I hope you understand that. I hope you understand that your sense of right and wrong and your need to know are the least important anything here!

All this and more races through Sophie's mind. But she says only, "I'll see you tomorrow afternoon, then."

Sophie sits in her locked car for ten minutes before her mind, painfully over-revved on anger, frustration, and dread, can think about anything practical. She decides to go to the store anyway, because Elise might still be awake when she gets back and, knowing Elise, she will want a cookie or two.

She drives to a larger H-E-B closer to her house and buys fifty dollars' worth of groceries. The brisk walk in a 100,000-square-foot establishment helps—she feels a little calmer, like she might be able to fall asleep in a couple of hours.

The worst has not happened. She has a problem on her hands, yes, but not a catastrophe. Or at least, not yet. Jeannette has poked her nose where it doesn't belong but she is still operating within semi-normal bounds. Linguistically, lightning does not strike the same spot twice, but in nature, it does. And Sophie just might prove lucky again, should Jeannette hold her secret long enough for Elise to turn eighteen.

She gets back to her car, loads the groceries in the trunk, and sees that there's already a canvas bag there—the stuff she and Elise take with them every time they volunteer for park cleanups. It's Elise's job to take it back home to the garage but it's one of those chores Elise sees as optional.

Sophie sighs and gets in the car—she can't care about this right now. But she does glance at her phone, in case Elise texted about why she's taking so long.

But the only new message is from Jeannette, whose number, though not in Sophie's contact list, has now seared into her brain.

After an initial onslaught of panic—Jeannette has decided to condemn Sophie without listening to the recording and will call the police imminently!—Sophie sees that Jeannette has shared her location.

Without any explanation as to why.

A different set of alarm bells clangs in Sophie's head.

Is this Jeannette demanding another meeting? Has she changed her mind? Is she a sociopath who pretended to be reasonable just so she could yank Sophie's string harder? Or a fragile snowflake who was annoyed that Sophie wasn't humbler and more obsequious in her demeanor?

Will she demand money? How much can Sophie afford to give her to keep her quiet for the next twenty months?

Oh, God, what if Jeannette doesn't want money? What if the woman just wants to watch Sophie burn?

Sophie hangs on to her self-control. She resists the overwhelming urge to type *What do you want?!* in response. There must not be any trail of traceable writing from her to Jeannette.

Fine, so she's been sent a location. It's not that far, somewhere in Astrid's neighborhood. She will go there, on the off chance that Jeannette made a mistake. These days people inadvertently send stuff to their contact list all the time.

She drives back in the library's direction, crosses under the highway, and turns into an apartment complex half a mile further on. But she doesn't see Jeannette's distinctive orange RAV4—not at the exact spot indicated by the shared location, nor elsewhere in the complex.

The emotional whiplash of this day is taking a toll on her—her brain feels as sludgy as a drying-up mud puddle, yet she is also jumpy and paranoid. Her reaction to Jeannette's car not being there is equally bifurcated: She is dying to go home to bed; she is convinced something is wrong.

She tries to tell herself that it was a prank.

But what if it's not so simple?

She drives out of the apartment complex. It is located on a street that leads out of a neighborhood onto a thoroughfare. If she turns left, she will reach the thoroughfare roughly fifty yards away and be on her way home. If she turns right, she will head deeper into a large subdivision from which the library draws a good share of its patrons.

She heads right, not because she knows what she's doing but because the matter feels unfinished.

Northwest Austin is well-off and the entire district is generally considered safe. Still, it can be spooky to visit an unfamiliar neighborhood at night. The sprawl of streets, carefully designed to never be straight for long—to discourage speeding—starts to take on a warren-like quality, making her question whether she's driving in circles. Some of her agitation transmutes into uneasiness—or rather, an even greater uneasiness.

She makes another turn and suddenly an orange SUV looms ahead, parked in a shadowy spot, yet so gaudy it still gleams in the scant light.

Does Jeannette live here? Why is her car on the street?

Sophie parks but is reluctant to get out: This is Texas; no matter how quiet and sleepy a street looks, it's always possible that a homeowner will materialize, firearm in hand.

Okay, she is going to peek into the RAV4, just to make sure that Jeannette hasn't somehow dropped dead inside. Because if she did, then Sophie, probably among the last people she contacted on her phone, is going to be in a lot of trouble.

Sophie knocks on the rear of the car. No response. She inches closer, but it's too dark to see much.

After a moment of hesitation, Sophie turns on the flashlight on her phone and shines the beam of light into the car—and screams, a short, shrill sound that immediately disappears, leaving her with her mouth open, her legs shaking.

A woman is slumped over on the back seat. Peasant dress, orange scarf—it's Jeannette.

What happened? Did she go to a bar and get drunk in the time Sophie did fifty dollars of grocery shopping? Can anyone black out in that little time?

Or... did Jeannette get roofied? As in, she was lucky enough to realize that something wasn't right and leave the bar just in time? And if so, was it because Sophie's number was at the very top of her messages that she sent her location to Sophie? But why send Sophie one location when she was going to drive to a different one?

Gritting her teeth, Sophie pulls on the door and almost screams again when it opens readily.

Jeannette lies on her side, her legs drawn up. The orange scarf is on the floorboard. Her head pushes against the opposite door, her face obscured by her now loose hair. Sophie leans down and shakes her by one calf. "Jeannette, are you okay? Jeannette?"

No response. Sophie types *Can you OD on Rohypnol?* into her phone. Apparently so. And if that Rohypnol is mixed with alcohol and other central nervous system depressants, it can be fatal.

Sophie reaches in further and grabs hold of Jeannette's limp hand. Does her skin feel slightly cool to the touch? Sophie digs her thumb into Jeannette's wrist and fails to find a pulse. That can't be true. She must be pressing in the wrong place. She tries again. Bottom of wrist, near the thumb. But the familiar throb of the radial artery is missing.

Sophie shines her phone's flashlight on Jeannette's wrist to visually confirm that she is holding the correct spot—and tries one more time. Still no pulse.

Her heart thuds. She rounds to the other side of the car, opens the car door, and pushes the hair off Jeannette's face. The beam of light from her phone casts harsh shadows on pallid, slack features. No blood; she just looks passed out. And—at least, judging by her clothes and the lack of a metallic smell—there seem to be no injuries on the rest of her.

"Jeannette!" Sophie calls her name sharply.

Maybe she should call 911?

But what if—what if Jeannette's already dead? And if she's already dead—under questionable circumstances—can Sophie trust the police not to pin the death on her?

Goddamn.

Sophie sprints to her car and takes her compact out of her purse. She runs back to Jeannette's SUV and holds the compact under Jeannette's nostrils.

Nothing.

She holds it under her own nose. Almost immediately a film of vapors obscures the mirror.

Her fingers shake. She holds the compact right up to Jeannette's nose. Still nothing. Oh, God. She feels around Jeannette's neck for a pulse. Nothing. She places her hand directly over Jeannette's chest. It does not rise or fall. And there is no heartbeat.

She should call 911. Or the police. But can she do that without implicating herself? What if Jeannette left behind notes at home or on her devices? What if as soon as the police start the investigation, they find Jeannette's musings on the greedy librarian who stole another woman's child?

Low wails penetrate her consciousness. It's her, keening in fear.

She dashes back into her own car again. Holding the steering wheel, she forces herself to breathe slowly, deliberately. Okay, she'll probably still call 911—her conscience will not allow her to just walk away if there's an off chance that the woman is still alive. But she has to first erase all signs that she's ever been here.

How? How?

The bag of stuff for park cleanups that's still in her trunk. She climbs into her back seat and grabs it from the cargo area. Among other things, the bag contains two pairs of rubber gloves and a pack of isopropyl alcohol wipes. And—she looks into her purse—her emergency manicure repair kit is there, with its small bottle of acetone.

She takes out her phone and composes a list, looking stuff up as she goes.

1. Wipe down Jeannette's left wrist, face, neck, leg—and any other part that I touched—with alcohol and acetone.
2. Wipe car door handles and any other part of the car I might have touched with alcohol, acetone, and a good rub with tissue.
3. Unlock her phone with her thumbprint and remove her phone from her car.
4. Use her phone to text 911 and give her location.
5. Disconnect battery from her phone and turn it off.

The police cannot find Jeannette's phone, because that would lead them to Sophie. And just turning it off isn't good enough, according to seemingly legitimate sources online. She must detach the battery altogether to avoid third-party tracking.

Sophie shakes worse than ever, but it's time to execute her exit strategy.

CHAPTER TWENTY

It is half past ten. Sophie has been speaking for almost an hour. Jonathan and Astrid, mouths agape, are still trying to digest what they've heard. Hazel, who has known for some time that something was the matter, if not precisely what the matter was, brings Sophie some water.

Sophie drinks gratefully. The table before her is a junkscape of open salsa containers, discarded tea bags, and half-eaten food. It has been like that the entire time Sophie talked: Nobody ate, nobody cleaned up, nobody did anything at all.

Sophie picks up her thoroughly cold breakfast taco and bites into the now soggy tortilla.

"Does—does Elise know?" asks Astrid.

Sophie isn't sure whether her question concerns Elise's parentage or the hole to the center of the Earth Sophie has dug for herself. But the answer is the same. "Not yet."

Jonathan gathers up a handful of trash and pitches everything into the wastebasket behind him. "So you still have Jeannette Obermann's phone?"

"Unfortunately so. At first I was paranoid about getting all traces of my DNA wiped off. Then I was like, 'Oh, no, if they had her phone, they'd know right away she contacted me just before she died'—which had me really conflicted since I want the police to have whatever other evidence might be there on her phone.

"But the worst is—" The sinking feeling from the night before engulfs

Sophie again. She gulps for air. "In my panic that night, between doing everything else, I read one crucial piece of information wrong. I thought I had weeks before the police would have her phone records. But they might have them already—and if not, they must be very close.

"And once they get them, once they see what Jeannette Obermann texted me that night, they are going to zero in on me like a heat-seeking missile."

The walls of the Den of Calories are already closing in on her. "My life flashes before my eyes three times a day. I don't know what to do once the police get their hands on the phone records. And above all I'm petrified the truth about Jo-Ann and Elise will come out and I'll lose Elise."

Silence. Even the roof seems to be lowering ominously.

Ever since she made the choice to honor Jo-Ann's dying wish, Sophie has steeled herself for the day it could blow up on her. The passage of the years might have made her less wary, but a pool of fear has always rippled quietly in the depths of her mind.

But still, she's unprepared for the destruction being found out like this would unleash.

And while it was such an overwhelming relief to unburden herself to Jonathan, Astrid, and Hazel, panic, like quicksand, is rising around her again. In fact, she might have done them a great unkindness. Now if the police question these three about Jeannette Obermann—or about Elise, if it comes to that—they will no longer be able to plead ignorance.

"So . . ." says Hazel, her voice remarkably even, "I guess it would help if we knew who actually killed Jeannette—and Perry."

The library is open on Sundays from noon to five.

Sophie and Astrid, who are not on the schedule, leave together a little before eleven—Sophie has invited Astrid to stay for a few days at her house until Astrid feels comfortable going back to her condo. Jonathan sleepwalks through the first couple hours of his shift, straightening up the rolling carts next to the circulation area every time he's completely distracted by the revelations of the day.

At three o'clock, Hazel, coming off an hour facing the public, signals that she wants to talk to him. They walk outside under the guise of a quick break.

The day is sunny and mild. Hazel looks tired. For the first time he notices tiny lines at the corners of her eyes.

"You wouldn't happen to smoke, would you, Jonathan?" she asks.

He shakes his head. "I stopped when I got out of the navy. You?"

"Not anymore, either. But right now I could really use one, or even half a cigarette."

In her place, he would have gone through a pack by now.

Whatever she wants to talk to him about would most likely involve finding out what exactly Conrad was doing on Game Night. He feels a great reluctance. Part of him wonders whether in doing so he will burn all his bridges with Ryan. But more than that, he is in a strange agony for her. The uncertainty must eat at her, yet the actual knowledge could prove ten times worse.

"What's your plan?" he says after a moment.

She pulls one sleeve of her argyle sweater straight, then folds it up an inch. "You remember last night I left my dessert container behind in Conrad's house and had to go back and get it?"

He nods.

She stills, then starts on her other sleeve. "I left it by design. I wanted an excuse to see Conrad again, even if it was a flimsy excuse."

His heart aches for her, for all those hopes withering on the vine.

"But when I saw Ryan's car," she continues, her words as considered as her motions, "I decided to question him alone."

So that Jonathan wouldn't be thrown into this potentially seismic knowledge about—at that time—Ryan?

"Unfortunately, as a result of that, now I no longer have anything I can retrieve from their house. Did you, by any chance, also leave some items behind?"

Jonathan shakes his head. No such idea had occurred to him. Then again, he had not been outright refused by Ryan. He still had hopes of being invited back.

She tilts her head and smiles at him. "Can you pretend, then, to have left something behind?"

Her idea ignites a flare of excitement. But—"Wouldn't Ryan have already seen it by now, if I'd left anything behind?"

"Tell him it's a really small item. A flash drive. A location tracker from your wallet. Something that can fall into nooks and crannies."

She is not throwing ideas at the wall to see what sticks. The woman is as committed as a kamikaze pilot.

"So we go back to Conrad's house." And then what?

"But only you will go through the front door. When you get in, ask to use the bathroom. You used the guest bathroom when we were there last time, right?"

He nods, already tense.

"It has a casement window—you know, the kind that opens out, instead of a sash that moves up and down?"

He didn't really notice. The only time he was in that bathroom, he was in a hurry to finish, wash his hands, and get back to Ryan.

"There is no screen. Last night I opened it out of curiosity and didn't hear any alarm going off. If you can unlock the window and leave it open a crack, I'll be able to get in from there."

"So you're going to search Conrad's house, like they do in movies?"

Her jaw moves. "I don't want to, and I don't think it'll be useful. Conrad isn't going to leave a printout of his guilt lying around and I'm neither a hacker nor a safebreaker. But if I don't at least try, then I'll have to ask him outright at some point, which—"

She takes a breath. "Which could be even more unsafe."

It becomes Jonathan's turn to take a deep breath—and whip out his phone. "Okay, might as well get it done now. Tell me what exactly I should have left behind at Conrad's place."

> Hey Ryan, sorry to bother you. My wallet tracker might have fallen out at your house. At least that's what my app says.

Ryan's response comes twenty minutes later, well after Hazel and Jonathan have returned to work. Jonathan finds Hazel, who is at the drive-through checkout station, handing a stack of books to a patron on a Harley, and shows her Ryan's reply. You want to come and look for it yourself? I'll be home tonight.

"Does that work?"

Hazel hesitates only a moment. "It should. Thank you, Jonathan."

"Hey, we're all in this together."

"You actually don't need to be involved at all." She takes his hand, her fingers cool yet strong. "In case it's not yet clear, I am supremely grateful."

Elise is delighted that Sophie brought Astrid home. After a few questions about the "foundation fumigation" that forced Astrid from her condo, she quickly ropes Astrid in for an afternoon of board games. Or rather, one game in particular, Elise's current obsession, called *Trails to Table*, which combines foraging with gourmet menu planning.

At first Sophie worries that Elise has taken Astrid hostage. But Astrid gets into the game before too long. By the time Sophie reminds Elise to finish her homework, it's Astrid who stands up more reluctantly, still hankering for another round.

"This is really interesting and complex, but not in a way that hurts your brain," she says to Elise as they pack up.

"I know, right? The props are cute, but it's the gameplay that's really propulsive." Elise hugs the box to her chest. "I love it. And thank you so much for playing with me!"

"Oh, gosh, don't thank me. I might not leave now—I might just squat here to play games."

"Don't say that, Astrid, or Elise will start praying for the carpenter ants in your neighbor's foundation never to go away!"

They all chortle at that. Elise bounces upstairs, humming a tune that Sophie is too out of pop culture to recognize.

"Come on," Sophie says to Astrid, "let's go for a walk. It'll be dark soon."

"Ooh, on the golf course?"

Sophie's town house is situated in a cluster of tightly packed units at the edge of a sprawling neighborhood of single-family homes. And her front door, much to Astrid's—and frankly Sophie's own—marvel, opens onto a golf course.

From her tiny porch, they step almost directly onto the ribbon of asphalt originally intended for golf carts. The sun is low in the sky, the wind is rising, but it's not cold yet and a lager-pale light drizzles upon a long expanse of tall grass. In the distance there are trees and in the even greater distance the land dips and rises again in a broad green slope.

The country club stopped watering the course several droughts ago. And it was thanks to the golf course falling into disuse—not to mention depressed real estate prices in the wake of the subprime meltdown—that Sophie was able to afford the town house on her librarian's salary.

She loves the view: golden grass undulating in the breeze, dark green clusters of ash juniper, a grazing family of deer scattering upon their approach.

"Wow," exclaims Astrid. "Everybody always tells me that Austin is full of deer, but it's the first time I've seen so many at once."

"Good thing I'm not a gardener." Sophie laughs a little. "I love deer as wildlife but gardeners around here have to jump through hoops to make sure their plants don't get eaten."

The path dips and they enter a small green tunnel made by tree branches meeting overhead.

Astrid turns toward Sophie. "You've built a good life for yourself and Elise. You really have, Sophie."

Sophie knows this. Of course she knows this. But to hear it after days of relentless self-castigation . . .

"Thank you," she says, a catch in her voice. She desperately needed to be reminded that while she might have put her foot in it on Game Night, she has not, by and large, messed up either her own life or Elise's. "Thank you, Astrid. It means a lot to me."

And then, not wanting either of them to feel too self-conscious, she keeps talking. "But it's been good for me, too, to be Elise's mother. Left to my own devices, I probably would have been a hermit."

But she couldn't have inflicted such isolation on Jo-Ann's daughter. Jo-Ann would have been the pillar of any community. She would have hosted neighborhood barbecues, organized school supply donations, and given out dozens of rum cakes at Christmas. Everyone would have known and loved Jo-Ann and everyone would have cared about her kid.

Sophie, nowhere near as extraverted as Jo-Ann, nevertheless served as school crossing guard when Elise was little, coached Elise's soccer teams even though she was a track-and-field athlete and not a team sport player, and to this day is still involved with the HOA.

And in this area, where the Claremonts are demographic outliers, all her neighbors know and love Elise.

A pair of young does dash across the man-made prairie, leap through someone's unfenced yard, and disappear into the residential street beyond.

"Can I ask you a question, Sophie?"

The wind tousles Astrid's red-streaked hair. Her eyes shine with curiosity and—a second passes before Sophie recognizes it as admiration. Astrid has always approached Sophie with deference, but Sophie had attributed it to a girl from overseas feeling intimidated by a no-nonsense Black woman.

Now Sophie's shield of invincibility lies in shards, yet the warm acclaim in Astrid's gaze remains undimmed.

"Sure, go ahead."

"I was—I was trying to escape my pretense, but you needed to make yours a permanent reality. I guess my question is, when did this stop being a pretense for you?"

On the drive from the library to Sophie's place, Astrid told Sophie the reason she no longer has a Swedish accent—that she was never Swedish to begin with.

Sophie glances back in the direction of her house, the direction of her reality. "In one sense, it became all too real right away—in the criminal sense, I guess. I could go to jail for my impulsive decision to honor Jo-Ann's wishes.

"As for when I started to think of Elise not as Jo-Ann's child but my own, that took a good bit longer."

Thrusting a child on a woman with no maternal instincts does not instantly turn her into supermom. It just makes her a frazzled mess with a bawling baby, desperately trying to regain a semblance of control.

This is not an admission that Sophie makes lightly—Mommy Judgment is real and fearsome. But that solid baseline of approval from Astrid makes it easier to speak the truth. "Children are such vectors of chaos and uncertainty and I've never been a fan of either. I'm pretty sure that if, when Elise was one, Jo-Ann's mom had turned up and said, 'I won't report you to the police, I'll just quietly take the baby off your hands,' I would have handed Elise over and told Jo-Ann's ghost that I tried.

"But by the time she turned three I would have spent my last penny to hold on to her. I'm an okay communicator at work, but not so much in my personal life. I think Elise learned to say 'I love you' from Barney, frankly. She loved to say 'I love you' and she taught me to say it back."

Sophie's voice thickens. "She made us a reality. She made us into a family. How do you ever give up the person who taught you everything about love?"

Astrid hugs Sophie, a warm, comfortable hug, like when Elise made Sophie embrace her favorite teddy bear. "You'll stay a family, always."

"I hope so," Sophie murmurs. She again looks in the direction of her house, her reality. "I really hope so."

CHAPTER TWENTY-ONE

In the navy, Jonathan was trained in insertion and extraction. But tonight, his role is eye candy: He is to keep Ryan otherwise engaged while Hazel slips into the house and searches Conrad's office and bedroom.

They went over their plan several times—or what passes for a plan.

"In movies people usually have an impressive plan at the beginning," Hazel said at one point, "but as contingencies arise they must improvise. We've saved ourselves time by committing to improvisation right away."

Jonathan wasn't completely sure whether Hazel was joking. But she was right. They had very little to go on. The house is huge and he failed to pay adequate attention to Conrad's side when Ryan gave them the tour.

He barely focused on Ryan's side either, come to think of it, only on Ryan himself, never imagining that he'd need to infiltrate the place the next evening.

Without a good understanding of the terrain, everything is a crapshoot. But Hazel assured him that she remembers the layout of the house very well, especially the approach to Conrad's private quarters.

She also reassured him that she's had plenty of training in hand-to-hand combat, but that only makes Jonathan more nervous. Not that he doesn't believe her, but if she needs to use those close-quarter fighting skills then they will have failed resoundingly in their goal of stealth information gathering.

He pulls into a cul-de-sac not far from Conrad's house. After the time change, night comes early and swift. Which is fortunate, as the cul-de-sac seems the kind where residents do not look kindly upon strangers coming into their little cove of exclusivity.

Somewhere nearby someone is grilling—the air is redolent with the aroma of mesquite smoke and searing protein. But tonight these otherwise appetizing smells make Jonathan's stomach twist into a hard knot.

Hazel gets out of her car and slips into the rather cramped rear seat of his truck. They'd considered putting on the tonneau cover and smuggling her onto Conrad's property in the bed of the pickup, but decided in the end not to bother because if there are exterior cameras on the house, she would be caught on film either way—they only need to make sure that she isn't seen at the beginning, in case Ryan meets them out in front again.

I'm almost there, he texts Ryan.

Ryan replies right away. I'll open the gate. The front door is unlocked. Just come in.

Jonathan reads Ryan's text aloud to Hazel, then guides the truck away from the curb. "You okay back there?"

"I'm fine. Thanks."

He exhales. "I don't know how you're fine, Hazel. I'm sweating bullets for you."

His hands are not clammy yet, but his antiperspirant will be in for the battle of its life tonight. And he wonders whether her apparent calm is as much a facade as his own.

"But we should be okay," he says, as much to himself as to her. "Even if Ryan kicks me out after a few minutes, he'd still have no reason to check Conrad's rooms."

They are out of the cul-de-sac now. In the rearview mirror, Hazel lies down on the back seat.

"My opinion on this hasn't changed," she says. "In case you aren't invited to stay, you should leave and head home. I can pass for an ex-girlfriend. An ex pawing Conrad's things is bad, but I might get away with it, even if the cops show up. The two of us in this together would look like we're casing the joint."

That is the reason she insisted on bringing her own car. Jonathan understands her rationale, but he won't be able to leave her behind, not until he knows that she is also safely out of the house, driving away.

They fall silent. He doesn't need to persuade her. He only needs to do the right thing when the time comes.

His palms do perspire as he parks the truck by the front door of Conrad's house.

"I'll let you know when the window is open," he murmurs, and steps out.

The door chimes softly as Jonathan walks in. Amazing what different details you pay attention to when you are committing a crime.

Ryan appears in pajamas—army fatigue green, slightly oversized but soft-looking.

Impossible dreams of domesticity inundate Jonathan. He can do nothing but watch Ryan's smiling approach.

"Hey. I looked around a bit, but I didn't see your tracker," he says.

Right, the tracker, the nominal reason for Jonathan's presence. He's never been a great liar and can only hope his body isn't going to betray him with a horrific white-man blush that turns him into a beet from forehead to collarbone. "It's—ah—kinda small, but I should be able to find it with my app. And is it okay if I use your bathroom real quick?"

He has one job and he wants it done.

"Sure."

Ryan sounds amused by the limited size of Jonathan's bladder but Jonathan is too nervous to be embarrassed. Thankfully he opens the guest bathroom's window without incident—and almost cries out loud when a balaclava-covered figure, all in black, materializes outside. He thought Hazel would stay in the truck until he texted.

She climbs in and signals him to carry on. So he flushes the unused toilet, washes his hands, and opens the door to reconnoiter. At his gesture of all-clear, Hazel slips out and disappears into the depths of the house like a wisp of smoke.

Ryan is waiting for Jonathan in the soaring living room library. Jonathan feels like a cheap windup toy, his motions herky-jerky. He has his phone out in his right hand, pretending to use it for guidance. But he knows where he was seated that night: under the double-story bank of windows that would have offered a panoramic view of the lake during the day, there is a smaller, plumper sofa.

He gropes the sofa for a bit, then thrusts his left hand, with the tracker Hazel had handed him earlier held tight between middle and ring fingers, into the space behind the cushions. "Aha! Here it is."

Then he takes out his wallet and pops the tracker inside.

"Well, that was easy."

Is there a teasing edge to Ryan's words? Has he guessed that there are ulterior purposes behind Jonathan's "search" for this bit of technology? Jonathan's cheeks scald, but it's not as if Ryan's wrong. He's only wrong in thinking that Jonathan has come all this way to hit on him.

But now Jonathan must. "So . . . what do you do on a Sunday evening?"

Ryan shrugs. "Look through profiles on Grindr."

Jonathan wants to chortle, but no sounds emerge.

Ryan laughs. "Just kidding. It's NBA season; I watch hoops. Want to catch a game with me, since you're here anyway?"

This is *great*, right? Jonathan *wants* to be here. Then why does his heartbeat suddenly feel like a hammer at the back of his head, cracking his skull apart?

His reply barely clears his vocal cords. "Let's do it."

Hazel enters Conrad's office, locks the door from inside, secures the curtains, and proceeds to his desktop.

Last year this time, she would have known nothing about hacking into someone else's personal computer. But last year, she did not know yet that her husband had committed financial crimes. In the days and weeks immediately after Kit's death, instead of dealing with loss and betrayal, Hazel gathered up all the devices in his London apartment—and even a couple of derelict CPUs in his mother's house—and took them back to Singapore.

There she found a hacker to help her break into them. For a little extra money, the hacker taught Hazel the basics and threw in some tools she'd developed herself, in case Hazel would find them useful in the future. Hazel almost didn't take the offer—she was not planning on having another dubious husband. Or any husband, for that matter. But in the end she did, because the girl seemed to need the income.

After Sophie and Astrid left together this morning, before the library opened at noon, Hazel spent the entire hour on the phone with the girl, reviewing what she'd learned and what she'd forgotten. As she turns on Conrad's desktop, she dials the hacker again. The phone is picked up right away—it's the middle of the day over there.

Hazel does not speak, but only shows the hacker what she is dealing with and follows the hacker's directions carefully. She knows enough about Conrad—name, birthday, parents' names, etc.—to mount a dictionary attack. But her efforts yield nothing—he must use a strong password even for his own home desktop.

She connects the laptop she brought to the desktop and sets the hacker's program to a brute force attack. This is not what she hoped for—there's no telling how long it might take.

She glances at her phone. Jonathan's latest text is time-stamped five minutes ago. Watching basketball with Ryan. 2 min left in first quarter.

So he'll be here another hour and a half? She's tempted to remove the balaclava she found in Nainai's box of old Halloween costumes—her nostrils are filled with its dusty, musty smell—but she only scratches her face through the itchy material.

Leaving the tool to do its automated hacking, she ends the call and gets up. Behind the desk on the wall is a large, framed image of a sailing catamaran—the one on which Conrad cabin-boyed his way around the world?

The office, like elsewhere in the house, has its share of books, mostly tax and contract law. She locates a filing cabinet, but the documents it contains are paperwork related to the bequest of the property from Romy Lonstein to Conrad's mother, and plans and contracts for the subsequent renovation.

Through a connecting door she enters the bedroom. The space is large but spare. Instead of books, the faint illumination of her flashlight reveals a whole shelf of vinyl records.

She has yet to get a true sense of Conrad in this house. According to Ryan, he inherited most of the books that form the backbone of the house's character. The vinyls probably belonged to Romy Lonstein, once upon a time—there were piles and piles of them in the background of some of her social media posts.

What belongs to him, then, in this entire place? The ship in a bottle? The jar of tickets?

On his nightstand she finds—what else?—a stack of books. A volume of poetry by Cavafy, another by Margaret Atwood, a paperback copy of *The Fifth Season* in French, and what looks to be a wuxia epic in complex Chinese.

She picks up the copy of *La cinquième saison* and gently thumbs the edges. There is something tucked in the pages, acting as a bookmark—a postcard.

Of Madeira. Her fingers tighten.

She sits down on the edge of the bed and presses on her flashlight's controls for stronger light. The front of the postcard is composed of smaller images: green peaks and gorges, glistening waterfalls, hikers walking alongside narrow, picturesque irrigation channels.

The corners of the postcard are slightly bent. There is a dent along the left side, too. Otherwise the cardstock is still smooth and shiny. She turns it over. To her surprise, there is writing on the back, the handwriting sharp and handsome but not easy to read.

She peers closer.

A click. A cold metallic barrel presses into her temple.

"Don't move," says a man.

Says Conrad.

CHAPTER TWENTY-TWO

The basketball game, naturally, fails to hold Jonathan's attention—and would have failed even if Hazel weren't upstairs breaking the law.

For all intents and purposes, he and Ryan are alone, for the first time in twenty years. Jonathan is grateful for the TV, for the sonic blast and frenetic motion of the match in progress. He is also grateful for the beer in his hand, which gives him something to hold and something to do.

"Oh, I almost forgot," says Ryan and leaps up.

He seems to have lost none of his agility. Jonathan can easily overlay onto him the image he still carries from those varsity b-ball games—yellow flooring, burnt orange bleachers, a lithe young Ryan levitating for a jump shot.

Ryan comes back with a plate of food. "Ever had karaage? Japanese fried chicken?"

With an H Mart not far from where he lives, Jonathan's had *Korean* fried chicken. But the karaage is new to him, and its crispy, salty deliciousness penetrates even his current level of inner distraction. "Wow. Did you make this?"

"It's frozen food. My mom bought two boxes at the Japanese store and gave me one." Ryan grins. "For me to put a little Asian gloss on my American ass."

Jonathan can also overlay this smile on his mental recollection of high school Ryan. The same charm, the same mischief.

But how does he come across to Ryan? Has he changed enough in the past twenty years that Ryan *cannot* reconcile the current him with his memories? God, he hopes so.

The final whistle blows on the second quarter.

Ryan tsks. "It's been three weeks since the season started and everybody still looks rusty."

"Too much bunching," concurs Jonathan. "Nobody's rotating properly." He did see a bit of the play and it was not inspiring.

Ryan shakes his head. He takes out his phone, frowns, puts it back into his pocket, and turns off the TV.

Jonathan holds his breath. Is Ryan about to evict him?

But Ryan only asks, "Do you want some ice cream?"

"Ah, thanks but no. My doctor isn't entirely satisfied with my lipids panel and I already had fried chicken."

This might be the most middle-aged thing he's ever said. And damn it, he's not middle-aged yet. Just a man in his prime with a slightly elevated triglyceride count.

"Do you mind if I do?"

Ryan doesn't wait for permission but leaves again and returns with a pint of Amy's Mexican vanilla ice cream.

"Now you're really tempting me."

"Adulting: Nobody to drag you away from temptations." Ryan smiles slightly.

An electric caress of a smile. Desire and yearning, wound together like the braids of a whip, lash Jonathan across the heart. He downs half a can of beer.

"So why are you here tonight?" asks Ryan.

Jonathan chokes on his beer and coughs. "I'm sorry?"

"I may not be a cop, but I still search for evidence for a living. There was nothing in that couch before you got here."

"I—" Jonathan's brain is functioning about as well as the fried egg in that ubiquitous antidrug PSA of his childhood.

He coughs some more. Ryan hands him a paper napkin.

Jonathan manages to catch his breath. *Oh, Hazel, I hope you find All The Things. I'm about to go over the event horizon here.*

"Thanks," he mumbles.

Ryan eats a spoonful of ice cream—he is still waiting for an answer. Jonathan feels naked.

"I—guess I just wanted to see you."

Ryan raises a cool eyebrow.

Shit. Jonathan's getting spaghettified. Is this going to be the last time he sees Ryan? "I wanted . . . to apologize."

"Really?"

Ryan sounds surprised. That bothers Jonathan but there is no stopping the words spilling out of him like guts from an eviscerated man.

"For all those years ago—the cruel and untrue things I said. I wasn't ready to face myself yet. I was still holding on to some illusions. You shredded those illusions and in that moment, I couldn't take it. I'm sorry. I was wrong. You don't have to forgive me, but you should know that I *am* sorry and that I've been sorry ever since that day."

That night.

Graduation was two months in the past. He and Maryam had parted ways but remained friendly and she was the one who told him about the pool party down the street from her house.

There must have been thirty, forty kids. The temperature had been a hundred and five earlier in the day and the water in the pool was almost warm enough to proof yeast. Jonathan sought refuge in the artificially cooled interior of the house and there was Maryam, sitting on Ryan's lap, the two of them whispering and giggling.

The sight of Ryan's arm around Maryam did something to Jonathan. But he wasn't angry that Ryan was maybe encroaching on his very recent ex. No, he was jealous of Maryam, her hand on Ryan's nape, her barely covered ass smushed into his groin.

The two spied Jonathan and broke into a fresh peal of laughter. Then Maryam leaped up. "I'm going into the pool."

She gave Jonathan a slap on the shoulder. Which annoyed him a little. Sure, they never did anything beyond kissing and a little light groping when they were together, but she could have felt his abs or something as she sauntered past, instead of that positively sisterly slap.

But with Maryam out of the way, Ryan's bare torso filled Jonathan's vision. He was just so . . . fit.

Ryan smiled. "You wanna see something cool? Maryam just showed it to me."

"What?"

Ryan beckoned. Jonathan, despite the alarm bells going off in his head, followed.

Ryan led him into an office lined on three walls with shelves. "Maryam said that she used to play a lot in this house when another Iranian American family lived here. And her favorite spot used to be—let's see if I remember it right."

He crouched down and pulled. A three-foot-high, eighteen-inch-wide lower section of the shelves swung forward, exposing a narrow set of stairs behind.

"What?" The exclamation shot out of Jonathan.

"Cool, right? You're not too big to fit in, are you?"

"Course not."

But Jonathan did have to shimmy in sideways. The stairs elevated only about five feet or so and he found himself in an octagonal reading nook, with shelves, a floor lamp, and a leather sofa chair facing a trio of large windows that had their blinds drawn shut.

He sank into the chair. Ryan came up, took a cushion from behind Jonathan, dropped it on the floor, and sat down at Jonathan's feet, between his splayed knees.

Jonathan tensed. The next second he lost his breath as Ryan ran the back of his hand over Jonathan's shin. It was as if Skynet had unleashed the nuclear apocalypse. Jonathan was scorched, burnt to a crisp.

Stop, he wanted to say. But he was afraid that if he opened his mouth, out would come, *Don't stop. Don't ever stop.*

Ryan peered at him. His hand moved up to settle at Jonathan's knee. Jonathan was paralyzed—and engorged to the limit. And when, with another grin, Ryan's hand settled on Jonathan's waistband, Jonathan's brain promptly short-circuited.

His still-dry swimming trunks ended up on the floor. Ryan took him inside his mouth. Jonathan's fingers dug into the armrests of the sofa chair. Ryan. Him. The two of them. It was all he wanted.

It was what he feared above all. The beginning of his worst nightmare. But as long as he didn't come, he didn't need to deal with it.

And then Ryan did something and Jonathan bucked and convulsed uncontrollably for a frightfully pleasurable eternity.

When he opened his eyes, still panting hard, Ryan was again smiling at him with that seductive gleam in his eyes. "Think you can return the favor, big guy?"

Jonathan jumped out of the sofa chair, knocking Ryan backward. He grabbed his swimming trunks and stepped into them, not caring that maybe he was pulling them on backward.

Ryan was on his feet now, rubbing his ribs where Jonathan had inadvertently rammed his knee. He studied Jonathan, a little puzzled.

Jonathan tried to explain that he wanted a life in which he never had to explain anything to his parents. A life in which he was never the butt of any locker room jokes. A life in which he was just a man, not a gay man.

But he shouted, "Don't try to make me a f— just because you're one. You're disgusting. Stay away from me!"

And then, instead of following that up with a righteous door slam, he had to go sideways down the narrow steps and crawl out of the hidden door that almost trapped him between its too-narrow frames.

Present-day Ryan slowly eats another spoonful of ice cream. "Apology accepted."

Jonathan blinks.

"Although, to be honest, I'm not even all that sure what you're talking about. I kind of remember that pool party as a good time—that's all."

"Oh," says Jonathan.

Now his brain is not only fried but hurled out of that pan to land splat on the kitchen wall, yolk dripping down in slow, sticky streaks.

"That's—that's good. I guess I didn't need to give myself such a hard time, then."

"No, not at all," says Ryan sincerely and, for the first time ever in their acquaintance, a little uncomfortably.

The significance of everything Ryan is saying doesn't sink in right away. Then it does and mortification flays Jonathan. He isn't upset that he's been fixated on his mistake all these years—he was cruel and dishonest and should have been tormented. But it is crushing that an outburst that has taken on such outsized significance in his life made no impression on Ryan at all.

Fuck. Where does one go from here? The possibility of catharsis is now just unbearable embarrassment. Even Ryan, in all his pajamaed, ice-creaming-eating splendor, isn't enough to lure Jonathan to stay.

But Hazel—Hazel is still here.

An enormous *bang* booms from upstairs.

———

Hazel hardly dares to breathe. The muzzle of the gun presses more forcefully into the side of her head. She blinks—and the handwriting on the postcard, which she had trouble deciphering a moment ago, resolves into legible words.

> *I bought this on my way back to the boat. Also bought another one—of the botanical garden—that I've taped up on the wall of my tiny, coffin-like cabin. I hope to be able to send this one to you soon. Thank you for a perfect day. I'm happy when I think about you.*

Does he know that it is she beneath the balaclava? Does she want him to know?

The postcard is still cradled inside the pages of *La cinquième saison*. She closes the book and slams it at Conrad's hand. He knocks it away, grips her by the wrist, and yanks her up. She uses the sharpness of his pull to ram her elbow toward his spleen.

He sidesteps her attack. She stabs her fingers at his eyes. He flings her away from him. She cries out as she sails through the air—and lands on the bed.

She scrambles up. He seizes her by the ankle. She kicks with her free foot. He grunts but grabs her by the knees. She pulls back to strike with both feet. He flips her whole person over.

The air is knocked out of her lungs as she lands on the mattress again, this time on her front. What feels like his entire weight jams into her lower vertebrae as he twists her arm over her back.

She lets out a whimper of pain.

"Hazel?" comes Conrad's hesitant question.

Her heart pounds. He would have seen her automated tool working on his desktop but isn't sure yet who she is. If she can escape the house and make a getaway, can Jonathan claim he has no idea what was going on upstairs?

Making use of his momentary distraction—and the easing of pressure on her spine—she jabs the elbow of her still-free arm toward his head. He lets go of her and narrowly avoids her elbow. She turns over and sits halfway up. But before she can scramble off the bed, he comes down on her like a mountain, grabs both her wrists, and pins them above her head.

And then he manages to free one hand. The barrel of his gun nuzzles the bottom of her balaclava.

Her flashlight is on the floor but still emits enough light for her to see the outline of his heavily shadowed features. And if he gets her balaclava off, he'll see her just as clearly.

She thrashes. He presses her harder into the mattress, his cheek brushing against hers. She would like to headbutt him but can't rear up with enough velocity to do that. Instead, she captures his mouth with hers.

Shock reverberates along her nerve endings. The softness of his lips, the warmth of their contact, the peppery taste of the kiss—it's as if she's reliving her own best memories, memories the accuracy and reliability of which she had begun to doubt years ago, precisely because of their pristine loveliness.

The kiss turns scorching. Heat simmers under her skin. Heat radiates from his hands, now cupped around her face and the back of her head. Heat palpitates between them, as roiling and inexorable as stellar expansion, evaporating entire planets in its path.

Her arms lock around his shoulders. Years drop away and they are just two very young people who have fallen under each other's spell. In the near darkness she can almost hear the Atlantic Ocean, swirling around the rocky precipices of Madeira. Almost smell the salt and happiness of a different eon.

She heaves him off her with all her strength. He lands on the floor with a thud. She leaps off the foot of the bed, runs to the door, and yanks it open. Only to have herself wrenched back and the door slammed shut with a thunderous crash that shakes the entire house.

"You're not going anywhere until you tell me what you're doing here."

He flips a switch. Light floods the room. Hazel squints. Something feels odd about her face. It's bare—her balaclava is gone.

She lifts the Glock he dropped on the bed in the middle of their kiss— and which she'd grabbed while getting off. "I will go and stay as I wish."

Coolly, he pulls another semiautomatic pistol from behind him. "The one in your hand isn't loaded. But this one is."

She should have groped him more thoroughly while they were still in bed. "That's fine. I'll keep this one for now. It's pretty handy for smashing into someone's skull in an emergency."

He is silent for a moment, his eyes down, his lashes casting shadows. Her gaze dips to his lips, still flush from their kiss, and she has to suppress an urge to put a fingertip to her own lips, tingling with remembered sensations.

He moves abruptly and opens the door. "Come on. We'll have to explain the noise to Ryan and Jonathan."

She doesn't have to wonder why he isn't worried that she'll attempt to flee again—Ryan's and Jonathan's footsteps, pounding up the stairs, echo against the walls.

She walks into the passage, lined with large, framed prints of islands and seascapes, just as Jonathan emerges on the stair landing, breathing hard, looking both frantic and grim. Ryan appears a moment later; his expression grows more puzzled as Conrad comes out of the bedroom to stand next to Hazel.

Hazel glances at Conrad. When he doesn't say anything, she realizes *We'll have to explain* means *she'll* have to explain.

"Hi, Jonathan, hi, Ryan," she says, putting all her heiress training to use.

"Conrad and I ran into each other and thought maybe we should talk over things a little more."

Ryan looks from Hazel to Conrad, then back again, and seems to make a conscious decision to take things at face value—for now. "Didn't know you were coming back so soon, Conrad," he says.

Conrad shrugs. "Last-minute change of plans."

"So . . . everything's okay?" asks Jonathan, his voice tight.

Hazel nods. "Everything's fine. We saw your pickup truck and didn't want to interrupt you and Ryan, so we came in from the side." This house has to have a side door or several, right? "But in the dark we tripped."

Jonathan evidently doesn't believe her—he knows why she is really here. She's pretty sure Ryan doesn't either.

"Okay then. You guys talk things over."

Ryan turns to leave, giving Jonathan little choice but to follow. But at the top of the staircase, Jonathan turns around and looks again at Hazel.

Go, she mouths. *You can go.*

———

Jonathan is not at all reassured, but Ryan is already halfway down the stairs, looking back expectantly at him, and Hazel clearly does not want him to be further involved.

But what is going on? Was Conrad lying in wait? Has he managed to entrap Hazel with a ruse about being out of town this week?

"Hazel, do you want something to drink?" asks Conrad all of a sudden. But his voice is low. And the way he studies her, with such undiluted attention—Jonathan could almost forget that he has just caught her housebreaking.

She glances at him. Is she also surprised by his apparent solicitude? "I could use a glass of wine," she says, deadpan.

"Could you get that for Hazel, Ryan?" Conrad calls toward the curving staircase. "I have to check something on my desktop. I'll meet you guys in the kitchen in five minutes."

Without waiting for an answer, he disappears into his bedroom. Hazel stares a moment at the now-closed door, then turns to Jonathan and smiles slightly. "Well, let's go."

Jonathan loved the kitchen in this house last night. Ryan before the stove, Ryan draining pasta, Ryan's head-tilted smile as he extracted the cork from the bottle of red Jonathan had brought. But right now all he can think about is whether Ryan and Conrad are in this together. The hell Conrad is looking at his desktop. What is he doing? Loading a bazooka?

No, actually, maybe "desktop" isn't a euphemism. Maybe he really has to wipe his hard drive after Hazel has rooted around in there.

Ryan pulls out a pale pink bottle from the fridge. "How about a glass of Kylie Minogue's Prosecco for you, Hazel? I was at a gay wedding this afternoon and they gave everybody a bottle."

"It will do," Hazel answers.

She trails her fingertips along a row of hefty cookbooks, looking for all the world like she's on a casual, or at least a normal, visit. Wait, is that a Glock in her pocket? Jesus, Jonathan thought they'd agreed not to bring firearms to avoid unnecessary escalation.

While Ryan fetches stemware, Hazel unwraps the foil atop the bottle and twists and pops the cork, her motions quick and efficient. "How was the wedding? Did you have fun?"

Ryan tilts a glass and pours carefully into it. "Wedding was nice. Not one hundred percent sure though that at my age I still have 'fun' at weddings."

"Oh?" says Hazel, accepting the glass of prosecco from Ryan. "What do you have, then, instead of fun?"

Ryan pours another glass and frowns slightly, an unusual expression for him. "If I think the couple isn't gonna make it, I wonder why everybody is there wasting their time. If I do think the marriage will last, then I'm forced to ask myself: 'Do I want to be married? Am I going to make a disaster of it? And do I want it just because it's *the* most patriarchal, heteronormative thing under the sun?'"

Hazel picks up the glass he's just finished pouring and gives it to Jonathan. "What about you, Jonathan? Do you like weddings?"

She's doing her Jedi mind trick, diverting attention from herself, and once again doing it so successfully that Jonathan dives headlong into the topic. "I love weddings—I can't help it. I don't even mind those that I'm sure will end in tears, as long as in that moment I can feel a sense of genuine hope and commitment."

This earns him a long look from Ryan.

"Hey, Conrad," says Ryan, shifting his gaze. "Do you want to get married?"

Jonathan turns to see Conrad walking into the kitchen, in head-to-toe black like Hazel.

"Is that a proposal?" he replies casually. "I'll think about it after you learn to load the dishwasher properly."

Ryan chortles.

Conrad picks up one of the remaining glasses of prosecco from the island and turns to Hazel. "Can I show you the alcove, Hazel?"

He speaks to her in the same low, gentle tone, but Jonathan remembers the stupendous door slam from earlier.

"You'll love the alcove," Ryan says immediately. "And oh, Jonathan, I think the second half of our game probably already started."

The alcove turns out to be right off the room where Ryan and Jonathan have been watching basketball, a glass-enclosed balcony accessed through a pair of French doors. With its lights turned on, the ribs between the glass panes of the alcove make Jonathan think of a large, beautiful birdcage.

From his spot before the TV, the alcove is visible, but at an oblique angle that doesn't let him see much of anything. The second half of the game has indeed started. Jonathan can't concentrate on the playmaking at all. He can't even pretend to pay attention: His gaze strays to the alcove every few seconds.

Ryan glances at him occasionally. After a while it dawns on Jonathan that even if Ryan has no idea what's going on, he must wonder whether Jonathan is there for Hazel rather than him.

He must wonder how much of what Jonathan said is true.

It's all true, but it hasn't really mattered, any of it. So maybe in the end, whether it's true or not doesn't matter either.

There is no traffic on the dark expanse of the river-turned-lake. A sprinkle of illuminated houses dots the hills of the far shore. Hazel wonders whether anyone can see the two of them, suspended in this glass aerie, lit like a sky lantern drifting aloft.

And if anyone does, would they marvel at the Instagram-worthiness of the scene, the woman seated on the thickly cushioned bench, the man standing opposite her? They are looking at the wineglasses in their hands and not at each other. Still, the unspoken awareness pulsates, a physical sensation upon Hazel's skin.

He sets down his stemware on a wall shelf by the doors, alongside a line of small potted succulents. Next he pulls the semiautomatic from the back of his waistband, drops out the clip, and racks a bullet from the chamber.

She does the same, except the magazine she drops out is empty, and the chamber too—unloaded, as he told her.

"Can people own guns in Singapore?" he asks abruptly.

"You can't keep firearms at home, but you can belong to a shooting club."

Hand-to-hand combat was not the only type of self-defense in which Hazel received training.

Conrad pushes his Glock and magazine onto the shelf, picks up his wineglass again, and sits down. "I'm sure you have an excellent reason for breaking into my house tonight. I'm all ears."

Human memory is unreliable. *Write everything down*, her mother used to tell her, *if you want a more accurate record*. But under her pen, he became a stick figure with none of the ineffable allure of a winsome adolescent on the cusp of manhood.

She gave up the endeavor around the time she gave up any realistic hope of finding him again. But always she was sure of one thing. As the finer details of his words and even his features faded, as she drifted further in a life propelled more by inertia than anything else, she remained convinced that he was adorable.

Or maybe "adorable" was simply a synonym for "safe." His youth, his frankness, his bright-eyed admiration of her—everything her memory embroidered and embellished—had made him ever safer and ever more adorable.

"Adorable" is not the first, second, or tenth descriptor that comes to mind now. As she watches him play with the cartridge he extracted from the chamber, "safe" is so far down the list that she'd have to scroll a whole minute to reach its vicinity.

He waits, patiently, lightly whirling the rosé in his other hand. And then he glances at her and sensation rampages through her like a violent weather system.

She swallows half of the contents of her glass, trying to tamp down that inconvenient shock of awareness. "I assume you know about the recent deaths connected to the library where Jonathan and I work?"

He frowns at his wineglass, but nods.

"Another librarian is currently implicated in Perry Bathurst's death. We found out that you and he were in business together. I also found out, last time I was in this house, that you took Ryan's car out the night of Perry's death." She takes a deep breath. "I was interested in who drove it because I saw it at the library at a time that would be of interest to the police."

For two seconds his expression remains unchanged. Then he again looks up. "You think *I* might have killed Perry?"

This time his gaze is sustained. It is not hostile, not even adversarial, only sharp and demanding. She has said something outlandish at a meeting, and he, the CEO, is waiting to see how she will justify that position.

His reaction is exactly right for someone who hadn't the least inkling that he could be a suspect. Or he might be a fantastic actor.

She never thought of the boy from Madeira as a good actor. But Valerian de Villiers comes from a wealthy family on his mother's side. *Succession* is not a bad introduction to the internal dynamics of enormous family fortunes, which are cutthroat and dispiriting at the same time. The constant jockeying for position, for the patriarch's or matriarch's favor, turns family gatherings into theater, and siblings and cousins into trained thespians.

"I wouldn't go so far as to say I suspect you personally," she answers. But she does, doesn't she? That was exactly the conclusion she leaped to when she first learned his full name. "But right now you're the only lead we have."

"You could have asked me about it."

"True," she says slowly. "But what if it *was* you who did it? As far as we can tell, you didn't speak about Perry to your roommate, the best possible source under the circumstances, until Perry had been dead for days."

He remains perfectly calm. "Still, your course of action seems extreme."

"I apologize for invading your privacy. It's no excuse, of course, but I wanted to have a definitive answer."

"To what question?"

Are you somehow responsible for Perry Bathurst's death?

"Lots of questions. The nature of your association with him. The reason you were near the library—and therefore near the site of his death. What you've been doing recently that might have led you there that night."

She's found nearly two dozen entities registered in his name in various parts of the world: UK, France, Taiwan, the United States. That by itself is not necessarily incriminating. Her mother has some eight or nine companies just to manage the great dowry she belatedly received when she was re-embraced by her parents.

Even Hazel, upon her mother's advice, created a company. And it is the company that enters into contracts with her publisher.

Conrad's companies have vague descriptions, little more than category selections to satisfy registration requirements. Again, not something incriminating in and of itself. Hazel's company is listed as an investment vehicle, even though its only assets are her intellectual properties.

But it bothers her that she has trouble finding specifics on him. Maybe, if Sophie weren't running out of time, Hazel would have achieved better results in French- or Chinese-language media. But Sophie is running out of time and it feels as if Conrad has deliberately obscured his digital footprint. Why? What is he trying to hide?

"I went to school in the UK. Perry and I met when we were kids, playing rugby for our respective schools," he says. "But we didn't become mates until my second contract on the *Pelagios*."

It takes her a moment to realize that he is answering her questions; another to catch the significance of his words. Assuming *Pelagios* is the name of the sailing catamaran—*second* contract? She thought he was desperate to resume land-based life.

"It was Perry's gap year," he continues. "His parents booked a trip from Southampton to Hong Kong. He came aboard in Malta and used to join me for watches, because he had nothing to do. We got to know each other then and kept up in the years since.

"Perry was always interested in filmmaking. When he learned that my mom was going to marry a filmmaker and that I was planning to put some money into my future stepfather's next documentary, he wanted in too. That's why we have an entity together."

He's been turning over the cartridge between his fingers; now he places it on the bench's cushion, under his palm. For a moment he appears extremely peaceable, as if he hasn't been playing with a round of ammunition. Then he again looks at her.

And makes her think of a man about to tell his wife that he knows all about her affair—and has known it for months.

"What do you know about Perry?" he asks.

That for sure she's never slept with the man. Ever.

Only then does it strike her, the oddity of the question. "Nothing," she answers, feeling strangely defensive.

He raises a brow. Is he waiting for further clarification? What is there to clarify?

But she does anyway. "I saw him for the first time this past Monday, when he came to the library. He asked me a few things. Then he walked up and down the stacks for a while. He came to the library again the next day and got in an altercation with another patron. He was roughed up a bit; Jonathan offered him some bandages.

"That was the last time I saw him. And then the police came to interview our colleague, who knew him biblically, so to speak."

Something flickers in Conrad's eyes. Consternation? Or maybe frustration?

"Other than that, all I know is what my colleague has dug up, because she wants to figure out what happened."

"So you've never heard of Perry before?"

She can no longer ignore his scarcely subtle subtext. "Should I have? You clearly think so."

"What are you doing at the library?"

Why is *he* asking all the questions? Sure, she owes him some answers, because he did catch her hacking into his laptop, but what does her entry-level work at the library have to do with anything?

"My grandmother made me apply for the job as soon as I told her I planned to stay with her for a while. She didn't want me hanging around the house all day."

"Why are you in Austin?"

"Because she's getting old."

"She doesn't have other kids or grandkids who are closer?"

"She does, but none of them are heiresses who have no other obligations in life."

He is silent, a thorny silence, as if she drew lipstick hearts on her final exam in lieu of supplying actual answers. Then he tilts back his glass and downs its entire contents.

As he swallows, her eyes fasten to the column of his throat. She wants to rip the wineglass from his fingers, throw it aside, and kiss him again. She wants to be in Nainai's car, speeding away. She wants him to have the decency to keep her in the dark forever and ever, because he knows something she doesn't and she is afraid of it.

Their gazes meet. Eight feet of air separate them, but they might as well be nose to nose.

She drains her own glass, pushes it away on the bench cushion, and sticks the empty magazine into the Glock she took from him. "You think I'm hiding something from you."

He picks up his cartridge and holds it between the thumb and forefinger of his left hand. "You aren't?"

There is an edge to his voice. It isn't a question but a jab. She gapes at him, trying to make sense of his provocation. "No, I'm not. I have no idea what you're talking about."

There is information asymmetry here, but not in the way he imagines. "You're sure about that?"

He is . . . mocking her. But there's something fatalistic to his tone, a bitterness that is nevertheless not directed at her. Or not directed *only* at her.

"I am sure about it, but you seem convinced otherwise. Why do you think I'm withholding something? *What* do you think I'm withholding?"

"Tell me again why you're here tonight."

She would like to throw her Glock through the glass wall of the alcove. "My colleague Astrid is currently, as far as I can tell, the only lead the police have on Perry's death. But I found out about your connections to him. And I wanted to know more before I make up my mind as to whether to mention you to the police."

"Why do you care?" he asks coolly. Coldly. "You should have passed my information directly to the police."

Why does she care?

Hazel rarely gives in to anger, and she tries to remain calm, but some banshee inside her howls and shrieks. *Why do I care? Do you, of all people, not have a fucking clue why I fucking care?*

"When I was engaged, I wondered obsessively what I would do if you were to suddenly reappear in my life. And when you didn't—"

She drags in a ragged breath. She should stop right here—this needs to go no further. But she can't. Her self-control has undergone a rapid unplanned disassembly and is streaking through the atmosphere in hundreds of fiery fragments.

"Let's just say, when reality failed to validate my wishful thinking, what I experienced was not a profound sense of relief. To this day, I carry no small amount of guilt toward my husband, because I would have ditched him at the altar if you'd only shown up."

He rises to his feet and looms above her, his expression unreadable.

"You don't need to be so alarmed." She speaks through clenched teeth. "I know very well that the person I'd have left my then-fiancé for isn't you but a construct of my own making. All the same, there isn't a single day in the last twelve years when I haven't thought about you. And there isn't a single time I think about you that I haven't regretted letting go of your number. Not because I lost a soul mate but because in the vacuum created by your absence you became untouchably perfect. You became whatever my psyche and my neuroses needed you to be."

Maybe he's standing because she has pointed the Glock at him, as if with a pull of the trigger she can destroy the illusion. She tosses the unloaded firearm aside, this thing that is as useless as her willpower.

"The kind of weight and relevance I've poured into the idea of you does not dissipate in a few days."

The opposite.

She's learned to live with her yearning and her regrets. And she's come to believe that they have not only collected as sediments but cemented into stone—after all, twelve years is a geological era. And she, an occasional visitor to the depths of her own heart, would run her fingers over fossilized memories caught in those prehistorical strata.

His reappearance overturned that tidy fantasy. Her yearning and her regrets have been locked away, yes, but like those children of the Khaleesi forced into the dungeon, they emerged instead as full-grown beasts, ravenous and more feral than ever.

"And when I was faced with the possibility that you might have something to do with Perry's death . . ."

She couldn't handle the cauldron of emotions; she had to channel her dread and confusion into concrete action, however stupid.

Silence.

He closes his fist around the bullet, the goddamn bullet. "What did your husband think of this idea of me?"

He didn't bat an eye when she mentioned that she'd been married. "Do you—did you know my husband, by some chance?"

"Never met him."

Never meeting someone is not the same as not being aware of someone's existence.

And if he knew of Kit . . . "Did you know who I was before Saturday?"

He drops the bullet into a pocket of his black tactical pants. "If you mean whether I knew you're Bartholomew Kuang's granddaughter before we ran into each other in the noodle shop yesterday, yes, I did. I've known for a while. Not in time to create drama at your wedding, I'm afraid, but yes, for some time."

How? How had he found out?

Then again, such a discovery is far from inconceivable. She's always kept the lowest of low profiles, but from time to time she does show up in group pictures on other people's social media, from attending weddings, birthday parties, and other such rites and rituals.

With his mother's ties in Taiwan and his stepfather's sphere in Hong Kong, it's more than possible that they or someone in their circle might have business dealings with her family. Business relations turn into social relations. People scroll through their feeds and show others nearby what they are looking at.

What had passed through his mind—and his heart—when he saw her? Had he felt any surge of wonder and hope? Any pang when he realized that she was already married?

He studies her—and betrays little of his thoughts other than a stark wariness.

The same wariness that has characterized his demeanor ever since their reunion.

"You *do* think I have something to do with Perry's death," she whispers.

In the Far East, the idea exists to this day, culturally, if not legally, that if a single member of a family perpetuates an act counter to the collective good, then the entire family is—at least partially—at fault.

Her grandfather, as head of the family, has long been considered fair and wise—or at least fair enough and wise enough. And the Kuang clan, consequently, enjoys a relatively unsullied reputation as ethical in business and decent in personal dealings. But every barrel has its rotten apples and Hazel has one second cousin who has been officially disowned and another skating on thin ice for his gambling problem.

She struggles, however, to connect their localized malpractice to Perry Bathurst.

And then a ghost wraps its ice-vapor hands around her spine and yanks it right out of her back.

Her fingertips, without anything to hold on to, quake. "Are you implying that my husband is—was—involved somehow?"

Conrad's lips curve in a mirthless smile. "Yes, that's exactly what I've been trying to say."

CHAPTER TWENTY-THREE

"How?" The question escapes Hazel before thoughts can form in her head. Then all at once ideas coalesce. "Was Perry involved in my husband's schemes—or a target of them?"

Dear God, the entire time they sat across from each other in that cupcake shop, Conrad had viewed her with suspicion, while she'd beamed heart eyes at him like a love-drunk Sailor Moon.

"Both, you could say. Kit convinced Perry to sink three million pounds into what he was doing, and Perry never saw the money again."

The value of the pound has cratered in the last ten, fifteen years. Still, three million pounds come to about four million dollars. The Bathurst family is well-off, but nowhere close to counting their money in billions. According to Astrid's web spelunking, their net worth is estimated to be somewhere between fifty and seventy million dollars. And of that, a good chunk must be land, manor, and production facilities. In other words, highly illiquid assets.

"Perry had that much of a cash position?"

"Good catch. No, but with your husband's help, he secured a short-term loan with the family Picasso as collateral. It was supposed to be a quick investment, ten percent return in ninety days, but—"

"Ten percent return in ninety days? Kit was promising an APR of more than 40 percent and Perry believed it?"

"We're in the era of casino capitalism. Perry wasn't always immune to its siren call."

"And you didn't advise Perry against this foolishness?"

In the reflection of the glass, her face is ghostly yet hard-edged. Angry. Kit's misdeeds are no longer victimless crimes. And by the long-standing tradition of her people, she too is now partly to blame for Perry's lifeless body in a cold cabinet.

Strangely enough, faced with her combativeness, Conrad's expression loses some of its earlier implacability. "Perry didn't say anything to me about his troubles until ten days before he had to either pay up or cough up Daddy's Picasso. By then he was in a blind panic."

The slight softening of his stance makes her feel even more wretched. She rubs her temple, trying in vain to prevent the onset of a throbbing headache. "Who was my husband to Perry that he would entrust that much money to him?"

"They knew each other all their lives—dads went to school together, moms at the same college in Oxbridge, that sort of connection."

"I don't remember meeting any Bathursts at either of our weddings."

She and Kit held one set of ceremony-and-parties in Singapore and another in England.

"Perry's parents' divorce was hardly a conscious uncoupling—they didn't go because they didn't want to run into each other. Perry wanted to go but he was under a forty-five-day house curfew for driving under the influence. His sister went, but as she once dated your husband, I don't imagine he paraded her in front of you, his new bride."

There might be more than a little bite in the way he said those last three words.

She slumps against the back of the bench. "I had no idea that even without you showing up, my wedding was that close to turning into a soap opera."

"Perry's sister wouldn't have wanted to make a fool of herself in front of you: You are far wealthier and infinitely more beautiful than she."

He does not look at her as he gives this compliment. It is a compliment, right? At least the more beautiful part?

She revives slightly. "You seem to know a lot about my wedding."

"Perry became obsessed with Kit when he couldn't track down either Kit or his money. And when he confessed his troubles to me, he dug up Kit's wedding on social media. Imagine my surprise when I saw you walk down the aisle with the man Perry swore defrauded him out of three million pounds."

She says nothing. What is there to say?

"I remembered your cargo shorts and big visor from Madeira," he murmurs. "At one point I almost convinced myself that this elegant creature with terrible taste in men couldn't possibly be you."

She draws in a long breath. "I didn't know about Kit's fraudulent business dealings until the police raided our place. I thought he was having an affair."

Conrad sits back down and stretches his legs out. He looks as tired as she feels. "Perry made me study Kit's wedding because he couldn't understand why Kit, who married into a family of extraordinary wealth, bothered to swindle a mere few million pounds."

She drops her face into her hands.

The same thought had crossed her mind when Detective Chu first brought up Kit's failed cryptocurrency speculations. But the digital forensics she'd commissioned—as well as the one undertaken by her grandfather's people—confirmed that Kit had indeed made wrong bets.

Or rather, he had read the trends correctly and shorted certain overinflated and problematic coins. But coincidentally, or perhaps not so coincidentally, the exchange in which he placed his put options shut down due to "technical issues" just as his gains shot through the roof. No one could log on to their account to buy or sell or do anything.

By the time the "technical issues" had been fixed and the exchange was once again operational, not only had Kit's gains evaporated but the shitcoins he'd counted on to lose their values had stabilized, leaving him to face an astronomical margin call.

That would be when he embezzled close to twenty million pounds from the prominent and highly successful art investment fund he worked for. The amount he took from Perry might have been taken in good faith, as seed money to recuperate his prior loss and to pay back his employers. But then he bet that the buoyed-up shitcoins would shoot up higher in value, only to see them fall to next to nothing, this time with no "technical issues" to prevent the cratering.

Kit's family, though still privileged, is no longer wealthy. He'd had to work hard to get ahead. To lose his life's savings would have been horrifying enough. To become a pauper when he was married to Bartholomew Kuang's granddaughter must have been unbearable.

But as it turned out, stealing from his employer and his personal friends to cover his shortfall so that he would not face the excruciating ordeal of accounting for both his crime and his new poverty to his in-laws was not the only thing Kit did.

As the police investigated the embezzlement, they uncovered something else altogether. They found out that he had been selling fake signed pop art prints from his art galleries to the tune of almost a million dollars.

That predated his crypto troubles and spoke not to momentary lapses in judgment but to a profound lack of character.

And *that* had been the one thing that became public knowledge. That the grandson-in-law of Bartholomew Kuang had taken two whole years to swindle a piddly one million dollars from chiropractors and accountants who wanted signed pop art prints in their suburban offices.

In the wake of the scandal, Hazel did not disappear. She went to the usual number of birthday and anniversary parties, where, a glass of wine in hand, she shrugged any number of times to variations of *I guess this is what can happen when you marry a foreigner, when you don't know the family inside out.*

Some people said it in sympathy, some in mockery disguised as commiseration. She accepted the sympathy and smiled at the mockery, numb to its sting.

Numb to the entire business. She, the perfect heiress, brought low by her very Instagrammable husband.

But now, in front of Conrad, she burns with shame. Not for Kit's crimes but because she was so cavalier in her choice of mate. She had not cared enough to be more thorough in her scrutiny.

She had so easily accepted the narrative that it was time for her to get married and then said yes to the first man who looked and sounded the part.

"In case you wonder why Kit didn't come to me or my family for help," she said into her hands, "before we were married, my grandfather invited Kit to lunch, just the two of them. I never asked what was said at that meal, but I wouldn't be surprised if my grandfather warned Kit not to fuck up and told him that as soon as he fucked up he'd be gone, swept out of my life like so much refuse."

Her grandfather did not deal in idle threats. Kit would have understood that very well. But as with most such things, rules are made by people, and people's minds can be persuaded to change. Her mother, through the independent and honorable life she led, had eventually changed her parents' mind. Kit too could have bought himself grace, if he'd put in enough time and shown enough personal integrity.

But there wasn't enough time, and Kit never had enough integrity.

Conrad is again silent.

She pushes against her knees and straightens her torso—when she would prefer to remain in a fetal position for the foreseeable future. "Do you believe me, that I had nothing to do with Perry's death?"

Through the cotton twill of her cargo pants, her nails dig into her kneecaps.

He pulls something out of his pocket—not the cartridge, only his phone, which he taps, scrolls, and scrolls some more. Then he hands the phone to her. "I hope this is enough to show that *I* had nothing to do with Perry's death."

On the phone is his WhatsApp chat with Perry. Conrad has scrolled back to a date shortly before Kit's death.

> Conrad, are you there? I need help. Can you ring
> me asap?

She scrolls back a little more. The texts before that were from two months earlier, and concerned dinner plans. No mention of Kit, no sign of anything wrong.

She scrolls down. After Perry sent up the Bat-Signal, there is indeed a voice call forty minutes in duration. And then a video call that lasted fifteen minutes.

Like I said, typed Conrad afterward, transferring this much money overseas is going to be a bloody nightmare, much better I take over your loan. Confer with your banker as soon as possible tomorrow. I'll see if I can fly in by the end of the week. Also, I'll need to speak to your dad about that Picasso. I need collateral, too.

Oh God. My dad is going to have my hide.

Perry, you kissed your hide goodbye when you used the Picasso without permission. Go talk to your dad this minute.

Just did. I feel like rubbish.

I'd comfort you but at the moment I have more sympathy for him.

The few exchanges after that are Perry informing Conrad that he was already at the airport, waiting.

The day after, Hey, you looked out of sorts when we were looking at Kit's wedding pics last night. Are you okay?

Hazel's heart thunks. In his place, how would *she* have felt?

Conrad's reply? Jetlag.

This is certainly the exact answer she'd have given.

Perry messaged: Get some rest. Banker tomorrow morning and dinner with my dad in the evening.

A flurry of voice calls took place over the next few days and then, Bugger, Conrad. Kit's dead. His plane went down.

Hazel braced herself for this moment. Still, she feels as if Kit's plane plowed into her.

That text is followed by more voice calls and even a few video calls, which convey the intensity of the situation but offer her, an after-the-fact voyeur, no additional insight.

Until Perry texts, ten days after Kit's death, I know you don't want me to, but I have to go to Austin.

She looks up. "So why *did* Perry have to come to Austin?"

CHAPTER TWENTY-FOUR

Tuesday
Two evenings later

Astrid bites her lower lip as she turns the key. She feels sick, the way she did the last time she ran the Cap10K, one of the hundreds of runners in costume so that Austin could go on being weird, except the day was too hot and she was all lightheaded and dehydrated inside her foam-and-polyester armadillo suit.

Come on, she implores herself, *you already slept in your own bed for the past two nights, so it's not as if you're walking in for the first time after you hid from the intruder.*

But what they will be attempting tonight . . .

Astrid casts a glance over her shoulder. Behind her, Sophie is opening and clenching her left hand. Hazel looks grave but calm—as calm as the eye of a storm.

They both nod at Astrid. Now Astrid has no choice but to open the door to her condo. "Come on in."

In her own ears, her voice quavers, like a guitar string plucked too hard.

Sophie's attention immediately goes to the five sixteen-by-twenty-inch framed blackboards on the two walls around the dining table. "But that is gorgeous lettering, Astrid! Are those your own fonts? I don't recognize them—and I window-shop fonts all the time."

Some of the boards are occupied by a large single letter—a particularly swishy capital *Y*, a capital *T* that looks like it's built of steel beams—but a couple of other boards have whole lowercase alphabets written out, one in an angular script font, another a rotund, friendly sans serif.

Sophie's compliment makes Astrid feel as if she's just seen the first snowdrop emerge from, well, under the snow. "I didn't know you liked fonts," she says, trying not to preen.

"I love fonts—always have." Sophie turns halfway around, a rueful expression on her face. "There's too much we don't know about each other."

"I know," Astrid murmurs, a pang in her heart.

"I cannot pick out Comic Sans in a lineup," says Hazel.

Astrid pivots toward her in horror. "Comic Sans is—I'm sure calling it a crime against humanity would be too much but . . ."

"But it deserves to be known as the typographical equivalent of failing upward," Sophie says authoritatively.

"Yes, omigod, yes!" Astrid cries—and high-fives Sophie.

Hazel chortles and walks over to the board that declares *Live, Laugh, Love* in a font that was Gothic horror except listless, practically comatose— Astrid wrote the slogan after Perry's desertion in spring.

"At least I can tell that this combination of text and font is ironic," Hazel says, tracing a finger over the first *L*, which is melting into a puddle of despair.

The relief and camaraderie Astrid feels at the discussion of fonts evaporate and she almost has a heart attack. Is Hazel doing too much? Will she give them away? And when Hazel turns around, there is a feverish gleam in her eyes, which could denote either a wild hope or an equally untrammeled panic—and does nothing to soothe Astrid's agitation.

Astrid pinches the back of her neck and clears her throat. "Let me get something for us to drink."

A few minutes later, she has a bottle of red wine uncorked and a halfdecent cheese board—grapes, olives, and a few slices of salami in addition to the last of the Hushållsost from her fridge—on the table.

Sophie's glass of wine is almost full to the brim. But she doesn't drink, only hangs on to its stem, her thumb pressed hard into her knuckles. "So . . . you said you need our help, Hazel?"

Hazel takes a swig of her club soda—the ice cubes in her glass clink loudly. "I do. You know that I'm a widow."

"I still can't believe it," says Sophie.

Hazel's lips curve into the sort of smile women give when they want to reassure those around them that things are all right, an expression more determined than sanguine. "The day my husband died I found out he embezzled a lot of money. Twenty million pounds, to be exact. More recently I learned that he also took three million pounds from Perry."

"What?!" Astrid's cry echoes sharply against the walls.

"That's . . . so much money," murmurs Sophie. "When our library was remodeled, it only cost one point eight million dollars. Twenty million pounds—how much is that in dollars?"

"Between twenty-five and twenty-six million, I'd say."

Astrid rubs her hand over her thumping heart. "That would have been enough to open a couple of whole new branches."

"It's too bad Kit wasn't more public-minded." Hazel picks up a grape from the cheese board and peels it, a look of blank concentration on her face. "We thought that was it—he played his cards wrong, he got in trouble, he ran, he died in a plane crash."

The peeled grape looks exposed and vulnerable. Is that how Hazel must feel, someone so self-contained forced to share so much that is painful and humiliating?

"The thing is, he'd accumulated a good deal of Bitcoin—the reason he embezzled was to meet a margin call so that the exchange wouldn't start liquidating his Bitcoin positions. But when he died, no one could find his Bitcoin.

"The current belief is that he took them offline, so that they couldn't be discovered or hacked. People have been looking for his cold storage, which can be a flash drive or even a piece of paper with his private key written on it."

Astrid covers the lower half of her face with her hands. "Perry, too?"

"Perry, too."

Astrid breaks out in goose bumps, even though this is not the first time she's heard this. "Was that why he came to Austin time and again? But why Austin?"

"In March of this year, my grandmother got COVID for the first time. I came and stayed with her for three weeks. Kit joined me for a few days." Hazel picks up another grape. Sliver by sliver, more pale green grape skin drifts onto the small white plate before her. "It was a strange thing for him to do. We'd already discussed a trial separation; my grandmother's illness hastened its implementation, but not by that much. Yet after two weeks, Kit showed up. He said he didn't want Nainai to think that anything was the matter—not yet."

Her lips crook in an ironic smile.

"He left before I did. By the time I reached Singapore, he'd already departed on a trip to the UK. So our goodbye, when he left in an Uber for the airport from my grandmother's house, was the last time I saw him. Recently, however, I was made aware of footage that showed him at the library, several days running."

"At *our* library?" asks Sophie. Her hands have come up to her upper arms, her wrists crossed defensively over her rib cage.

Astrid looks down and sees that she herself is holding almost the exact same position. At this point, some details are new to her, but not the gist of the story. Yet the potency of the whole is amplified by the all too close wall behind her and the ever so slightly sinister light from the ceiling fixture above.

"At our library," confirms Hazel. "This was before the surveillance cameras broke. On his last visit, Kit walked in with a box of books—and then walked out with what seemed to be the same box. And apparently he looked directly at the camera and did a chin lift, a sort of *I see you.*"

She pops a grape she's peeled into her mouth and chews meditatively. Astrid doesn't understand how she can eat at a time like this—the woman must have an esophagus of steel. "Now that I think about it, he mentioned the library to me. He said he found it a good place to work. Had I paid more attention, I'd have found it odd: So much of his work involved talking to artists and clients; a coffee shop would have been a much better spot than a library.

"But at the time his remark barely registered. I was not happy that he arrived at my grandmother's house without prior notice; I felt that his presence in fact made my grandmother more suspicious about the state of our marriage than she would have been otherwise."

Sophie, at the head of the table, reaches out and squeezes Hazel's hand. Astrid might have done the same if she didn't feel so paralyzed—even if Hazel no longer loved her husband by the time he perished, she would still have been horrified by his fate, would still have agonized over the lack of closure on their relationship, especially since his criminal offenses came to light at the same time.

Hazel downs some of her club soda and looks up, as if hoping for strength from above.

Astrid's heart pounds. She dares not follow the line of Hazel's sight—there is no way she can make it appear natural.

Sophie, more hard-core than Astrid, does glance up, but only fleetingly. She finally takes a sip of her wine. "Are you sure that the cold storage for Kit's Bitcoin is at the library?"

"I don't know. I don't even know that it's ever been there. And even if it was at one point, most likely it's already been found. Possibly Perry found it—and was killed for his trouble."

But if the cold storage—and the millions it holds—has been found, then why was there an intruder at Astrid's place in the middle of the night?

"All the same, I'm going to mount a search," declares Hazel softly.

She is as beautiful and resolute as Daenerys Targaryen, standing at the bow of her ship, sailing to Westeros—except the khaleesi should have stayed the fuck home!

Astrid sets her knuckles against her lips. Her teeth are chattering. "Are you sure?"

"I don't think I have a choice. If it can be found, then the money should be used to pay back Perry's family and everyone else Kit embezzled from or swindled."

"What are you looking for, exactly?" asks Sophie, leaning forward, her hands on the edge of the table. "A piece of paper, a flash drive hidden in a book, or..."

"It could also be a book with an RFID tracker," explains Hazel, "the kind that does not emit any signal until it's been activated."

Radio-frequency identification is hardly cutting-edge technology at this point—in fact, books in larger library systems often have RFID tags affixed as part of their processing. But the kind of tracker Hazel is talking about does not make its presence known until it is scanned with a particular frequency.

"Whatever it is, wouldn't Perry and those others have already tried to find it?" asks Astrid.

Hazel, mirroring Sophie, also leans forward, her hands spread. But unlike Sophie and her perfect burgundy manicure, Hazel's unvarnished nails are nearly white from how hard they are digging into the oak veneer of the dining table—the only real sign of tension on her part. "Perry and whoever else might have searched the stacks. But we have thousands of books that are not out on the shelves or on carts waiting to be shelved."

Astrid sucks in a breath. "The donations?"

"Precisely. Kit entered the library holding a box and exited holding the same box, apparently. But what was in the box? The library's CCTV cameras, back when they still worked, covered the public terminals and other areas where patrons gathered. But they didn't point toward the corridor where donated books are dropped off."

And if Kit's hoard has been sitting among the donated books all this time...

"This is where I need help from you two." Hazel looks from Sophie to Astrid, and back again. "I've sorted the three huge boxes of donations that came in last Tuesday and have no more reason to be in the storage room during normal hours. Can you lend me your keys so I can go after hours?"

"You mean, at night?" Astrid ventures.

"Tonight, if possible." There is a hint of lunacy in the brilliance of Hazel's eyes. "Now that I know Perry's death is linked to Kit, I can never sleep easy again unless I get to the bottom of it."

Astrid bites on her knuckles. "Are you sure that's safe?"

"It's the library. It doesn't have any valuables and I won't be visible to anyone outside when I'm in the storage room."

"Should I come with you?" Astrid squeaks.

"You two have to work in the morning; my hours don't kick in until afternoon." Hazel loads a cracker with cheese but does not eat it. "Will you let me borrow your key?"

Astrid licks her numb lips. "Umm, if it's okay with Sophie, I can, but I have to make a request, and that's the reason I want to come with you. You know that the CCTV cameras haven't worked for a while at the library, but there are a bunch of other peripheral things that are not working as intended. The door to the Den of Calories, for example—it doesn't lock anymore."

"I'll lock the front entrance when I go in. Then it doesn't matter if the Den of Calories can't be secured."

It feels really stupid to be talking about the mundane realities of municipal housekeeping when there are tens of millions of dollars and multiple lives at stake. "But that's just it. That's the problem. You see, the front entrance used to log when it's keyed open and locked. But a few months ago—maybe forty days of one-hundred-ten-degree weather messed it up last summer—it broke so that it no longer logs when you open it, only when you lock it."

Hazel looks at Astrid blankly.

"What Astrid means is that if you don't lock the front door, then nobody will know you've been there overnight," says Sophie. She takes a deep breath. "Here, I give you executive permission. Go tonight, if you need to. And then just leave. Don't bother locking up. I'll make sure I'm the first person at the library tomorrow morning so nobody else will know it's been opened at night."

"All right." Hazel rises slowly, as if struggling against a great weight. She once again settles her hands on the table, to steady herself. "Guess I'll be off, then."

CHAPTER TWENTY-FIVE

Conrad's house
Two nights earlier

With three minutes left in the fourth quarter and with the visiting team having already given up, Ryan turns off the TV.

Jonathan, once again looking in the direction of the alcove, turns his head at the ensuing silence.

"I was right, wasn't I?" Ryan murmurs. "You never lost your wallet tracker here."

Jonathan flushes, even though it's far from the worst thing Ryan can say. "I—it's possible."

"Did Hazel come with *you*, and not with Conrad?"

"That—is also a possibility."

Ryan perks up. "So there could have been a shoot-out between you and Conrad tonight?"

"I didn't bring a firearm—it would have been a one-sided gunfight, if Conrad wanted one."

Ryan snickers. Then he looks at Jonathan for a long moment. Jonathan stops breathing. Is he going to ask whether Jonathan was also lying about the apology?

The click of a doorknob turning: Hazel and Conrad drift in from the alcove. Hazel appears dazed, as if a sinkhole had cracked open and she'd driven right into it.

Jonathan stands up.

"Coffee, anyone?" says Conrad. He looks a little better than Hazel, but not by much. Whatever shocked and dismayed her got to him too.

As everyone follows Conrad into the kitchen, Jonathan sidles up to Hazel. She smiles wanly at him. Conrad opens a cabinet and pulls out a barista machine that looks a little banged up. Ryan takes everyone's coffee orders and retrieves a ceramic canister from the pantry.

"Ryan," says Hazel, her voice low but steady, "I already apologized to Conrad, but I owe you an apology too, for intruding on you tonight."

For a moment, Ryan looks surprised that someone is actually addressing the elephant in the room. Then he says, rather seriously for him, "Not gonna lie—I love apologies. But I'd like an explanation too, if you're in the mood to offer one."

Jonathan fidgets—Ryan has been very patient in not demanding that explanation from him.

Conrad takes the canister from Ryan and glances in Hazel's direction—he looks at her as if he can't help himself, not because he means to.

"Of course," says Hazel, speaking to Ryan, seemingly unaware of Conrad's attention. "I believe Jonathan consulted you on the death of one Mr. Perry Bathurst?"

"That's right. One of the librarians was tangled up in it, but I didn't think that was you."

"No. Or at least, at the time, none of it seemed to have anything to do with me. But I recently learned that my late husband owed Perry three million pounds, and Perry died while trying to recoup that sum."

Ryan has been pulling out coffee cups from a glass-front cupboard; Jonathan, trying to be useful, has been rinsing some of the dishes Ryan brought back from the TV room. Now they both go still. Only Conrad remains in motion, pouring roasted beans into the grinder at the top of the espresso machine.

The rich, nutty aroma of freshly ground coffee fills the kitchen.

Hazel stands with her back to the shelf of old cookbooks and carries on with her narrative. Jonathan is sure she has trimmed it down to bare bones, but still he is overwhelmed. He scarcely notices Conrad bustling about the kitchen, except when Hazel asks him to provide a missing piece of the picture, or when she relates how she found out about his connection to Perry.

After Hazel describes Astrid's ordeal the night before, Conrad hands her a cup of mocha and Jonathan a cappuccino. Jonathan belatedly realizes that they are at the beginning of a possibly sleepless night and that coffee is being offered out of not just hospitality but necessity.

Hazel swirls a spoon in the thick foam atop her mocha and finishes her account, which includes the events of the past couple of hours.

"I am beyond grateful nobody shot anybody," says Ryan, sipping his own cappuccino. "I'm not the sort of doctor you'd want in an emergency."

Everyone chuckles, but the underlying tension in the room remains unbroken.

"I'm also grateful to be included in your confidence," Ryan continues, his expression now grave. "But as much as I'm always telling everyone to spill the tea, this is way more tea than I can handle. So . . . I'm guessing you need something from me?"

"We do," says Conrad. He turns around from the stove, flips a beautifully golden-brown quesadilla from the pan in his hand onto a plate, and then cuts it with a few rolls of a pizza knife—while Jonathan and Ryan have stood in place, transfixed by Hazel's account, Conrad has not only made four cups of espresso-based coffee, but cooked up a meal besides. "We need to know how Perry Bathurst and Jeannette Obermann died."

Ryan nods. "Let me go double-check everything for you guys."

Jonathan watches Ryan until he disappears. When he looks back, both Hazel and Conrad are studying him, the former sipping her mocha, the latter biting into a wedge of quesadilla.

Jonathan vows to work on his chill.

In the meanwhile, he clears his throat and casts about for something to take the focus off his unrequited sentiments. "We're lucky you happen to live in Austin, Conrad. There's so much stuff we never would've learned if it weren't for you."

Conrad washes down his quesadilla with half a cup of black coffee. "I didn't *happen* to be in town. My cousin left this house to my mom. My mom was going to sell it, but I asked to have it for a few years—Hazel once told me that she lived in Austin."

The walls of Jonathan's chest expand in an oddly painful yet oddly gratifying way. He's been worried that Hazel had invested too much in Conrad—the way she looked at this house on their first visit, it was as if she stood before a magic mirror that had lost its ability to transport and was now only a beautiful piece of furniture, nothing more.

But this confession from Conrad? The man basically said, *When I had no realistic chance of ever seeing you again, I still planned and prepared, in the hope that miracles might happen.*

Jonathan glances at Hazel, who seems to have eyes only for her mocha.

"Did I?" she responds after a few seconds. "I don't remember mentioning Austin at all."

"You also said your name was Meimei," says Conrad drily.

"That's right," says Hazel. "Meimei Pickfair is my porn name."

Conrad reverses another round of quesadilla onto a plate and aims a half-incredulous, half-resigned look at Hazel. "What was Meimei, your hamster?"

"My mom's cockatoo." Hazel gives her mocha another stir. "She's still alive, actually, forty going on fourteen. Very moody and has an opinion on everything."

Conrad is silent a long moment. And then he says, "I have a copy of *Trails to Table*. According to the box, it's designed by a company named Monte Unlimited."

Hazel slowly sets down her cup. "How long have you had it?"

"For a few months. It's still in its shrink-wrap."

No one speaks after that. Jonathan has no idea what this last exchange concerns, but the unfinished business between these two thrums and percusses, drowning out everything else.

Ryan returns with his laptop. He props it open on the kitchen island, grabs a wedge from the latest batch of quesadillas, and says, "Okay, I already looked up Perry's cause of death before I met with Jonathan. Jonathan, do you remember what we said at the time?"

Jonathan is relieved by the resumption of normal conversation, despite the morbid subject. "You said it wasn't natural causes but also that there was no reason to suspect that it might have been homicide."

"Because he died of a fentanyl overdose, which I still see far too often."

Conrad rinses out the bowl in which he's beaten eggs. "And his family said no, absolutely not."

"That's what I understand," concurs Ryan.

Conrad wipes his hands with a dish towel. "It might sound contradictory, given that Perry has done his share of stupid things, but he was scared of hard drugs—never wanted to try any. In fact, after his house curfew for driving under the influence, he gave up alcohol too. Last few times I saw him, he drank only soda water. He was not someone who decided to acquire a cocaine habit one day and then proceeded to buy the bad shit."

"That was the reason his case was eventually assigned to homicide," says Ryan. "That and the fact that he didn't have any other substances in him, not even alcohol or marijuana."

Jonathan rubs his arm—it's spooky, a man who didn't use drugs dying of an overdose. "How, then, did the fentanyl get into his system?"

Ryan shrugs. "His nose was completely clean and there were no puncture marks on his body made by needles."

"What about Jeannette Obermann?" asks Hazel. "How did she die?"

"Carfentanil."

Hazel and Conrad both suck in a breath.

"Is that the synthetic one that's a million times more potent than regular fentanyl?" asks Jonathan.

"Fentanyl is synthetic too," Ryan points out. "It's fifty times stronger than morphine. Carfentanil may not be a million times more potent, but it's unbelievably powerful stuff. You only need thirteen milligrams to sedate a literal one-ton elephant. One milligram of the stuff will kill an adult human—that's a milligram, one thousandth of a gram. And Jeannette Obermann did have a tiny but rather deep puncture on her gluteus maximus."

Silence.

Jonathan has never been less inclined to die of unnatural causes than at that moment. He is sure the last thing Jeannette Obermann wanted was to have her ice-cold skin examined inch by inch on an autopsy table.

"Ryan, you listed how fentanyl *didn't* get into Perry. Any ideas on how it did get in?" asks Conrad.

"He could have ingested it or come into contact by touch. But there was no sign that he was forced to swallow anything, nor was trace fentanyl found on his hands."

"My grandmother enjoys a bit of alarmist news from time to time," says Hazel. "She told me once about children dying from picking up their caretakers' fentanyl patches."

"Fentanyl patches?" Jonathan's understanding of the substance is largely limited to news of overdoses. "You mean, like nicotine patches?"

"It's used in long-term pain management for patients who are opioid-tolerant," answers Ryan. "But we didn't find patches on Perry—nor were there any telltale adhesive rims left on his skin. But as a theory it's not half bad. The children who pick up grandpa's fentanyl patches and earn themselves a trip to the ER can do that because those patches are left on for three days and sometimes fall off without the wearer's knowledge. A patch on Perry could have similarly quit well before he was found."

Hazel taps at the side of her coffee cup—she makes no sound but her motion is agitated and arhythmic. "So either he ate it or it entered his system via skin contact. You sounded pretty sure, though, about how the carfentanil got into Jeannette Obermann."

"She did have marijuana in her system and a touch of psychedelics—not as clean as Perry. But likewise no hard drugs of any kind. And yes, the jab did it."

"Where does one even get carfentanil?" wonders Jonathan.

"At the vet's, I'd imagine," says Conrad—he's been looking at Hazel and glances around at the company only after she stops fidgeting. "My stepdad did a documentary on wildlife vets in various parts of Africa. But even then it's only for the real heavyweights, like elephants and rhinos, that you'd use carfentanil in your tranquilizer darts."

Ryan drains his cappuccino. "I'd answer the same. I imagine Detective

Hagerty has already inquired at large-animal vets around town to see if anyone is missing any Wildnil."

Jonathan is flabbergasted. "Are there elephants and rhinos in Austin? The local zoo is hardly of that scale."

Ryan shrugs. "There's a preserve outside Fredericksburg with a few elephants, last I heard."

But Fredericksburg is ninety miles away. "What about for horses? Do they use carfentanil for horses?"

"Not that I know of. There are already perfectly good tranquilizers for horses—and of course people shoot it up too. It's nasty what can happen. If you've never seen necrotic ulcers, ignorance is bliss."

For a moment Jonathan feels relief for Sophie: Sophie has never burgled a large-animal vet's office. But then again, if Detective Hagerty can't find any direct evidence in the murder of Jeannette Obermann, he could put even more weight on circumstantial evidence.

"Any other carfentanil deaths at the medical examiner's office lately?" asks Hazel, frowning.

"No—and of that I'm confident. There have been other fentanyl overdoses in recent weeks, but the deceased were habitual cocaine users and their deaths, while unfortunate, did not appear criminal."

A longer, even heavier silence descends.

"I don't know what we can find out on the carfentanil front—for sure I personally shouldn't commit any more breaking and entering without a great deal of further training," says Hazel with a self-deprecating pull of her lips. "But I do know of two people who were in enough contact with Perry on that day to have put a small patch on him. Actually—"

She turns to Ryan. "Ryan, can you pull up Facebook and do a search for Gus Anderson?"

The name sounds familiar to Jonathan. "Do you mean the patron who's always trying to engage female librarians in a conversation about *Fifty Shades*?"

Conrad casts yet another glance at Hazel.

Hazel smiles slightly at Jonathan. "That's the one. Yesterday, before I went into Peng's Noodles, I stopped by the Indian grocery place next door.

Mr. Anderson was there—he's a fan of their samosas—and he wanted to show me a recording of the altercation Perry was involved in."

"Okay. I have a bunch of Gus Andersons," declares Ryan. "Which is the one we're looking for?"

It takes a little head tilt from Hazel for Jonathan to remember that he could assist with the effort at least as well as Hazel.

He approaches the island; Ryan slides over his laptop. Jonathan takes care not to stand too near Ryan, but a curious Ryan brings himself closer—and taps Jonathan, indicating that he should hunch down a little so Ryan can look over his shoulder.

Have they ever been so close to each other since that day at the pool party? Ryan braces a hand on the island. Jonathan restrains himself from letting his eyes travel up the flannel sleeve, which smells wonderfully clean, as if it were line dried in a summer breeze under concentrated sunlight.

He finds their quarry on the second page of Gus Andersons—the patron uses a headshot as his avatar. Thankfully his Facebook output isn't too toxic—mostly he complains about his favorite businesses moving away or becoming too expensive—and Jonathan quickly locates the video of the library brawl.

After an obligatory caption of *Libraries used to be nice, quiet places*, Gus Anderson lets the video speak for itself. The footage starts when the guy looking for trouble was pushing Perry into the public terminals. Perry unsuccessfully tried to get away, his expression one of complete bewilderment just before he was punched in the face.

Whoever took the video murmured, "Holy shit." The attacker pivots and runs out of the library. The camera follows his progress until the sliding doors shut behind him and then swings back toward the interior of the library. Here the cinematographer rounds the bank of public terminals to get a better look at Perry on the carpet, and the army medic with two fingers on his neck, taking his pulse.

Ryan plays the video again, a scowl of concentration on his face. With regret Jonathan yields his place so Conrad can get a look. And then Ryan plays the video one more time.

Conrad casts him a sidelong look. "Caught something interesting?"

Ryan looks up from the screen. Jonathan cranes his neck and sees that he has paused the full-screened video on a shot of the attacker, who happens to be marching toward the camera on his way out of the library.

"Is this dude known at the library?" Ryan asks tightly.

More choreography takes place. Now it's Hazel and Jonathan standing before the laptop.

"I've only ever seen this man on the occasion this video was taken," Hazel states.

Jonathan looks the man over for a full minute. "I *have* seen this man before, but not recently. Hazel wouldn't have been here for it, but do you guys remember a few years ago, when tent cities popped up everywhere?"

"That was right around the time I moved here," says Conrad. "I'd get on the trail downtown and it would be lined with tents."

"The phenomenon wasn't limited to downtown. The library is almost fifteen miles north of downtown and there was a tent city under every overpass in the area, including the one nearest to the library. I'm pretty sure around that time I saw this man a few times in the library. I didn't have any occasion to interact with him, but some of my colleagues did and they said that he always brought back library books on time."

Ryan's expression turns grim. A feeling of foreboding creeps over Jonathan. "My God, Ryan, I hope you haven't seen him at work recently?"

A silent Ryan pulls the laptop in front of himself and types in several spurts. He then turns the screen toward them. The blue-lipped face that fills the screen stares out blankly, a dead man's unseeing gaze.

The homeless patron. Jonathan swears.

"I not only saw him at work, he was one of my most recent postmortems. Manny Vasquez—I could be wrong, but I think he was on one of the junior varsity basketball teams we played against way back when. Showed signs of being long-term unhoused. Died of a single shot to the back of the head."

"I hope this is a coincidence," murmurs Hazel.

"I hope so too—life on the street is dangerous," replies Ryan. "But I wouldn't count on it."

"How is he possibly related to Perry and what Perry was looking for?" Jonathan mutters, as much to himself as to anyone else.

"What about the other guy?" Hazel and Conrad ask in near unison.

It takes Jonathan a moment to remember the army medic who examined Perry while Perry was unconscious.

"Haven't seen *him* at work," answers Ryan with obvious relief.

"Not at the library either, except for on that day," says Jonathan. "But he did show me his military ID. Can't remember his name anymore but I wrote it down that afternoon and gave it to our administrator for her incident report. Let me see if she has it."

Sophie answers his text straightaway. Let me log in to my laptop. I always keep a copy of incident reports.

Barely two minutes later, she texts, His name is Tarik Ozbilgin. And what's this for?

> Talking over the case with Hazel. I'll tell you more later.

"Tarik Ozbilgin," Jonathan reads the name aloud, hoping he's not butchering it.

Conrad types into his own phone, a frown on his face. "I can't get a good hit on his name—most of what's pulled up is in Turkish. He looks about thirty-five in the video. How old would you say he was in person, Jonathan?"

"Thirty-five would be my estimate too. Why?"

"I want to give that information, as well as the link to the video, to a private investigator I've worked with in the past. I think we can use a little professional help at this point—other than Ryan's outstanding contribution, that is."

Conrad looks at everyone in turn. "Are we okay with farming this bit out?"

Jonathan and Ryan nod.

"Tell your PI to be careful," says Hazel.

Conrad gazes at her a full second. "I will."

Conrad is gone for nearly half an hour, during which time Ryan, Hazel, and Jonathan polish off all the food, clean up the coffee machine, and load the dishwasher.

Mostly in silence.

"Hey," Ryan calls out when Conrad returns, "you were on the phone with your PI for that long?"

"No, I talked to her for all of five minutes. But this whole thing about fentanyl and carfentanil made me uneasy so I did a little online search to make sure I'm not misremembering things."

Ryan, who's been passing around fruits to the guests, tosses Conrad a fig. "What things?"

Conrad catches the fig. "Have you guys ever heard of the Skripals?"

Only Hazel answers in the affirmative. "The ones poisoned with Novichok—those Skripals?"

"Novichok?" exclaims Ryan. "The same nerve agent that was used on Navalny?"

Conrad nods. "Papa Skripal was a Russian double agent who settled down in Salisbury, in the UK, for what was to be a nice, uneventful life for himself and his family. Then one day, he and his daughter were found unconscious in a park. Before the authorities figured out it was Novichok, they first suspected fentanyl.

"Because of that, the article I was reading brought up that in 2002—remember the Moscow theater hostage crisis?"

Jonathan vaguely recollects having walked by a TV with the story blasting. "Sorry, I was in high school and not exactly paying attention to world events."

"I remember it," says Hazel. "I was already in Singapore and the rest of the world is much closer to Singapore than it is to the contiguous United States. The story was on TV for days. And didn't Russian security forces pump some sort of gas into the theater, which allowed them to storm the place and kill the hostage takers but also killed a bunch of hostages?"

"Over a hundred hostages. And guess what was in the gas?"

"Jesus, not fentanyl?" whispers Ryan.

"Possibly a mixture of carfentanil and remifentanil, aerosolized."

The violent death of the homeless patron made Jonathan feel as if he's barely holding on to a storm-tossed dinghy. But this—this is the cold shock of seawater engulfing him.

Ryan swears and taps a button to reveal a hidden bar. On the glass shelves, bottles gleam darkly under recessed lighting. He pours himself a shot of gin. "Are you really talking about weaponized carfentanil, Conrad?"

"I would love for it not to be the case, but at this point, it would be irresponsible not to consider the possibility."

Ryan downs his shot. "The *Kremlin* wants Hazel's husband's Bitcoin?"

"Hardly. American military weapons are smuggled all over the world. The Russian military—and intelligence service—are far more corrupt. I would not be at all surprised that weapon-grade carfentanil is sold to civilians or otherwise fenced."

"Okay, slightly better," deems Ryan. "But still, what are we supposed to do with this information?"

Jonathan feels equally dazed.

For the first time since they came out of the alcove, or so it seems, Hazel gazes directly at Conrad, who frowns and says, "We need to talk to Astrid."

"You're pretty good at this," says Conrad as he studies the direction from which they came.

They are parked right next to the steps that lead to the top of Mount Bonnell, which offers a panoramic view of Austin during the day but is now dark and deserted. Hazel has driven Nainai's Miata up the steep, winding lane at nearly unsafe speeds. Then turned off the headlights, shifted to neutral, and drifted to a parking spot.

"Defensive driving is for others. My mom believes in evasive driving for heiresses."

They continue to wait. If they are being tailed, they will know soon.

An SUV zooms into sight, headlights blazing, and swings into a parking spot with a screeching of tires. Hazel tenses, but a gaggle of young people spill out. They are tipsy, judging by their raucous laughter—and the fact that they plan to leave their ride unattended in a place notorious for smashed windows at night.

Conrad's watch beeps. "That's five minutes," he says. "We can go now."

Hazel reverses and shifts into first, making as little noise as possible, while longing for the resolute silence of an electric vehicle.

Brake. Downshift. Turn. Accelerate. Upshift. She tries to keep her mind focused only on the mechanics of driving as the inadequately lit road dips and swerves through the opening folds of Texas Hill Country.

Beside her, Conrad looks out of the window. In the kitchen of his house she was always aware of his attention. But now that they are alone in this tiny car, his presence a constant sensation of pinpricks on her skin, he seems to be distancing himself.

And then he turns toward her and asks, "What are you afraid of?"

Her stomach clenches—so does her heart. In that moment, it almost feels as if they are back on Madeira and the deeply perceptive young man she's just met is asking *What makes you happy?*, the question no one has posed to her before or since.

A minute passes before Hazel can bring herself to say, "Kit had Russian clients."

"And?"

She accelerates to beat a yellow light. "And nothing. Every British and European art dealer worth their salt has Russian clients. Besides, he didn't steal from his clients—he embezzled from his employer, a British establishment."

Does she feel a hint of warmth just above her right hand on the gear shift? Is he about to take her hand? But he only leans more toward the window and says, "But?"

They are on a local highway now and the illumination is adequate. Yet she feels as if she's driving into fog and shadows. She bites the inside of her cheek. "What if we find Kit at the end of it?"

There, she has named her fear. But the fear does not lessen, it only coils tighter around her, a python bent on suffocation.

"Kit is dead, Hazel," Conrad says quietly.

Or so she—and everyone else—has been told.

But is it the truth, or is it just something they are supposed to accept at face value?

CHAPTER TWENTY-SIX

About half an hour after Sophie gives the army medic's name to Jonathan, he calls—and asks her to say nothing until she is out of her house.

Standing at the very edge of the golf course, a sea of darkness before her, she nearly screams when a herd of deer sprint past her. But she repeats the directions Jonathan gives her, then goes back inside and gathers up Astrid, who is nonplussed to be asked whether she knows not just her home Wi-Fi network's name and password but also the IP address of her router. And by the way, could she pass along the code to her condo community's gate too?

They drive Sophie's Cooper to a park halfway to Jonathan's house. There they stop and perform a thorough inspection of the car before continuing on their way.

Sophie's never been to Jonathan's house, which sits nearly at the doorstep of Elise's high school—Jonathan's too, back in the day. The subdivision, built in the '70s, features smallish—for Texas—cookie-cutter structures that in less topsy-turvy times would have been perfect starter homes. Now they list for prices that make Sophie's head spin.

On the driveway, they are met by the handsome and charming Dr. Ryan Kaneshiro. Sophie likes him right away: He greets them with cheer and delight even though the occasion is sadly lacking in both; he relinquishes his bug scanner immediately when Sophie asks for it and gives her the time—and the illumination—to figure it out for herself; and he does not hesitate to get down on the concrete and shine more light on the undercarriage of her car.

She also can't help but feel a stab of anxiety that he will hurt Jonathan without even trying to.

"We should also take apart the dashboard to look behind it," says Astrid. "In case there's something hardwired to the battery."

"Wow," says Ryan, "you know how to do that?"

Astrid shrugs, even as she smiles with pleasure. "I grew up in the country. My parents taught us all these things. My mom used to fix tractors, back when her family had a farm."

"My mom was just thrifty—didn't believe in paying anyone to do anything," says Sophie. "Changed her own oil until a few months before she died."

Jonathan comes out of the house. "Thanks for coming on such short notice."

Astrid goes up and hugs him. Sophie does the same, but she has to first imagine herself as Elise to open her arms wide and not end up with a fist bump or some such. But ah, Jonathan gives five-star hugs—she feels completely enfolded, completely embraced.

"You okay?" Jonathan murmurs in her ear.

"Hanging on," she tells him.

"That's all any of us can do," he says before letting her go.

"Your house is clean?" asks Astrid, biting her lower lip.

"I think so. No unauthorized devices hitching a ride on my Wi-Fi network. We shut off power and I did a sweep inside with this phone app for anything that emits radio or infrared frequencies and didn't find anything suspicious there either."

Sophie shakes her head. "How did this become *Mission: Impossible*, all of a sudden?"

"At this point, better safe than sorry," chips in Ryan.

They walk into Jonathan's house and Sophie feels as if she's boarded the DeLorean and gone back in time. The dark paneling, the shag carpet, the framed covers of *Life* magazines—she hasn't visited a house this '80s since January 1, 1990.

"Wow, is this a set for *Stranger Things*?" marvels Ryan.

Sophie agrees. She half expects to see a first-gen Apple Macintosh on a desk, and maybe an empty pouch of Capri-Sun behind the floral-patterned couch.

"It's my mom's house and she wants everything to stay the way it is. I'm not going to fight with her over décor when I get to live here for free."

"Oh, I'd have fought her tooth and nail," says Sophie. "No old woman is allowed to cramp my style."

They all laugh, Ryan uproariously.

The doorbell rings. Ryan checks his phone and leaps up. "It's them."

Hazel and her long-lost beau glide into the living room. Sophie considers herself to have met plenty of genetically blessed individuals. Still, what a fantastic evening to have functioning eyes.

Besides her, Astrid looks beauty-drunk, and doesn't recover her concentration until Hazel says, "Astrid, we need a huge favor. Would you consider going back to your condo? Tonight itself, if possible."

———

Outside her condo, Astrid keeps backing out and reparking her car until it is exactly equidistant between the two white lines that delineate the spot.

She turns off the engine and closes her eyes.

The drive back to Sophie's place for Astrid to pick up her Prius was silent. It was only at the very end that Sophie said, *You know, I'd probably have done it too, if I could. Made myself out to be a hot, Creole-speaking babe from Reunion Island to live without my own baggage for a while. Of course, my cousin was at the same college so it never happened. But that version of me, she would have been a lot more chill.*

Sophie did not absolve Astrid of the stupidity of her choices, but for her to say she got why Astrid did what she did—a thunderbolt of happiness had struck Astrid despite her thoroughly frayed nerves.

Now let's get this behind us, so you can enjoy your new life, Sophie had added, before pulling Astrid in for a tight hug.

True, telling other people that she's been an ass doesn't seem all that daunting anymore. Now Astrid is only scared of how to put "this" behind them.

She elbows the car door open, grips the overhead bar, and hoists herself up and out. Inside her condo, she puts away her purse, changes into her pajamas, and brushes her teeth. All normal activities for someone who comes home late in the evening on a Sunday night, right?

Then she turns on her TV—a bit of streaming at this hour is also perfectly understandable. But before she sits down on the couch, she grabs a spray bottle, a microfiber cloth, and her potted aloe vera.

With one eye on the screen, she sprays and wipes down the plant, taking care not to scrape her fingers on the teeth of the spear-like leaves. Then, frowning at the spots on two of the leaves, she pauses her K-drama, picks up her aloe vera and her phone, and ambles about the condo, turning on the lights in each room she enters.

Eventually she places the aloe vera on her dining table. Her phone buzzes. It's a text from Hazel.

> Could you give me a call if you haven't gone to bed yet?

With an index finger that's almost not shaking at all, Astrid jabs at the phone. Hazel picks up after a few rings.

"Hi, Astrid. Thanks for calling me. I hope it's not a bad time for you."

Hazel sounds strained. No, overcome. Astrid's stomach twists. "No, not at all. I was just going around my house looking for a better spot for my houseplant—I think it needs more light."

"Did you find it?" asks Hazel.

Astrid shakes on the inside until Hazel adds, "That better spot for your houseplant?"

"I've decided to put it on my dining table for now, because there's a skylight overhead, but I won't know for a few days whether that'll solve the problem."

Hazel is quiet for a moment. "You sure you can talk now?"

"Of course. I still have a couple of plants to clean—so it's a perfect time for talking, actually. Hold on, let me turn on my speakerphone and bring them over."

"Lucky houseplants." Hazel's voice, not just low, but almost hoarse, emerges from Astrid's phone.

"Oh, they are—the pandemic taught me that I'm a great plant mom." Astrid sets a spider plant and a snake plant on the dining table. "So, what's going on with you?"

"Nothing really, I'm just . . . uneasy. But I don't know. Never mind—I should go to bed. I'll feel better about everything after a good night's sleep."

"No, no. Don't keep it bottled up, Hazel. Let it out. What is it? And trust me, I'm not at all sleepy."

She's in a worse state: tired yet hopped up.

Noises arise on Hazel's side—it sounds like she's taking off a jacket in a small, confined space. Is she in a parked car?

"Has Jonathan told you, by some chance, that I'm a widow?"

"No, he hasn't."

But Hazel did, tonight, when they were all at Jonathan's house.

"And I'm so, so sorry," Astrid hastens to add.

Hazel is silent for close to ten seconds. "The police raided our apartment in April, looking for evidence of financial crime. They arrived at midnight and didn't leave until well after sunrise. It was while they were there that my mom came by and told me that my husband died in a small plane crash off the coast of Scotland.

"It always felt like too much of a convenient coincidence for him to perish just as he was wanted by the law. I don't think I was ever fully convinced of his death. And part of the reason I moved to Austin—not a huge part, but still, it figured into it—was that I thought here, where nobody knows us, he'd find it easier to approach me.

"I wanted to see him face-to-face one more time; I wanted some kind of closure. But with everything that's happened, now I'm terrified of that possibility, even as—even as it begins to feel more and more inevitable."

It takes Astrid a moment to realize that her fingers are hooked tightly around the edge of a ceramic pot—this is not at all what she expected to hear. "Oh, Hazel," she murmurs, to cover for the fact that she's completely lost her place in the script.

"You're right," says Hazel's disembodied voice, "I actually do feel a little better now that I've said it aloud, now that I'm no longer turning it over in my personal dark cave like Gollum under the Misty Mountains."

What happened? Why is Hazel telling all this to Astrid? Astrid pushes her snake plant a few inches to the side and picks up her phone. "And it's not inevitable, Hazel. That your husband might be alive is only a possibility, and not a very likely one. It's fear that's making you think like this."

"I hope you're right. More than anything else, I would love to be worried over nothing."

Astrid brings her phone closer to her lips, as if that will somehow help Hazel. "Would you—would you like to talk this over in person? Sometime after work this week?"

"Yes, I would. I'm going to call my hacker friend in Singapore and see if she can find out anything that might either put my mind at ease or confirm my suspicions. And then I'll dump it all on you. So thank you in advance, Astrid."

"What are friends for?" says Astrid, something she has waited eons to say. "Good luck and don't stay up too late."

"Thanks. Good night."

"Wait!" Astrid cries.

"Yes?"

Astrid rubs her temple—the tiny vein beneath her skin jumps madly. "Hazel, have you thought about what you are going to do if we do find your husband?"

"I don't know," says Hazel, her voice taut yet heavy. "I used to imagine that I'd listen to his excuses in great silence, passing judgment without ever uttering a word. But now—now I'm just afraid."

CHAPTER TWENTY-SEVEN

Astrid's house
Tuesday night

After Hazel leaves for the library, Astrid and Sophie exchange a look, and then reach for the cheese board at almost the same time.

"Swedish cheese?" Sophie asks, scraping some Hushållsost onto an almond flour cracker.

"Yep, from IKEA," Astrid answers.

They burst out laughing, but their mirth quickly subsides into a choked cackle. Sophie shoves the cheese and cracker into her mouth; Astrid does the same with a piece of salami, chewing nervously.

When they have calmed themselves down some by demolishing half of everything on the cheese board, Sophie asks to see more of Astrid's fonts. As it turns out, she is perfectly knowledgeable about typography, and they discuss x-height and kerning like two old friends reminiscing over childhood memories.

So much so that Astrid is startled when her phone beeps. It's Hazel, messaging their three-person text group.

> Inside the library. All good. It's a bit creepy but doesn't really bother me.

Astrid immediately texts back. You see anything promising?

I'm pretty much searching for a needle in a haystack. So, not yet.

This time, Astrid and Sophie do not find it so easy to lose themselves in the finer points of finials and ball terminals. Their exchange peters out gradually, until Astrid closes the last of her stack of lettering-filled notebooks.

"I still feel iffy about Hazel being alone in the library," she says.

Sophie looks at her watch. "Let's call her. Put it on speakerphone."

Sophie comes to sit next to Astrid. Astrid makes sure that the phone is right in front of Sophie.

She glances at Sophie. Sophie has her hands under the dining table. She nods at Astrid. Astrid taps at her phone.

A ring tone reverberates.

"Hey, Astrid." Hazel sounds puzzled. "Are you okay?"

"I'm fine. Sophie and I are worried about you, that's all."

"Yes, why don't we keep this line open?" says Sophie. "That way we'll all feel a little less jumpy."

"Sure, thanks for thinking about me," answers Hazel. "I definitely feel safer with you guys on the line."

"Are you still in the storage room?" Astrid asks.

"Yep."

The answer is accompanied by crisp sounds of pages being flipped and then small thuds of stacks of books being moved about.

Sophie rotates her neck. "Any luck?"

"Not yet."

Astrid's heart rate, which has yet to return to normal, spikes again. "Let us know if you see anything interesting."

It becomes mostly quiet on Hazel's end, with the occasional minor interruptions of filliped paper and gently colliding volumes. Astrid startles once at a crash, but Hazel assures her that it's only that she inadvertently knocked some books onto the floor.

Time passes as slowly as if Astrid were staring at a pot of water on the stove, waiting for it to boil. She and Sophie split the remaining grapes. Her head feels heavy, despite her agitation. Drowsily she wonders whether she ought to get up and make some coffee when Hazel says, "Hmm, there's a box that says 'For Central.' The central library?"

"Should be," Sophie answers, her voice sounding preternaturally calm. "From time to time we get interesting items donated, things that could constitute primary material for local history. We send those downtown and see if central might want them for their collection, or even forward them to the history center."

From the other end, the shrill slide of a box cutter slicing through packing tape, followed by the pulling and snapping of incompletely cut tape. "I see why these were potentially of historical interest. There's a stack of Austin and Texas maps from the forties and fifties."

"Practically antiques," concurs Astrid.

"Look at that, a couple of first edition historical romances from the 1970s. I think my grandmother had these books at one point—maybe she still has them in the attic. Oh, what's this?"

There's now wonder in Hazel's voice.

"What's what?" demands Sophie.

"A yearbook from my old elementary school. I have this one—it's from my fourth-grade year."

Astrid moves closer to the phone. To Sophie. "It's not yours, is it?"

"No, mine is back home in Singapore." The sound of pages flipping again. "But it's definitely from the time I was in the States. There I am, Mrs. Rodriguez's fourth-grade—"

Hazel's silence is abrupt and complete, like those moments when a movie's soundtrack suddenly stops when characters plunge into water. Or deep space.

"Hazel? Are you okay? Are you still there?"

"I'm here, it's just that—under my picture, someone wrote 'Hi' and drew an arrow pointing to the right."

"Shit!" The word escapes Astrid. "Oh my God, do you think—is it possible—"

The rub of glossy paper on glossy paper grows more strident—Hazel is paging through the rest of the yearbook at a breakneck pace. Astrid's hand comes up to her throat. Beneath her thumb, her jugular throbs like an EDM rave. Next to her, Sophie's knees knock together.

"I'm on the last page," whispers Hazel, "you know, that blank flyleaf for people to write on."

"What about it?" Astrid's voice shakes.

"There is a huge character string." Half a minute passes. "Fuck. It's exactly sixty-four characters. That's how long a blockchain private key is."

"Lord Almighty," squeaks Sophie. "You think you found it?"

"I don't know. I need to FaceTime my hacker friend—she'll know more than I do. If this is it, I need to hand it in to the police."

"Okay," says Sophie. "We'll hang up now. Let us know what you find out."

"I will—in the morning. But if you don't see me at work tomorrow, you'll know why."

The line goes silent.

"Everything will be fine, right?" asks Astrid.

Her hands shake. She places them on her chair, under her thighs, to keep them still.

"Yes," says Sophie, sounding only half-convinced. "Everything—and everyone, too."

～

But everything—and everyone—is not going to be all right this night. That was always a given. The only question is, *who* isn't going to be all right?

The library is not brilliantly lit at night. But between streetlamps, exterior lights on apartment buildings across the parking lot, and exterior lights of the shopping center to the other side, enough illumination is provided for a midnight visitor to see clearly, without the aid of flashlights.

A man dashes out of the apartment complex and streaks across to the long, extended porch in front of the library. He counts only one car in the lot, an incongruously cheerful red Miata. Strange to conceive of Hazel Lee in such a symbol of suburban midlife crisis.

He hopes she will cooperate. He doesn't want to hurt her. But it's so much money. What else matters in the end? Nobody loves him anyway, so he might as well have as much money as possible. Money is loyal—unconditionally so—it will provide better than any parents and be more dependable than any children. It will form the bedrock of his future.

The front entrance slides open soundlessly, as does the next set of automatic doors. The interior of the library is shadows upon shadows, but he's familiar enough with its layout to skirt the darkened public terminals and head for the staff breakroom.

The door opens. There is another door in the wall opposite, under which a fluorescent glow creeps. He takes a deep breath and wraps his gloved hand on the handle.

The storage room is a cave full of book stalagmites rearing up from the floor. A woman with her back to him sits on a knee-high stack of books. The hood of her jacket is pulled over her head but the slender volume on her lap is visible, with little rectangular headshots of children—that particularly American publication, the primary school yearbook.

He extends his weapon, points it at the back of her head, and commands, "Give me that if you don't want to die."

CHAPTER TWENTY-EIGHT

Jonathan's house
Two nights earlier

As Hazel pauses at the edge of the den to remove her sneakers, Conrad, standing to her side and a foot or so behind, turns his head toward her.

And Astrid falls instantly in love with their love story. In the gravity and patience of his gaze, she sees a man who has searched a hundred airports and a thousand crowded intersections, not from hope but from a deep-rooted obduracy that even he himself cannot do anything about . . .

Lost in her own musing, Astrid is only vaguely aware of introductions going around. She might have even shaken Conrad's hand.

Hazel says something in a gentle but urgent tone. Astrid realizes, a few moments later, that those words have been addressed to her.

"Sorry. What did you say?"

Hazel regards her a moment, then smiles apologetically. "We need a huge favor. Would you consider going back to your condo? Tonight itself, if possible."

Astrid blinks. "Wh-what?"

Why?

"I wish I could give you more details, but the short version is, we think whoever broke into your place did so not to take anything—or not just to take something but also to install spy devices."

Goose bumps raise up all along Astrid's arms. Was that why the intruder didn't care where she was last night, since her absence made their work easier? "Because of Perry?"

"Because of Perry, or possibly because of me. I just learned from Conrad that Perry and those who intruded upon your privacy were all looking for money my late husband might have hidden. If those intruders believe the two of us have become friends, they are likely to think it's because we have banded together to look for the cache."

"So . . . I should go back there now. Otherwise they might think it's suspicious that I started to stay away as soon as they put the devices in?"

Astrid digs her toes into the brown shag carpet. It's comforting underfoot. Jonathan's house—with everyone here—feels so much warmer and safer than her own.

"I worked with a local private investigator some time ago," says Conrad. "Today after I got back to Austin, I put her on retainer out of an abundance of caution—didn't think we'd need her service so soon, but here we are. May I have her join us?"

He has a reassuring demeanor, not that of a brisk, time-conscious man of business but more like an expedition guide who is invested in everyone's safety and well-being, willing to explain everything at length.

His question was asked to the whole room, but also to Astrid in particular. She nods tightly.

Conrad calls the PI. "Madeleine, I'm putting you on speaker. Miss Sorenson is here. Please tell her what you texted me."

"Right, thanks, Conrad," says a youngish-sounding but efficient voice. "Miss Sorenson, with the information you provided, I did a network scan of your home Wi-Fi network. I am texting you some screenshots now. Can you please take a look?"

Astrid finally bought a Wi-Fi-enabled TV after her roommate Becky moved out, to keep Hulu on in the background so the condo wouldn't be so quiet all the time. She took a picture of the information on the side of her router to connect the TV to the network, and still has it in her phone. Apparently those strings of letters and numbers were what Madeleine needed to perform the audit.

The PI's screenshots arrive. Astrid zooms in, trying to make sense of what looks like a spreadsheet.

"The fourth column lists the MAC numbers of the devices on your network. I have checked. Most of the devices, according to their MAC numbers, are normal household items, but there are two I cannot account for."

Astrid's throat closes. "Spy devices?"

"I can't be entirely sure, not having done a sweep myself, but the likelihood is there."

Sophie, seated next to Astrid on the couch, places a hand on her shoulder. Astrid reaches up and grips it tightly. "So . . . what should I do?"

"From what I understand, you don't wish to alert those who planted these possible surveillance devices that you have become aware of their existence. In that case, you will need to do the sweep yourself."

"But I've no idea how to do any such thing."

"That will be a drawback, but at least you'll be in your own home, not someone else's Airbnb where cameras are concealed inside wall chargers or a speckled-looking piece of decoration. Do you have any pictures of the interior of your home on your phone?"

With unsteady fingers, Astrid scrolls through her album and forwards several recent portraits of her houseplants, which have become a pleasant and largely non-fraught topic of conversation with her mom, who enjoys regular photo updates of her plant grandbabies. But in those pictures, much of her condo can be clearly seen behind the plants.

"I'm going to say the devices are most likely in the living-dining area," pronounces Madeleine's authoritative voice. "The people who installed them had no assurance that you weren't at home, so there is a good chance they steered clear of the bedrooms. And if they have installed the devices in the public areas, then they would want a spot that has a clear, unobstructed view of everything.

"A camera wouldn't be stuck on your window, for instance, because if you shut your blinds, it becomes useless. But it could be on the end of your curtain rod, facing toward the dining table. Or it might be on the frame of one of those blackboards behind the dining table—people typically don't look closely at curtain rods or picture frames."

"And if there's a listening device?" asks Sophie.

"Those don't need to see so they might be hidden behind stuff. I see you have a frosted glass light fixture above your dining table; that would be a favorite spot. The back of the face frame on your bookshelf would be another. But remember the camera and don't go looking for anything in an obvious manner. And assume whatever you say will be transmitted and recorded by a remote device."

Astrid swallows. "I might hyperventilate, but I think I understand everything. I should be there so they don't think I'm deliberately avoiding my condo for some reason. And while I'm there, I should try to find out where the spy devices are, but without coming across as if I'm looking."

"Exactly. If you choose to return to your condo tonight, I'll be on hand. I had to leave your cute little gated community when some lady tapped on my window. But I'll bet she's gone to bed now, and I'll drive in after you and be near enough in case you require assistance."

Madeleine proceeds to give detailed instructions on how to use the two bug scanners Conrad borrowed from her earlier in the day. All the trained librarians take copious notes—Astrid writes down every word, keeping her nerves in check by keeping her hands busy. When Madeleine hangs up, Sophie hesitates a moment and wraps an arm around Astrid's shoulders.

"You okay? You don't have to look for the bugs tonight. Just go home and go to bed—take something to help you sleep, if you need to. That should be good enough for tonight."

Around the room, everyone nods in agreement.

It's tempting, but the thought of not knowing the location of the spy devices bothers Astrid even more than the idea of a surreptitious search.

"I'm okay," she says. "I'll be even better after I get a general notion of where the bugs are. It's just that—"

She realizes she forgot to ask Madeleine an important question. "It's just that, can anyone tell me how long I'll have to live like that, with those bugs in my place?"

The four people who came from Conrad's house exchange glances.

"That will depend," says Hazel, "on how charming and persuasive Jonathan can be."

Astrid leaves with Sophie to pick up her car from Sophie's house. Jonathan decides that he will join forces with Conrad's PI—or at least, be close enough to make a difference, if push comes to shove. Ryan, after a look at Hazel and Conrad, walks away with Jonathan.

At this point, more reinforcement probably wouldn't be of any use. But Hazel, like Jonathan, doesn't want to be too far away. So she takes Conrad to a neighborhood bar a mile or so from Astrid's place, an old and slightly run-down place where her parents used to attend trivia night.

It's the second time in three days she and Conrad face each other across a table. Last time she was full of wonder and hope, but this time she's jittery, her facade of nonchalance peeling and cracking. She takes a sip of her mocktail, not really tasting anything.

He studies her. She is momentarily distracted by the sight of his close-cropped hair. Memory rushes back of her hand on the back of his head, the smooth yet prickling sensation on her palm, the heat of the kiss, his weight on her—

"I need to tell you something, Hazel," he says, stirring his drink with an agave fiber straw.

"You, sir, need to tell me a lot of things," she answers more severely than she needs to. "What were you doing at the library on Game Night, for instance? And why are you back so soon, when you told me you were going to be gone for a week?"

The ice in his glass clinks. "I said I'd be gone a week because at the time I didn't have the bandwidth to deal with Perry's murder, your possible involvement, and seeing you in person on top of that. I wanted to take care of everything on Perry's end first and I hoped a week would be enough."

He'd lowered his eyes to his drink, but now looks back at her. Her heart quakes, not from the intensity of his gaze but from its simple honesty. "As for what I was doing at the library, I thought it would be obvious by this point. I had no idea Perry came to Austin again but I knew you were in town because your grandmother posted about the cookies you made for her book club. And then she wrote that you'd be starting at the branch library.

"I went to the library's website, saw that there would be an evening of board games, and knew you'd be there. I bought a mask, then chickened out and left town. The day of, I changed my mind and came back. Got to the library fifteen minutes before it closed—and lost my nerve again."

Has she ever heard anything that so closely resembles the music of the spheres—that is, apart from when he said he'd moved to Austin in part because of an old white lie on her part?

There's also the quesadilla, which she finally tasted when he was doing a sweep of his house after speaking to Madeleine. On Madeira, when she told him about the dish—to burnish her largely expired Texan credentials—he'd never heard of it. What he made tonight—scrambled eggs, pepper jack cheese, diced tomato, and avocado between crispy flour tortillas—was exactly as she'd described, exactly her dad's recipe.

"*Now* can I tell you something?" asks present-day Conrad, his expression solemn.

She takes a sip of her mocktail. She's already forgotten what fancy name it goes by—it's just ginger ale, club soda, lime juice, and grenadine. Yet the combination of sweetness and bright acidity, with the sharpness of ginger and the deep, puckering fruit notes of pomegranate and black currant—she's never tasted anything so complex and so beautiful.

"Yes?" she says.

He doesn't need to tell her anything else. Tomorrow the melancholy will come back. But that's tomorrow. Tonight, right now, she feels like vigorously shaken champagne, full of tiny bubbles of joy inside.

"I hope it will not come as a huge surprise that I hired Madeleine after I learned that you were married to Kit," he begins.

She already guessed as much. She was able to glean a great deal from hacking into an old laptop she found at Kit's London apartment, carefully hidden under a box of twenty-year-old issues of *The Economist*. But what Conrad was able to tell her—the existence of the surveillance footage showing Kit at the library, for instance—clearly indicates that he and Perry, or the PIs they'd hired, undertook a much deeper investigation.

Also, the fact that he is well-versed in Nainai's social media presence.

"Did you hire only Madeleine or did you also have someone in Singapore?"

"I had someone in Singapore. Between him and Madeleine, I got a deep background on you but I didn't have you followed. If I hadn't known you I would have, but I did, and I'd have felt like too much of a creep."

"Okay," she says.

At this moment, if he said that he'd indeed had her tailed, hell, even if he told her that he climbed through her window to watch her sleep, she'd reply, *I am willing to be gratified by your obsession, provided you dial it down a notch in the future and do not attempt to exert undue control over my life.*

Perhaps her response is too cheerful, or perhaps she is peering at him with too much unabashed interest—he looks away. The half-lit signs on a nearby wall cast neon shadows across his features, a chiaroscuro of copper and electric blue.

He tugs at the corners of a tiny napkin, situating it exactly flush with the edge of the table. "At one point, I was doing everything to find out what I could about you, with Kit's misdeeds as a cover. And then news came that Kit's plane went down. I didn't believe he perished in the incident any more than you did. So I hired yet another PI, this one based in the UK, to audit every second of that flight, from whether Kit boarded, to whether the plane followed its scheduled flight path, to what exactly happened weatherwise along that flight path."

All things she should have done but didn't, because she was convinced that it was all a lie.

"When His Majesty's Coastguard declared that they would halt search efforts, I booked a remotely operated underwater vehicle and carried out a search based on our own analysis. It took five days to find the debris field in the Rockall Trough, at a depth of more than five thousand feet, about as deep as the ROV could go. We weren't able to perform recovery, but we managed a detailed survey."

The tightness in his voice. The tension in his shoulders. The careful blankness in his eyes as his gaze meets hers again. All at once she feels as if she's been plonked down back in her apartment in Singapore, on the day of the raid, with her mother at the door, ringing the bell with all her might.

"What are you saying?"

"Bodies decompose more slowly in water, because of the anaerobic environment. Water that far down is cold, right above zero centigrade. And salt water will further delay decomposition." Conrad watches her closely, as if she's a hothouse flower that will wither after ten seconds in real nature. "Therefore, even though by the time we found the debris field, nine days had passed since the flight's last communication, the footage we obtained clearly showed your late husband in the wreckage, still strapped to his seat."

Hazel has just taken a sip of her mocktail. At his words, like Cinderella's coach at midnight, the magical concoction on her tongue turns back into nothing more than high fructose syrup and artificial flavoring.

"Are you sure?" Her question is barely audible.

"One hundred percent, unfortunately. If you'd managed to hack into my desktop, you'd have found the footage. I also have it on an external drive."

A Boeing 747 takes off inside her skull, 140 decibels of jet engine roar. And then deathly quiet, all her cerebral functions stunned into inertness.

"Are you okay?"

A quarter century of being a major heiress makes her pick up a tortilla chip and eat—the first rule of appearing okay is movement; nobody will believe you're okay if you're frozen in place. But all she tastes is the whey protein concentrate in the queso.

And why is she pretending to be okay in front of Conrad? He is the one who has been crushing her illusions left and right. Even if she were one hundred percent normal yesterday, she'd have become fucked-up by now.

"I'm . . ." She rubs her forehead. "I feel . . ."

It takes an endless moment to recognize the awful sensation inside. "I feel guilty. He's already dead. Yet here I was, suspecting him of having perhaps killed his friend—and a pair of strangers besides."

Conrad takes a sip of his own mocktail, grimaces, and sets it aside. "Kit's crimes managed to outdo your imagination. Of course your imagination had to kick into high gear, to prevent you from being caught unawares again."

She twists her lips. "Groundless suspicion as self-defense."

"I didn't believe Kit died until I was watching feedback from the wreckage in real time. Perry didn't believe it either. The only person who believed it might have been Kit's mom—Perry was convinced even Kit's dad secretly thought he'd run off somewhere that didn't extradite to Commonwealth countries."

Hazel breaks a chip in half, then into quarters. She was so convinced that Kit would crop up again, she'd practically taken it for gospel.

Silence, or what passes for silence with classic rock coming out of the bar's speakers.

"Do you want to collect his remains?" comes Conrad's abrupt question. "It will be tricky, but not impossible."

Dear God, she hasn't even given any thought to that. "I don't know. I suppose I should—since I never did anything else for him."

Conrad's expression sharpens. "Your love—had you loved him—would not have fixed him."

She sets her elbows on the table and drops her head into her hands. "I know. That doesn't mean I won't feel guilty for not having loved him. I should've at least been at the edge of the precipice, trying to keep him from falling in."

"And what would that have accomplished? The love of a good woman amounts to nil when a man's problem is that he doesn't feel validated by the world. When there's an insecurity in him that no validation can erase."

Slowly she raises her head. "Who are you talking about?"

He isn't speaking of some hypothetical example—there's too much aversion in his tone.

The neon lights on the wall flash and now flicker a reddish tinge across his cheeks. His voice turns heavy. "You've tried to find me online, haven't you? And it's as if I don't exist—or as if I've deliberately deleted all traces of myself?"

She doesn't understand why he is changing the subject—and that sends a chill down her spine. "It has felt like that at times," she says carefully.

"It's because of a French law that allows for certain personal information to be suppressed. The information is still there, at the original sites of publication; it just doesn't show up in search results. If it wasn't for that and you searched for my name, for pages on end you'd have news articles about my father. He was a former diplomat and he killed himself when an investigation began as to whether he'd accepted bribes from countries that did not have France's best interest at heart."

"Shit," she murmurs, unable to better articulate her futile sorrow. What must he have felt when he found out? A close kin of the helpless yet furious shame that drowned her—that still drowns her—in the wake of Kit's scandal?

"I know." He places a napkin on the condensation left behind by his mocktail; dampness spread in a perfect circle on the napkin. "It took years, but now a casual search of our names won't bring him up anymore. Or anything about us, really, because after his death, everyone involved—except for my mum—has kept an extremely low profile."

As difficult as it has been for Hazel, Kit could be and has been—at least by others—dismissed as a romantic mistake. But a father's sins cannot be disregarded so easily. His blood flows in Conrad; his name is the one Conrad will always carry.

Conrad looks back at Hazel, his amber gaze direct, forceful. "My dad had the love of not only one but two good women, two great women in fact. And if you want to be a wanker and argue that maybe my mum was too successful, theirs was a starter marriage. By the time he began taking bribes, he'd been married to my stepmother for more than ten years. She looked like a young Catherine Deneuve, was devoted to him, and had the most spectacular home-cooked dinners on the table every night. And what did he do? Demanded palm grease to support a series of mistresses while she made sure everything was perfect at home.

"Your love would not have changed a thing for Kit. Maybe he felt poor being married to you, but trust me, he would have felt poor regardless. Because he looked down on himself and his family's relative penury, and the cure for that was never yours—or anyone's—to give."

It takes Hazel a moment to understand that Conrad's ire was aimed less at his father than at Kit—he is upset not for himself but for her.

But *she* is upset for him. "When did your father commit suicide?"

"A few months after Madeira."

And she was able to meet a young man as of yet unmarred by scandal and tragedy. "Would you have told me this, under different circumstances?"

One corner of his lips lifts, a rueful smile. "Under different circumstances you'd still be married."

"Well, you know what I mean."

With his buzz cut, he couldn't look more different from the boy she remembered from Madeira. He's leaner, grimmer, and so much warier. But as he says, carefully, "Yes, I'd have told you—not so soon, but yes," she is suddenly reminded of that younger, more trusting man.

Her phone buzzes. She grabs it. Astrid has texted.

That is the signal for Hazel to text her back, then Astrid would call and they would lay the groundwork for the much longer conversation they would have in the very near future, in Astrid's house, where every word they speak will be transmitted to a remote listener.

That they will have to lure the hidden killer into the open has been obvious to Hazel since the moment Conrad pointed out that the intruder who entered Astrid's place might have been there to install a few surveillance devices, in case Perry did find Kit's cold storage and entrusted it to Astrid without her realizing its significance. Or, should the intruder be desperate for further leads, of the two people connected to Kit's crypto, Astrid lives in a place that is far easier to access: More than a dozen cameras keep watch over Hazel's grandmother's house; Astrid's had, until recently, none.

So Hazel and Co. need to take advantage of the fact that—if spy gadgets have indeed been placed in Astrid's condo—now they have a direct conduit to the intruder, who is most likely also the murderer of Perry Bathurst, Jeannette Obermann, and the homeless patron, bribed with a meal and a few dollars to make trouble for Perry, and then executed to avoid any leak.

Hazel's phone rings. She takes it and goes out to her car.

When she was sure that the secret audience would be—or at least include—Kit, she'd planned to play up her fear of Tarik Ozbilgin, the supposed army medic who might have stuck a weaponized fentanyl patch on Perry. To let Kit know that while they were not quite on him yet, they were getting close. And that he should act without delay.

But now that Kit has gone to his eternal rest in the stygian depths of the North Atlantic, and her words will be carried to the ears of a dangerous stranger, what should she say? Most certainly not that she is frightened of Tarik Ozbilgin, especially if he's listening. She wants to lure him in, not to send him running or make him think he should kill her—or, God forbid, Astrid—to keep himself safe.

"Has Jonathan told you, by some chance, that I'm a widow?" she says to Astrid.

She doesn't really hear Astrid's response. Astrid must be surprised that she's bringing up Kit, but Astrid is meant to be astonished, in any case. So Hazel presses on and dumps it all on Astrid, syllables spilling out too compressed and too fast.

Conrad stands guard outside the car, staring down into his phone, and lets himself in only after she hangs up.

"You okay?" he asks.

She doesn't answer for a while. Anyway, who's really okay? Everyone is just carrying on as best as they can. "So, Tarik Ozbilgin . . ."

"Madeleine sent an email about him just now."

She turns toward him. In the little two-seater, there is hardly any distance between them. But the light from the front porch of the bar isn't quite enough for her to make out his expression. She can only feel the leashed energy within him. "What is it?"

"She's found him."

"Already?"

"She has a buddy who is also army medical personnel and confirmed, after logging into something called"—Conrad glances down at his phone—"CHCS—Composite Health Care System—that there *is* a Tarik Ozbilgin, army medic, with the 10th Mountain Division. But when she looked up Tarik Ozbilgin's social media profile, his timeline indicates that he hasn't been anywhere near Austin around the time of Perry's death—or within the past few years, for that matter. Not to mention, he looks nothing like the man we saw in the video."

Her head throbs, from the coffee, the overload of information, and the dread that only bores ever deeper into her cortex. Her hand, of its own will, lands on Conrad's forearm. "Then who is the man in the video?"

CHAPTER TWENTY-NINE

Monday

Because of their two years together in high school, Jonathan has always thought of Maryam as soft and cuddly. FaceTiming her first thing in the morning does not greatly alter his opinion. She is still rubbing sleep out of her eyes and yawning behind her hand, her old casual and approachable self. Even as he narrates what he's learned about the people and circumstances around Perry Bathurst's death and her eyes turn grim, it remains a conversation among old friends.

But once they get on Zoom and bring in the others, she becomes all business, cool and assertive. She grills Conrad for close to forty minutes and Hazel for at least a quarter hour—recorded—and only then turns off the recording and asks, "Okay, I know you didn't offer me your accounts solely out of the goodness of your hearts. What is it you want from me?"

Jonathan, the only person who has a prior relationship with Maryam, swallows and begins. "We—we've been working since last night to set things up so that the murderer will come to us."

He lays out the plan as cogently as he can, calling on the others for backup when he needs something explained in greater depth. As he speaks, some of his anxiety drains away. They will be taking a risk, of course, but their plan is logical and not too complicated, and they have made careful preparations along the way.

When he finishes, a resounding silence greets him.

Maryam's resounding silence, as everyone else is already on board.

She raises a brow, and he suddenly feels like a seventh grader who forgot to do his social studies homework.

"You want to do *what*?"

Jonathan clears his throat and repeats carefully, "We would love for you to arrest a trespasser at the library, who will most likely also turn out to be the one behind Perry Bathurst's murder."

"No, I mean, you expect me to put a civilian's life in danger?" Maryam says with a frown.

For the first time in his life, Jonathan connects the word "formidable" with her and feels little beads of perspiration gather on his nape. "No, no, not at all! Hazel will come through the front entrance and go into the storage room. But then she will immediately exit the storage room from the back.

"She won't leave the library, because she might be observed, but it will be dark inside the library. From the back of the storage room, she can slip into the meeting room, or even the passport office, without being seen.

"We tested it last night. From outside the library, even advanced infrared sensors cannot detect the movement of a person through the walls—so Hazel's whereabouts, once she's inside the library, should be completely hidden from the would-be trespasser."

The furrow between Maryam's brows is deep enough for planting seeds, but she waits for him to continue.

Jonathan takes a quick breath and hurries on. "That is point number one: Hazel will not come into direct contact with the trespasser. Point number two: We will place several small cameras outside the library, to achieve advance warning of anyone approaching. Point number three, Conrad and I will be there, one of us outside the library, the other in the building with Hazel."

"Oh, great, more civilians to put in harm's way."

"Come on, Maryam, you know I was a Navy SEAL." They lost touch a few years after high school, but when he'd first made it into the elite forces, he'd told her and she'd sent congratulations.

"Fine, so you've had some relevant training. But Mr. Fancy Clean Energy Investor here?"

Jonathan did not know, until this morning, that Conrad had already met with Maryam twice before, first on Friday, at the behest of Perry Bathurst's family, then again yesterday, as soon as he landed, before he paid a visit to Madeleine, his PI.

It so happened that on Saturday, when Conrad stepped into Peng's Noodles, where Jonathan and Hazel unexpectedly ran into him, he had indeed been bound for the airport, for that afternoon's direct flight to London. He turned around and flew back to Austin immediately with Perry's phone, which had been left behind in Perry's flat in London and found by his parents, who then sealed and signed the package in front of witnesses before handing it over to Conrad.

"I would hardly label what I do fancy—most of what we support is established technology that needs to be put into practice more widely," says Conrad. He is in a crisp, blue button-down, looking slightly better rested than he was last night. "But I was a marine for a bit—mandatory military service in Taiwan."

Hazel, who attends the call from a somewhat nondescript bedroom—the neatly made bed is right over her shoulder—looks surprised. Maryam purses her lips, an okay-you-win-this-round expression.

Jonathan presses on. "As I said, all we need is reinforcement for when the trespasser shows up. But if the APD is willing to join us, we are more than happy to defer to your expertise and modify our plans."

Maryam narrows her eyes.

"It's true that we might net nothing at all, that what we think of as a nice trap is just a bunch of sticks on the ground that wouldn't catch a rat, let alone a fox. But if it does work, you'll solve not one but possibly three murders in one fell swoop. Don't you want to stick it to Hagerty?"

Maryam's expression loses all humor. "I will have you know, Jonathan, that Detective Hagerty is a man of unimpeachable personal integrity, respected and admired by all his colleagues."

Shit! Jonathan wishes he could travel back in time to ten seconds ago to shove a sock in his mouth.

"Not to mention," continues Maryam, "we are working closely together. For what you are proposing, the approval process has to go up the chain of command, and I will be sure to inform Detective Hagerty before someone else does."

Jonathan listens meekly, feeling again like a homework-deficient seventh grader.

"But I'll still be one up over him." Maryam relaxes into a slight smile. "Opportunities to stick it to Detective Hagerty are few and far between and I will never forgive myself if I fail to exploit this one to the fullest."

―――

After the end of the Zoom call, Hazel texts Conrad. If you have time, I'm ready to see the footage.

She isn't ready at all, but she will never be less unready so she might as well do it now.

Conrad replies, Driving right now. Give me about 20 minutes.

Twenty minutes later, she glances again at the phone. Nothing yet. She walks to the front of the house and looks out—this is typically the time Nainai's exercise buddies drop her off from their Monday morning Zumba class.

Nainai is back, in her windbreaker and athleisure, admiring what looks like a Porsche Taycan while talking to a man in a slightly slouchy, caramel-colored suit, a large gift bag in his hand.

Conrad.

After the chaos and upheaval of the past few days, by the time she finally returned home at two o'clock this morning, she thought she had no idea how to feel about him anymore. Was she standing in the rubble-strewn remnants of Tokyo after an incursion by Godzilla, with him as Godzilla? Was Kit the rampaging beast and Conrad but a fellow plaster-covered survivor, trying to find his bearings?

Or has *she* been Godzilla all along, heedlessly stomping through these men's lives in her immense privilege, leaving a trail of destruction that barely registers on her awareness?

But the moment she sees him, she rushes toward the front door, remembering only at the last second to strip off her housecoat and put on a jacket.

At her running approach, Nainai turns around. "Hazel, you didn't tell me your boyfriend was in town."

Hazel skids to a stop.

Conrad holds up his free hand. "I just said we know each other."

But he does not appear displeased by that appellation.

His suit, worn over a white tee, is the kind that men in Milan, Tokyo, and New York might wear to buy a pack of cigarettes at the corner store—and get photographed by chroniclers of street fashion. In a city as casual as Austin, it should be considered much too formal, especially for this early in the day. Yet on him it feels exactly right for a first meeting with her family elder.

And he even comes with a pretty correct gift—inside the gift bag is a large Fortnum & Mason boxed set, probably acquired at Heathrow airport.

"He's not my boyfriend," she tells Nainai, "only my dream lover."

This earns her a lingering look from Conrad and a cackle from Nainai.

"I see your taste in men has improved," says Nainai.

"It's the opposite." Conrad smiles. "We met a long time ago; she used to have good taste in men and then lost it."

Hazel cocks her head. "I . . . actually can't argue with that."

Nainai cackles some more. "Let's go inside. We are just about to have some breakfast."

Over steamed bao and congee, Nainai extracts biographical data from Conrad. Hazel learns that right before he began his military service, he dumped most of the funds his mother had set up for him in an investment vehicle into two friends' cybersecurity start-up, intending to lose his shirt, only to have the opposite happen. He bankrolled several more ventures by those same friends and then needed a meaningful way to deal with his windfall.

She also learns that he's never dated an Asian woman. "It wouldn't have been fair to them—to be compared to Hazel. Actually it wasn't fair to the women I did date, but I didn't realize it at the time."

By the end of breakfast, Nainai appears completely satisfied. But Hazel knows that she will pass on what she knows to Hazel's mother—her former daughter-in-law, with whom she remains close despite the death of her son. And then her family in Singapore will find out about every last parking ticket he's ever been issued—and of course his father's scandal.

"Okay," says Nainai, setting down her spoon. "I'll leave you young people alone in a bit. But what are you two doing getting together first thing Monday morning? Not exactly a conventional hour for a hot date."

Hazel has been wondering whether she ought to come clean to Nainai. Now that Nainai has asked a direct question, she answers—at least about Perry and Kit's connection, and how Conrad came across her wedding photos because of that connection.

"This morning I asked to see some more of the evidence concerning Kit, and I assume Conrad has brought it?"

Conrad nods gravely.

Nainai sighs. "Okay, go look at your evidence."

Her veiny hand settles on Hazel's, a papery warmth. "But be careful. Be very, very careful."

Conrad seems to sense that Hazel doesn't want to study the evidence he brought with Nainai nearby, now that Nainai knows the purpose of his visit. "You want to go to my place?"

In his house, Hazel stands before the two-story window of the library. Knowing what is to come, she is barely aware of the rippling lake outside or the green hills on the far shore.

Conrad offers her a palm-size device. "The complete footage, which is mostly ocean floor and dispersed wreckage, is more than six hours long. Kit's part is about twenty minutes. You can start roughly five hours and ten minutes in."

"Thanks," she murmurs, the device smooth and heavy in her hand.

"I'll be around if you need me."

He leaves quietly. She sits down and plugs the drive into her laptop. With fingertips that don't seem to feel anything, she puts in her earphones, drags the time marker to 5:10:00, and hits play.

She expects darkness, eeriness, water pressure so palpable that steel creaks and pops. But the footage is unexpectedly bright and completely silent—the underwater vehicle must have been equipped with powerful search lights and perhaps no microphone.

The ocean floor sprawls, desolate and moonlike—a desert. A ribbon-shaped fish wriggles across the screen, its shiny scales surprisingly orange. Ahead, wreckage looms. She can make out letters and numbers to the side of the fuselage. The camera navigates around wires and sharp, broken edges to enter the fragmented core of the plane, a three-row section, two seats to a row. The first body that comes into view is that of a woman in her sixties; in the same row, a man of about the same age.

An empty row.

Has someone poured mercury into Hazel's trachea? Dread infiltrates her lungs, branching coral-like over her rib cage.

The camera crawls over a small hill of spilled carry-ons and tilts up. And Kit is there, his features graven, as if he has been chiseled from blue marble. He does not look dead, but as restful as she's ever seen him. Only the movement of his hair, a testament to the shifting currents, acts as a reminder of his watery grave.

When the camera swims away from the wreckage she blinks, as if she's been yanked out of a strange yet consuming dream, and her real life is, for the moment, distant and gray.

She watches Kit's part of the footage again, closes her laptop, and sits for some time, her brain heavy but blank. Then she gets up, steps out to the terrace beyond the library's windows, and descends into a garden with bright mosaic planters that hold sages and cornflowers.

"You want some hot cocoa?" asks Conrad, standing on the terrace, a mug in each hand. He's changed out of the grandmother-visiting suit into a dark blue tracksuit. Earlier he looked like a producer attending the premiere of his own film; now, a trophy husband even someone as wealthy as her mom might not be able to afford.

Does she want hot cocoa? She supposes it can't hurt. "Sure."

He comes down into the garden and hands her a cup, piled high with whipped cream. She takes a sip and is momentarily jolted out of her funk—

this is seriously luxe hot cocoa, not from a powder, or even a bomb, but made the old-fashioned way with milk, cream, and freshly grated chocolate.

She searches for something to say. "I thought you only drank black coffee."

"To impress you, I guess," he answers, smiling a little to himself, and she is struck anew by the lyrical timbre of his voice. "I'm pretty sure I never drank black coffee before Madeira."

He leans against the edge of a raised flower bed, looking up. It is a crisp autumn day, puffs of cloud drifting across a high blue sky.

I don't seem to care whether I'm happy today, but I worry over whether I'll be happy when I'm forty-five or fifty.

He'd sensed, hadn't he, well before his father's suicide, that Hubert de Villiers's life had become profoundly misguided? His stint as a mariner hadn't been just a young man's thirst for adventure but an escape, however temporary, from the ultimately ineluctable.

He turns toward her, once again looking serious. "You okay?"

She sighs. *Is* she okay? "Kit is the one who will never be okay again. I will be, eventually."

He only gazes at her.

She hesitates, holding tight to the mug in her hands, the heat it emanates. "But now I'm forced to acknowledge how angry I've been at times. And not even for what Kit did but because I imagined him hiding out in some remote, beautiful place, enjoying his stolen riches with a local girlfriend while I endured the pity and ridicule of my peers."

Even a criminal deserved a little grace from those closest to him. But she, once betrayed, dealt exclusively in the worst possibilities.

Conrad continues to gaze at her. She is reminded of their time on Madeira, of his curiosity that felt embracing but never intrusive. "At least now you can be angry with him, if you still wish to, for what he did do."

The image of Kit's seemingly sleeping form comes back, embalmed by the deep sea. She doesn't feel anger, only a leaden sadness. "Why was everyone still strapped in their seats? Why didn't they try to swim out before the fuselage sank?"

"They would have been told to buckle in and hang on while the plane was in free fall. The two forensic pathologists I spoke to in the UK agreed that all the passengers would have died instantly upon impact—at sufficient velocity, hitting water is almost the same as hitting land."

Everyone wants an instantaneous death, if death must come, but who would have chosen the panic, chaos, and utter loss of control of a plane crash? Had Kit realized what was about to happen? Or had he been too stunned by the sudden development in what should have been a routine small-plane flight?

She clasps a hand around her upper arm. "After my dad died, I had a hard time, because I was convinced that if he'd survived, at some point he and my mom would have reconciled. His death destroyed that possibility. Kit also has no more possibilities left—he will always be known first and foremost as a financial criminal who died while trying to escape justice."

Conrad is silent for some time. "How's your mom, by the way? On Madeira you said she wanted to protect you from life itself. I imagine she did not take kindly to Kit's misdeeds."

This is a rather Asian question, inquiring after the parent of an acquaintance, a parent he's never met. "She's still furious at Kit. She's even angry at her parents because they were the ones who most wanted me to settle down."

"I must be getting old," he says. "Of everyone involved, she's the one I really feel for."

His comment startles Hazel into laughter, a much-needed release after the oppressive underwater footage.

"I should leave soon," she murmurs after a minute. "You probably have a lot of work."

"I do, but I've shoved it off to my assistants." He runs his fingertips along a row of purple asters and peers at her from beneath his eyelashes. "Would you like to stay for lunch?"

⁓

After ramping up her heart rate and unleashing a flood of wild sensations in her, Hazel's dream lover does not proceed to seduce her but instead informs her that he must examine the contents of Perry's phone—apparently before Perry's parents sealed the phone for APD, they allowed Conrad's people to extract its data.

Hazel chooses to go over videos accumulated by Nainai's DIY security system: Now that she knows she must be of interest to the same person who installed surveillance devices in Astrid's condo, it behooves her to double check whether Nainai's cameras might have caught someone lurking.

At first she doesn't think she'll get any real work done, with Conrad in the same room. But they settle on the opposite ends of the two extra-long sofas and after a while, she becomes absorbed in her task.

Lunch is country pâté sandwiches on good, generously buttered bread, accompanied by a small bowl of crispy cornichons. Conrad slices two pears for their dessert. After lunch he simply goes back to his work; Hazel, who is again pondering the question of her departure, hesitates a moment then does the same.

She comes across the video of herself sashaying down Nainai's catwalk two nights ago, just before the first time she visited Conrad's house, and smiles a little. Maybe she'll download the video and send it to her mom at some point, if Nainai hasn't already done so.

The next one is from the same night, of Nainai voguing as she slides into the camera frame, blue steeling as if she gave birth to not only a doctor and two engineers but also Zoolander himself. This one Hazel will definitely save.

Between spring and autumn of this year, Nainai seems to have shrunk a whole inch in height. She walks slower, the rims of her eyes are always dry and red, and her hair is so sparse that half of her scalp is visible. Hazel wants to hang on to every piece of evidence that Nainai's heart is still as young as ever and her zest for life just as undimmed.

"My God," exclaims Conrad.

She looks up. "What is it?"

"I went through Perry's camera roll on my way back from London, but at the time I didn't even notice this."

He comes over with his laptop, places it on the wide armrest next to her, and crouches down beside it. Her gaze strays to his hair. Her fingers dig into the sofa's cushion. She wants to rub the inside of her wrist against his beautiful, bristly skull; instead, she wrenches her attention to the pixels he wants to show her.

The image is that of Astrid, smiling widely, her eyes shining. The date indicates that the photo was taken during Perry's first visit to Austin, back in spring. Astrid, in a floral dress and a cute, matching coral cardigan, leans over the back of a chair in the library's reading area. Behind her, standing by the DVDs, looking over his shoulder, is none other than the man who tried to pass himself off as Tarik Ozbilgin.

Hazel grips the edge of the screen.

"Madeleine has been trying to find the fake Tarik Ozbilgin," says Conrad, "but she says Google changed something and reverse image search isn't what it was. It used to be a piece of cake for her to figure out for her clients if someone they met online was catfishing; these days it's a matter of luck. Let me send this one to her and see if it gets her better results."

He takes the laptop and rises to his feet.

"Is—is he the one, then?"

The one who killed Perry Bathurst, and possibly two other people? The one they are trying to entrap?

Conrad does not answer her question. He only says, "When the time comes, I'll stay with you."

To distract herself from the onslaught of fear, Hazel goes back to watching clips recorded by Nainai's motion-activated cameras. And deletes what feels like a hundred raccoon clips in a row—as if she can obliterate all the dangers barreling toward her by getting rid of useless pixels from the past.

A much longer video coming up the queue snares her attention. Usually the clips are three to five seconds—wildlife don't stay in frame very long—or ten to twenty seconds—the amount of time needed by most delivery personnel to move into camera range, set down their loads, and move out of range again. But this one is over a minute in length.

In the clip a lithe, tanned blonde woman approaches the house holding a stack of paper. She spies the camera and studies it for a moment. Then she reaches out a hand to press the doorbell, just out of view.

Hazel pauses the clip and plays the next one, from inside the house, which shows an unhurried Nainai, coming out from the kitchen, looking at her phone. From her phone app, she can get live feed from her cameras and would have seen it was a woman outside, and presumably she was in the mood to speak to someone.

That clip ends quickly: Nainai moves out of camera range when she reaches the door. Hazel goes back to the previous clip. The woman waits some more and then her mouth starts moving. She speaks enthusiastically for fifteen seconds or so and hands Nainai a piece of paper. Hazel can't gauge an unseen Nainai's reaction. The woman starts talking again, this time pointing to the camera. As she listens to Nainai's reply, her face is alive with interest. She then waves at Nainai and leaves, driving off in a small SUV.

The woman looks vaguely familiar, but Hazel can't think where she might have met such a person, with a thick head of platinum blonde hair.

The next clip again comes from inside the house and shows Nainai going back into the kitchen, now holding a piece of paper—the one she received from the woman?

Hazel has a vague recollection of such a piece of paper on the formal dining table that is hardly ever used. It was about a fundraiser of some kind.

She pulls out her phone and dials. "Nainai, do you remember a blonde woman who came to our door"—she double-checks the time stamp—"Monday last week and gave you a piece of paper?"

"Was that the first day you went to work? Yes, a woman came and said her son was fundraising to go on a class trip to DC next spring."

"Do you still have the paper?" Hazel asks.

"I put it to recycle—and I don't want to hurt my back fishing it out of the bin. But I checked out the link and my browser might still remember it. Hold on, let me type in GoFundMe and see if it brings anything up. Yep. Johan Schweiger is the kid's name, and only one person donated twenty dollars. That was the reason I threw away the paper. If the kid won't hustle for his own funds, and the mom can't get people to donate, then I'm not going to bother either."

Hazel asks Nainai to send her the link and hangs up, half expecting

Conrad to be listening in on her conversation. But he's on the phone too. He hangs up, a grim look on his face. "That was Madeleine. She said she couldn't obtain a good match from reverse image search. But she was able to feed the new image of the fake Tarik Ozbilgin, which is high-res enough, through a program she just got for beta testing."

"What does the program do?"

"Match people by eye shape alone, even if they wear cosmetic lenses that can fool biometric iris scanners."

Hazel tenses. "And?"

"And according to her program, the fake Tarik Ozbilgin was at Game Night."

Hazel feels like a set of train tracks, reverberating with oncoming disasters. "Can you do me a favor? I'm going to do a screen grab. Will you send it to Madeleine and ask her to also run this woman through her beta software?"

CHAPTER THIRTY

Monday evening

Unless there are special events, Sophie usually doesn't stay at the library until close. But tonight is an exception. Tonight, she is in the storage room, sorting through things.

Books, stacks, carts—she tries to clear some space in the center of the room and scoot everything closer to the walls.

Books are heavy—little wonder, they used to be trees—and Sophie is grateful for her back brace. After twenty minutes, she sits down for a while to breathe: Her instructions say that she should include some intervals in her sound recording during which she does nothing.

Five minutes later, she gets up: She is also supposed to open boxes. She decides to look at some forgotten donations that have been shoved behind the couch—a layer of dust has accumulated over these boxes.

Low-fat cookbooks from when fat was the enemy. Two dozen Fodor's travel guides, a decade out of date. A case of audiobooks on cassette—hoo boy, they will either all go to that single reader who still has a real boombox at home or be complete wallflowers at the book sale.

The next box, though . . .

Underneath a bunch of celebrity memoirs, she spots a copy of *Beloved* by Toni Morrison. It looks almost new, but the cover—Sophie quickly flips to the copyright page. It is indeed a first edition, first printing copy. And signed too, in the great writer's loopy script.

Sophie is no rare book dealer, but somewhere out there someone would cough up a couple of Benjamins for this. She doesn't know if the branch could open an eBay account but surely it would be a sin—as well as a waste— to let this one go for two dollars, the price of a typical used hardcover at the library.

She sets it aside.

The next book in the box turns out to be a copy of *Sense and Sensibility* published in the 1820s—definitely not a first edition, but still, ancient enough and spiffy enough to warrant a pretty penny.

She can't tell the exact publication date of the next two volumes because they are in Chinese, the text arranged vertically. But the dark covers are faded and frayed at the edges, and the bindings are not glued but sewn— they, too, are probably more than a century in age.

The remaining five books in the box comprise poetry by Sappho, Elizabeth Barrett Browning, and Christina Rossetti, *Histoire de ma vie* by George Sand—all published toward the end of the nineteenth century—and a third edition copy, dated 1777, of the first volume of Edward Gibbon's *The History of the Decline and Fall of the Roman Empire*.

Despite the obvious antiquity of most of the books, they are not nearly costly enough to discharge Hazel's late husband's debts—or even buy Sophie's little town house. But her monthly salary would not be enough to purchase them.

No collector would pack such a valuable reserve into a cardboard box with a bunch of titles by the Real Housewives and dump the whole thing on the library.

Unless . . . has Sophie found the box of books Hazel's late husband brought in shortly before he died?

The library
Tuesday Night

Next to the meeting room is a perennially closed door that hardly anyone notices. Behind it rises a flight of narrow metal steps clad in blue thermoplastic. The steps lead up to a hidden gallery overlooking the circulation area, which serves as access to ducts and machinery essential for the smooth running of the building.

In the darkness inside the gallery, Hazel sits on a folded blanket, her back against a wall. The air is slightly stale up here, stale and warm. She racks the Glock in her hand.

A similarly deadly sound issues from two feet away.

After saying good night to Sophie and Astrid, Hazel left Astrid's condo and reached the library twenty minutes ago. She went into the storage room via the Den of Calories, then out from the storage room's back door into the bathroom corridor. Conrad was already there at the corridor's other end, holding open the door to the hidden gallery.

Hazel has sent the agreed-upon texts to Astrid. And now Astrid, seated with her back to the camera, will give Sophie the signal and Sophie will press a button on a small device hidden from view. A pre-produced audio will play and it should sound, to those listening on the other end, as if Astrid and Sophie are on a prolonged call to Hazel, who is looking for El Dorado in the storage room.

The same recording is also playing in the storage room, in case their quarry somehow makes it past all the perimeters without alerting anyone and is at this very moment standing outside the storage room, listening.

But those ambient sounds with bits of conversation spliced in cannot be heard in the hidden gallery, its door shut tight. All Hazel can make out is the occasional low hum of the HVAC and the inevitable pops and creaks of a building cooling and contracting at night.

"No movement in the parking lot," comes Jonathan's voice in her ear. "Everything normal so far."

"Same here," answers Conrad.

A part of Hazel would feel wretched if after this whole song-and-dance they net nothing. But the other part of her—ninety-nine percent and rising—deeply regrets ever choosing to be more involved than absolutely necessary.

"You okay?" murmurs Conrad.

Their recent conversations all seem to start with this question from him. Hazel exhales and checks the safety on her firearm. "I feel like a damsel in distress in an action movie. Like it's the Terminator out there or something."

"Watch your example, Ms. Lee," admonishes the shadowy silhouette that is her dream lover. "Those movies were before my time, but I'm pretty sure the poor human protector from the first *Terminator* bites the dust."

She would laugh if her viscera weren't compressed to the density of white dwarfs. "What if I compare you to Jason Bourne?"

"Even worse," he retorts softly. "All Jason Bourne gets for his trouble is his girlfriend shot dead in a tropical paradise."

Well, shit. "Is there a good action movie that ends happily for everyone involved?"

He is silent for a few seconds. *"Everything Everywhere All at Once?"*

Hazel remembers the movie primarily as the struggle of an immigrant family coming to grips with the everyday trauma and alienation that had come to define them, but there were indeed action sequences—some with dildos and butt plugs, no less.

Not to mention an extravagant, expansive multiverse.

If the multiverse truly exists, there must be at least a few realities in which she never tore up Conrad's number. In those realities, did they meet in Charleston, South Carolina, two giddy young people caught off guard by love? Did she, groupie-like, follow him along the coast of South America, stealing a few hours every time his ship dropped anchor? And did she dip into the funds her maternal grandmother set aside for her, which she was not supposed to ever touch, to buy her way onto his ship, so that they could sit under starry skies together, as the *Pelagios* hurtled ever toward the next horizon?

As if he heard her thoughts, he says, "After my father's funeral, I changed my phone number."

Her heart stops beating. The sound of her sharply indrawn breath bounces off the too-close walls. So he had given her up, just as she had given him up.

"I wasn't in a good place—and didn't believe I ever would be." His words are slow and heavy, as if they are underwater wrecks that must be brought up with great care, lest they trap the diver or give him decompression sickness. "All throughout my second contract on the ship and even during military service afterward, I believed I was right to cut you off, to spare you the person I became."

People will try. They don't want to accept that pain is simply a part of life; they still think, after thirty, sixty, or even ninety years on this earth, that something can be done, if not for themselves, then for those they love.

The old pain returns. Not like a knife, but like a fog. A fog of obliterating vapors, the sensation that she will be lost no matter which direction she chooses.

"But for some reason, I never gave up on running into you again—you would not believe the number of botanical gardens I visited. You would not believe how many botanical gardens there are under the sun. Except I always thought that I wouldn't say hi when I eventually saw you. I would simply watch you go by, husband and children in tow, and that would have to be good enough."

She clutches the Glock in her hand as if it were the last flower in a desert world.

"You'd think, given my certainty that I had not seen the last of you, that I would have been better prepared to come across your wedding photos. But I was . . . shell-shocked. Perry sat next to me, theorizing endlessly about why Kit did what he did, and all I could think was that you finally became what you were running away from."

She bites into her lower lip. She had, hadn't she? Where had all the secret determination to remain herself gone? Certainly on the day of her wedding she had been completely subsumed by her identity—and performance—as Bartholomew Kuang's granddaughter.

"I thought that glossy version of me was your ideal woman."

"I was—obsessed with her. But . . ."

Is their underwater wreckage so tricky that he's not even sure where to attach cables? He sighs. In the darkness, with him close enough to touch yet somehow unreachable, she has the sensation that he is speaking to himself, and she is only the accidental eavesdropper.

"But I was also obsessed with my father after his scandal came to light.

I went through every single record he left behind—much as I did with everything I could find out about you."

Was he engaged in emotional forensics—piecing together all the evidence so he could figure out how to feel? Or had he already decided how he felt and was simply looking to shore up his beliefs?

She clips her Glock back into the holster strapped across her chest. "Why are you telling me all this?"

She hears a shrug, a push-and-pull of fabric against weapons, ammo, and communications equipment. "Isn't the moment before mortal danger the time to lay out stuff like this?"

Her phone is on the floor beside her, counting down. Ten seconds remain before "she" discovers the yearbook, which Madeleine found in her deep dive on Hazel's life in Austin—all part and parcel of Conrad's quest for information earlier in the year.

"Are you expecting a response before mortal danger hits?" she asks, after the countdown disappears from her phone screen.

"No need. It's enough that you know."

But what does she know, exactly? And why doesn't he want a response?

Because it is an end, rather than a new beginning, warns the fatalist part of her.

"If we survive tonight . . ." she says—and doesn't know how to continue.

"Someone's approaching," comes Jonathan's abrupt whisper.

Hazel is light in the head and heavy everywhere else.

Conrad turns on his microphone. "Roger. Be careful out there."

Then he turns off the microphone, pulls Hazel close, and kisses her on the forehead. "You'll be fine. *We'll* be fine."

Jonathan's feet went to sleep a long time ago. The rest of him is jumpy and over-caffeinated.

The recording has just finished playing. "Hazel" is about to call the hacker she worked with before, to "verify" whether the made-up sixty-four-character string could be the private key to Kit Asquith's blockchain fortune.

It's now or never.

In the infrared view on his phone, a figure dashes out from the apartment complex, its heat-emitting windows brightly lit against dark cold bricks. There are no walls or fences around the cluster of generic three-story buildings. The moving figure, face and hands losing the most heat, swerves around a clump of blackish trees, leaps down a low retaining wall, and runs over the small depression that serves as storm drainage between the apartment complex and the library.

"Someone's approaching," Jonathan whispers into his headset.

He darkens his phone. It has served its purpose and is best put away so that it won't give away his location. But without it, he, on his stomach atop the extended front porch of the library, is blind.

Footsteps come to a stop directly below him. Silence, then the front entrance opens with a pneumatic hiss as loud as a train whistle.

Jonathan's heart pounds. This would be the moment a *Star Wars* character declares, *I have a bad feeling about this.*

The operation isn't set up quite the way Jonathan wants it. Not that he is an expert on police maneuvers, but he would have allocated both more manpower and more equipment. Maryam wanted the same. But Detective Hagerty insisted that the entrapment be conducted with as few personnel as possible, to avoid alerting those they wish to catch. And he got his way thanks to his seniority and pull within the department.

So Hagerty and his partner are staking out the suspects' apartment. Leaving only Maryam and Detective Jones, her partner, to face an extremely dangerous individual.

Jonathan forces his thoughts out of their dark spiral. It will be fine. Maryam and Detective Jones are both seasoned cops. They will handle it. It will be over in the blink of an eye and then they can all go home.

How long has the intruder been in the library? Ninety seconds? Two minutes?

He imagines the intruder listening outside the storage room and then slowly pushing open the door. He would see someone in a hooded jacket with their back to him, and a genuine yearbook from a quarter century ago on their lap.

"Give me that if you don't want to die."

Jonathan's teeth clench. Finally.

"Drop your weapon and put your hands behind your head. You're under arrest," comes Maryam's cool voice.

Silence.

"Don't look so surprised," she continues. "Hunters can become prey, too."

Her breezy confidence is reassuring. Still, Jonathan's heart revs at a dangerous rpm. Adrenaline floods him; he digs the toes of his boots into the top of the porch to hold still.

"Fine, so I walked into it, I'll give you this," answers a man's voice. He speaks fluent English and sounds British, but with an undertone of elsewhere.

That's a capitulation, right? Is it all over except for the handcuffing and eventual fingerprinting?

"But I didn't come unprepared," continues the man. "Your flak jacket and tactical masks are all well and good, but the carfentanil in this tranquilizer gun doesn't require hitting the heart or even any major arteries. Look at your colleague's big, strong, undefended thighs. If my finger slips, he'll be dead by the time you finish talking to an emergency dispatcher."

Jonathan's ears ring.

"Now, both of you," says the man, a trace of smugness in his voice, "put down your weapons, hands behind your heads."

By the lack of a subsequent scuffle, Jonathan has to assume that the detectives have complied.

Shit. This is what he was afraid of. But at least Hagerty and Gonzalez are close by. They will come to their colleagues' aid, right?

"Now walk," says the man. "You, lady, two steps ahead of me."

"There's a vehicle moving in the apartment complex," Conrad speaks in Jonathan's ear, his voice low and tense. "Might be our guy's partner in the getaway car."

Why didn't Hagerty and Gonzalez stop the driver of the getaway car? What are they doing?

Hagerty's voice booms in his ear. "Individual in the gray Honda CRV, Texas license plate BVF 7725, is highly armed." He sounds panicky. "I repeat, individual in the gray Honda CRV is highly armed."

Fuck. The guy in the library will most likely use one of the detectives as hostage and human shield until he makes a successful escape—and the highly armed individual in the SUV has practically guaranteed that escape. The thought of an unconscious Maryam being kicked to the side of some desolate stretch of I-10 is bad enough, but what if they don't let her live?

"Tell your guys outside not to be stupid," says the man.

"My partner and I came alone," answers Maryam. She might be quaking in her boots, but her voice is even, if flat. "There's nobody else here from the force."

The man snorts in derision. "And where is Hazel Lee?"

"At home. We drove her Miata here."

The CRV nears the exit of the apartment complex and disappears behind some utility buildings.

Conrad comes around the side of the library at that exact moment—thank goodness they disabled the alarm on the emergency exits in case anyone had to leave during the wait. He sprints to Hazel's Miata, and crouches down.

The CRV covers the scant hundred feet of road distance between the driveway of the apartment and the entrance into the library's parking lot, banking two sharp left turns in succession.

The sliding doors underneath Jonathan hiss again, opening. His heart migrates to his throat, each beat a hard thump against the base of his skull. Being atop the porch gives him a certain amount of surprise factor, but he can't see anyone until they emerge from under the structure—and if he crawls too far forward, he might be seen by the driver of the getaway car.

Maryam is the first to become visible, her hands behind her head. She looks toward the CRV, then back at her partner, careful not to glance up toward Jonathan.

The CRV draws closer. The driver's-side window rolls down; a dark muzzle sticks out.

Detective Jones and his hostage taker step into view, the tranquilizer gun held much too close to his neck. Jones also happens to stand between the Miata and the man, making it difficult for Conrad to take shots.

Jonathan exhales and squeezes the trigger. Dark blood blooms on the back of the man's left hand. He screams and drops the pneumatic device.

The muzzle from the SUV sprays bullets—Jonathan's silencer is good but in real life a shot is never soundless and now he has revealed his location. He scrambles back, sliding on his stomach, then rolls toward the edge of the porch. Shots erupt like dozens of champagne bottles popping, overlaid by the shattering of glass, grunts, more screams, and the sickening crunch of fist on bone. He drops down behind the second of the two brick pillars to the side of the entrance.

Conrad, firing from behind the Miata, has forced the driver of the getaway vehicle to scoot out the passenger-side door to use its bulk as a shield—only a few jagged bits of glass still cling to the cowl of the SUV's windshield.

On the ground, Jones crawls, dragging one leg behind him. Maryam and the man grapple over a handgun in the man's uninjured hand. Even though he has only one good hand, Maryam is barely holding even. Worse, she has her back to the Miata and Conrad would have to shoot through her to get to the man.

Jonathan is in a much better spot. But no sooner does he peek out than a barrage of fire forces him behind the safety of the brick pillar again. A few feet behind him the glass panels of the library's sliding doors crack and crash in a shower of shards.

Jonathan tries again. The muzzle raises from behind the CRV. But this time, Hazel, who materializes from nowhere, slams the butt of a handgun into the driver's temple. The driver cries out in pain—a woman!

Before the woman can react, Hazel pistol-whips her again, grips the assault weapon in her hands, and kicks her in the chest. The woman goes down with a grunt.

Jonathan, belatedly coming out of his astonishment, takes aim and lands a shot to the man's arm. But his partner's peril must have pumped the man full of adrenaline. He wrenches the handgun free from Maryam, shoves her in Jonathan's direction, and uses the second he buys himself to run toward the back of the CRV.

If he rounds it, Hazel will be exposed!

"Watch out!" Jonathan screams.

But Conrad is already by Hazel's side, firing at the man.

The man goes down. Jonathan is astonished. At that angle and with nearly the whole of the CRV between them, Conrad's rounds shouldn't have been able to do much beyond stalling the man's approach.

Jonathan stares at the downed man. And only then does he see the tranquilizer dart sticking out from his calf—and the pneumatic device, now in Detective Jones's hand.

The chaos isn't over. Hazel holds the woman down on the ground, her knee on the latter's spine; Conrad shouts for handcuffs. Maryam throws him a pair even as she cries out for bandaging for Jones. On rubbery legs, with the siren of oncoming police backup in his ears, Jonathan sprints into the library in the direction of the first aid kit, grabs it with trembling hands, and runs back out.

He pants hard, his heart pumps wildly, he can barely feel his fingers, and he worries that he might pass out. But what a wonderful rush of euphoria and relief—the worst of the danger is over.

They have made it.

CHAPTER THIRTY-ONE

The image Hazel had screenshot from her grandmother's home security video was not high-res enough for Madeleine's beta-testing app to ID the platinum blonde woman. But the match Madeleine got with the man in the back of Perry's picture pointed to Ahmed Khan, the husband of the South Asian couple who came to Game Night, to be the fake Tarik Ozbilgin in disguise.

Which made it likely that his "wife," Ayesha Khan, who "rescued" Hazel from the *Fifty Shades* patron's unwanted attention, might have been following Hazel and did not want her to see the video of the altercation, which showed her partner's face, even if it's not "Ahmed Khan's" face.

The address the Khans gave to Detective Hagerty was an apartment in the complex nearest the library, the residents of which are heavily South Asian, many working for Austin's numerous high-tech companies.

A young policewoman of South Asian descent ventured into the complex under the guise of an apartment seeker and found out that the Khans in fact lived in a different building, on a sublet that was against the apartment's rental policy—though that was hardly anyone's focus. Theoretically, at that point the police had enough evidence to search the Khans' apartment and make arrests, but the higher-ups hesitated, as they were dealing with dangerous individuals and the apartment complex is dense with residents.

So the entrapment scheme was given the go-ahead.

Astrid spends the day after the entrapment giving evidence downtown.

Then she and Sophie join Jonathan and Conrad in a visit to Detective Jones in his hospital room—thank goodness the officer is recovering well and in good spirits.

When Astrid finally reaches home and turns on her TV, she is assaulted by breathless local news coverage. "Our reporters are hard at work investigating the midnight shoot-out that resulted in one suspect dead and one APD officer injured—not to mention untold damages to one of the city's most popular branch libraries!"

Astrid winces at the shot of the library, covered in black tarp and neon police tape.

Another channel seems to have slightly better sources. A reporter standing before the apartment complex announces, "It is my understanding that police discovered guns, cash, weaponized narcotics, and a veritable trove of wigs and silicone prosthetics for use in disguises, not to mention a stack of passports for each of the suspects."

A third channel interviews Sophie. Sophie, looking dignified and authoritative, reassures the library's patrons that work crews will be in place as soon as the police give the go-ahead and that the library will reopen at the earliest possible date.

The newspaper, thankfully, goes into some actual detail.

> The suspects, known as Ahmed and Ayesha Khan while in disguise as South Asians, are said to be Russian nationals from the Caucasus region. It is highly likely that they worked as FSB (Russian security agency) contractors. But with funds tied up in the war with Ukraine, they needed an alternative source of income and turned to work as recovery agents, who typically seek stolen artwork and earn a commission when they return the artwork to their rightful owners.
>
> It is also possible that the suspects were lying low in Austin, as sources inform *The Statesman* that the suspects were, under various aliases, wanted in France, Spain, and the UK. The same sources assure *The Statesman* that European authorities will need to be patient: The NSA and the CIA are vying to interrogate the surviving suspect.

But consuming news about the case makes Astrid feel strangely hollow. Perry is gone. Whatever the infotainment sources have to say about the individuals responsible for his death or the circumstances around it, she can never bring him back.

When she and Hazel had their first good talk and she'd confessed a certain numbness where Perry was concerned, Hazel had told her that she might miss that numbness in the days to come.

Hazel was right. Numbness is infinitely easier on the psyche than the hot burn of shame brought on by the indifference she'd felt toward Perry's fate. Had she accepted his distressed avowal that there was a reason behind his ghosting, had she let him stay at her place, maybe, maybe he would have been safer. Maybe he'd still be alive.

When the noises in her head and the pain in her heart become too much, she picks up her phone to call Hazel, only to remember that Hazel is currently thirty thousand feet in the air, flying to San Francisco. Singapore police want to interview her again and local law enforcement, after interrogating her all day, has granted the all-clear for her to leave the country.

But Sophie and Jonathan check in and make her feel less alone—as does Hazel, right before she boards her seventeen-hour San Francisco-to-Singapore flight.

The next afternoon, an unexpected text comes from Conrad. He is house-sitting for Hazel's grandmother, who is on a tour of California wine country with her book club. Would Astrid care to come for tea? He has some information about Perry that she might like to have.

The drive to Hazel's house is short, but it's long enough for all kinds of dire possibilities to cross Astrid's mind.

Conrad welcomes her to a dining table laid out with tea and scones. He pours her a cup of tea and nudges a cream-and-sugar set toward her. "I'm not quite sure how to begin—"

He isn't as gregarious as Ryan, or as naturally embracing as Jonathan, but there is a stillness to his presence—reminiscent of Hazel's—which convinces Astrid that she would have to fuck up far worse than she ever has to incur his disapproval. That he's seen too much to be bothered by blunders like hers, however stupid and unforgivable they may seem to her.

"I really loved him," she blurts out. "Being with him felt like opening a window in a room that was boarded up for ages. It was all sunshine and spring breezes. But when he left, it was as if that window became bricked over. Then, when he came back, made a beeline for Hazel, and asked her all the same questions he asked me when we first met—even now, knowing why he did that, I still feel this scalding mortification. I really hated him at that moment and wished he would disappear forever."

Her voice catches. "And he did—and now I keep thinking about everything I could have done differently."

Conrad, seated across from her, bows his head. "With regard to Perry, I will always carry a measure of guilt. The moment I found out that Hazel was married to Kit Asquith, I threw everything I had into digging up everything about him—and her. And I had far more connections at my disposal than Perry did—I made my friend in cybersecurity stop everything he was doing and put his entire team of hackers on this. Without that we wouldn't have found the footage of Kit at the library, and without *that*, Perry would have never set foot in your workplace."

She tries to imagine what that would have been like—her spring without him, her summer without heartbreak—and cannot.

"But at the time I had no idea how that information would change his life—all our lives. I was away from Austin on his first visit and didn't pepper him with questions—I figured if he found anything he'd let me know; otherwise I could ask after I returned. But I got a text from Ryan instead. Ryan hardly saw Perry for a week and then came back from work one day to find a note on the kitchen island from Perry saying he'd already packed up and left."

Perry's abrupt departure has long been a debilitating secret for Astrid; it's disorienting to hear it brought up from the perspective of a puzzled friend.

"I texted and rang and got no response. Two weeks later I kicked down the door of his London flat and found him, well, not quite depressed but highly dejected.

"He'd gone teetotal eighteen months before and that was the only occasion I wished I could just pour a few pints down his gullet. It must have taken the two of us gallons of soda water, six different kinds of chaat, and forty overs of cricket on telly before he confided that he'd received an anonymous text that threatened your safety if he didn't vacate Austin immediately. The sender included photos taken of you leaving home and arriving at work."

Conrad's voice seems to come from a hundred miles away. Here it is, at last, the legitimate reason Astrid has always hoped for. Legitimate and terrible. All the fear and frustration Perry must have felt crowd into her airway. She can barely breathe.

Conrad sighs and pours himself a cup of tea. "That was the first I heard of you. I was not thrilled with his decision to leave you in the dark, but to explain the matter would have involved telling you about the money he lost to Kit Asquith, and that was a *sore* point with Perry—he hated that he was exploited, especially since his family and friends had been telling him for years that he was a little on the gullible side."

"Did you also think of him as gullible?"

Astrid can't help but feel defensive on Perry's behalf. Maybe he was gullible, but he was also open and curious. And what is the point of human interaction without at least a modicum of faith?

"I didn't think of him as overly credulous, more . . . untested," answers Conrad, his voice low, his tone contemplative. "He was generous by nature, and from time to time an acquaintance might take advantage of that. But Kit was someone he'd known since he was in nappies. Their mothers served as bridesmaids for each other. He wasn't conned by Kit; he was betrayed. And he had a really hard time working through that.

"Also, he believed you'd be spooked if you knew someone had locked in on you as a target."

She would have been. She thought she would die of fright that night, hidden above her utility room, but being left all alone with only her imagination to fill in the void would have been just as bad.

"So there he was," continues Conrad. "He'd hurt you, he despised himself, he was still out three million pounds—and he couldn't even drink himself to oblivion. I forced him to take a shower, take a walk, and get some essentials in his fridge, and then I had to leave for work.

"But before I left, I made him promise that he wouldn't go back to the library again. If someone wanted Kit's money badly enough to threaten you, then they could just as well harm Perry."

Astrid bites the inside of her lower lip. "But he came back anyway."

"He came back anyway." Conrad excuses himself, leaves the dining room, and returns a minute later with a manila folder and a tablet. He pulls out three sheets of paper from the folder and hands them to Astrid.

"These are from the Notes app on his phone. He's been trying, on and off, to compose an apology slash explanation to you."

Some of the drafts are quite short, others are much longer. On a quick scan, Astrid sees a sea of "I'm sorry," "I wish I hadn't," and "I don't know how to explain everything without sounding like a complete idiot—maybe because I have been one."

Anguish and gladness collide inside her, a bittersweet vortex of emotions. She's desperate to read Perry's words more closely, but maybe not with Conrad looking on.

"I'd like to draw your attention to the final note," says Conrad.

Astrid switches to the last sheaf of paper and skips to the very bottom.

Or have I been mistaken all along? Maybe the warning had nothing to do with Kit's hoard but was simply some crazy ex of Astrid's, in which case—

Astrid's heart sinks, even though the worst has already happened.

Conrad rounds the dining table to stand before a large black-and-white canvas on the wall. Earlier Astrid thought it was an art print; now she sees that it's a portrait of a nearly unrecognizable Hazel, her hair short and spiky, her gaze brooding.

"I think that was the reason Perry came back," says Conrad, "this new belief that maybe he conflated the causality of two unrelated things. That and the fact that he probably kept tabs on Hazel's grandmother's social media, which I'd shared with him as part of our collective scrutiny of Kit Asquith and everyone around him. He would have interpreted Hazel's arrival at the library as an unmistakable sign that Kit had indeed left something there."

And so he rushed back . . . to his end: Those who had threatened and later killed him had rushed back too, for the exact same reason.

Conrad touches a corner of Hazel's portrait. "Until this morning, these notes were all I had to share with you. But then I heard from Perry's dad—a private detective Perry was working with contacted him.

"It would seem that after Perry came out of his funk, he became determined to find out who had threatened him. He engaged the PI. The number that was used to text him the threats didn't yield anything. He turned over all the photographs he took in Austin; the PI didn't get anywhere with those either.

"Until the PI met with an old friend a few months later. The old friend has a flat in central London. In the same block lived a defected former Russian spy. The friend only learned about this neighbor after the spy died under suspicious circumstances. As he was talking to the PI, the topic came up and he showed the PI the CCTV footage that was sent around to all the residents of the flat block in the hope that they might be able to help with the investigation."

Conrad next hands Astrid the tablet he brought. A video is on the screen, ready to play. She presses the button.

A man emerges from a door in a long corridor. He wears a fedora, its brim pulled low. The video cuts to footage from a different camera inside an elevator. It is located much lower and manages to capture a full-frontal image of the man's face.

Recognition hits Astrid with a flash of prickly heat in the centers of her palms. "But that's the fake Tarik Ozbilgin! So—so he really was a Russian agent."

"He and his partner were mercenaries who took commissions from the FSB, most likely. Maybe they were cut loose, maybe they also acted as recovery agents on the side. I'm pretty sure they weren't going to surrender Kit's crypto fortune to the art fund he embezzled from—they were looking to swallow the whole thing themselves and did not want Perry's fingers in the pie."

Conrad hands her another two pieces of paper. One shows two pictures of her, along with *If you don't want anything to happen to her, leave Austin within twenty-four hours.*

The next was her again, standing forlornly in the children's area, a stack of books in her hands. And the text that accompanied it reads, *Do we really have to repeat ourselves?*

Tendrils of cold dread curl around Astrid's lower limbs, as if a revenant, emerging from underground, hooked its claws around her ankles.

"This second one, it was sent last Monday, the day before Game Night. Did Perry ever get it?"

"No, he left his phone behind because he was afraid whoever sent him the threat would be able to track his movement via his phone—at least he mumbled something about that back in spring. He must have enabled message forwarding for some people in his contact list—yours were forwarded to his burner phone. But this one was from an unknown number and he never got it.

"What happens next, unless the accomplice gives a full confession, we can only guess. But given that Perry never saw the text they sent him Monday before Game Night and showed up at the library the next day, it's more than conceivable he then received an in-person threat to get the hell away."

Astrid vaguely wonders what the mercenary looked like when he came face-to-face with Perry. According to Jonathan, the man they fought the night of the entrapment, as befitting the owner of a "veritable trove of wigs and silicone prosthetics," didn't resemble either Ahmed Khan or the fake Tarik Ozbilgin.

But no matter what he looked like, the moment he opened his mouth to threaten Astrid, Perry would have connected him to the previous threat, and to the man captured in his camera roll who also happened to slip out of the London flat of a former Russian spy on the day the latter died under mysterious circumstances.

Dear God, what did that sweet fool do next?

"He should've left—they only wanted him gone so he wouldn't find the private key before they did." Conrad rubs a hand over his face. "Or he should have gone to whatever security agency that could have hunted down the mercenary and protected him too. But judging by what happened, Perry might have confronted his eventual killer with the knowledge that he is a wanted man, believing that he'd checkmated the man."

What did Conrad say about Perry? *Untested.* The greatest travail he'd ever faced had been his parents' divorce and Kit Asquith's theft. He'd been too well sheltered, and had not understood the danger he faced.

"So that was the reason they opted to kill him that day itself," she murmurs. "Because he'd become a threat to them."

They found a homeless man to make some trouble. The mercenary, disguised as an army medic—taking advantage of an ID card likely stolen from the real Tarik Ozbilgin and subsequently altered—used the opportunity to stick a patch of weaponized fentanyl on Perry. A clever plan: An overdose of fentanyl would scarcely draw any attention and an executed homeless man told no tales.

Conrad gives the entire manila folder to Astrid. There's only one piece of paper left and it is a photograph Astrid has never seen. But she does recognize the setting—atop Mount Bonnell—and she recognizes herself from the back, her hair, with blue streaks in it last spring, and her blue cardigan that she thought to be so cutely matching.

She took Perry to Mount Bonnell to see the sunset. It was a gorgeous evening and the stony hilltop teemed with tourists and locals alike. Several drones hovered overhead, lots of toddlers sat on parents' shoulders, and the entire vibe was relaxed and happy. Or maybe it was just her, projecting her joy outward onto everyone and everything.

They took several selfies together. She wanted to use the best one as the lock screen on her phone but refrained—she didn't want to spook him. And then he left and she deleted all their selfies, even her favorite ones.

"This was his lock screen when I was in his London flat last spring. It was still his lock screen when my friend's hackers accessed his phone last week to download all the data," says Conrad. "I won't make excuses for him—he should have handled the threat to your safety very differently. But I hope, well, maybe closure is overselling it, but I hope that this is something you would like to know. That he was loath to leave and never forgot you."

Astrid caresses the edge of the picture. She imagines Perry looking at it—looking *through* it to happier, simpler times. "Conrad, have you ever met any of Perry's ex-girlfriends?"

Conrad raises a brow at the abrupt change in subject. "Some, yes."

"Did they ever wish they could hit him upside the head?"

Conrad chortles. "A lot. His friends too, frankly."

Then mirth disappears from his face, replaced by wistfulness. "But in the end we all remember him fondly, because he was good and decent through and through—a dumbass at times, but our beloved dumbass."

~

Conrad leaves, telling Astrid that he has some stuff on the stove.

Alone in the dining room with the contents of the manila folder, Astrid sits for a while with its slender weight in her hands. It's all evidence, evidence that she didn't open her heart and love in vain.

She almost doesn't dare dive into Perry's notes to her, but after a couple of scones and two cups of tea—liquid courage for librarians—she pulls out those sheets of paper and reads, line by line, word by word, syllable by syllable, all the communication she will ever have from this man.

After eight different attempts to make her understand why he did what he did, he seemed to have given up on the ninth try.

> *Dear Astrid,*
>
> *It's no use. In my mind, you've already moved on—because what man with half a brain wouldn't want you in his life? I'm too late and whatever apology I can offer at this point will always be insufficient.*
>
> *And I have no one to blame but myself—the bitterest pill to swallow.*
>
> *It's raining here—hardly surprising as it's October in London. The city is gray, noisy, and unlovely. But sometimes, when I'm out and about, I think of how a dull, ordinary street would have looked to you, had you come for a visit. Maybe you would have thought it equally dismal. Or maybe you*

would have seen fresh, interesting details that I long ago stopped noticing. In any case, I would have liked to see my city—my country—through your eyes.

I've taken to frequenting the two public libraries closest to my flat—did you know London has over three hundred libraries spread across its thirty-two boroughs? Neither did I—I was never much of a reader, let alone a patron of libraries. But I so relished those quiet hours in your library that I've been trying to replicate that peace and contentment.

It's not the same, of course, yet I do feel a little closer to you when I wander the stacks. I've even been making my way through your recommendations—found them on your library's blog. Last week, I read one of your favorites, Ted Chiang's "Story of Your Life," and am still thinking about it.

Had I known the consequences of approaching you that afternoon outside the library, would I still have done it? For your sake, probably not. But if I had only myself to consider, then yes, despite how difficult these weeks and months have been, I would still have held on to those scant days.

I would still have fallen in love.

Next time I'm in the library, I will borrow the movie version of the story and

The note ends abruptly on that conjuncture. Greedily, Astrid reads it again, but it still ends in the same place, with the same unsettling, unfinished finality.

Her tears fall.

So many emotions—in such overwhelming quantities—have besieged her, like the legions of Mordor coming to sack Minas Tirith. Yet her tear ducts have remained stubbornly dry, even as the walls of her city fell into ruin. She couldn't cry—at least not for Perry.

But now, because she will never know what else he meant to say—or if he himself had ever finished the thought—she weeps.

For what seems like days.

When she stops, she slips into a nearby powder room to wash her face and freshen up. Then she finds Conrad in the kitchen, straining a thick, buttery-looking liquid.

"Can I help?" she offers. "What are you making?"

"Crème brûlée."

"Wow, just like that?"

He smiles. "I've invited your colleagues and my roommate for dinner—to celebrate the relative success of Entrapment Night. Hazel's grandmother actually instructed me to trash the place by having a legendary party—she is going to be disappointed."

Conrad studies her a moment. "You are, of course, invited too. But if you'd prefer to be by yourself..."

For a moment Astrid thinks seriously of declining. But she recalls her red-rimmed eyes in the powder-room mirror. She's been alone so much already—why choose more seclusion when she finally has friends, wonderful friends?

"I'll stay," she tells him.

She is glad to see Ryan when he saunters in. And when Jonathan and Sophie arrive together, she runs to greet them, wallowing in Jonathan's mountainlike hug and then glorying in an equally sustained embrace from Sophie.

"You all right?" asks Sophie.

"I will be," Astrid whispers back. "I can feel it."

While Conrad finishes things up in the kitchen, Ryan entertains them with an account of a blue-black bruise on Conrad's chest that Ryan is sure resulted from a physical altercation between Conrad and Hazel the night Hazel stole into Conrad's house.

"Oh, I almost forgot," says Ryan. "Take a look at this."

The guests gather around the dining table. *This* is infrared footage from the night of the firefight. The camera was placed on a tree near the front of the library, at a perfect angle to capture Hazel sneaking up on the fake Ayesha Khan.

Astrid heard from Jonathan about the unexpected but crucial role Hazel played, but even Jonathan is surprised to see that after the fake Ayesha

Khan went down the first time, there was a vicious bout of hand-to-hand combat behind the CRV. Astrid feels as if her own skull is cracking as she watches the two women slug it out before Hazel emerges victorious.

"You're lucky she didn't break a few of your ribs last Sunday!" Ryan calls to Conrad, still in the kitchen.

"What can I say, she loves me too much," replies Conrad, walking into the dining room with a large salad bowl and the enviable confidence of a man who has decided on his path.

Dinner is green salad in vinaigrette, a rib-sticking cassoulet with crusty bread—perfect for the first real cold front of the year—and rich, silky ramekins of crème brûlée that Astrid torched under Conrad's supervision.

After they clear all the dishes and load the dishwasher, the company returns to the dining room with coffee and cocktails and talk about everything under the sun. Astrid has never been so sad in the midst of such a wonderful evening, and never so glad to be alive.

When Ryan asks if anyone wants to play a board game, she is the first one to say yes.

She decides, at the same moment, that when she returns home, she will watch the movie version of "Story of Your Life" again.

That from now on, it will always be their movie, hers and Perry's.

CHAPTER THIRTY-TWO

The summons that Sophie has been waiting for—and dreading—comes the next day.

Jonathan and Astrid drive downtown with Sophie, all three quiet. Sophie holds on to the steering wheel in a death grip; her stomach feels as if an alien creature is clawing its way out.

She can see clearly how Jeannette Obermann must have been killed. Perry Bathurst was not found at Twin Courtyards but at an apartment complex less than a mile to the north. Sophie, however, is almost one hundred percent sure he had parked his rental car at Twin Courtyards, across the street from Astrid's gated condo community.

The mercenaries, who must have planted a tracer on Perry Bathurst's car or his person, tracked him down after Game Night to make sure that he was dead and to remove the fentanyl patch and the tracer.

Jeannette Obermann arrived back at Twin Courtyards. And whom did she see when she got out of her car? The nice couple who had been at the game of Clue with her that very evening. Extremely curious person that she was, she went up to them to say, "Hey, fancy seeing you two again so soon" or "Oh my goodness, do you guys live here too?"

With Perry Bathurst's dead body right there in the car they were all standing next to. Did she see the body? Did she have questions? Did she realize the danger she was in and turn to run?

Whatever happened, with her final bit of clarity and strength, she sent her location to the last number she texted. And her killers, after unlocking her phone with her thumb, must have decided to leave the phone behind because it would confuse the police to see that she'd contacted someone else right before she died.

But they did drive her car elsewhere—they didn't want her body discovered right away if the person she contacted came looking. And then they must have decided to move Perry's body, too, just in case.

Yes, *Sophie* can see it all with diamond-bright clarity. And the firefight at the library—her heart still aches for her library, caught in a hail of bullets—exposed the murder weapon used on Jeannette Obermann, the tranquilizer gun with its deadly load of carfentanil.

But how will *Detective Hagerty* view everything? Like Hazel, Conrad, Jonathan, and Astrid, Sophie was interviewed extensively in the wake of the firefight—but only concerning the events leading up to the entrapment. That she's been called in again, this time by Hagerty, means that Hagerty has obtained Jeannette Obermann's phone records and now knows that she reached out to Sophie repeatedly right before she died.

From what she's heard from Jonathan, Detective Shariati will receive the bulk of the credit for solving the murders of Perry Bathurst, Jeannette Obermann, and the homeless patron Manny Vasquez, used and discarded by the mercenaries. Hagerty's prestige in the department is further eroded due to the mistakes he made with regard to the entrapment operation, insisting on fewer officers and then letting the female accomplice leave his sight too easily.

But his weakened position makes him not less dangerous but more. If he can successfully pin Jeannette Obermann's death on the quiet librarian, what is Sophie's—and Elise's—future compared to his glory and success?

A warm hand clasps around her shoulder. "Breathe, Sophie," says Jonathan quietly.

Sophie looks up to see concrete floor and concrete pillars—they've arrived in the parking garage and she has scarcely any memory of the drive.

"You'll be fine," says Astrid from the back seat.

Sophie stares for a moment at her bright lemon manicure—Elise's favorite, for its beaming cheerfulness. "Yes, I'll be fine," she concurs.

She has no choice but to outsmart Hagerty.

The interview room is cold, sparse, and smells of stale coffee. The metal desk in front of Sophie has a disconcertingly deep scratch along its right edge.

Detective Hagerty wastes no time. "Ms. Claremont, you lied to me."

To the side, Gonzalez, his partner, looks accusingly at Sophie.

The back of Sophie's head rings, as if she's been hit with a baseball bat. She prays desperately that muscles at her temple will not leap—Hagerty must not sense her state of abject terror.

She lifts the corners of her lips in approximation of a sheepish smile. "I know. I'm sorry, Detective, but in my place, wouldn't you have done the same thing?"

She can't bring herself to bat her eyelashes, and that is probably a good thing. She would not want to disrespect the law.

"No, in your place I would have told the truth," Hagerty says firmly. Harshly.

Is she grimacing or smiling placatingly? She can only hope it's the latter. "Well, Detective, I hate to bring it up, but my people have had less than stellar luck where the law is concerned—the law has always tried to bind us but has rarely attempted to serve us. Would you declare aloud and in good conscience that perfectly innocent Black people have nothing to fear from the police?"

This is a gamble. She has no idea what Hagerty will say.

His jaw moves. He frowns. But in the end, he only says, "You had nothing to fear from *me*."

"But I did not know you, Detective. I only know the directive handed down from my grandmother and my mother—and my own experience living in this skin—that I should always, always have as little to do with the police as possible, especially if I'm innocent."

Her throat burns. Her nape burns, too. But she forces herself to smile again. "I was wrong, of course. And I apologize. I'll tell you the whole truth today, but you'll see that the whole truth would only have sent you down a fruitless path."

"I'll be the judge of that."

"Very well." Sophie adjusts the cuffs of her navy blazer—she is dressed more formally than anyone else in the room. "My daughter spoke to Ms. Obermann Saturday before last, when they happened to be both standing in front of some graphic novels. But I never saw Jeannette Obermann until she arrived at Game Night with the third eye on her forehead.

"During the event, my attention was on my daughter—and how the evening progressed as a whole. It was as we were leaving that Ms. Obermann approached me and asked if she could have a word in private."

If only she'd known . . . if only she'd agreed to Jeannette Obermann's suggestion to talk again on a different day, then the woman would have gone home at an earlier time, missed the Russian mercenaries, and lived.

"You told me—and your daughter—that she was interested in volunteering at the library."

"For which there is a whole process to follow, starting with an online application form. No, what Ms. Obermann expressed was a personal interest in me."

Hagerty's right brow lifts up half an inch. "As in . . ."

Sophie sits up straighter. "As in a romantic, or perhaps solely sexual, curiosity."

Hagerty reschools his expression into one of impassivity. Sophie has the sensation that he's restraining himself from looking her up and down. "Are you queer, Ms. Claremont?"

"I am. People might know me for years without knowing that, since dating hasn't been a priority for me, but I've never misled anyone about it."

"Then how did Ms. Obermann know? Surely she wasn't shooting darts in the dark?"

Six feet to his left, even Gonzalez's permanent poker face betrays a trace of interest. At least neither cop looks outright incredulous.

"I'm sure you're aware, from your investigation, that Ms. Obermann lived for some time in Albany, New York?"

"Yes?"

"My ex-girlfriend, right after we broke up, worked for a while in Albany and, according to Ms. Obermann, joined a hobby group in which Ms.

Obermann was also a member. Also according to Ms. Obermann, my ex, still not over me, showed our pictures to everyone around her.

"Now, a little bit after nine p.m. on Game Night, in the library's parking lot, Ms. Obermann told me this. She told me how beautiful she always thought I was, how envious of my ex she'd been, and how she would have given me the moon and the stars, if only I'd been hers."

Sophie feels queasy—she's twisted the truth into a Möbius strip. "I haven't dated much in recent years. To have an attractive woman tell me that from a glimpse of my photos almost two decades ago she remembered me to this day and wanted nothing more than a chance to get to know me better—it was dizzying, frankly.

"But I had a slight problem—my daughter was still with me. I wanted Ms. Obermann to keep telling me how dazzling I was, but I also needed to get Elise home. And I, not being a woman who had a regular nightlife—or any kind of nightlife—had zero idea what places—other than McDonald's—would be open after nine. So I asked Ms. Obermann if she could meet me back at the library after I dropped my kid home. The library is my turf. I know it's safe. And if push came to shove, we could always go inside.

"She agreed. I rushed home and rushed back. We met again in front of the library—it was all extremely promising. Unfortunately, as she kept talking, I started to have a sinking feeling that it wasn't me she was interested in. The one she couldn't forget was my ex."

Detective Hagerty, who has never jotted down a single word on the occasions he interviewed Sophie, now opens the notebook in front of him on the desk. It's full of writing. But before Sophie can make out any of the upside-down words, he closes it again and looks back at her, expectantly and with great severity.

Sophie's heart rattles, an overworked machine about to jolt apart. Under the desk she grips her fingers. Her words emerge slower, more cautious, as if they too are afraid. "I'll grant you this. My ex was a remarkable woman—she was also impossible to live with, you know the sort. I was willing to leave the comfort of my home at what I considered a late hour to be adored and worshiped, but I wasn't there so Ms. Obermann could feel closer to my late ex."

"Excuse me, did you say 'late'?" But Hagerty does not sound surprised.

"She died unexpectedly of a pulmonary embolism the year after we broke up. Everyone was shocked—but that's life, I guess." Sophie shrugs—her shoulders seem to weigh a thousand pounds each. "The point is, as much as I loved my ex, as much as it hurt to break up with her, I'd already mourned both her departure from my life and her departure from this earth. I'd moved on.

"I lost all interest in Ms. Obermann at that point. She, too, could probably tell. Before it got too awkward we went our separate ways.

"I went to get some cookies for my running group and didn't see the location she texted me until I came out from the grocery store. It struck me as extremely odd. Was she inviting me to go over? With just that? Why would I want to?

"The whole evening was too much, one thing after another. I drove around for a while, thinking about my ex, about the different life I would have had if our relationship hadn't fallen apart."

Hagerty lifts a finger to stop her. "When I spoke to your daughter, she said that you told her you would discuss her father with her after she turned eighteen. She says she suspects that you might have used a sperm donor."

Not her, but Jo-Ann.

"I have never in my life stepped into a sperm bank, Detective. My mother, may she rest in peace, would have killed me. No, my daughter, lovely and worthy an individual as she is, was conceived the old-fashioned way, in a drunken haze. Nothing so clean and clinical as a vial of disembodied sperm."

Sophie absolutely cannot risk Hagerty demanding to know where she got the donated DNA and being unable to provide the name of the establishment.

Hagerty actually looks a bit discomfited.

"Librarians make mistakes too—as much as anyone else. My poor child will be disappointed when we have that actual conversation." Sophie sighs—and takes advantage of the moment to make her thesis statement. "I got a text and a location sent to me by a woman with whom I had a disappointing conversation. Next thing I knew she was dead, and people are looking for her murderer. It scared the living daylights out of me. I didn't want to be mixed up in it. I had absolutely no idea why anyone wanted her dead and wouldn't have been of any help to you even if I told you everything. So I kept my head down and hoped that without this red herring, you'd find the real killer. Or killers. And it looks like you have."

Hagerty pulls his lips.

Sophie flexes her toes—can the arch of a foot get a charley horse? What is Hagerty going to say? What holes will he knock in her story?

"Is your ex's name Jo-Ann Barnes?"

Can one shudder while being completely paralyzed? Sophie does. "Yes."

So Jeannette Obermann did use her other devices to look up Jo-Ann.

"I mean," Sophie adds, trying for a measure of insouciance she didn't feel, "I've had other exes, but Jo-Ann was the one Ms. Obermann was obsessed with."

"Jeannette Obermann ran a number of searches. Looks like she also spent some time on Ms. Barnes's old Facebook account, and on accounts of Ms. Barnes's family and friends."

Dear God. Did that woman search for Jo-Ann Barnes's child? If she input anything that would lead Hagerty to believe Jo-Ann might have a kid on the loose somewhere—

"I suspected as much. Ms. Obermann told me she obtained a copy of Jo-Ann's will because she wanted to know if Jo-Ann ever got married—that's when I said to myself, nope, Sophie, this woman isn't interested in you, she's still in love with Jo-Ann's ghost."

"So you know she looked up the will?" Hagerty sounds surprised.

A bubble of optimism bursts inside Sophie's skull. She's doing okay, isn't she, striking Hagerty as completely candid? "Ms. Obermann was nothing if not forthcoming. Too much so, if you ask me—toward the end I was backing away from her. But she didn't deserve to die. She was happy to be in Austin, happy for a new start. She should've had the chance to enjoy her new life."

As she utters her formulaic and practiced words, an unexpected wave of sadness buffets her. For Jeannette Obermann, the wellspring of stress and agitation in Sophie's life ever since she pulled Sophie aside on Game Night. She hopes that wherever the woman is, she saw what happened to her killers a few nights ago and derived a measure of satisfaction.

All her wistfulness evaporates the next second as Detective Hagerty says, "Ms. Claremont, it is always a mistake, a huge mistake, to lie to the police."

Fuck, she's done nothing but lie today.

Pain drills into her head, her heart, her stomach. Is he going to tell her that he knows about Elise and throw the book at her for child abduction? She didn't even tell Elise that she was going to talk to the police again today. Elise will expect her to be home when she comes back from school, she will expect them to have dinner together and—

"But yes, I think I see why you were not more forthcoming," continues Hagerty, his eyes tired and defeated. "Please still consider this a solemn warning to cooperate with the law in the future. You are fortunate that the woman you knew as Ayesha Khan has confessed to the killing of Jeannette Obermann—or at least pointed the finger at her dead partner. If the entrapment hadn't worked the other night, you'd be in a world of trouble now."

But she isn't. And he won't look any deeper into this. And she and Elise will remain a family.

Sophie's head rings again, this time because it has been brushed by the wings of an angel.

She starts to bawl right in front of Detective Hagerty.

Sophie manages to pull herself together enough after a couple of minutes to shake hands with the detectives and thank them for their understanding. Then she ducks into the nearest restroom and bawls for another quarter hour.

She doesn't remember crying like this since Elise was two. She also doesn't remember ever crying from so much relief and happiness.

She texts Jonathan and Astrid and joins them for a stroll on the boardwalk along Town Lake, the chill of the November day dispelled by the sun shining high in the sky. But after she reaches home, sitting alone in an empty house, she feels unsettled again.

At four thirty, Elise bursts through the door. "We've got a huge package. What did you order, Mom?"

Without waiting for an answer, she hauls a large box to their dining table and cuts it open. "Omigod, these are the other two games by Monte Unlimited! You know, the designer behind *Trails to Table*. Did you buy these, Mom? Did we win the lottery?

"Oh wait, there's a gift message. It's from Conrad—is that Miss Hazel's boyfriend? He says he's a huge fan of Monte Unlimited and loves to share their games. Did you tell him that I'm a die-hard stan? This is so lit, Mom. Mom—"

Elise finally glances at Sophie, still stuck to the couch. She abandons her new favorite games and comes over. "Mom, you okay? You look kind of peaky."

Sophie leaps up and hugs her so hard she might have bruised a couple of Elise's ribs. "Oh, Elise. We're going to be okay now. We're finally going to be okay."

Elise pulls back. "What's the matter, Mom?"

Sophie cups her face. "I have to tell you something, sweetie. I mean, I have to tell you a lot of things. I was hoping to wait a little longer, but it's past time that you're prepared for certain eventualities. You're smart, you're mature—"

Elise takes hold of Sophie's elbows. "Mom, calm down."

What? But Sophie is perfectly cool and collected. She is—

Her fingers are shaking against Elise's soft cheeks.

Elise shrugs off her backpack and tosses it onto the couch. It lands with a solid *whump*. She goes into the kitchen and puts a cup of water into the microwave.

Sophie slowly sinks back down to the couch. She stares at her still trembling fingers—she had no idea she was so worked up.

Elise returns from the kitchen with a cup of chamomile tea, sets the mug on the coffee table, and sits down next to Sophie. "Mom, I have something to tell you."

Sophie is instantly on high alert. "What? Did something happen at school?"

"No, school is fine—Ana Maria is going to run for class president next year and I'll handle her campaign, but that's not what I need to talk to you about."

"What is it, then?"

Elise, the straightest of straight shooters, hesitates, then clears her throat awkwardly. "Were you—were you going to tell me about Jo-Ann?"

Is there a kind of bomb that explodes and sucks up all the sound in the vicinity? Elise's lips are still moving, but Sophie can't hear a thing.

How? How does Elise know? Did Detective Hagerty—or, God forbid, Jeannette Obermann—somehow get to Elise—

"—heart attack and we all thought she wasn't going to make it? Well, she probably thought the exact same thing."

"Wait. What?" Sophie's voice is as thin as a needle in her own ears. "Are you talking about *Grandma*?"

"Yeah, five years ago when she had that scare. We flew up to Chicago. The next day you had to run some errands and it was just her and me in the hospital."

"She—"

Sophie can't believe it. Aubrey Claremont promised Sophie—swore—that she would carry her secret to the grave!

Elise grips Sophie's hands; Sophie belatedly realizes that she is shaking again. But Elise's hands are warm and steady, her gaze solemn and mature. "I don't blame her, Mom. I don't blame Grandma."

"I do! You were eleven. You were—"

"I was becoming spoiled. And I was definitely taking you for granted. Grandma could see that I was going to drive you up a wall when I became a teenager—"

"Still!"

She'd tried so hard to give Elise the kind of upbringing Jo-Ann would have wanted for her child. And that did not include making her face the pain of being an orphan alone or instilling in her the constant fear that child protective services might show up at her door.

"It's okay, Mom." Elise presses the cup of chamomile tea into Sophie's hands. "Grandma and I texted each other a lot after that—she helped me come to grips with everything. And it was good for me to learn the truth—everything you went through—it changed my perspective forever."

The sincerity in Elise's eyes, the certainty in her voice—Sophie's heart expands almost beyond what she can endure.

Elise jumps up and fetches herself a cup of iced tea from the pitcher in the fridge. When she returns to the couch, she grins from ear to ear, again the irreverent young girl Sophie can't live without.

"Your turn, Mom. Grandma told me I could tell you that I know everything as soon as she went to a better place. But I, well, why rock the boat? I have, though, been all kinds of curious about your version of the events. The way Grandma told it, Jo-Ann was one sandwich short of a picnic."

"I still can't believe she told you all that. You were so little!"

Elise touches Sophie on the sleeve. "Don't worry, Mom. I never doubted that you loved me. Not even for a minute—you loved me too much for that."

Sophie thought she'd wrung her tear ducts dry, but now her eyes sting again, filling up.

"And now I can at least say thank you, Mom. I mean, that's what I've meant every time I've said thank you for the past five years, but now you know, I'm not just thanking you for packing my lunch or folding my laundry but for everything. For my whole life."

"But that's just the thing," Sophie manages thickly, "I don't know that in the end I have given you a better life. You're not queer, as far as I can tell, so you would have had a great life with your real grandmother, with aunts and uncles and a lot of cousins. You would have grown up surrounded by Black people—in a whole country of Black people."

Sophie envied Jo-Ann lots of things—her optimism, her charm, her natural affinity for people—but none more than the fact that Jo-Ann had grown up with her psyche largely unmarred by racism. Colorism, yes; other ills of colonial vestige, of course; societal problems endemic to Jamaica, absolutely. But she'd emerged without the same discrimination-bred mistrust and self-doubt that weighed down Sophie.

"I can always go to an HBCU to immerse myself in the Black experience, if I want to," says Elise. "And Grandma pointed me to one of Jo-Ann's sisters on Facebook. I've checked in on her over the years."

Would shocks never stop coming? Vaguely, through her stupefaction, Sophie realizes that Elise has called Jo-Ann by name three times. Obviously she's failed to instill respect for one's elders in the girl.

"There have been times when we've been at loggerheads and I have fantasized about living with her," continues Elise, "or with Cora Barnes, when she was still alive—"

"What? She's dead?"

"From the flu, right before the pandemic began."

"Oh," says Sophie, a muddle of confused emotions. For so long she was terrified of the specter of Cora Barnes, coming to snatch Elise away. Yet . . . "I always hoped you'd be able to meet her someday, after you turn eighteen."

Elise shakes her head. "She suffered from dementia. Jo-Ann's sister took care of her and wrote that she sometimes asked about Jo-Ann. She was upset when they told her Jo-Ann passed away, so in the end they took to reminding her that she banished Jo-Ann because Jo-Ann was queer, and Cora would say *Good riddance* every time. So maybe she wouldn't have wanted to meet me."

This brings back Sophie's old sadness for Jo-Ann, Jo-Ann who was so dynamic, so can-do, yet so powerless before her mother's implacable rejection.

"Poor Jo-Ann," says Elise.

Decades of Aubrey Claremont's directives finally kick in. "She's your mother," Sophie says, "don't call her by name."

"She gave birth to me. *You* are my mother." Elise takes Sophie's arm and places her head on Sophie's shoulder. "I don't regret the path not taken. I only hope—I only hope you also have no regrets. If you didn't take me on, maybe today you'd be working at New York Public Library—Grandma said that was your dream when you were a kid."

Sophie doesn't know whether she ought to thank her mother or cuss out the woman who defended and protected Sophie in her own harsh ways. To lay all that guilt on a child—they were lucky that Elise, strong and ebullient, was able to turn that psychological pressure into changes for the better.

"I also wanted to be an astronaut when I was a kid, until I tried a human gyroscope for the first time and almost passed out." Sophie pulls back a little, so she can look Elise in the eye. "I don't need the NYPL to be happy. Everything I need to be happy is already right here, in my life."

For the first time since Elise was two, mother and daughter cry together. Afterward, to calm themselves down, they bundle up for a walk on the golf course.

The sun, reclined upon the horizon, gilds the expanse of long grass and turns it into a veritable field of gold. Sophie fluffs the pom-pom atop Elise's beanie. "Do you remember all those old, old board games you pored over when you were a kid? They were all Jo-Ann's. You've always been her daughter too."

Elise is silent for some time. And then she says, "Mom, remember when Game Night just got over and you were mulling over another one in January? Do you think there will ever be another Game Night at the library?"

"In January, probably not. But I think I'd recover enough by March or April. What do you think?"

Elise snuggles more tightly against Sophie. "I think that'd be great."

And then, like in the old movies, they ride—or walk arm in arm, rather—into the sunset.

CHAPTER THIRTY-THREE

Saturday is day one of the Texas Book Festival.

Jonathan, who has long been involved with the festival, moderates a panel on queer love stories in the morning and a second one on the Marvel Cinematic Universe early in the afternoon. Both are well attended, the second especially so. At the end of the MCU panel, after he shepherds the panelists to the signing tent where they can meet their newly acquired fans, he turns around to find Ryan, with a varsity jacket hooked over one finger, standing only a few feet away.

Jonathan's heart leaps. "Hey! What are you doing here?"

Ryan is wearing his dark-rimmed glasses again, which just might prove to be Jonathan's greatest weakness. "I came with Conrad. We were at your panel, but he had to go to the airport—he's taking Perry back home to England. He was sad about missing a panel on romance."

"Does he read romance?" Men do read genre romance but Jonathan hadn't figured Conrad for one.

"I don't know for sure but he was curious about the socioeconomic topics that might come up at such a discussion."

It looks like the people who bequeathed Conrad their book collections chose the right person.

"Anyway," says Ryan, smiling, "do you have more stuff that you need to do for the festival?"

"Not today."

"Cool. Want to take a walk?"

Jonathan's backpack is still in the green room set aside for authors and moderators, but he answers without hesitation. "Absolutely."

They head south on Congress Avenue, toward Town Lake—or Lady Bird Lake, as newcomers call it. The last time they were alone, they were parked a quarter mile from Astrid's house, tensely waiting to get an okay from her, whether she found any spy devices or not. And before that—good gracious, on the same night—they'd had the basketball game on TV to act as a buffer. This time, it's Ryan who keeps up a running commentary on the hotels, bars, and eateries along the way, Ryan who seems to have visited every single one of the establishments.

Jonathan is openly astonished.

"I used to live downtown, I didn't cook, and I went out a lot." Ryan shrugs. "It would be odd if I didn't know the places around my own neighborhood."

Jonathan shakes his head. "They don't pay librarians enough for me to sample all the places around *my* neighborhood."

"So you cook?"

Jonathan nods.

"And you read?"

Jonathan nods again, intensely aware that Ryan is looking at him.

"And you're handy around the house?"

"I wouldn't charge for my services but I can take care of the normal stuff."

"Why haven't you settled down yet?"

Jonathan's heart zips around his rib cage, like a pinball hitting all the reflectors on the board. Why is Ryan so interested all of a sudden? "I've tried. Dated a couple of techies. They were fine. Just didn't work out."

They were coming up on Congress Bridge, famed for its bats, more than a million strong. But despite multiple attempts over multiple decades, Jonathan and his parents never managed to catch a good look at the largest urban bat colony in the world. Every time they took the trouble to come all the way downtown at sunset, the listed time for the bats to begin their nocturnal hunt, the bats emerged only when it was fully dark. Instead of a vaguely apocalyptical funnel of winged mammals upon a still bright sky, they witnessed the merest wisps of shadows against the deepening night.

Ryan doesn't make any comments on Jonathan's lack of romantic success but guides Jonathan off the road to the hike-and-bike path that rings Town Lake.

The trees are turning colors, gold and red against determined evergreens. The sun, squatting toward the horizon, casts long, leafy shadows.

"You haven't made much of an effort to settle down either, have you?" Jonathan ventures to ask.

They are walking past an upscale hotel, with terraces full of guests enjoying an afternoon beverage. Ryan hops onto a huge round lounger that's been placed near the trail and pats the seat, inviting Jonathan to join him.

The steel-framed lounger can accommodate three, possibly four, relatively slender individuals. Jonathan gets on, feeling tentative. Feeling too close to Ryan, though there's still a good eighteen inches between them. Ryan leans back against a pile of throw pillows, but Jonathan sits cross-legged—even the half-reclined position feels too intimate.

He's been trying to get closer to Ryan for what feels like a geological era, yet here he is, jumpy and scared at the first hint of greater proximity.

Ryan glances at him. "To answer your question, I came out to my mom when I was fifteen. I told her that I liked boys the way most boys liked girls. She didn't cry or get angry, she was just flabbergasted. The next day, she asked me very seriously, and in exactly so many words, whether I'd have many liaisons but never settle down."

He shrugs. "That was what? Twenty-three years ago? *Brokeback Mountain* hadn't even come out yet. I was a kid in the suburbs. I knew what I was, but I had no idea what kind of life I'd have—or be allowed to have.

"Most likely I'd have had 'many liaisons' even if my mom had never said anything. But she did and I've always felt somewhat ashamed about those 'liaisons.' Once in a while I turn into Mr. Ready-to-settle-down."

"I see," says Jonathan.

So whatever impetus Ryan feels toward monogamy—or even serial monogamy—is predicated on placating the ghost of maternal disappointment.

Ryan shrugs into his varsity jacket—it's chillier in the shade. "There's something else I want to tell you."

Jonathan wishes he had a pair of AirPods on full blast. What Ryan just told him doesn't make him feel all that great. In fact, there's a heavy stone where his stomach used to be.

He braces himself. "Yeah?"

"Do you remember your apology?"

Jonathan feels broadsided. The apology that he's spent half of his life crafting . . . "Please don't think I wasn't sincere because I happened to be serving as Hazel's lookout—"

"Of course not." Ryan, who flopped down on the throw pillows after putting on his jacket, sits up straight again. "I believe in your sincerity. You're not a flippant person, like I can be."

Jonathan doesn't consider Ryan flippant. It's more that Ryan excels at appearing cool and carefree, leaving Jonathan unsure as to what he truly thinks and feels.

The Ryan sitting across from him, however, looks rueful, even hesitant. "Do you recall that after you apologized, I said I didn't remember being mistreated, that I had a good time at that pool party?"

Jonathan nods tightly. Different individuals recalling common experiences differently is to be expected, but their diametrically opposite recollections unsettle him.

"Do you remember Davoud Asadi?"

Jonathan heard that name on the night of the reunion. What was the context again? Maryam also mentioned him when Jonathan asked her on Zoom what she might know about Detective Hagerty's investigation. Davoud Asadi, Maryam's second cousin, was in their class. Jonathan has a vague memory of a shortish kid with chubby cheeks and a thick neck—and nothing more.

"He and I were"—Ryan's fingertips scratch against the weatherproof material of the large round cushion under them—"we were a thing half of junior year and all of senior year."

Jonathan more or less expected that, but it still fazes him. "Okay . . ."

Ryan's gaze is on his own hand. "Davoud thought we were in a relationship. I objected strongly to the idea because he had cleidocranial dysplasia."

"What?"

"Genetic condition—basically he had no teeth." Ryan still doesn't look up. "He'd made peace with it, but I was mortified. I never even let him say hi to me at school."

Jonathan tries hard to recall Davoud's features, so that he doesn't have to think about what Ryan is saying. "I . . . don't remember anything about his teeth."

"He wore dentures. Sometimes he took them out when we were together. I was probably the only man alive who wished the person blowing him had more teeth."

Jonathan coughs.

Ryan lifts his head—and stares at a tall hotel downstream. "It might have been funny if I wasn't beside myself. I didn't mind being gay but I was convinced I'd die if anyone ever found out I was doing it with Davoud Asadi.

"I couldn't wait to graduate and break up with him. And when I did, I made sure not to mention his teeth, but he was devastated all the same—he thought he'd meant something to me. And maybe he did. Because I've never been able to forget the pain I caused him. And I felt rotten, far more horrible than any real or imagined humiliation at his naked gums."

Ryan grips one hand with the other, the beautifully trimmed nail of his right thumb digging into the edge of his other palm.

Hey, Davoud Asadi isn't coming. So you can be straight now.

Jonathan at last remembers what Ryan said to Conrad on the night of the reunion. "You took Conrad to the reunion because you were afraid Davoud might be there?"

"Very mature, right?" Ryan looks at Jonathan, but only for an instant. "He has an Instagram. For years it was vacation pics plus an occasional quote. Then he locked down with someone just as the pandemic began. They make a good-looking couple. The other guy is clearly smitten—as he should be. Davoud is a good person. He deserves someone who loves him."

Jonathan looks down at his own hands. Is Ryan trying to tell him that he only got together with Jonathan because he was trying to forget what he did to Davoud?

"Where was I?" Ryan sounds puzzled. "Right. The pool party. The pool party was a week after I broke up with Davoud. That evening Maryam told me that you and she never went beyond first base and I thought, what the hell, let me give it a try. I succeeded beyond my wildest dreams. I, who was a complete shit to Davoud, got together with the perfect blond, blue-eyed all-American boy of my dreams."

Jonathan's head snaps up. What? What did Ryan call him?

Ryan is again leaning back against the throw pillows, but this time, with his arms around one knee. "It's not that I didn't hear what you said afterward, it's that it didn't matter. Of course you were upset—we cracked your hetero facade. And of course you would disappear from my life—I had already committed the original sin of unkindness and didn't deserve a prize like you."

"A prize," Jonathan says slowly.

"Back then I fixated on you because of a combination of my own shallowness and the cultural hegemony of Middle America. Now at least I see that your character has caught up to your physical appeal, that you are as good a person to know as you are to look at."

Ryan smiles, not the brilliant, glamorous smiles Jonathan has come to expect but a smile so wistful it's very nearly forlorn.

Jonathan's heart pinches. "Wh-what are you trying to say?"

"I'm saying that I've been trying to stay away from you because I don't deserve you any more than I did twenty years ago." Ryan is once again looking down, his index finger drawing figure eights on his knee. "But my willpower might fail at some point. I might show up at your house one of these days and not leave. Then you will need to remember what I told you today, that everything I've ever felt for you and will ever feel for you is fucked-up, and my desire to settle down is always deeply suspect."

Silence. A pair of children laugh and chase each other past the lounger, their parents in hot pursuit. Beyond a screen of trees, kayakers glide by, orange streaks on the lake. The wind picks up, carrying with it the scent of water and fallen leaves.

Jonathan feels as if he's floating above the lounger and being melted into it at the same time.

Maya Angelou said, *When someone shows you who they are, believe them the first time.*

But what about when someone *tells* you who they are? What about when they decant all their self-loathing and defensiveness together, believing it to be the world's most repellent mixture, not realizing that they've also poured in a gallon of hope and longing and fearful anticipation?

Ryan shoves his hands into the pockets of his varsity jacket. The next moment, he withdraws his left hand and frowns at a clementine in his palm, as if he has no idea how the fruit came to be on his person.

Sophomore year in high school, toward the end of football season, one day, after practice, Jonathan was waiting in front of the school to be picked up by his mom. After a minute or two, Ryan sauntered into view. Jonathan was instantly a tangle of nerves, trying not to look at Ryan and trying not to flee.

"Hey, you want one?" Ryan asked.

Jonathan glanced up. Ryan lobbed over something, his motion that of someone at a free throw.

Jonathan caught it, a clementine almost as tiny as a marble. "Thanks," he mumbled.

"You were at all the JV basketball games last year," said Ryan, peeling open his own clementine.

A sharp, citrusy tang filled the air. Jonathan breathed in deeply. "Yeah," he mumbled again.

"Are you coming to the varsity games this year?"

"I don't know."

But of course he'd be there. To watch Ryan.

Ryan's dad arrived then to pick up Ryan. Ryan lifted his chin in Jonathan's direction, a gesture of goodbye, then he was gone. Later Jonathan found out that Ryan usually went home after practice with a senior on the basketball team who lived three doors down from his house. But that day the senior was out and Jonathan got to see him for a few minutes.

He kept the clementine in his nightstand drawer for two days before he ate it. It tasted like his favorite orange juice, except fresher and tarter and a hundred times more delicious.

Ryan in the present day drops the clementine back into his pocket and exhales. He is waiting for Jonathan to say something.

"So . . . you just want me to tell you no?"

A net made of vinyl cords hangs from the steel frame of the lounger, forming a protective circumference. Ryan plunges his right hand into the net. "Yes."

For the first time, Jonathan notices a strand of white in Ryan's otherwise thick, black hair. Ryan can pass for twenty-nine any day, but time has tiptoed up to him too.

Jonathan hasn't quarterbacked in almost twenty years. But in that moment, he reads the field and knows exactly what to do. "We don't need to wait until your willpower fails another day," he says. "Go ahead and tell me that you want us to get together. I can refuse you right away."

Ryan's hand tightens around the net. "I'm not sure I want to be refused right away."

"You do, trust me. You didn't bring everything up for me to react in six weeks. You wanted an answer today."

Ryan gazes at Jonathan, as if he's trying to commit every last detail of Jonathan's appearance to memory. For the first time, in front of Jonathan, he looks openly apprehensive, openly vulnerable. "Okay, here goes. Jonathan, you want to spend the night at my place?"

Jonathan pulls him close by the lapels of his varsity jacket and kisses him softly, carefully. Not only because they are in public, but because he wants to let Ryan know that even though they are fucked-up and failure hangs by a thread overhead, he will still approach their relationship with all the attentiveness and diligence of an archaeologist starting on a new dig. Sure, there might be nothing worthwhile, everything ransacked by tomb raiders long ago. Or there could be enough buried treasures to astonish the whole world.

Ryan breaks free, breathing hard. "What happened to refusing me right away?"

"What for?" says Jonathan, his heart pounding so hard he can barely hear himself. "So I can go home and think about you all night?"

They have been thinking about each other since they were fifteen. That's long enough.

Ryan studies him. Does he see the years on Jonathan's face—the beginning of crow's feet, the incipient lines on his forehead? "You're right," he says solemnly. "Let's not be wusses anymore."

He places his hand against Jonathan's beard. His thumb traces over Jonathan's left brow, his ring finger behind Jonathan's earlobe. "Let's not waste any more time."

CHAPTER THIRTY-FOUR

Upon Hazel's return to Singapore the humidity immediately wraps her in a moist blanket. It takes her a couple of days to adjust to the tropical heat, the metric system, and the cars coming from the wrong side of the road. And then she is back in the flow of things, buying coconut rice from holes in the wall and freshly squeezed guava juice from her favorite stalls.

She has not gone back home, however, for a change of climate and the abundance of street foods. Or even to see her mother and grandparents.

The day after her flight lands, she greets Detective Chu of the Singapore Police Force in her penthouse apartment. Not in the soaring two-story reception area in which he'd interrogated her in spring, but in a more modest living room on the other side of the building, overlooking, a little further northwest, the Singapore River, which meanders through the heart of the city.

Hazel stands with her back to a glass wall, a cup of tea in hand, bleary-eyed from jetlag. Halfway across the room, Detective Chu, a pair of cotton gloves on his hands, examines the old books spread out on a large coffee table, a doubtful look on his face.

"This one is worth at least five million American dollars, you say?"

He gingerly lifts the cover on *The Birds of America* by John James Audubon, one of the 119 complete copies known to exist.

"Five million is a conservative estimate," Hazel informs him. "Most likely it will go for at least eight million at an actual auction."

Yesterday her mother met her at the airport with three bodyguards in tow. They drove directly to her grandparents' house, where two antiquarian experts waited to authenticate the books, which included, among others, three fifteenth-century volumes of the *Yongle Encyclopedia*, not one but two copies of the First Folio, a mostly complete copy of the Gutenberg Bible, a 1478 edition of *The Canterbury Tales* printed by William Caxton, and a Quran handwritten on paper that seems identical to the gold-flecked reams beloved by Chinese calligraphers.

"Altogether, these books should fetch thirty-three million US dollars—again, by conservative estimate."

Detective Chu, who has read the affidavits signed by the antiquarian experts, carefully lowers the cover of *The Birds of America*. "So you allege that your husband exchanged his Bitcoin for these books?"

"It's the best conjecture we have at this point."

That Kit, whether because he felt the law breathing down his neck—cryptocurrency can be seized like any other assets—or because he was worried about crypto's volatility, decided to exchange his cache for rare and highly valuable books. There is a non-negligible likelihood that the books had been held by criminal elements looking to turn them into more liquid assets—art has been in use as collateral in drug deals for a while; it's only a matter of time before the same happens with antiquarian books.

Detective Chu reaches toward a volume of the *Yongle Encyclopedia*, a much smaller and slenderer treatise, but changes his mind: The great Ming Dynasty work once comprised over twenty thousand volumes, only four hundred or so of which have survived—and each of the three volumes on the coffee table can command more than two million dollars on the open market.

"My mother is a booklover and a casual collector," says Hazel, "not of books of this caliber, but she spends a few thousand dollars here and there. I've been trying to make a book-themed tabletop game for a while. From time to time, I would borrow a stack of books from my mother's rare book collection for inspiration.

"This past spring, my grandmother in Austin contracted COVID. When I went to look after her, I took a bunch of those titles with me."

Detective Chu stands up and retreats to where he placed his cup of coffee, the breakfast table by the glass wall where Hazel and Kit used to sit over their scrambled eggs, at first in affectionate banter, then, as time went by, in greater and greater silence. "The books your American colleague found in the storage room of the library where you've been working?"

"Correct. My husband, who visited me in Austin and left before I did, asked if he could help me pack away the books, since I wasn't working on the game. I said, 'Yes, thank you.' He then said he had plenty of room in his luggage and could lug them home for me. I said, 'Sure, why not.'

"When I got here, I heard from my mother that he'd gone to her house when she was out and entrusted a box of books to her staff. Given what happened soon after that, it was probably the last time anyone gave any thought to the books for a while."

How strange to think that the stranger before her, an even greater stranger then, had witnessed two of the most trying events of her life—the raid of her apartment and the news of her husband's death.

"After I went back to Austin in autumn, I saw that I didn't bring my game in progress. My mother said she hadn't bothered to unpack the books Kit returned on my behalf in spring, so if I would have someone bring over my game, she would have her staff ship the game and the books to me in Austin.

"I took a look at the package when it arrived, but I only looked at the game, not the books. My American colleague found my mother's books at the library and brought them to my attention. If Kit donated my mother's books, then what was in the unopened box I received from her?"

Detective Chu gestured at the books on the coffee table. "These."

Or rather, some of them—her mother's staff had chosen not to send the largest and heaviest volumes.

Raindrops pitter-patter against the glass wall—monsoon season isn't here yet, but the cloud cover hasn't lifted since her arrival. Has Conrad ever visited Singapore? In her younger days she used to stand on the bridges that spanned the river and imagine him wandering by, a new ex-pat in a city teeming with them.

"Precisely," she says. "Perhaps at some point Kit wanted to leave these books at my grandmother's place, but he changed his mind and decided that my mother's house would work better. In any case they escaped the search of this apartment."

"And now you have brought them back."

"To hand them in to your keeping, as the only right thing to do for an extremely law-abiding resident of our great city-state."

Hazel smiles. She can tell her smile makes Detective Chu nervous, because he understands she is about to set conditions.

And he is correct about that.

Hazel is not conversant with how long seized—or surrendered, in this case—assets typically remain in police custody, but with her grandfather's lawyers acting as go-betweens, they quickly broker a deal.

Kit's former employer accepts five of the rare books as repayment for the money Kit embezzled. The rest will find buyers through private channels—with some of the proceeds going to repay Conrad, who took over Perry's loan; some to compensate customers of Kit's art galleries who bought the fake pop art he peddled; and the remainder to fund scholarships both in the UK and in Singapore.

Originally Hazel thought she would have to budget for the retrieval of Kit's body. But Kit's parents do not view a watery grave as an undignified end—both families have sacrificed young men to the wars of the twentieth century and lost a number of them at sea.

"He didn't live the life we hoped for him," says his mother, "but maybe his money can still do some good in the world."

Hazel donates an additional million dollars of her own in the UK, not in Kit's name but in Perry's.

Her librarian friends keep her apprised of what they learn about the investigations still going on in Austin, but—not so surprisingly—it is her grandfather who tells her that Alina Kadeev, aka Ayesha Khan, is now answering questions for the NSA, and will later face MI5.

"Don't put yourself as bait next time. And absolutely stay away from firefights."

She doesn't ask how he knows—she's said not a word about either. "Sorry, Gonggong. At least it didn't become news here."

"I'm not worried for my old face," says Bartholomew Kuang, shaking his head slightly, "but for your safety. What am I going to do without my little girl?"

He places a large spoonful of stir-fried pork and wood ear mushrooms—her favorite—in her bowl. "Eat more."

Popo, her grandmother, follows with a scoop of marinated bamboo shoots—another perennial favorite. "And this too. It has hardly any carbs."

Hazel eats a great deal that night.

The day before Hazel's flight, her mother stays over at her apartment. They cook together while streaming a glass-blowing competition.

"How's Robbie?" Hazel asks.

Her dad's been gone almost a quarter century and Lillian Kuang has had several significant boyfriends. Hazel really likes the latest guy, who's been around a solid five years.

Her mother smiles slightly. "He's planning a vacation for us in December. Told me that it will be somewhere less hot and rainy. I suspect we were headed to Austin to see you, but he's a bit stumped now that you came back unexpectedly."

"Nainai would be happy to see you."

"I *should* pay her a visit. She's getting up there." Lillian pours soup into a pale green porcelain tureen. "What about you, Hazel? What are you planning to do?"

"I finally figured out the playing mechanism for my new game," enthuses Hazel, waving stems of fresh cilantro in the air. "There's going to be a criminal element. Some of the books in each round will have been stolen and players will be able to check one another's acquisitions to see if a book is of questionable provenance. It's a gamble, of course. If a challenger is right, they receive an amount from the bank equal to half of the book's value and the owner has the book confiscated. But if they're wrong, they have to pay pretty sizable penalties."

"It does sound interesting." Lillian laughs and shakes her head. "I'm still amazed—and delighted—that this is what you do. I would never have imagined it for you."

Hazel sprinkles chopped cilantro on top of the soup. She hesitates a little—she thought Nainai would have broached the subject for her, but Nainai has left the choice and the timing of it to her.

Is she ready?

"Actually," she says, "I never imagined it for myself either. Someone suggested it to me, someone I met long ago."

Dear Hazel,
I have a stack of postcards from all over the world that I never got to use to write to you. I looked them over and decided to buy a new one of Austin instead. Hope it finds you well in Singapore.

Yours,
Conrad

Dear Hazel,
I write from London, as you can see. I brought Perry's body back.
Astrid decided not to come, but to visit his grave at some point in the future.
It will be a sad day tomorrow at his funeral.

Yours,
Conrad

Dear Hazel,
Greetings from Edinburgh, where I brought my stepmum and my younger siblings over for a short holiday. They've never visited Scotland before.

I've had to refrain from introducing myself to the locals as your dream lover.

Yours always,
C.

CHAPTER THIRTY-FIVE

There is no one at Conrad's house.

Hazel texted him from five minutes away. He unlocked the gate and the front door remotely, but said he wouldn't be back for a quarter hour. Hazel pokes her head into the alcove for a moment—it's still pretty—and heads to the library for something to read.

There is already an oversize book sitting on the tree-slab coffee table, no dust jacket, no title on the solid blue cover. On the first page is the image of a large catamaran in port, its sails furled.

She hesitates a little and turns the page. Captions are sparse, but the dates affixed here and there confirm that this is a record of Conrad's time on the *Pelagios*.

Most of the photographs are of the sea, the ports, and sometimes the interior of the ship, which is richly appointed, as expected of an expensive private yacht. A month in, after various islands in the Aegean Sea, there is finally a picture of Conrad, leaning over one of the *Pelagios*'s bows. Hazel must have been blind, thinking him only cute. He was already beautiful then, tall and long-limbed, jawline sharp enough to cut glass, smile brilliant against healthy, tanned skin.

Pain plucks at her heart—this was him in the age of innocence, before his father's death. She flips the book to its midpoint and lands on a funeral under a leaden sky. There is a shot of him from behind, bareheaded, the edges of his long, black coat flying in the wind.

In the wake of the funeral, he became a better photographer—or perhaps he'd improved steadily in the months she's skipped over. But the nature of the photos changes. There are many more images of rain and storms. The sea seems colder, crueler.

The first post-funeral image of him comes after two months or so. Someone took a snap of him cooking in the galley. He looks up, a huge pot in front of him, his young face expressionless, shuttered.

The next shot of him is dated a few weeks later. He is trimming sails with a scowl of concentration, a cigarette dangling from the corner of his lips.

She comes upon a photograph of what must be his cabin—tiny and coffin-like, as he described—but wow, teenage-boy messy. She leans in. Is that the postcard of the Madeira Botanical Garden that he'd taped to his wall?

Some instinct makes her stand up and head for the terrace outside the library, just in time to see a single scull pull up to the boathouse at the edge of the property. Conrad, in a windbreaker and a pair of shorts, leaps up, stows the oars, and lifts the scull into the boathouse.

Then he sprints out of the boathouse and, halfway across the garden, finally spotting her at the balustrade, comes to an abrupt halt.

"Hi!" he says, smiling.

He is happy to see her and she is . . . strangely moved by that happiness.

He resumes walking and comes up to the terrace. "You should've told me you were coming. I'd have been waiting for you."

"Nainai didn't tell you I was coming?" By unspoken agreement they have refrained from electronic forms of communication, but he has been in touch with Nainai.

"Guess she didn't want to spoil the surprise." His smile becomes even more buoyant. "I like the surprise."

She certainly has no complaints about the surprise of seeing him post-workout, glowing with health and vitality. And those shorts show off some seriously glorious quads.

He pulls open the door for her to enter the house. "Let me take a quick shower. I'll be back in five minutes."

But he doesn't depart upstairs until he's poured her a glass of water and loaded a plate with French butter biscuits *and* Taiwanese wife cakes.

She eats one of each, smiling to herself all the while. Even the water tastes sweet, as if it formed when the world's hydrogen and oxygen atoms first met to produce the most life-giving elixir in the universe.

Her phone dings. She deletes a dozen emails and realizes that she missed one from her grandfather's people earlier. Even without opening the email, the two first lines of its content that show in the inbox make her cover her mouth with her hand.

She has just returned to the living room library and sat down when Conrad enters in a lightweight black sweater and a pair of black slacks that unfortunately show no quad at all.

"Did you see it?" he asks.

She looks at him askance. "If you mean your chaotic cabin, yes."

"Oh, God. I swear, the marines beat the messiness out of me."

He sits down next to her. Other than when they were grappling—or kissing—that one time in bed, or when he pulled her in to kiss her forehead right before they faced mortal danger, he's kept her at a literal arm's length ever since Peng's Noodles.

Now they very nearly touch from ankle to shoulder. And whatever he used in the shower smells divine, like Scandinavian rain.

"What I meant was," he says, "did you see the section on Madeira?"

"Not yet."

He lifts a thick section and flips it back, and the book—well trained to, apparently—opens exactly to a photograph of Hazel—three, in fact. She is climbing up a steep street in a white Cape Verde T-shirt, a pair of camo cargo shorts, and, of course, that gigantic visor. Yet somehow, through his lens, she doesn't look dorky but rather cool and breezy.

"When did you take these pictures?"

"When you were busy texting on your phone. I was looking for a panoramic shot though, not to creep on you." He sighs. "But then I saw you."

She raises a brow. "Are you going to tell me you weren't lost?"

"Not only was I not lost, I'd already walked around the botanical garden and left."

"I knew you were hitting on me." She really did.

He smiles down at the coffee table. "Thanks for letting me. I was—I don't think it was love at first sight, but I was struck by this impossible curiosity about you."

He turns two pages and there she is again, laughing uproariously at the ginormous beef skewer that has just been put on the table between them.

"Huh," she says. "I have a vague memory of you with your camera out at this point. I thought you were taking pictures of the beef skewer."

"Well, the beef skewer is there."

As foreground for her thorough hilarity. Come to think of it, she doesn't know if she's ever been captured in another picture laughing so hard, having such a good time.

"So you always had pictures of me," she murmurs. "I kind of forgot what you looked like, but . . ."

She opens her carryall and digs out a small box. "I remembered that you had pierced cartilage. So I got you an ear barbell every year for your birthday—except during the time I was married."

He looks at her, opens the box, and then looks back at her in astonishment. "I thought you meant some goth trinkets. These are—museum quality."

"It's nice to have visuals when I beat myself up over my mistake," Hazel answers, half-joking. She reaches into the carryall again and extracts a glass jar. "I also made these for you, one hundred every year, even when I was married."

The jar contains tiny lucky stars. The ones in this jar are folded from strips of pastel pearlized paper and shimmer with an iridescent sheen.

"I have a whole shelf of those jars in Singapore. I didn't bring them all."

He turns the jar in his hand and regards it with a fierce concentration. The soft-hued lucky stars inside shift and glide against one another.

"All I have is a jar of botanical garden tickets, at least three of them from Singapore," he says quietly. Then, after a moment, "And that."

He points to the large ship in a bottle that she noticed on her first visit because it's so intricately detailed that it has a sailor throwing a message in a bottle overboard. "Remember I changed my number?"

How can she forget?

"The message in the bottle has my new number—not the best way to give it to you, is it?"

No one speaks. After some time, she realizes that they are no longer almost touching, that somehow, in the giving and receiving of gifts accumulated over the years, they moved apart.

She casts about for something to say. "Where's Ryan?"

"Jonathan's hosting a poetry slam somewhere up north. Ryan will be in attendance."

This makes Hazel smile despite her uneasiness. "Ryan has it bad—but then again, so does Jonathan."

Conrad smiles likewise. "Last night I got home from the airport at about midnight and ran into Jonathan in the kitchen. Never seen a grown man blush like that. It was cute."

"So tonight Ryan will be at Jonathan's place." Hazel bites her lower lip.

"I imagine," says Conrad. He caresses the shoulder of the jar of lucky stars with his thumb.

She feels electrical currents zigzag across her shoulders. "Do you want to—"

Conrad glances up at her.

"—hear about the restitution of your three million pounds?"

He keeps looking at her. Then he sets down the lucky stars on the coffee table. Hazel's heart thuds.

"I would love to," he says, "in forty-eight hours."

"What are you planning to do for the next forty-eight hours?"

He looks her in the eye, his amber gaze unwavering. "You."

She is hot all over. *What are you waiting for?* But he is waiting for something, just as she is.

"That night at the library—" she begins.

Memories of that night have rushed back to her many times since, hugging herself in simmering anxiety after he left to reinforce Jonathan, pushing open the emergency exit to the rapid-fire popping of a machine gun, her feet as heavy as fifty-pound weights, slugging it out with Alina Kadeev in a white-hot haze of fury and desperation, not realizing until much later that she'd scraped her arm and bled through her sleeve.

But what she recalled most of all was sitting in the dark with him in silence, the trace of light creeping in from the view window to the circulation area just enough to delineate his silhouette. The greasy, slightly overwarm air. The thrum of the HVAC. And then, his words.

After my father's funeral, I changed my phone number. You finally became what you were running away from. It's enough that you know.

"That night . . ." she begins again, trying hard not to clamp her fingers into a fist. "I wasn't sure what you were telling me. At times it sounded as if you were listing the reasons we wouldn't—and shouldn't—be together."

He reaches down and picks up the hem of her ankle-length green dress. For all that he's declared that he would spend the next two days in the physical exploration of her person, his gesture isn't flirtatious but pensive. "What do you think would have happened to us, if we'd kept in touch?"

A question for the ages.

"Realistically, and forgive me for saying so, it would have depended on how good you were in bed."

He smiles slightly. "Let's assume I was eager to learn and willing to listen to feedback. And let's assume that I quickly achieved adequacy, if not virtuosity."

Heat licks her like a summer day in Austin. She swallows. "I used to think that we'd have had a memorable affair, three, maybe even five years together, leaving me sadder but much wiser at the end. And I'd have a book like this"—she gestures to the volume on the coffee table, still open to the page of her irrepressible delight—"of our entire time together, but wouldn't show it to anyone, not until I was really old.

"But that's what I thought in a vacuum." With him forever remaining the idealized version in her memories. "What do *you* think would have happened?"

He still has his fingers on the hem of her dress, as if the stitches on the reverse could convey a secret code if only he stroked them long enough. "I think we would have had a fantastic few months. We boarded only two guests at Charleston, instead of the scheduled three, so you could have bought a passage on the ship, for a reduced rate, possibly, and sailed with us around Cape Horn."

Rounding Cape Horn is the sailing equivalent of climbing Mount Everest—the waves there can toss a yacht end over end.

"Did your yacht somersault?"

"Not quite, but our first mate was swept out to sea. Fortunately he had a tether, so we hauled him back in and he suffered nothing worse than a torn rotator cuff."

She would have loved it, a real adventure. Until . . .

"San Diego was the end of my first contract and that was where I found out. We would have been okay until the funeral—I was in denial until then. But afterward I was a mess." He lets go of her hem. "It wouldn't have been a pretty breakup. I would have hurt you and you wouldn't have wanted to tell anyone about me in your old age."

She aches for him, for the boy for whom the sky was falling. "But that didn't happen. *We* didn't happen."

"No, we became beautiful ideas to each other." He reaches up and touches the ends of her hair. "And I didn't want just the idea of you any longer. If you never came to Austin I'd have gone to Singapore at some point to see if the heiress version of you would have me—and that woman makes me worry for myself."

"Why does she make you nervous?"

"Because—" He pulls her close—now they touch from shoulder to ankle—and kisses the corner of her lips. "She would have an affair with me and move on with the rest of her life."

It is the lightest contact, his lips to her skin, yet she is singed. She wraps her hand behind his head—at last, the sensation of his bristly hair upon her inner wrist again—and kisses him below his ear.

He sucks in a breath.

"And you wouldn't move on?" she murmurs, her lips against the helix of his ear, right where it had been pierced.

"I can't." He bends his head and kisses her neck. "I've never been able to move on."

Pleasure jolts her.

He cups her face and speaks with his lips two inches from hers. "And I don't plan to move on ever again."

Her lips part. She stares into his eyes, and then down at his lips. He traces his thumb over her lower lip. But instead of kissing her, he reaches over for the box of ear barbells. "Do you want to put one on me? Which one says *Man over thirty with career, house, and extremely beautiful girlfriend?*"

She has a sudden insight into the kind of lover he would prove to be: Her adorable young man has grown up into a tease. But also, it dawns on her that unlike what she thought earlier, he isn't waiting for anything—not anymore, in any case. He is simply enjoying this hard-earned moment, this grace from the universe.

She yanks the box from his hand, tosses it aside with un-Hazel-like abandon, and pushes him down on the couch. His look of astonishment quickly turns into one of pure masculine glee. "Are you sure I can't offer you some dinner first? Or at least a drink that isn't just water?"

She straddles him, settles her hands on his deltoids, and marvels at how strong and lovely those rower's shoulders feel under her palms. "You can offer me both. But first I need to hear something else from you."

He gazes up at her, his extraordinary eyes crinkled playfully. "Are you going to make me say 'I love you' this early?"

Would he say it if she asked him to? Her heart flutters. "You can hold that one up your sleeve until the time of your choosing. I'm looking for something different."

He studies her, one hand trailing up her arm. "If you're afraid what happened to your mum will happen to you, we can waive the forty-eight-hour waiting period and talk about those three million pounds now. Afterward you can always throw extra money at me—I don't have a problem with sugar mummies."

She snorts.

He pulls her lower, so that he is again speaking with his lips only two inches from hers. "And I can promise you I will never make you choose between me and something else that is important to you. I will always conduct myself so you can have more of what you love in your life, not less."

At some point since she arrived in his house, possibly when he said, *I can't. I've never been able to move on*, she understood that she too is all in. That the commitment has been made, today and long ago, and she doesn't need to wait for any further signal from the universe.

But what he said just now—and the thought behind it—she kisses him deeply, solemnly, with all the resolve and devotion of her heart.

And then, when he would kiss her again, she raises herself up and punches him on the chest. "Liar."

"Ow, careful. That's where you kicked me."

She has no choice but to fuss over him and lift up his sweater to kiss him on the fading bruise. "Asshole. When we met you said you'd turn nineteen in three days. That was in early October. Your birthday isn't until the end of the year."

"Kiss here too." He points at an entirely unbruised part of his torso. And when she complies, he adds, "And here. And here. And aren't you glad I did? If you learned I was still solidly eighteen, you'd have bought me a binkie and sent me home. Besides, you lied too. Your birthday isn't a month from early October. It's also in December."

True, none of it matters, except now there will never be that slender portion of the year during which she is only three years older than him and not four.

"One minute." He pauses in the unbuttoning of her dress—when did he start to do that? "Are you telling me that your family back home is already looking into me? You told them about me?"

His eyes are all lit up. She's never seen anyone so happy to be investigated. Her heart melts into a puddle. "I told them I don't want to know anything, but they still sent me an email and your birthday showed in the preview."

"Let's look at that email together in forty-eight hours. I want to see how I come across in a PI report."

She snorts once more. "I don't have forty-eight hours. I need to be at the library tomorrow."

"Should I drive you home now so you can sleep early?" He sits up. "Let's feed you first. And don't forget to give me the jigsaw puzzle that—"

Once more she pushes him down. "Young man, how well we do in our future together still depends on how good you are in bed."

"Ah, why didn't you say so?" He wraps his arms around her and kisses her again. "For the record, I've never been so motivated to be an extraordinary lover."

CHAPTER THIRTY-SIX

The library's reopening thrills Astrid. She arrives a full hour early to work, walks three circles around the building, and traces her hand everywhere that was once damaged but is now made whole again.

Fifteen minutes before the start of business hours, the parking lot is already half-full, with patrons chatting to one another before the brand-new sliding doors. Once those doors open, one patron after another tells Astrid how happy they are to have their library back, how much they took its services, its convenience, and its lovely ambience for granted until it was suddenly out of commission. And to one patron after another Astrid confesses that she feels exactly the same—as much as she loves the library, she too has taken its existence for granted.

What a miraculous place it is, a haven for anyone who passes through, and a refuge for the individuals who have dedicated their working lives to its excellence and betterment. Astrid does two storytimes back-to-back and must have high-fived Sophie three times during the first half of her shift and Jonathan at least as often.

In the middle of the afternoon, however, in comes Gus Anderson, the *Fifty Shades* patron, and Astrid happens to be on the last few minutes of her public-facing hour at the checkout station.

If only Hazel were here to play him like a fiddle!

The old man manages to talk like a human being for a couple of minutes, before he shows his real interest. "That new librarian, the pretty one, she mentioned she likes male-male romances. That got me thinking"—he tee-hees—"is there such a thing as a female-female romance?"

Wanker, as Perry would have said.

Think of Hazel. Think of how she handled this wanker.

"Of course," Astrid says with great professionalism. "There are many wonderful women-loving-women stories to choose from. Do you have any other parameters for me to narrow the search for you? Do you like stories set on the high sea? In the Old West? Or maybe with a speculative element, you know, like—"

"Like in *Barbarella*?" Gus Anderson's eyes light up.

Astrid has only the vaguest impression of a young Jane Fonda in a skimpy outfit on the *Barbarella* movie poster, an image that serves the male gaze as its raison d'être.

"Comparable titles in the sense that these stories are also set in the future, or in space, or sometimes both," she says firmly. "Would you like some recommendations?"

"Absolutely." The old man sounds giddy. "Bring them on."

Astrid writes down *This Is How You End the Time War* and *Gideon the Ninth* for him, and then personally takes him to the stacks to retrieve *The Stars Are Legion*, by Kameron Hurley. "There isn't a single man in this book. Everybody on this planet is a woman."

"Oh, my!"

Gus Anderson, his head probably brimming with images of thousands of chicks making out with one another for his delectation, checks out the book and leaves happily.

Hazel comes into the library then, dressed simply in jeans and a gray hoodie, yet looking gloriously vibrant. Astrid rushes out from the circulation area to embrace her. "I thought you don't start working until tomorrow!"

"I don't, but I can't miss the first day of the library's reopening." Hazel points unobtrusively toward the sliding doors. "Saw our friend leaving with *The Stars Are Legion*. I think he's going to pass out."

"I know." Astrid giggles. "That's the hope, at least."

Hazel grins. "Good job, you, expanding our patrons' horizons."

Astrid basks in that compliment.

Everyone else also gathers to welcome Hazel back, Sophie especially, as Hazel left for Singapore with not only a box of books worth almost as much as the most expensive house in Austin, but also Jeannette Obermann's phone.

Hazel loads bags of salted egg yolk–flavored chips, interesting cup ramens, and Tim Tams—which are apparently available in Singapore—onto the Wall of International Snacks. Then the four of them gather briefly in Sophie's office.

"Is it all taken care of?" asks Jonathan.

"All taken care of," answers Hazel. "That phone doesn't exist anymore."

Sophie rubs her knuckles lightly across her sternum, as if she is releasing the last of the pressure from her chest.

Everyone quietly hugs her.

"Oh, I almost forgot," says Astrid. "Hazel, I've been waiting to invite you in person to Friendsgiving this weekend. I'm making ham balls and Jell-O salads, Midwestern classics."

"Oh, cool. I'll bring a store-bought Peking duck—and see if I can find a good recipe for sticky rice with shiitake mushrooms and Chinese sausage. Those were what we used to eat at Thanksgiving when I was a child."

"I'm already drooling," murmurs Jonathan. "What about Conrad? I'll bet he does a mean casserole if he puts his mind to it."

Everyone is still chortling as they file out of Sophie's office.

The staff pose together in front of the library. The pictures come out beautifully. Sophie says she will frame her favorite and hang it up in her office, to commemorate the reopening of the library.

Everyone else must go back inside to their duties, but Hazel, who isn't on the clock today, has the luxury to linger for a few minutes.

Go on. Start a new life for yourself, Nainai had told her before her first day at work. At the time Nainai's exhortation had seemed much too lofty a goal for Hazel, who was only trying to get through the day.

Have a wonderful life, Conrad once inscribed those words to her. That day on Madeira she hadn't the least idea how to live a wonderful life, hadn't even believed in the possibility.

Now she has a new life and she is beginning to wonder how one might go about achieving a wonderful one.

And she still doesn't know how to do that. But maybe, she can learn to have wonderful moments instead.

A wonderful moment is her standing by the bike rack before the library, her shadow stretched out before her in the light of golden hour, breathing in the scent of live oak and green grass, a muted roar of traffic rumbling across the overpass eight hundred feet away.

Her grandparents' health, her mother's happiness, the longevity of her brand-new relationship, the state of the country, the fate of the world—the potential for future distress is endless.

But in this moment, she is happy for her colleagues and she is happy for herself. In this moment she trusts in the kindness of others and the kindness of the universe. In this moment she does not need anything beyond the air she is breathing and the peace in her heart.

In this moment, she has a wonderful life.

ACKNOWLEDGMENTS

This book would not exist had Berkley, my publishing house, not pitched me the idea of a feel-good mystery featuring a cast of crime-solving librarians. Always happy to secure real deadlines, I said yes even though I was not the most logical or obvious person for such a task: I'd never written ensemble casts or workplace stories, and only one of the twenty-odd books I'd produced up to that point was set in contemporary times.

But, ah, now that the book is done, I am beyond thrilled that I got to write it. Thank you, everyone at Berkley, for the brilliant idea and for trusting that I could make something of it.

Since I am no librarian, I relied on the librarians in my life to guide me along the way.

My deepest gratitude to my lovely friend Amanda Charles of Los Angeles Public Library, who, at my very basic queries, returned a veritable treatise that served as valuable grounding for this entire endeavor.

I am forever indebted to Patrick Walz, until recently one of Austin Public Library's most spectacular librarians, who helped me in innumerable ways during the writing of this book. I tried my darnedest to put a body in the hidden gallery he showed me; failing that, I put two living, breathing characters up there because a secret location in a library absolutely cannot go to waste. Good luck in San Antonio, Patrick—they are so lucky to have you there!

John Charles of the Poisoned Pen has long been one of the guardian angels of my career. Early on, when he was still a librarian, he gave me such meticulous help when I wrote an article on how genre romance made its way into public libraries. This time he generously read an early draft so I could be sure I wasn't going down completely wrong paths.

My beloved Sara Ramsey also read an early draft of the book. She is not a librarian—as far as I know—but she saved me from the grievous error of using a corkscrew on a bottle of prosecco in this book. Who knew that corks on sparkling wines can be simply twisted out by hand!

Now I can finally copy and paste my usual acknowledgments:

Kerry Donovan, my saintly but also marvelously effective editor.

Kristin Nelson, Super Agent.

Janine Ballard, my critique partner, proving once again with this book why she is utterly invaluable.

My family and friends, who, much to my delight, are still my family and friends.

And you, if you are reading this, dear one, thank you. Thank you from the bottom of my heart.